find

Susanne O'Leary was born in Stockholm, Sweden. After graduating from the French lyceé in Stockholm, she married an Irish diplomat. She has spent most of her adult life either on diplomatic postings with her husband or in Dublin. They now live in County Tipperary. Susanne trained as a fitness teacher and has published two books on health: *Look Great, Feel Great for Life* (Gill & Macmillan 1999) and *The Life in Your Years* (Gill & Macmillan 2000). Her first novel, *Diplomatic Incidents* (Blackstaff Press), was published in 2001; *European Affairs* (also Blackstaff Press) followed in 2003. Her bestseller *Fresh Powder* was published in 2006. *Finding Margo* is Susanne's fourth novel and she is currently working on her fifth.

www.susanne-oleary.com

FINDING MARGO

SUSANNE O'LEARY

NEW
ISLAND

Copyright © 2007 Susanne O'Leary

Finding Margo
First published 2007
by New Island
2 Brookside
Dundrum Road
Dublin 14

www.newisland.ie

The moral right of the author has been asserted.

isbn 978-1-905494-47-7

British Library Cataloguing in Publication Data.
A CIP catalogue record for this book is available from the British Library.

Printed in the UK by Athenaeum Press Ltd., Gateshead, Tyne & Wear
Book design by Fidelma Slattery

10 9 8 7 6 5 4 3 2 1

For Björn

Acknowledgements

Many thanks to all at New Island, especially my editor Deirdre Nolan, as always a delight to work with, Fidelma Slattery for the beautiful cover and Tom Cooney for his hard work on the marketing.

To the Irish Girls, fellow writers and friends, in particular Marita Conlon-McKenna and Catherine Daly. Also to the members of www.writeon-irishgirls.com for all their support and enthusiasm.

Thanks also to Pat O'Brien at the Chapter One bookshop in Cahir for his huge support and to Lucy at Eason's in Clonmel.

A huge thank you to my husband, Denis, for his never-ending patience and support and the rest of my family for making my life such a rich tapestry.

And, finally, I'd like to thank my readers, especially those who have sent me emails of appreciation.

1

The silver BMW travelled smoothly along the motorway, the soft purring of the engine barely audible over the Beethoven sonata that wafted from the CD player. Margo looked idly at the French countryside gliding past the windows, the music and the gentle movement of the car making her drowsy. She glanced at her husband to make sure he wasn't falling asleep too, but he looked reasonably alert, driving the big car expertly, as always.

They had arrived in Calais by ferry in the early morning and headed south straight away to avoid the worst of the heat and the traffic. Now it was late afternoon and Margo was tired of concentrating on the map and directing Alan through the maze of motorways. She leaned her head against the soft leather of the headrest and closed her eyes. The road map and guidebook slid off her knees. As her head lolled forward, she realised falling asleep would be a bad idea. She opened her eyes, fighting to stay awake.

'Could we change the music?' she asked drowsily. 'Or put on the news or something? I'm beginning to nod off here.'

Alan frowned without taking his eyes off the road. 'You'd better not, or we'll end up going the wrong way.'

'And that wouldn't do, would it,' Margo said, imagining what would happen if they missed even one minute of the medical conference in Cannes.

'It certainly wouldn't.'

'Maybe we can get the news on the BBC?' Margo put her hand out to switch the CD player to the radio setting.

'No, I like this,' Alan said in a voice that didn't allow argument. 'I find it relaxing while I drive.'

'OK.' Margo settled back into her seat again. Maybe I'll feel less sleepy if I talk to him, she thought, trying to think of a topic of conversation. 'Do you realise,' she said after a while, 'that we haven't been on a trip like this for over three years?'

'Three years?' Alan asked incredulously. 'It couldn't be that long.'

'It is.' Margo nodded. 'The last time we went anywhere together was...' she thought for a minute, 'America. We went to New York for that meeting. Don't you remember that lovely weekend in the *fall*?' she said with an exaggerated American accent. 'We drove to Vermont and stayed in that cute little country inn, and...'

'I got terrible backache from that horrible bed,' Alan grunted.

'That wasn't from the bed, it was from making love in the bath,' Margo said with a little smile. 'You got such a cramp, remember?'

'God, yes. I had to go to hospital.'

'And we had to explain to that elderly nurse what you had been doing to be in such pain,' Margo laughed.

'I don't know why we found it so funny,' Alan said. 'But we did. We couldn't stop laughing.'

'I know.' Margo's smile died on her lips as her thoughts went back to those happy days. We don't laugh together like that any more, she thought. She turned to look at Alan, admiring his profile. Still handsome, still the same tall frame, broad shoulders and gleaming blond hair. He looks nearly exactly as he did when we got married. It's my fault, she thought. I haven't managed to keep him interested. I haven't made the effort to be fascinating and sexy and feminine and whatever else men want you to be. But I will, she promised herself. I'll change my hair and buy some really sexy underwear. And now I have the chance. After all, this is France, what better place to get something really fabulous? We're still young, she thought, not even forty, we should be able to rekindle that hot flame. She felt a stir of excitement at the thought of surprising Alan.

'We should be there soon.' Alan's voice dragged Margo out of her reverie.

'Mmm.'

'About twenty minutes, would you say?'

'Something like that.'

'Great.' Alan smiled and shifted his body in his seat. 'I'm beginning to feel a little stiff.'

'But you'll be able to have a swim in the hotel pool soon,' Margo said. 'We'll have plenty of time before dinner.'

'I know. I can't wait. My back is really beginning to get to me. Maybe we shouldn't have driven so far in one day.'

'That was your idea,' Margo reminded him. 'I would have been quite prepared to have stopped much earlier.'

'What's that supposed to mean?' he asked, giving her a sideways glance. 'I told you so? OK. I admit it probably would have made more sense to have stopped earlier, but I'm not that bad. Not worse than usual, in any case.'

'If you took some exercise and tried to cut down on your workload…'

'Yeah, yeah, I know,' he interrupted. 'But you know I can't work less at the moment. This break was only possible because of those cancellations and the fact that the conference is being held in Cannes this year. Which also gave us the opportunity to stay in this fantastic place on the way. And, as you might have noticed, the traffic wasn't as bad as you thought. We seem to have managed to get ahead of the posse. You did a good job directing me.'

'I hope I can keep it up,' Margo said, leaning her head on the headrest again.

'So do I.' Alan paused and shot her another glance. 'You weren't thinking of taking nap?' he asked, a hint of irritation in his voice. 'You know I need you to keep an eye on the map.'

'I am,' Margo assured him, picking the books off the floor. 'I have both the map and the guidebook right here.'

'Great. Just make sure you don't miss the exit. It should be coming up shortly. As far as I can remember, we go up a hill and through a round-about. Then I think there's a right turn over a bridge and we should be on the road straight to the hotel.'

'Mmm.' Margo stifled a yawn. 'Sorry,' she laughed, 'it's the sun and the motion of the car. Makes me sleepy.'

'We'll have dinner as soon as we arrive and then a swim and an early night,' Alan said.

'Good idea,' Margo agreed, beginning to look forward to the evening. And tomorrow they would arrive in Cannes and she would be able to relax, have some time on her own while he attended the conference. She would laze on the beach, swim, read, maybe do some shopping. There was that nice lingerie shop just off the Croisette, where they had the most amazing things. She'd buy that sexy underwear. Maybe I should go a bit kinky, she thought, that might do the trick...

'Exit 22,' Alan suddenly said as a road sign whizzed past. 'Is that the one I should take?'

'Mmm? What? Exit 22?' Startled, Margo picked up the map. 'No, it should say exit 8. Hold on, I'll have a look.'

'Wake up!' Alan shouted. 'Tell me quick! What should I do? We're coming up to the exit now!'

'No! Don't take that one!' Margo yelled. 'It's wrong. Keep going until I find out.' She studied the map with a feeling of dread as the car swept past the exit. 'Oh God, I don't believe it.'

'What?' Alan demanded.

'Well, there shouldn't be an exit 22 here.' Her mouth suddenly felt dry and her hands clammy. 'Unless…'

'Unless you've made a mistake again?'

'Yeah, well.' She swallowed nervously, staring at the map, trying to figure out how she could have got it so horribly wrong. 'Oh God. I must have made a mistake back there at the spaghetti junction. It was so difficult to figure out.' Margo bit her lip, her stomach churning, ready for the stream of abuse she knew would come now.

'We're on the wrong motorway?' Alan asked, his voice dangerously silky. 'Are you telling me we're going in the direction of Grenoble?'

'Eh, I'm afraid we are.'

Alan's hands gripped the wheel, the knuckles white, and a muscle twitched in his jaw. 'Fuck,' he muttered.

'Sorry,' Margo whispered.

'That junction you're talking about – was that the one we went through just after Dijon? A fucking *hour* ago?'

'Yes,' she stammered. 'Oh Alan, I'm really sorry.'

'Moron.'

'I know. It was really silly of me, but it was so confusing. And there were no proper signs and—'

'You stupid bitch! We have lost a full hour, do you realise that? And we're nearly out of petrol as well. Shit! We have to stop at the next petrol station. And then we'll have to figure out how to get to where we're supposed to be. We won't be at the hotel until at least ten o'clock at this rate. Do you understand what you've done?'

'Yes,' she replied.

'I can't hear you.'

'Yes,' Margo murmured, 'I do understand. But I did say I was sorry.'

'Sorry? You think you can fix what you've done by just saying *sorry*?'

'I didn't do it on purpose.'

'Yeah, right.'

'It was a *mistake*,' Margo whispered, her chin trembling.

'Mistake?' There was a pause and a sharp intake of breath. 'A fucking mistake that has cost us half a day's driving and God knows how much money in petrol. My back is killing me as well. You're useless, do you know that? I should have known better than to ask you to read a bloody map. You couldn't direct a child on a tricycle to playschool!'

'I know. It was really stupid.'

'You bet it was.'

'Sorry,' Margo said again even though she knew she sounded as stupid as he thought she was. Oh, how I hate this, she thought. How I hate his temper and his swearing and shouting. And it always comes out of the blue like a bolt of lightning. One minute he's so charming and sweet, and the next…

'How long are we married?' Alan suddenly demanded.

'What?'

'You heard. How long are we married?'

'Ten years.'

Alan shook his head and sighed. 'Ten years,' he snarled. 'Ten *fucking* years. I can't believe I've been stuck with such a half-wit for ten fucking years.'

Margo felt suddenly trapped. She wanted to open the car door and throw herself into the road, so strong was her urge to get away from him, from the venom in his voice and the horrible insults. 'Stop the car,' she said.

'Stop the car? What the fuck do you mean? I can't stop in the middle of a three-lane motorway. I'm in the fast lane, can't you see that?'

'I don't care. I want to get out. I can't stand sitting here while you go berserk.'

'What? Me? Berserk? What are you going on about now?'

'You know very well. You're ranting and raving like a lunatic just because of one little—'

'Little?' he snapped. 'You call that *little*? You had the map, you knew where we were going, why the fuck couldn't you manage to do the one thing that was required of you instead of going to sleep?'

'But I…' Margo stopped. She clamped her mouth shut, deciding not to talk to him until he had calmed down. What was the point? Arguing only made him worse. He's so mean, she thought, hot tears stinging her eyes, so cruel and unforgiving. I know I was a little absentminded, but why can't he be more easy going, more willing to forgive? Why can't he understand how difficult it was to figure out that complicated mess on the map? Why couldn't we laugh about it and try to solve the problem together? But no, that would be too much to expect. There was a brooding stillness in the car as the last bars of the piano sonata died away and the heavy trucks roared past them outside.

'There's a petrol station a few miles ahead,' Alan said, sounding marginally calmer, as they passed a large sign. 'We'll stop there and fill up.'

Margo didn't reply.

'And I'll have a look at the map and try to find out where the *fuck* we are,' he continued.

Margo turned her head away and stared blindly out the window, trying to block the sound of his voice from her mind.

'Sulking now, are we?' Alan's voice dripped contempt. 'Feeling sorry for ourselves?'

Margo laughed bitterly to herself as she was tempted to ask him what his patients would say if they saw him now, all those women who found him so caring and wonderful, the best plastic surgeon in London with the wonderful bedside manner, the miracle worker who can make an ageing woman look young again.

Alan shook his head. 'Jesus. Women,' he muttered. 'Can't read a fucking map.'

Margo rummaged in her bag.

'What are you doing now?' Alan demanded.

'Nothing. Just looking for a hanky.'

'You're going to turn on the tears now, I suppose. Jesus Christ, you really are pathetic.' He tightened his hands on the steering wheel and the car suddenly surged forward.

Margo closed her eyes, humming a little tune to herself. Alan said something she didn't hear, his voice only a distant murmur as the car swept around the next bend.

*

'Here we are,' Alan said as he slowed the car and turned into the entrance to the motorway station. 'But look at that queue. Shit! I should have known it would be like this at this time of year. Why does everybody go on holiday in July? We'll have to wait at least half an hour now.'

Margo looked around. It was one of those huge stations with about twenty petrol pumps, a picnic area, a playground for children and cafeteria, restaurant and shop in a separate building. She took her handbag and started to get out of the car. 'I'm going to the loo,' she announced, taking her black leather tote bag as well, thinking she could change her sweaty T-shirt for a fresh one.

'Yeah, sure,' Alan muttered, staring ahead, drumming his fingers on the dashboard.

'I'll see you in the cafeteria when you've finished filling the car,' Margo said as she left.

Alan just glared at her without replying. She shrugged and hurried away from the car, across the hot tarmac baking in the afternoon sun, into the coolness of the restaurant.

*

Margo looked at herself in the mirror as she dried her hands on the paper towel in the surprisingly clean ladies' toilet. God, I look a mess, she thought. Her face was pale and there were traces of mascara under her eyes. She pulled out the scrunchie that held up her hair and the dark blonde curls tumbled onto her shoulders. She dampened a tissue to wipe away the smudges under her eyes, but to no avail. She still looked tired and dishevelled, despite having changed into a fresh blue T-shirt, and her white linen trousers were more wrinkled than fashionably creased. She sighed and took a comb from her bag, trying to fluff up her hair. I'll have to wash it as soon as we get to the hotel, she thought, tying it up again. She put away the comb, took out a lipstick and quickly touched up the colour on her mouth, which made her look only slightly better. A good night's sleep, she thought, that's what I need. Can't wait to get to the hotel. Alan will have calmed down and we'll have a nice dinner, some wine and then I'll do my best to cheer him up. And tomorrow, we'll be in Cannes. The conference will keep him occupied and maybe improve his mood.

Margo wandered out of the ladies' into the shopping area and started to walk around the aisles. There was an amazing amount of luxury goods for sale – perfumes, soaps, expensive choco-lates, even bottles of wine and champagne. She chose a small box of Belgian chocolates and a tray of tiny soaps, not because she needed them, but because it cheered her up to buy something.

'That's forty-four euros and fifty cents,' the girl at the checkout said.

Margo handed her a fifty from the euro notes Alan had given her early that morning when they had gone to the cash machine at the ferry port. He had told her to keep the European 'funny money' in her purse for emergencies, as you never knew when you might need to pay for something in cash. She didn't have a credit card. Alan wouldn't allow it. Not that he was stingy, but he didn't want her to buy things he hadn't approved of first.

Margo put the change away, picked up her purchases and walked toward the restaurant. He must still be in that queue, she thought. I'll have something to eat while I wait. I'll order him a salad or something, that'll cheer him up, he hates waiting around for meals. Or maybe he doesn't want anything to eat? He might get irritated again if I buy him a meal he doesn't like and then he'll be in a mood for the rest of the evening. She idly picked up a tray and went to the buffet, where an array of rather tired salads and sandwiches were displayed. She picked up a plate of chicken salad, a bread roll, a piece of apple tart and a bottle of water. But what if he's really hungry, she thought, then he'll be annoyed that I didn't get him something…

'*Madame?*' the man at the cash register looked at her questioningly. '*Vous voulez autre chose?*' Then he asked if she wanted something from the hot buffet.

'*Non*,' she said, shaking her head to emphasise her words, and paid the bill. She sat down at a Formica table and tucked into the meal. The salad, followed by the apple tart and a cup of strong coffee from the espresso bar, improved her mood and she felt more hopeful. He's just tired, she thought, all that driving would exhaust anyone. If only we could share the driving, it would be so much better. But he never wants me to drive.

Where was he? She looked toward the entrance, but all she could see was a group of Italians arguing about who should get the last pasta salad and a couple with two children choosing ice cream. She looked out the grimy window and spotted Alan standing by the car, which had inched forward only two spaces since she left. He looked hot and irritated and Margo could see him wiping his forehead with his handkerchief. Oh God, this will make him even worse, she thought. She lifted the cup to her lips to finish her coffee, but found her hand was shaking so much she couldn't hold it steady. Oh, I hope he'll be able to fill the tank soon, she prayed, so we can get going…

A few minutes later, Margo looked out again and saw Alan gesticulate in an evident rage at a uniformed youth holding a bucket and mop. Hit him, she silently willed the bewildered young man, hit him right in the face. But the young man just backed away. Margo turned back to her coffee.

How is it possible, she asked herself, for a man with such charm to be so horrible when he's angry? And he has been a lot worse lately, losing his temper for no apparent reason at all. The week in Cannes should be good for us both. We'll be able to talk things through, really get close again…

Margo turned her gaze to the window opposite and looked at the view of the motorway, crossed by a footbridge that led to the lay-by on the opposite side, where a large number of trucks were parked. She stared at the footbridge, at the motorway with the traffic roaring in both directions, turned around and glanced at Alan again. Now he was kicking the wheel of the car. He looked up and peered at the windows of the cafeteria and she could see his face, still scowling. She knew he couldn't possibly see her, but she cringed all the same. She looked through the other window again, at the footbridge and the people walking across it. She wished she was one of them, someone, anyone who didn't have to get back into that car with Alan in the mood he was in. She wished she was back in London, at work, out shopping, anywhere but here in this café waiting to confront him again.

I'd better go back to the car, Margo thought. He'll be even worse if he has to wait for me. She sighed, slowly gathered her things and started for the main entrance. But when she was halfway across the restaurant, she suddenly stopped, turned and, on an impulse, walked out the side door instead, around the back of the building, across the tarmac, away from the petrol pumps and the line of

14

cars. She kept walking, staring ahead, as if guided by an inner voice that kept telling her to keep going. Suddenly, someone shouted somewhere nearby, but she walked on, her heart pounding, afraid to look around. The shouting stopped. She glanced behind her. A man had caught a small boy by the shoulder. Margo clapped her hand to her chest as if to slow her heart and stood for a moment, trying to catch her breath and regain her cool. She breathed in deeply and, like a sleep-walker, started to walk again, across the car park, through the playground and the picnic area, up the steps and over the bridge.

2

The small green truck was parked in the shade of a tree a short distance away from the group of big articulated lorries. The paint was flaking off its sides and the lettering spelling the word 'horses' above the front windscreen was barely visible. Margo had been wandering around the parking area in a dazed state, wondering what to do next. She kept looking over her shoulder, expecting to see Alan coming across the footbridge ready to drag her back to the car. The urge to get away was the only thing on her mind now. I have to get a lift quickly, she thought, studying the truck drivers, mostly big, swarthy, unshaven men who were laughing, joking or snoozing in the shade. She tried to spot the one that looked the least likely to attack her the first chance he got. But none of them looked in any way friendly or even particularly appealing. But I have to get out of here before

Alan finds me, she said to herself, panic rising in her chest. Then she saw the small truck. Margo tightened her grip on her bag and walked toward it. She went around the side, where a young man, his back to her, was drinking deeply from a beer can. He was short and stocky, with dark, slicked-back hair, dressed in a loose blue shirt and jeans and he was flicking ash from a cigarette held carelessly in his other hand.

'*Excusez-moi, monsieur,*' Margo said politely.

The young man whipped around. 'What the fuck?' Despite the hoarseness, the voice was not male.

'Oh, sorry,' Margo smiled nervously, 'I thought you were…'

'A fucking French guy?' The young 'man' put her cigarette in her mouth, tucked her shirt into her jeans with one hand, revealing an impressive bust, and crushed the beer can with the other.

'Well, yes, but I only saw you from the back, and…'

'I looked French?' The woman shook her head and laughed. '*And* you thought I was a man. Jesus, that's a laugh.' She stubbed out her cigarette against the side of the truck, looking Margo up and down. 'You look hot.'

Margo backed away. 'Well, I'm…'

'You in some kind of trouble?' The woman spoke with a strong Irish accent.

'No, not really.' Margo laughed nervously. 'I was…' she swallowed, trying to think of a likely story, 'on this…this bus, and we stopped for a break and then…then…it just drove off.'

'That's a pisser.'

'Mmm, eh, yes.'

The woman studied her for a moment through narrowing eyes. 'So now you're looking for a lift, is that it?'

'That's right.'

'Where are you going?' the woman asked, folding her arms across her ample bosom. 'I mean, where was that bus taking you?'

'To Cannes,' Margo blurted out without thinking. 'I mean, no, I mean…' She stopped, feeling both confused and embarrassed. 'I want to go to Paris,' she heard herself say.

'You were on a bus to Cannes and now you want to go to Paris?' The woman looked at her suspiciously with her small brown eyes. Like currants in a bun, Margo thought.

'Yes, that's right,' she replied, trying to sound confident. 'I've changed my mind about Cannes. I've decided to look up a friend in Paris instead.'

'You don't say,' the woman muttered ironically. 'Why do I have the feeling something really weird is going on here?'

'Weird?' Margo straightened her shoulders and gazed innocently at the other woman. 'I don't understand what you mean.'

'Like you're up to something. Like you're in some kind of trouble. You haven't killed anyone, have you?'

'Not lately, no,' Margo tried to joke.

'And the police aren't after you or anything?'

'No, of course not,' Margo replied with feeling.

The woman looked at her thoughtfully for a moment. 'Know anything about horses?' she suddenly asked.

'Horses?' Margo said, confused.

'Yeah. That's what I have in the truck here. Two of the best event horses in Ireland. I'm bringing them back from a competition in Grenoble. I had someone to help me, but the bitch let me down. Decided to go off with a groom from Italy and now I have to look after the horses on my own. So, if you think you could give me a hand with 'em, I'll be happy to give you a lift and drop you off somewhere near Paris.'

'Horses?' Margo said again. 'Well, yes, as long as it's not too complicated. I went to pony camp once when I was younger. But that was a long time ago.'

'Pony camp, eh? Well then you would know the basics, wouldn't you?'

'I suppose.'

'Great. OK.' The woman wiped her hand on the back of her jeans and held it out to Margo. 'By the way, I'm Gráinne.'

'I'm sorry? You're what?'

The woman laughed. 'I get that all the time. It's my name, very common in Ireland. Seems to confuse English people big time. Gra, rhymes with bra, for someone with your la-de-da accent, then "nya". Try it – "gra-nya".'

'Gráinne.'

'Brilliant. What's your name?'

'M—' Margo started. 'Maggie.'

Gráinne grabbed Margo's hand and shook it. 'Pleased to meet you, Maggie. Are you ready?'

Margo nodded, feeling oddly excited, as if she was embarking on some kind of adventure. 'Yes, I'm ready,' she said.

'Want to nip into the jacks before we go? It's just across that footbridge.'

'No!' Margo exclaimed. 'I'm all right. And thank you so much for helping me.'

'No bother. OK, let's go then,' Gráinne said and opened the door to the driver's side.

Margo ran around to the other side, opened the door, climbed up and settled into the passenger seat. Gráinne put on her seat belt, turned the key in the ignition and the truck's engine came alive. 'OK?' she shouted over the rumble. Margo nodded again, clutching her bag and looking straight ahead, a feeling of elation making her heart beat faster.

'Here we go,' Gráinne yelled as she put her foot on the accelerator. 'Next stop, Paris.'

*

The truck shook and rattled as it made its way through the dark woods. They had left the motorway nearly an hour earlier, and Gráinne had explained that they would spend the night near a farm, where they could let the horses out in a field and Gráinne and Margo would sleep in the truck. Margo held onto the handle of the door, trying to keep herself steady, having absolutely no idea where they were. She had been trying to make polite conversation with Gráinne for a while, but now the CD player was on full blast, playing country and western music. Gráinne had smoked at least five cigarettes since the beginning of the journey, and the heat and the twisting motion of the truck combined with the smoke were beginning to make Margo feel queasy. 'Are we there yet?' she asked like a child when there was a lull in the music.

'Nope,' Gráinne said.

'Maybe we could stop for a moment?'

'What for?' Gráinne asked, the cigarette in the corner of her mouth, her eyes squinting through the smoke.

'I don't know. Fresh air? Those cigarettes are making me sick.'

'You don't say,' Gráinne muttered, but the cigarette stayed stuck in her mouth.

'Smoking is very bad for you,' Margo stated. 'But I'm sure you're well aware of that.'

'Yeah, right.'

'And passive smoking is just as bad.'

'Is that supposed to be a hint?'

'Maybe.' Margo shrugged and looked out the window, staring into the gathering dusk.

'You some kind of nurse?' Gráinne grunted.

'I'm a physiotherapist,' Margo replied. 'I mean, I was. Before I got married.'

'I see. A fucking health freak.' Gráinne stubbed her cigarette out in the overflowing ashtray. 'So you're married, then?'

'Not any more. And I don't want to talk about it.'

'OK.' They drove in silence for a while. 'He bought you that ring?' Gráinne asked after a few minutes.

'Who?'

'Your husband. Did he buy you that rock you have on your finger? Must be two carats at least.'

'Four,' Margo said and turned the ring around.

'Jesus. So what is he, some kind of millionaire?'

'Plastic surgeon.'

'No shit?'

'I don't want to talk about him,' Margo snapped.

'OK. Sorry.'

'Never mind.'

'Right.'

They were silent again while the truck bounced on the uneven road.

'He's dead,' Margo suddenly said into the darkness.

'What? Who? Who's dead?'

'My husband.'

'That's a pisser. When did he die?'

'Oh, a long time ago.'

'I'm sorry.' Gráinne took another cigarette out of the packet on the dashboard and lit it.

'Do you really have to do that?' Margo asked with a sigh.

'What?' Gráinne blew out a plume of smoke.

'Never mind. I suppose you're going to smoke no matter what I say.'

'You bet.'

'But don't you realise,' Margo insisted, 'that you're hooked on something highly addictive? A drug that will eventually kill you? Not to mention what it's doing to your skin and your teeth. You have no idea how much better you would feel if you stopped. And if you changed your lifestyle just a little, cut down on fat and sugar, maybe did a little exercise, you could look—'

'Shut up!' Gráinne suddenly shouted.

'What? You don't want me to talk to you?'

'I don't care about fucking lifestyles!'

'Yes, but…'

'If you don't fucking well close your mouth, I will throw you out!'

'OK, don't get excited,' Margo said. 'I just thought I'd tell you…'

'Just shut the fuck up.'

'Charming,' Margo muttered to herself. 'Lovely manners.'

Gráinne glared at her.

'OK. I won't say another thing,' Margo promised.

'Good.'

The truck rattled on while they both stared out the window, the potholes becoming more frequent, making the truck bounce and lurch and Gráinne swear even louder.

'You know, you remind me of someone,' Margo said despite herself a little later.

'Who?' Gráinne demanded.

'My husband.'

'The one who died?'

'That's right. You use exactly the same vocabulary. Amazing.'

23

'I talk like a fucking plastic surgeon, now?'

Margo smiled. 'That's right. Exactly like him.'

'Shit, that's f—' Gráinne glanced at Margo. 'OK, I get it.'

Margo leaned her back against the seat and closed her eyes. It's a nightmare, she thought. I'm not in this horse truck with this weird woman, I'm in the hotel, I went to sleep and had a really strange dream. There'll be a knock on the door and the waiter will bring us breakfast – coffee, orange juice, fresh croissants…

*

They had met at work. Margo had been twenty-two, just qualified as a physiotherapist, and had started working at the orthopaedics ward in one of London's biggest hospitals. She felt very lost at first. When Ted, the registrar on her ward, asked her to join him at his table in the cafeteria on her second day, she was delighted. She took her tray and walked over to the table.

'Here,' Ted said and pulled out a chair, 'sit down.'

'Thanks.' Margo sat down and smiled at him. 'I hate eating on my own.'

'It's always tough when you're new,' he replied. 'But I'm sure you'll make friends very soon.'

'I hope so.'

'Of course you will.' He looked at her with admiration in his eyes. 'I have to say, you're the best-looking physio we've had for a long time.'

'Oh, that's…I mean, thank you.'

'How about you and me—'

'Well, well, well,' a voice interrupted him. 'What have we here?'

Margo looked up at the tall man standing by their table.

'Oh, hello Alan,' Ted murmured, sounding deflated. 'Margo, this is Dr Hunter. He's on Mr Major's team.'

'Mr Major?' Margo asked, shaking the man's hand. 'The plastic surgeon?'

'That's right,' Alan replied, sitting down beside Margo. 'What's your speciality, Margo?'

'I'm a physiotherapist. I've just started working in orthopaedics.'

'How nice,' Alan said and draped his arm across the back of her chair. 'I'm very pleased to meet you. You have livened up an otherwise rather dull day. I love blondes with…' he looked into her eyes, 'dark green eyes.'

Suddenly a shrill bleep could be heard. 'Damn.' Ted took out a pager from his pocket and got up from his seat. 'Have to go. A patient in recovery kicking up a fuss. But I'll see you later? Maybe we could go for a coffee, or a drink, or a pizza or…' He looked somewhat sheepishly at Margo. 'Think about it. I'll be in touch.'

Margo looked at Ted as he sprinted out of the cafeteria, his white coat flapping around his tall, skinny body. She turned back to find that Alan was still looking at her intently. There was an air of arrogance about his bearing and a hint of conceit in his slightly protruding pale blue eyes. Margo looked back at him levelly.

'So.' A little smile played on Alan's lips. 'Margo.'
'Yes?'

'Lovely name. Margo,' he said again, propping his chin in his hand. 'You're going to have dinner with me tonight.'

'What? I mean, I don't know if I'm…'

'Free?' He took her hand. 'Of course you are.'

His touch made her feel both hot and cold at the same time. His eyes were hypnotic.

'All right,' she heard herself say. 'I am free. I mean I will. Have dinner, I mean.'

He patted her hand and then let go of it. 'Good girl.' He rose, put his stethoscope around his neck and buttoned his white coat. 'Champagne at the Ritz?'

She laughed out loud, thinking he was joking.

He looked at her without smiling. 'You do know where that is, don't you?'

'The Ritz?' she stammered, feeling suddenly very stupid. 'Of course, but…'

'Good. See you there at eight?'

'Eh, fine.'

'And we'll have dinner somewhere nice and then go to a club. Wear something slinky.' He flashed her his practised smile, which was to become so familiar, and strode out of the cafeteria.

*

The truck bumped across cobblestones on the road that had suddenly become very narrow.

'We're here,' Gráinne announced as they drove through a set of gates into a yard with an old barn and another gate that led to a field. 'Finally.' She pulled up the truck and switched off the ignition. 'Great. Now all we have to do is let out the horses and make sure they have hay and water and then we can turn in for the night.' She stretched her arms above her head and yawned. 'I sure am tired. What about you?'

'Exhausted,' Margo replied, leaning her head against the back of her seat.

'You look half dead,' Gráinne said with a little laugh. 'But never mind, we'll soon be able to nod off.' She opened the door and started to get out. 'Give me a hand with the horses, will you? There are a pair of wellies behind your seat. Stick them on. I can't see you going far in those bits of string you're wearing.'

Margo glanced down at her Prada sandals. 'You're right. Not very practical. But I didn't think I would be doing farm work when I put them on.'

'I suppose you thought you'd be swanning around Cannes.'

'Yes. Something like that.' Margo suddenly realised how different the evening would be if… 'So what do you want me to do?' she asked, sliding off her seat onto the cobblestones.

'Put those wellies on like I told you and come around the back of the truck,' Gráinne ordered. 'I'll take Daisy. She's a bit of a bitch when she's been tied up for a long time. Then you can lead Stan. He's a darling. No problem at all. We'll turn them out into this field here, see? And there's hay in the barn and I'll check the water. Won't take a minute.'

There was suddenly a commotion inside the truck and a horse neighed loudly, then a kind of screaming. 'Shut up, you bitch!' Gráinne shouted, lowering the ramp at the back of the truck and walking in. 'Stay back,' she ordered, 'she might decide to charge.' She swung back the partition to reveal a big black horse trying its best to break loose. 'There now,' Gráinne soothed, untying the rope that was attached to a ring in the wall. 'Calm down.' The horse rose on its hind legs and kicked at Gráinne, who jumped back. 'Shit! Will you stand, you bastard!'

Margo backed away as Gráinne led the frisky mare out of the truck and into the small paddock. The horse broke free just as they were inside the gate and, rearing and bucking, galloped into the paddock, where it proceeded to roll in the dust.

'OK. I'll just check the water trough,' Gráinne said. 'Go get Stan, will you?'

'Oh, but, I'm not sure if…' Margo felt more like hiding behind the barn than approaching the other horse.

'Don't worry. He's as good as gold,' Gráinne assured her. 'He wouldn't hurt a fly.'

Margo tiptoed into the truck and peeked over the edge of the other partition. A pair of big brown eyes met her gaze. She slowly opened the partition, ready to flee at the slightest hint of trouble. Her heart was pounding in her chest and her sweaty hands slipped on the latch. The big chestnut stretched his head toward her and nuzzled her cheek. His gentle eyes met hers and Margo knew he wouldn't cause her any problems.

'Hello, Stan,' she murmured. 'What a nice boy you are.' Stan's warm breath on her face and the velvet touch of his muzzle suddenly felt very comforting. As Margo put her hand on his silky neck and breathed in the horsey smell, she was instantly transported to pony camp when she was a child. She put both her arms around the horse's neck and her face against his shoulder. 'Oh, Stan,' she sighed. 'You have no idea how nice it is to meet you.' Stan sighed, shifted his weight and blew into her hair. Margo stood back. 'I'll take you outside now, darling,' she said, 'and you'll get some nice hay and some fresh water and then you can sleep under the stars until tomorrow. How's that?'

'Have you got a grip on that horse yet?' Gráinne yelled from the paddock. 'Get him out of the truck before tomorrow, will ya?'

Margo untied the rope and led Stan down the ramp and into the paddock, where Daisy was trotting around, rolling her eyes.

'Great,' Gráinne said when Margo had let Stan loose and closed the gate, 'that's them settled. Now we can have a bite to eat and then organise the sleeping arrangements.'

'Eat?' Margo said, suddenly realising she was very hungry. 'Is there a village nearby? Maybe we can have dinner there, then?'

'Nah,' Gráinne shook her head. 'The nearest village is miles away. And there's no restaurant there, only a kind of bar. But I have some stuff I bought this morning. Sausages, cheese, a bit of bread and some apples. That do ya?'

'Well, if you're sure there's enough for both of us?' Margo said. 'I wouldn't want to…'

'No bother. There's plenty.'

'Oh, good. But…'

'What?'

'Is there…' Margo hesitated. 'Would there be a bathroom around here?'

Gráinne laughed raucously. 'Bathroom? Jesus, where do you think you are, the bloody Hilton? If you need to go for a pee, you have to go in the bushes. And there's a stream down the hill, just behind those trees there. Very popular with the ducks and not bad if you want to wash.'

'Oh, great.' Margo felt suddenly more alert at the thought of cool water against her hot, sticky skin. She took her bags and started to walk toward the trees.

'Don't worry about stripping off,' Gráinne called after her. 'There's no one around and the cows have seen everything by now.'

Margo stopped. 'But who owns this place? Is there no farmhouse or people looking after the animals?'

'It belongs to the château. You can see it from the hill on the other side of the stream.'

*

As she walked toward the stream, Margo glimpsed the towers of the château against the darkening summer sky. A soft breeze lifted her hair and caressed her face and she enjoyed the coolness and the smell of flowers and grass. A few stars glinted in the sky and the thin crescent of a new moon rose above the trees. Water gurgled over a weir into the stream, the sound enticing in the hot evening. Margo walked down to the edge of the water. She took off the wellies, pulled her T-shirt over her head and stepped out of her trousers. Her bra was stuck to her skin and she took it off with a sigh of relief and dropped it onto the pile of clothes. She started to ease her knickers over her hips, but froze when she heard Gráinne coming down the path. In the cover of the near darkness, Margo quickly finished undressing and stepped into the black water. She sighed happily as she sank down into the weir, swimming away from the edge, turning onto her back and floating, her hair in the cool water, her face to the sky. 'Heaven,' she murmured to herself. 'This is truly heaven.'

'How is it?' Gráinne asked, pulling off her shirt. 'Hope it isn't too cold.'

'It's lovely.' Margo turned away as Gráinne stripped off the rest of her clothes. 'You know,' she said, her eyes on the trees opposite, 'I just remembered. There are some soaps in my bag. The big leather one. I bought them...well, never mind. Help yourself.'

'Great.' Margo could hear Gráinne rummage in the bag. 'Jesus, this is really fancy. Smells like a whole whorehouse. Want one?'

'Yes, please.' Margo swam closer and caught the soap Gráinne threw her.

'This is nice.' Gráinne lathered up her soap and rubbed her breasts. 'I never buy this kind of thing. A bar of Palmolive usually lasts me months. But these little guys seem to melt...oops, dropped it down my...'

Margo swam away again. She trod water while she discreetly washed herself under the surface.

'What are you doing over there?' Gráinne shouted. 'I can hardly see you. I have to stay in the shallow end. Swimming is not exactly my favourite sport.'

Margo swam a little closer. 'Don't you know how to—' A shout from the trees, accompanied by loud barking, interrupted her. A man's voice called out something in French. Margo sank deeper into the water, suddenly aware of her state of undress.

'*Qui est la?*' the deep voice called.

'It's only me, Jacques,' Gráinne yelled back. 'I'm bringing a couple of horses back from the championships in Grenoble. And I have someone to help me and we're having a swim, OK? It's the farm manager,' she whispered to Margo. 'Probably come to have a peek, the bloody pervert.'

'Ah, Mademoiselle O'Sullivan,' the voice said, sounding more friendly. 'And you have a...a... friend?'

Margo looked up and saw the outline against the sky of a man holding a dog on a lead.

'That's right,' Gráinne replied. 'And we're just cooling off before dinner.'

'*Ah, oui.* I understand.' The man stood there, looking at them for a while, then turned and walked back the way he had come.

32

'Bloody peeping Tom,' Gráinne muttered. 'Well, he can keep his thing in his trousers, I'm not interested.'

Margo swam away again. She moved slowly through the water, enjoying the cool silkiness against her skin. She looked up at the crescent moon and the stars and felt as if she was in some kind of odd twilight zone. The real Margo had continued in the car and was now at the hotel, sorting out their luggage, soothing Alan, humouring him, apologising, taking more abuse and finally in bed, weeping quietly to herself, her tears sliding into the pillow. What am I doing? she thought, where am I going? She stared at the moon as if it could give her an answer, but it looked silently back at her, the mystery of the universe in its silvery light.

3

There was a smell of cooking in the air as Margo shuffled back to the truck, the big wellies chafing the skin of her heels.

'There you are,' Gráinne said as Margo came around the side of the barn. 'I'm cooking up a storm here.'

'So I see.' Margo put her bag down and walked over to a camping stove Gráinne had rigged up on an upturned wooden crate under the headlights of the truck. She sniffed the air hungrily. 'What's that I can smell?'

'Sausages. I found some of these in a super-market this morning. Not like Irish sausages, though, but they seem all right. What do you think? You don't mind eating warm food? I know something cold would be better in this hot weather, but this is all I have apart from bread and cheese. Not your three-course gourmet dinner, but...'

Margo's stomach rumbled in anticipation. 'They smell lovely. I'm so hungry I could eat a horse.'

'Shh, not too loud. You might upset you-know-who,' Gráinne whispered, waving her fork in the direction of the paddock. 'Fuck!' she jumped back as the sausages suddenly spat in the pan. 'Sorry. I mean, damn. Oh shit.' Gráinne looked apologetically at Margo, rubbing her hand. 'Those bloody things spit like hell.'

'Are you all right?' Margo moved closer and peered at Gráinne's hand.

'Yeah, fine. I think they're cooked now in any case. Why don't you grab some of those paper plates over there and help yourself to some sausages and bread. I think there are tomatoes in the shopping bag and a big piece of cheese.'

A few minutes later they were sitting on a bale of straw, eating Gráinne's improvised supper. Apart from a soft rustle from the paddock and the odd cry of an owl, the dark, velvety night was still. Food never tasted so good, Margo thought as she bit into the sausage. It reminded her again of pony camp, of picnics in the woods, of feeling content and safe and not needing much more than the comfort of food, companionship and a good night's sleep. 'Lovely sausage,' she muttered through a mouthful.

'Yeah, not bad. Pity the bread is a bit hard. But that's French bread for you. Doesn't stay fresh for more than half an hour.' Gráinne chewed laboriously. 'Tough as old leather,' she mumbled.

'I know. French people buy bread three times a day. I always thought it was such a chore having to go to the baker's all the time.'

'How come you know so much about it?'

'I spent a year in Bordeaux as an au pair when I had just finished school. I thought I might do a degree in French or something.'

'But you didn't?'

'No.' Margo cut herself another wedge of cheese. 'This is nice. What kind of cheese is it?'

'Haven't a clue.' Gráinne studied Margo. 'What are you going to do when you get to Paris?'

'I'm going to look up a friend, well, acquaintance, really. She's been asking me to visit since she moved there from London.'

'Oh? What's she doing there? Working?'

'No. She's a solicitor, but I think she took a career break when her husband was posted abroad. He works at the British embassy. He's the agricultural attaché there.'

'What? In Paris? I didn't think they had any agriculture there.' Gráinne bit off another piece of bread with her small white teeth. 'I've only been there once and I've never seen any cattle. Lots of pigs though, but only of the two-legged male kind.'

Margo laughed. 'I know what you mean.'

Gráinne peered at her. 'Not too fond of them either?'

'Men? No, not at the moment. In fact, I think I might give them up altogether.' Margo broke off a piece of bread.

'Good idea. I never could figure out what use they are, actually. Apart from the obvious.'

'You haven't had much luck with men?' It was Margo's turn to study Gráinne.

'Do you want another beer?' Gráinne asked. 'There's a can left and I'll split it with you if you like.'

'No, you have it,' Margo said, feeling that one can of lukewarm Irish beer was as much as she could handle. 'Thanks for supper. It was great.'

'Glad you liked it.' Gráinne took Margo's plate and put it with her own into a plastic bag. 'And no washing up. Do you feel like turning in?'

'Oh, yes. I'm really tired.'

'OK. Let's get organised, so. The sleeping quarters in this truck are not exactly five star. Hope you can cope with that.' Gráinne opened the door to the truck and climbed in. 'Here, I'll show you.'

Margo got onto the step behind her.

'This is my bunk here behind the front seat,' Gráinne explained. 'And that's where you'll sleep tonight.'

'No, I couldn't take your bed,' Margo protested.

'Yes you will and no arguments. I'll set up the camp bed in the back of the truck. That's where that bitch who ran off used to sleep. It's quite all right, really.'

'Are you sure?'

'No bother,' Gráinne assured her, taking a bundle of blankets from a stack on the bunk. 'Here.' She handed some white fabric to Margo. 'Hang those over the windows. They'll stop the midges. Buggers would eat you alive.'

'Mosquito netting?' Margo turned the fabric in her hands. 'You're very organised.'

'Nah, just a couple of net curtains from Dunnes Stores back home. Try to get comfortable. Here's a blanket and there's a pillow over there. That's all you'll need in this heat. I'd take off those clothes and sleep in the buff if I were you. Much cooler.'

'Actually, I have a nightie,' Margo, said, suddenly realising that she had all her overnight requirements in the leather bag.

'Good. OK. That's you organised.' Gráinne jumped down onto the ground. 'I'm going to have a last fag and then I'll turn in as well. Good night, love.'

'Good night, and thanks a lot.'

'Ah sure, it was nothing.'

Margo secured the net curtains across the open windows and changed into her pretty white cotton nightgown, the kind she had thought Alan would like, with lace around the low neckline and a slit to the thigh. She had hoped it would turn him on. Margo suddenly felt herself shiver. She lay on the hard bunk and pulled the blanket over her. She closed her eyes, but even though she was exhausted, she was too tense to sleep. She could smell faint cigarette smoke and hear Gráinne moving around on the other side of the partition, muttering to herself. Everything that had happened that day flashed through her mind – the row in the car, Alan's rage, her sudden urge to run away, Gráinne, the truck, the horses… 'Stan,' she mumbled, 'the stream, Gráinne, Paris…'

*

'Are you OK?' Gráinne asked, lighting up her first cigarette of the day as they rumbled up the motorway. 'Not too tired?'

'I slept quite well, really.' Margo smiled and scratched a midge bite on her arm.

'Really? I wonder how, I must have snored like a fuc— fecking elephant.'

'You did. But that didn't really bother me.'

'You must have been really wrecked if you could sleep through my snoring,' Gráinne remarked.

'I was. But now I feel great. And I had a lovely dip in the stream this morning.'

'You seem to be hooked on cleaning yourself.'

'I thought you went in as well.'

'Nope. Last night was enough.'

'But I could have sworn…' Margo stopped. 'Do you smoke French cigarettes?'

'You mean those fat ones that smell like old socks? No way. I prefer a good old Marlboro.'

'Oh.' Margo stared ahead without seeing the cars and trucks, remembering getting out of the water and a faint smell of a Gauloise.

Gráinne glanced sideways at Margo. 'So, you're going to stay with these friends in Paris, is that it?'

'That's right.'

'Then what?'

'What do you mean?'

'Jesus, I mean what the feck are you going to do when your visit's over? Are you going back to London or what?'

'I don't know.' Margo suddenly felt butterflies in her stomach. 'I might stay on for a bit. I like Paris. It's my favourite city.'

'You know your way around then?'

'Oh, yes. I've been there many times.'

'OK, here's the exit you asked for,' Gráinne announced. 'Are you sure that's where you want to get off? I mean, you could go with me a bit further.'

'No, this is fine. I can take a train to Paris and then the Metro to my friend's apartment. And this way you don't have to go all the way into the city centre.'

'OK. Suit yourself.' Gráinne turned into the exit and drove up the slip road to the roundabout. They could see the train station as they drove into the small village.

Gráinne pulled up the truck. 'Here we are,' she announced. 'Right at the station. Fecking brilliant driving, even if I say so myself.'

'Absolutely,' Margo agreed. She gathered up her bags. 'Well, this is it then. Thank you, and…'

'Hang on,' Gráinne said, rummaging around in the glove compartment. 'I'll give you my mobile number. Just in case, right? You never know when you might need to get in touch. Got to have something to write on somewhere…here we are.' She picked up a piece of crumpled paper and scribbled something on it. 'There. Give us a shout if, well, you know.'

'Thanks.' Margo shoved the piece of paper into her handbag.

'Well, that's it. See ya around sometime.' Gráinne hesitated and then suddenly held out her hand. 'Goodbye and good luck and all that crap. Thanks a lot for helping out with the horses.'

'No, thank *you* so much. For…for…every-thing.' On an impulse, Margo leaned over and gave Gráinne a kiss on the cheek.

'Oh, shit,' Gráinne muttered, 'it was nothing.'

Margo opened the door and climbed down onto the street. She looked up at Gráinne for a moment. 'Goodbye,' she whispered, and, without looking around, walked swiftly across the street into the railway station.

*

Margo rang the bell and heard it echo inside the apartment. There was no sound for what seemed like an age and she pressed the button again. Still nothing. She was about to turn around and leave when the big door suddenly swung open. She smiled expectantly as a slim woman in a black dress, at least five rows of pearls and her dark hair swept up in a French twist came into view.

'Fiona! Hi!' Margo stepped forward, ready to kiss her friend on the cheek, but Fiona stepped back, a look of horror on her face, and stared at Margo as if she had seen a ghost.

'Margo,' she gasped, putting a hand to her chest. 'You're alive. Thank God.'

'Alive?' Margo said. 'Of course I am. What's the matter? I know it must be a huge surprise and I should have called first to tell you I was in town, but I thought—'

Fiona grabbed Margo roughly by the arm and pulled her into the apartment, slamming the door shut behind her.

'What are you…' Margo protested, trying to shake loose.

'Shut up,' Fiona hissed. 'Come with me.' She propelled Margo through the hall, down a corridor and through a large kitchen where two waitresses making canapés looked at them curiously. 'Just carry on,' Fiona snapped at them and pulled a door open. She dragged Margo into a small sitting room. 'We can talk here.'

'But Fiona,' Margo panted, trying to catch her breath after the sprint from the front door, 'what's wrong?'

'Sit down,' Fiona ordered as she locked the door.

'OK.' Margo sat down on a small sofa and stared at Fiona. 'But, please, why are you so—'

Fiona twirled around. 'Why am I so *what*?' she snapped. 'Are you out of your mind? Don't you know everybody's looking for you?'

'Everybody? What do you mean? Who is looking for me?'

'Christ, I don't believe this.' Fiona wrung her hands. 'How can you not know that there is a huge manhunt for you? The French police have been looking for you all over the country since you disappeared yesterday. Alan thinks you were kidnapped from some motorway café! Your picture has been on every news programme on television and the papers are full of…' Fiona turned around and took a newspaper from a table beside the television. 'Look, you're on the front page of *Le Figaro*!' She held it up.

'Where did he get that?' Margo stared at the picture, feeling confused. 'I look terrible in that picture.' She took the newspaper from Fiona. 'Oh God,' she muttered as she read, 'this is awful.'

'You bet it is. You have no idea how—' Fiona stopped suddenly and waved her hand in front of her nose. 'Sorry, darling, but what *is* that smell?'

'What smell? Oh, horse, probably,' Margo replied with a little laugh. 'I'll tell you about it in a minute.' She frowned at the picture. 'But why did Alan phone you if he thought I had been kidnapped?'

'I don't know. He said he remembered that you had mentioned looking us up while you were in France and thought you might have come here to ask for my help or something. He was not very pleasant, I have to tell you.'

'I can imagine,' Margo muttered as she continued to read the article. 'Oh God, the police seem to think I was taken away by force by some truck driver.'

'Weren't you?' Fiona stared at Margo with her huge Bambi eyes.

'No.'

'What happened?'

'We had a row, you see, and Alan was behaving like such a mean shit.'

'So? I mean, don't they all?' Fiona said, looking confused.

Margo put down the newspaper. 'No, this was too horrible. It was more like some kind of abuse. I just felt I couldn't take any more. We stopped at this petrol station and I went into the restaurant

43

for a cup of coffee. And then…I…I…just kind of, I don't know. Something snapped, I suppose. I just felt I couldn't face him. I left while he was filling the car. I walked across to the other side of the motorway and…'

Fiona looked startled. 'You just took off? Right there in the middle of the motorway?'

'Yes.'

'Oh,' Fiona said. 'I see. I know you've told me Alan has a bit of a temper, and I have to say it wasn't very nice to be on the receiving end of it this morning, but…' She stopped.

'But what?'

'You're not thinking of leaving him, are you? For good, I mean?'

Margo thought for a moment. She looked at the newspaper with her picture and the headline about a missing Englishwoman with a feeling that it was about someone else.

'Leave him?' she said, a little shocked at the idea. 'No, that really didn't cross my mind. I just felt like I needed some space. Just for a little while, anyway. It all happened so fast. I haven't stopped to think, really. I just walked away, and then…'

'But how did you get here?'

'That's what I was about to tell you.' Margo laughed. 'I got a lift with this rather quaint Irishwoman in a horse truck, or whatever you call it. We got off the motorway and drove…' She paused. 'I suppose that's why the police didn't find me. Anyway, we stayed the night on a farm and… Oh, Fiona, did you ever go to pony camp?'

'What?' Fiona looked confused again. 'Pony camp? What does that have to do with anything? But no, since you ask, I didn't.'

'Oh. Well, if you had, you'd know what I mean. It was just like that. You would have laughed if you had seen me, wearing wellies and working with the horses and eating sausages. It was fun, though. And this woman was really, eh, unusual, but nice.'

'Well, the Irish are charming, of course,' Fiona nodded, 'quite charming. But go on. What happened then?'

'Then I came here, because I thought I could stay with you for a couple of days while I...'

'Here?' Fiona suddenly looked very nervous.

'Oh, I know you're having a party and everything, but...'

'Yes, we are. A very important party, as a matter of fact. The *ambassador* is coming, you know. We've been trying to invite him for six months. It's so important for Marcus's career that we show that we can entertain at the very highest level.'

'Of course. I understand. And I won't disturb you at all. If I could just stay in your guest room for a couple of days.'

'And then you'll go back to London?'

'Yes, of course. Eventually.' Margo put the newspaper on the coffee table, got up and took Fiona's arm. 'Please,' she pleaded, 'let me stay. It'll just be for a few days. I need to get myself together. I need a bit of a rest, that's all. A holiday, I suppose. Yes, that's it. A holiday. Have you never felt like having a holiday on your own?'

Fiona pulled away and looked sternly at Margo. 'No, I haven't. And I have to tell you that it was very irresponsible of you to just take off like that. I've been out of my mind with worry, you know, thinking you were…oh God, I can't even say it.'

'I'm sorry,' Margo whispered, feeling guilty. 'I didn't realise this would have any impact on you or anyone else.'

'You just didn't stop to think, did you? I was so upset I…I nearly cancelled the party!'

'No!' Margo stared at Fiona in mock horror. 'You thought I was *dead* and you nearly cancelled the party? I'm *really* touched.'

'Stop it,' Fiona snapped. 'It's not funny.'

'No,' Margo agreed, 'it's not.'

'You're in a big mess, you know,' Fiona remarked. 'Alan is not going to be amused when you turn up and he finds out what you did. He's going to be so annoyed when it turns out that…'

'I'm not dead? That I wasn't kidnapped, raped and murdered and my body thrown into a ditch?'

'Yes. No. I mean…you know what I mean.' Fiona was red in the face. 'I think you should call Alan as soon as possible, if only to make him call off the police. You needn't tell him where you are. You could explain to him that you didn't know what you were doing, that you were having some kind of mood swing. Something hormonal. You're getting to the age when…'

'What do you mean?' Margo demanded angrily. 'Are you suggesting I'm menopausal? I'm only thirty-seven, for God's sake. And don't look at me in that patronising way! You're only a year younger, so if I'm menopausal, so are you!'

'Shh, there's no need to shout.' Fiona looked at the door as if someone would be able to hear them through the thick oak panelling. 'Calm down.'

'I'm perfectly calm,' Margo snapped. 'But if you don't think you can put me up, I think I'll be going now.'

'No, don't go,' Fiona said, looking suddenly contrite. 'It's all right. You can stay here for a little while. A few days. Until you feel ready to go back to Alan.' She looked at her watch. 'Shit! It's nearly seven o'clock. I have to go and make sure everything is OK and the chef has arrived. Marcus is supposed to have organised the drinks trolley in the drawing room. I have to go and check that too and that he has changed. It's black tie, but if I don't tell him he'll forget and put on a suit instead. And then I'll have to make sure Rufus is behaving and doing his homework and not driving the au pair mad, and...'

'Darling Rufus,' Margo said with false warmth in her voice. 'How is he?'

'Fine, just fine.' Fiona looked suddenly both sad and worried. 'It's just that he hasn't settled into school very well. We're having a few problems with discipline, but I'm sure that's just because he was quite upset by the move and losing his friends. They're very strict in this school and he isn't used to...'

'Doing what he's told?'

Fiona glared at her. 'I knew *you* wouldn't understand. Isn't it funny how people who have no

47

children always—' She stopped as she looked at Margo's face. 'Oh God. I shouldn't have said that. I'm just so stressed at the moment, I don't know what I'm saying any more.'

'It's OK. Forget it.'

'I'm sorry,' Fiona said and put her hand on Margo's shoulder. 'Look, I'll just show you the guest room and then…'

'That's fine. Thank you so much, darling. You really are a brick.' Margo wrapped her arms around Fiona. 'I'll be as quiet as a mouse, I swear.'

'Yes, all right,' Fiona said, peeling Margo's arms off her and smoothing her hair. 'Fine.' She unlocked the door and gestured silently for Margo to follow her down the corridor and into a bright, pretty room with a big double bed. 'This is it. Bathroom through there. Make yourself comfortable. I'll get you some sheets and towels.'

'What are you going to say to Marcus?'

'Oh,' Fiona shrugged, 'I'll just tell him you're staying the night and that you'll sort everything out in the morning. He's so occupied with the party and the ambassador and what he's going to say in his little welcome speech that he wouldn't care if an Iraqi terrorist was in the guest room. Don't worry.' Fiona walked to the door and opened it.

'By the way,' Margo called after her, 'love your dress. Terribly *Breakfast at Tiffany's*.'

'Thank you, darling.' Fiona smiled, slipped out of the room and softly closed the door.

*

48

Margo went to the window and looked out. The room had a view of the tree-lined street and a small square with a little pond where some ducks were swimming around, dipping their heads into the water from time to time. An old lady sat on a park bench throwing bread crumbs to the pigeons. Margo stepped away from the window and looked around the room, peered at a print of Paris, idly picked up a paperweight and finally sat on the bed, bouncing up and down as if to test the mattress. It was the first time she'd had a chance to think since her 'escape' the day before. She stared in front of her, going through everything that had happened and trying to get a grip on her feelings, but her mind was a blank. She didn't really know what to do next. But she enjoyed the peace and quiet all the same, the feeling of not having to do anything for the moment but stay here in this bright room and relax. Fiona would let her stay until she had decided what she was going to do. Very kind of her, Margo thought; in fact, surprisingly kind. Fiona didn't usually go out of her way for people if it didn't suit her.

They had met at the gym about ten years earlier when Margo was engaged to Alan and Fiona was newly married to Marcus. They had got into the habit of having a cup of coffee after the aerobics class and chatted about their respective lives – Margo about her job at the hospital and her forth-coming marriage and Fiona about her budding career as a solicitor, her little boy and her husband, who had a promising future as a diplomat. Not really close friends, Margo thought, but they enjoyed each other's company and being useful as dinner party guests at each other's houses. Margo admired Fiona's fashion sense and impeccable taste and Fiona seemed impressed with Margo's choice of husband. If she only knew the real Alan, Margo thought as she sat on the bed, she wouldn't find him so marvellous. But she's right about one thing, I'll have to get in touch with him. And of course I'm not going to leave him, whatever gave her that idea? He'll be furious, of course, but only for a while. But right now I'll just rest and try to get a good night's sleep. I must have a bath and get rid of the smell of horse. Maybe Fiona will lend me some bubble bath? She always has lovely bath products. I'll go and ask her.

Margo slowly opened the door a crack and tried to figure out where Fiona was. She could hear the maids in the kitchen chatting softly, and voices at the other end of the corridor. Fiona and Marcus. Talking about the party, probably. But the voices were suddenly louder, more intense, as if they were arguing about something. She could hear Fiona's voice, low and insistent, and Marcus's, indignant, protesting. Margo tiptoed closer, until she was right outside the half-open door.

'But she just arrived,' she could hear Fiona say, 'out of the blue. What was I supposed to do?'

'You have to call Alan,' Marcus said. 'He has a right to know. Can't you imagine what the poor man is going through?'

'Margo said he was absolutely beastly to her. That's why she ran away.'

'I find that hard to believe,' Marcus snorted. 'He's a very decent chap and a Harley Street specialist. Always very correct. A perfect gentleman.'

'I know. I find it really unbelievable too.'

'Did Alan say where he was when he called?' Marcus asked.

'He said he was in Cannes. At this conference they were going to. He said it helped him to have something to do.'

'He's very brave.'

'Yes, he's bearing up amazingly well,' Fiona said.

'So what are you going to do with her?' Marcus sounded annoyed. 'I hope you're not taking Margo's side in all of this. I don't think you should be involved at all, actually. Why should you? She didn't show any consideration for anyone else when she just took off like that. Where did she go? And how on earth did she manage not to get caught?'

'She hitched a lift with a truck driver,' Fiona said. 'Some woman transporting horses to Ireland. Margo seemed to have enjoyed it. Said it was just like pony camp. Isn't that sweet?'

'Sweet?' Marcus said. 'She's hysterical, can't you see that? She must be having some kind of breakdown. She might even be dangerous.'

'Don't be ridiculous.'

Marcus sighed. 'Well, maybe that was a little over the top. In any case, I really don't need this right now, Fiona. I thought we agreed that you would concentrate on me during this posting and not go off on one of your mad schemes.'

'But I have,' Fiona protested. 'I even took leave of absence from my job for you. I've done nothing but run around for you since we came here, and—'

'Oh, all right,' Marcus interrupted. 'I know all that. But this is a very important evening for me. You know I was hoping to tell the ambassador about this idea I have to make the French start buying British beef again since the BSE scandal. It's pure nonsense on their part to keep the ban.'

'I know, I know,' Fiona soothed. 'You told me. And everything is going to be fine. Don't worry about Margo, she won't ruin your evening.'

'You bet she won't. You're going to get rid of her right now.'

'But darling, that's not very kind.'

'I know, but she doesn't deserve kindness after all the trouble she caused. I'd call the police, but I don't want them here just when the guests arrive, so…'

'So?' Fiona asked. 'Throw her out into the street? She has no money and nowhere to go.'

'That's her problem,' Marcus said.

'You don't give a shit, do you?'

'Not really, no. Do you?'

Fiona sighed. 'I don't know what to think. I wish she hadn't arrived like this, tonight of all nights. I wish she wouldn't drag us into this…this fight she's having with Alan. It's so common, if you know what I mean. But she's here, so…'

There was a brief silence and Margo held her breath while she waited to hear what they would decide to do with her.

'OK. Let her stay,' Marcus said. 'For tonight. And we'll call Alan and tell him she's here.'

'But—'

'Shut up for a minute and think about it, Fiona. Alan has to be told that Margo is safe. They have to sort out their problems, you must know that.'

'You're right. Of course you are.'

'And if you tell her we'll help her, she'll keep quiet and not cause any problems tonight. So go back and tell her she can stay. Hand me the phone. I'll call Alan.'

Margo backed away from the door and padded silently back the way she had come, down the corridor, into the guest room, grabbed her un-opened bag and ran through the kitchen, smiling at the startled maids, towards what she hoped was the back door. It was. Margo stumbled past a bucket and mop and a garbage can, nearly fell over a stack of old newspapers and flew down the narrow back stairs to the ground floor, into the servants' entrance and finally outside. Breathing hard, she sprinted down the street, into the Metro station, through endless corridors, onto a platform and finally jumped on a train that was just moving away. Gasping for breath, sweat pouring down her face, Margo sank down on a seat as the train gathered speed. She didn't notice the elderly gentleman beside her as he wrinkled his nose and shifted uneasily in his seat before moving to another one in the nearly empty carriage.

4

The following night was the worst one of Margo's whole life. The small hotel she checked into, so quiet in the early evening, was heaving with noise all night. The sounds that emanated through the thin walls left no doubt about the activities of the occupants. Margo tried to block out the noise by stuffing tissues into her ears and putting the pillow over her head, but to no avail. The thumping, moaning and sometimes even *screaming* was impossible to ignore. My God, those girls work hard, Margo thought. Finally, at about five o'clock in the morning, the noise died down and Margo fell into an uneasy sleep, only to be woken up by the garbage trucks two hours later. Giving up on any hope of going back to sleep, she tidied herself up and went downstairs to pay for the room. She stared in disbelief at the price on the slip of paper the man behind the counter had handed her.

'What?' she exclaimed. 'There must be some kind of mistake. This hotel hasn't even got one star, and you're charging me this much?'

The porter, a swarthy, fat man with a huge moustache, glared back at her. 'The rooms are usually rented by the hour, you know. A whole night is a lot more expensive.'

'Oh, really? And what about breakfast? That wouldn't be included or anything?'

'That's right. It wouldn't.'

'Oh,' Margo said, feeling both angry and stupid. 'But I really don't think you're entitled to charge me this much, you know. I'm sure it's against the law.'

'You want to call *les flics*?'

They stared at each other for a moment. 'Eh, no, not really,' Margo mumbled finally.

The man shrugged.

Margo sighed and dug in her handbag for her wallet. Gritting her teeth, she paid the bill and walked out into the early morning sunshine. I've got to stop spending money like this, she thought, or I'll end up sleeping under one of the bridges like a tramp. She left the hotel, nearly running into the Metro station in her haste to leave the area and get back to civilisation. Half an hour later, she emerged from the Metro at a station near the Eiffel Tower with a feeling of great relief and went into a little café for breakfast.

Later that morning, as she walked down the street, feeling much better after a big cup of *café au lait* and some fresh bread and jam, but with no particular plan in mind other than trying to find a slightly better place to stay, she noticed a hairdressing salon with a big sign in the window. '*Coupe elève gratuit*,' Margo read. Free haircut by student. Not a bad idea. A shampoo and trim would be nice. She had managed to wash herself in the hotel, but not to shampoo her hair. The prospect of clean hair suddenly felt very tempting. And it was free. She pushed open the door and walked in. 'That offer,' she said to the receptionist, pointing to the sign, 'free cut?'

*

An hour later, Margo looked at herself in the mirror. She put a hand on her head to make sure it was really true, that she had allowed the girl to not only cut her hair shorter than she had ever worn it before, but to dye it a very light blonde. 'Champagne,' the girl had said, 'that's what the colour is called. Very sexy, no?' Margo had nodded, speechless, as she saw the result in the mirror. The tiny curls all over her head were more platinum than champagne. 'You like it?' the girl asked.

'Oh, eh, I have to get used to it.' Margo couldn't stop looking at the woman in the mirror.

'Oh but you are soooo beautiful, like this,' the girl said. 'So young and fresh. Marcel,' she called across the salon, 'come here and see what I did.'

A young man almost sprinted across the room and came to a stop behind Margo. He touched the back of her head. '*Fantastique*,' he declared, '*magnifique!*'

'Exactly,' the girl nodded.

'It makes her look like…like that singer,' the young man said. 'You know, the one who sings about angels. The English one.'

'Annie Lennox!' the girl exclaimed. 'You're right.'

'Who?' Margo asked.

'Don't you know her?' the girl exclaimed. 'But she is English like you and very beautiful. And like this, you look a little like her. With this new *coiffure*.'

'Really?' Margo turned her head and smiled at herself. It was certainly different, she thought. It makes my neck look longer and my eyes bigger. And I never realised I had cheekbones. With a sudden dart of fear, she tried to imagine what Alan would say if he saw her transformation. He liked her dark blonde hair dead straight and worn in a simple bob or tied back in a knot. 'That's what I call class,' he always said.

Still in a state of shock, Margo went to a nearby café, sat down at a table on the pavement and ordered a glass of *pastis* to help steady her nerves. The waiter smiled broadly at her as he handed her the glass with great flourish. '*Ecco signorina*,' he said.

'Oh, eh…' Margo felt suddenly self-conscious. '*Merci*,' she managed.

The waiter smiled again, put the bill on the table and left.

Margo sipped her drink and looked idly at the people walking past, enjoying the sunshine. When the waiter came back, she picked up the bill and reached for her wallet. There were no coins left, and she realised she would have to break one of the euro bills. But when she opened the wallet, it was empty. What? But where is that fifty I had? I could have sworn I had that and another two twenties... Oh God, no. The hotel...and the breakfast... She suddenly felt the blood drain from her face and cold sweat breaking out on her forehead and in her armpits as she realised she had spent every cent of her money without thinking. Her throat tightened and tears of panic welled up in her eyes. She looked up at the smiling face of the waiter. 'I...' she started, 'I can't...'

'*Que signorina?*' he asked, his voice full of concern. 'You not feeling very well?'

'I can't pay for this,' she exclaimed in English. 'I have no money left. Oh God, I'm so sorry.' Her mouth was so dry she could hardly get the words out.

'It's OK, *cara*,' the waiter soothed in very broken English. 'The drink is...how you say, on the house. But you have lost your money? Someone steal it?'

'Yes. No. I...' Margo didn't know what to say or do. 'I thought I had at least fifty euros left, you see, and...'

'You make mistake?' The waiter's eyes were sympathetic. 'I do all the time. But I have to work now. You sit here and do not worry. I will be back later, no?'

The Italians are so nice, Margo thought as she watched him weaving his way between the tables.

Then she tried to think of what to do next. Tears stung her eyes again as the full impact of her situation hit her. *Oh God, what am I going to do? Will I call Fiona and…? No, I can't. I can't crawl back to Alan, not like this. I can't, I can't*, she kept repeating to herself, feeling as if she had entered some kind of labyrinth she couldn't get out of. Tears kept welling up in her eyes and, feeling in her bag for a tissue, her fingers met a piece of paper. She pulled it out and glanced at it, the numbers not registering in her brain. She was going to crumple up the paper and put it in the ashtray when she realised what it was – Gráinne's mobile phone number. *I'll call her*, Margo said to herself, the thought of hearing a friendly voice suddenly very comforting. *She might still be in the country. She might even have an idea of what I should do next.* Margo took out her mobile, dialled the number and listened while the dial tone rang and rang. While she waited for Gráinne to answer, she turned the piece of paper around and started to read what was on the other side.

Dear Miss O'Sullivan, it said, *I am writing to you to enquire if you would be able to spend a few months at our estate. I have bought five horses for the French event team and we are very short of staff. I need someone to help out until the horses are fit and ready to be transferred to the team headquarters. If you are available, please contact me at the château, or at the Paris address above before the end of the month.* The letter was dated July 2 and signed J. Coligny de la Bourdonnière.

Margo stared at the letter as the dialling tone suddenly stopped. 'The number you are calling,' a tinny voice said, 'is temporarily out of range. Please try again later.'

*

'*Oui?*' the old woman said. She was wearing a white apron over a blue housecoat and her steel-grey hair was tied back in a severe knot. She stood squarely in the hallway, looking as if she was poised to close the heavy front door in Margo's face.

'Do you speak English?'

'*Non.*'

Margo breathed in deeply. 'OK. Well, eh, *bonjour*,' she said, 'I'm looking for a Monsieur…' she consulted the letter, 'Monsieur Coligny de la…'

'*Count* Coligny de la Bourdonnière,' the old woman corrected.

'That's right. Count Coligny de la Bourdonnière.'

'He's not here.' The woman started to close the door.

'Oh, but when will he be home?' Margo said and put a hand on the door. 'I could come back later.'

'What is it about?' The woman tugged on the door, but Margo was stronger.

'A job. He offered me a job a while ago,' Margo said, waving the piece of paper in the air. 'I have the letter right here.'

'What kind of job?'

'Looking after horses at the château. I know I should have gone there, but I happened to be in

Paris visiting a friend, and…' Margo paused and looked at the woman. 'I thought I would call in and see…'

'What's your name?' the woman demanded.

'My name? It's Gráinne,' Margo said, 'Gráinne O'Sullivan.'

'That's a strange name. Never heard it before.'

'It's Irish.'

'You're Irish?'

'That's right,' Margo replied, looking back at the stern face with what she hoped was confidence.

'Hmmm.' The old woman seemed a little less hostile. 'Madame is in,' she announced. 'I'll ask her if she'll see you.'

'Madame?'

'Yes, Madame la Comtesse, of course.'

'Of course.'

'Stay here.' The old woman closed the door, leaving Margo standing on the dark landing. A few minutes later, the door opened again. 'Madame la Comtesse will see you in the small *salon*,' the old woman announced. She led the way through the huge hall, down a long corridor and into a room full of antique furniture. Louis XV, Margo thought automatically. 'Wait here,' the old woman ordered and left the room.

Margo sat down gingerly on a gilt chair with an exquisite embroidered seat. The room was silent except for the ticking of a small ormolu clock on the mantelpiece. There was a faint smell of dried rose petals and the room seemed far removed from the hustle and bustle of the street below. Feeling suddenly tired, Margo rested her head against the back of the chair and closed her eyes.

'Mademoiselle O'Sullivan?' The voice was imperious.

Margo gave a start and jumped to her feet. '*Eh oui*?' She stared at the elegant, straight-backed woman who, seemingly from nowhere, had just materialised before her. The woman looked to be in her late fifties or early sixties, but her features were classic and her frame as slim as a pencil. Her beauty was ageless and Margo felt she would probably still be stunning at eighty. She was dressed in a cream linen dress and her dark hair, gleaming like polished ebony, was cut in a perfect bob. 'I am Comtesse Coligny de la Bourdonnière,' the woman said, holding out a hand.

Margo shook it limply. 'Good afternoon.'

'Please, do sit down.' The Comtesse's English was correct but heavily accented.

Margo sat down again and the Comtesse sat on another of the gilt chairs. She studied Margo for a moment with a penetrating look in her almond-shaped hazel eyes. 'So, you are looking for work?'

'That's right,' Margo replied, 'I received a letter from a Mister J. Col—I mean, Count—'

'My son. He manages our château.'

'Oh. I see. Well, I have this letter offering me work at the château for a few months. With the horses. I know I should have contacted him there, but I was in Paris and I thought he might be in town and I could talk to him…' Margo paused.

'You have experience with horses?'

'Well, yes, of course.'

'How did my son hear of you?'

'We've met many times at horse trials,' Margo lied. 'And when I was in Grenoble—'

One of the Comtesse's eyebrows shot up. 'Grenoble? You met him in Grenoble?'

'Yes. About a week ago.'

'How strange.'

'Why?'

The almond eyes were now colder than a Norwegian mountain lake. 'Because, Mademoiselle, my son wasn't in Grenoble this year.'

'Oh.' Shit, Margo thought. 'I mean, somebody gave me this letter from him while I was there,' she said, trying to sound confident.

'I see.'

Margo squirmed under the frosty stare. There was a long pause. Then the Comtesse spoke again. 'You're not Irish,' she said sternly. 'Nobody in Ireland speaks with that accent. Except for those dreadful Anglo-Irish. You're not one of them, are you?'

'Well, no.'

'Of course not.' The Comtesse looked at her with more interest. 'In that case, you can't be this, this Gray...what was that name again?'

'Gráinne,' Margo mumbled, 'rhymes with saw.' She added automatically, 'then nya.'

'I beg your pardon?'

'Never mind.'

'Very well.'

They looked at each other during what Margo thought giddily to herself was a very pregnant pause. The game is up, she realised, I might as well just tell the woman the truth and get out. 'No, I'm not,' she said. 'Her, I mean. Gráinne.'

The Comtesse stared at her incomprehensibly, then shook her head as if to clear her mind. 'Tell me then,' she demanded, 'who are you? And why are you here?'

'It's a long story.'

The Comtesse opened a lacquered box on the inlayed coffee table, took out a cigarette and put it in a long black holder. '*Racontez, moi,*' she ordered, crossing her long slim legs and lighting the cigarette with a Dunhill lighter. 'I'm sure it's very interesting.'

Margo looked on, fascinated, as the Comtesse blew out a thin stream of smoke through her perfect nostrils. The pungent smell of the French cigarette reminded her of something or someone, but she couldn't quite remember what or whom. 'Well,' she started, 'I was on holiday, you see. But I had a bit of bad luck with…with the tour bus I was on…'

'Tour bus?' One of the perfectly shaped eyebrows shot up again.

'Yes. It was going to Cannes.'

'A tour bus? To Cannes? *Vraiment?*' The Comtesse looked at Margo incredulously. 'I had no idea that sort of thing went to places like Cannes.'

'Well, yes, they do, but I never got there, because…because…' Margo didn't quite know how to continue, how to make her lie more convincing. 'The bus stopped to refuel at a motorway station. I got off to…to powder my nose, and when I came out again, the bus had left.'

'The bus had left? How very inconsiderate of it.' The Comtesse looked faintly amused. 'Then what did you do?'

'Well, I…I kind of changed my mind about going to Cannes and decided to try to get to Paris and then go back to London with the Eurostar or something. I was lucky enough to bump into a very nice woman who gave me a lift to Paris.' Margo was talking very fast now, as if this would make her story more believable. 'That was Gráinne O'Sullivan, actually.'

'When was this?'

'Yesterday.'

'Yesterday. I see. So what did you do when you arrived in Paris?'

'I, well, I looked up a friend who is living in Paris. Her husband works at the British embassy,' Margo babbled on, 'and I thought she might put me up, but…'

'But?'

'Well, she couldn't, as it turned out, because, well, that doesn't matter now, does it?'

'Not really, no,' the Comtesse said in a bored tone of voice. 'And where did you spend the night?'

'In a hotel in Rue St Denis.'

Now both the eyebrows shot up, nearly colliding with the hairline. 'Rue St Denis? In a *maison de passe*?'

'Well, yes, I suppose it was, but I didn't realise until…'

'Must have been an interesting experience,' the Comtesse remarked with the hint of a smile.

'Not one I would care to repeat.'

'I should think not.'

'No.'

There was another long silence, during which the Comtesse continued to smoke with utmost elegance. 'So,' she said finally, 'this, this, whatever her name was, that Irishwoman who gave you a lift, told you to come here and pretend you were her and try to get this job?'

'No, she knows nothing about it.'

'You stole the letter?' the Comtesse's lips curled.

'No, Gráinne gave it to me.'

'She gave it to you, but she doesn't know about the job?'

'No, she knew about *that*, but…'

'It's all a pack of lies, isn't it?'

Margo gave up. 'I'd better go now,' she said, getting to her feet. 'Thank you for seeing me, Madame.'

'Sit down,' the Comtesse ordered.

Margo sat again, startled by the sharp tone.

'*Allons*,' the Comtesse said. 'Let's forget about your story. How you got here is of no importance. I'm more interested in your skills.'

'My skills?' Margo asked, mystified.

'Yes. I might be able to use you. What is your profession?'

'Profession? Well, I suppose you could say that I'm a medical secretary.'

'Excellent. And you have a very nice accent. I take it that you would like to stay on in Paris for a while?'

Margo nodded, feeling a ray of hope.

'And that you might also prefer to be, shall we say, incognito?'

'Yes,' Margo mumbled.

'Are you involved in any kind of crime?'

'Absolutely not,' Margo declared.

'That, my dear, seems to be the first time you've told me the truth.' The Comtesse looked at Margo shrewdly. 'And what about your husband?'

'What makes you think I'm married?'

'Apart from your wedding ring and that rather vulgar diamond? Nothing. But you are quite attractive for an Englishwoman, and you're not a teenager, so I assumed…'

'I don't want to talk about it.'

'Fine.' The Comtesse removed what was left of her cigarette from the holder and stubbed it out in a marble ashtray. 'I'm not interested in your love life, or lack of it.' Her gaze strayed to Margo's hair. 'That…that *coiffure*…is it on purpose or are you recovering from an illness?'

Margo touched her hair. 'Well, no. It was a kind of accident.'

'I don't think I want to know. Let's hope it grows out very quickly. Now, about your position.'

'But what do you want me for?' Margo managed to cut in. 'I mean, what sort of job would it be? I don't think I want to do housework or anything like that.'

'You would be my secretary, of course. Or...' The Comtesse seemed to consider the question for a moment. 'Personal assistant? Yes. I had an assistant but she just left to get married, and, well, I was going to advertise the position, but now that you're here, I thought I might give you a chance. In any case, you're the same size as...' She paused. 'What do you think?'

'I...well...' Margo didn't know what to say. What was going on here? she wondered. She had been sure the Comtesse was going to throw her out when she discovered that she had been lying, but now...

'Room, board and three hundred euros a month,' the Comtesse breezed on. 'All right?'

It seemed like the worst deal Margo had ever heard of and she was about to say so, but considering the alternative, she managed a feeble 'yes'. What have I got to lose, she thought. I can always leave when I've had enough.

'Excellent.' The Comtesse nodded, looking satisfied. 'Now, all I want to know is your name. Now that we have established that you are not this Mademoiselle O'Sullivan, I mean.'

'Of course. My name,' Margo started, 'is Mar...Margaret...' she glanced around the room for inspiration and caught sight of the television set. 'Philips,' she ended. 'Margaret Philips.'

The Comtesse followed her gaze. 'That's a Sony. Never mind. I will just call you Marguerite.'

'And what do I call you? Countess?'

'Oh, I don't use my title these days. Nobody

does. It's because of the socialists.' The Comtesse paused. 'You may call me milady.'

'Very well.'

'And I expect you to be very discreet and not to gossip. Is that clear?'

'Absolutely,' Margo promised, wondering what sort of things there would be to gossip about.

'Good. Now, about your accommodation.' The Comtesse's voice took on a businesslike tone. 'There is a staff room on the top floor of this building. You will take your meals in the kitchen with Justine.'

'Justine?'

'My housekeeper. She let you in.' The Comtesse looked Margo up and down with a hint of distaste. 'Do you have any other clothes?'

'No. I left my clothes…'

'On the bus?'

'Yes.'

'Yes…?' The almond eyes bored into Margo.

'Yes, milady,' Margo mumbled, feeling like a twelve-year-old.

The Comtesse nodded, looking satisfied. 'Never mind your clothes. You will find your uniforms in the wardrobe of your room. One for daytime and one for evening. And some other things you might find useful. Give what you're wearing to Justine for cleaning.'

Margo nodded.

'I think that's everything,' the Comtesse announced, getting to her feet. 'If you wait here, I'll get Justine to give you some sheets and tell her to take you to your room. And I'll see you tomorrow morning.' Without another word, she glided out of the room and closed the door, leaving Margo feeling vaguely as if she had sold her soul to the devil.

*

The lift creaked and groaned, shook and rattled as it slowly rose through the building, and Margo wondered if they would ever reach their destination. She hugged the pile of bedclothes tighter to stop it from sliding out of her grip and looked at the small, sturdy figure beside her. Justine had not uttered one word since they'd entered the lift, looking straight ahead with an expression of great pain on her plain face.

'So, isn't this strange,' Margo said in French, trying to sound jolly, 'we're going to be seeing a lot of each other.'

Justine shrugged.

After a long silence, Margo tried again. 'Have you been working for the family long?'

'All my life,' Justine muttered.

'Oh. That's…a very long time.'

'Hmmm.'

'And are you happy working here?'

'It's a living.'

'The Comtesse seems very nice. A very interesting lady.'

'Hah.'

'What about her husband?' Margo asked, pretending not to have noticed the sour note in Justine's voice. 'Is he nice?'

'Dead. Died a long time ago,' Justine muttered.

'Oh no, how sad for her.'

'He was very old. A lot older than her.'

'Yes,' Margo said, 'but it's still sad to lose your husband.'

'She got over it.'

'I see.' Margo tried to think of something that would lighten the atmosphere, but the lift had come to an abrupt stop and Justine heaved the cast iron gates open and stepped out onto the landing. She walked up another flight of stairs and Margo followed. She looked around, amazed at the difference between the attics and the floors below. Up here, there was no oak panelling or marble floors, only peeling paint and creaking floorboards. They walked down a long corridor, past a number of doors through which could be heard a mixture of sounds – voices arguing, music from a radio, the occasional cry of a child. The heat was stifling under the low ceiling and the air smelled of cabbage, garlic and exotic spices. Margo walked behind Justine, the pile of bedclothes growing heavy in her arms, feeling as if she had stepped into some kind of time warp. Finally, Justine came to a stop. She took out a big key, put it in the lock and threw the door open.

'*Voila*,' she said, walking in, '*la chambre de bonne.*'

Margo followed Justine into the little room with the old-fashioned wallpaper, sloping ceilings and worn linoleum on the floor. 'Oh,' she said, looking around, 'it's…it's kind of sweet, really.' Justine didn't reply, but took a set of keys and handed them to Margo. 'That's the key to the door. This one is to the toilet and shower down the hall.' She paused, holding out a hand. 'Now, *Mademoiselle*, I would like your clothes.'

'My clothes?' Margo stammered, putting her burden on the old-fashioned mahogany bed.

'Yes. Madame said to take them and clean them at once. It would be better to burn them, in my opinion.'

'But I have nothing else to wear.'

'There are clothes in that *armoire* over there. And a dressing gown.'

Justine stood in the middle of the floor, her arms folded across her ample bosom, while Margo undressed.

'It's strange, though,' Margo remarked, handing Justine her T-shirt, 'how she offered me this job just like that. I wonder why?'

Justine didn't reply. She took the clothes one by one in her thumb and index finger, as if they were contaminated, and walked out, leaving Margo standing in her underwear in the middle of the room.

When she had left, Margo walked to the big walnut wardrobe, opened the door and surveyed its contents. A frayed navy blue dressing gown and a number of items of clothing, all wrapped in plastic, hung inside on wire coat hangers. Without looking at the rest of the clothes, Margo took down the dressing gown and wrapped it around her. Feeling totally shell shocked, she flopped onto the bed, asking herself what on earth she was doing there.

Is this really happening, she asked herself as she looked up at the ceiling with the cracked plaster and the light bulb hanging from an electric wire. Am I really going to live in this dump and work for that woman?

Margo sat up again, got off the bed and walked across to the open window. Peering out, she could see rooftops and windows and balconies all higgledy-piggledy, above them a patch of blue sky and, leaning out precariously, she caught a glimpse of the top of the Eiffel Tower. Two pigeons were cooing from the small terrace opposite, where a number of terracotta pots were spilling out geraniums in a profusion of colour. She stood there for a while and watched the sky turn from blue to pink, enjoying the cool breeze against her face. Then she made up the bed and put her few possessions into the cavernous wardrobe. She washed her face and hands, dried them on a towel that smelled faintly of cologne and, after taking off the dressing gown, crawled in between the cool linen sheets and put her aching head on the pillow. She closed her eyes, listened again to the soft cooing of the pigeons and, just as in the truck with Gráinne, fell into a deep sleep.

5

'Madame's breakfast,' Justine declared the next morning while she prepared the tray, 'is quite a tricky business.' Her stocky frame was encased in a blue cotton dress covered by a crisp white apron that crackled with starch as she moved. Her grey hair was pulled back so severely it looked as if the bun at the back of her head had been tightened with a wrench.

'Oh,' Margo said, feeling awkward standing there in the kitchen in the navy skirt and white blouse. 'Tricky? Why?'

'Because she is never happy.' Justine poured orange juice into a crystal goblet, placed it on the starched linen cloth and looked up at Margo. 'Those clothes fit you perfectly.'

'I know. I couldn't believe it when I tried them on. And all the other things fit me too, even the shoes. But why is Madame – I mean, Milady – never happy?'

'Milady?' Justine snorted. 'Has she given herself a new title, then?'

'Well, that's what she told me to call her. And that is also what you would call a countess in English,' Margo explained. 'But do go on. What is the problem with Milady's breakfast?'

Justine shrugged. 'Oh, you'll see. No matter how hard I try, she always complains.' She put a small basket of fresh bread rolls beside the orange juice, followed by a plate, a knife and a large cup which she filled with equal amounts of coffee and hot milk. She put one and a half cubes of sugar into the coffee and placed a small bowl with jam and a saucer with two tiny rolls of butter beside it. Finally, after having placed a single red rose in a small vase on the tray, she lifted it up and handed it to a startled Margo. 'Here, you take it in.'

'Me? But…' Margo backed away.

'Not fancy enough for you? Not the job of a personal assistant?' Justine almost spat out the last words.

'No, it's not that. I…'

Justine glared at Margo.

'Oh, all right.' Margo took the tray. 'Where do I go?'

'Go to the lobby, then take the corridor on the right, and it's the second door on your left,' Justine replied.

Margo found the designated door and, trying her best not to drop the tray, managed to knock gently.

'*Oui?*'

'Breakfast, Ma…Milady.'

'Bring it in then!'

Margo turned the handle, pushed the door open with her shoulder and walked into the still, dark bedroom. 'Good morning, Milady,' she murmured. I'm really good at this, she thought with delight.

'Where's Justine?' the voice from the large four-poster bed demanded.

'In the kitchen. She asked me to—'

'Open the curtains,' the voice ordered.

Margo put the tray on a table near the door and walked over to the windows. She pulled the heavy brocade curtains apart and the room was at once flooded with light. As she walked back to pick up the tray, she glanced around the huge room, noticing the beautiful Persian carpet, the deep red silk on the walls and the exquisite French antiques. There were some impressive oil paintings, but Margo's eyes were immediately drawn to a huge framed black and white photograph of a vaguely familiar woman. There was a big vase with fresh flowers and a silver candlestick on the table underneath. Margo nearly tripped on the carpet as she stared at the photo, trying to figure out who it was.

'Coco Chanel,' the Comtesse said. 'The pillar of French haute couture.' She was sitting up in the huge bed, propped up by a number of pillows in lace pillowcases. With her dark hair and pale pink silk negligee, she looked like a very beautiful ageing diva. Margo put the tray in her outstretched hands and the Comtesse put it across her knees. 'Thank you,' she said graciously, picking up the linen napkin and studying the contents of the tray. 'This looks to be in order.'

Margo smiled back and walked to the door, wondering what all the fuss had been about. Justine was just trying to frighten me, she thought, opening the door.

'Wait!'

Margo froze.

'The coffee is not strong enough,' the Comtesse announced. 'Take the cup back and make me some really strong coffee.'

Margo took the cup and brought it back to the kitchen. 'It's too weak,' she said.

Justine, who was sitting by the table enjoying her own breakfast while she read the morning paper, didn't lift her eyes from the front page. 'Give it a minute, then bring it back again,' she muttered through a mouthful of bread and jam.

'What? But shouldn't I...' Margo gestured towards the coffee pot.

'She won't notice. She only complains because she wants to be difficult. She thinks it makes her important.'

Margo walked back with the coffee, which, as Justine had predicted, the Comtesse accepted without question. 'No good, that woman,' she muttered, cutting her bread roll in half, 'getting too old and confused. I should get rid of her, but she has nowhere to go. Been in the family for genera-tions.'

'I see,' Margo mumbled. She turned to leave.

'Where are you going?'

'I thought I'd go and…until you've finished your breakfast…'

'The newspaper. Give it to me.'

'Oh, right. Where…'

'It should be on my tray. That woman has forgotten it again. Go and get it and come back here at once.'

'Right away.' As Margo walked out of the room yet again, she had the peculiar sensation of playing the part of some kind of a go-between in an elaborate minuet.

'I would leave, but she can't manage without me,' Justine said in the kitchen, handing Margo the newspaper. 'I should go and live with my cousin in Tours. She has been asking me for years.' Justine shook her head. 'But I can't leave the family. They need me badly.'

Back in the bedroom, the Comtesse was waiting impatiently. 'My eyes are a little dry this morning. I would like you to read the paper to me. Start with the first page. The headlines. Then the main stories, the theatre and book reviews and the social pages. Then the weather. In that order.'

'In French or English?'

'French,' the Comtesse barked. 'You might as well practise.'

Margo read the newspaper, having her pronun-ciation corrected at nearly every word. When the Comtesse was satisfied she was *au fait* with what was going on in the world, she announced she was getting up. 'Draw me a bath,' she ordered, 'and lay out my clothes. The blue linen Chanel today, I think. Cream shoes and handbag. Fresh under-wear. You'll find it all in the dressing room.'

It took Margo some time to find, first the dressing room, then the required items in one of the huge oak wardrobes that lined the walls of the dark and gloomy room. The wardrobes were full to bursting with beautiful clothes squashed together in no particular order. When she finally spotted a pale blue linen ensemble and rummaged around on the floor of the wardrobe for the shoes, she went back to the bedroom, where the Comtesse was pacing up and down on the carpet, talking rapidly into a mobile phone. Margo blinked and stared. The Comtesse was fully dressed in a blue linen dress and beige Chanel slingback shoes, and her hair and make-up were immaculate. She switched off her phone and stared at Margo. 'Where have you been?'

Margo held up the clothes. 'I went to get...' she stammered. 'You said the dressing room.'

'*Mon dieu,*' the Comtesse exclaimed, throwing her hands up, 'not *that* room! You must have gone in the wrong direction. That is my vintage collection you have been going through. Did I not tell you to go to the dressing room?'

'Yes, but I thought that *was*...' Margo's voice trailed away.

'No, no!' The Comtesse walked across the room and threw a door open. 'In here. This is where my current wardrobe is kept. What you have there is the pre-nineteen-eighties clothes.'

'Oh. I see.'

'Yes.' The Comtesse sighed with the exasperation of someone forced to be kind to a very small and very slow child. 'Hang those clothes back, please. *Exactly* where you found them.'

'All right, Milady.'

'Good. I am going out now and won't be back until late afternoon. I have written out a list of instructions and left it on my desk in my study. And by the way, my son will be home for dinner tonight at eight o'clock.'

Margo wanted to ask whether it was the dinner that was at eight o'clock or the return of her offspring, but the Comtesse had swept out of the room. Margo could hear her heels on the parquet as she walked swiftly down the corridor and the loud bang of the heavy front door as it closed behind her.

*

Margo tidied the bedroom, brought the breakfast tray back to the kitchen, managed to gulp down a piece of bread and some cold coffee and then helped Justine wash the breakfast dishes.

'How do I get to Milady's study?' she asked as they worked. 'I find this apartment and all the corridors so confusing.'

'Go to the inside lobby,' Justine replied, 'then take the corridor toward the hall. Turn left, then left again. Second door on the right after the *grand salon*. All the corridors start at the lobby, and if you get lost you can always go back there and start again.'

'Does this apartment take up the whole floor of the building?'

'That's right. It's the only one that is still the original size. The other ones have been split into two, and sometimes even three apartments.'

'How many rooms are there?'

Justine shrugged. 'Who knows?'

'But there are a *lot* of rooms,' Margo said.

'And a lot of locked doors,' Justine added with a strange look in her steel-grey eyes.

In the study, Margo stared at the list she had found on the polished mahogany desk. It consisted of two A4 pages. She sat down on the *Directoire* chair by the desk while she slowly read through her chores for the day. *Write invitations and address envelopes for dinner party next Thursday (list, cards and envelopes on small table by the window in* petit salon*)*, she read, *then post same. Collect dry cleaning, walk Milou* (a child? a dog?), *buy fresh flowers for dining and drawing room, help Justine with big table-cloths, iron silk blouses, press black linen trousers and jacket. After lunch –* 'Whaddya mean after lunch?' Margo muttered. 'It's eleven o'clock already.' She sighed. *After lunch*, she read again, *Galeries La Fayette...* There was a long list of things she was supposed to buy in said department store and charge to 'Milady's' personal account. She would find Metro tickets in a drawer in the hall table. Then another long list of things to do after that; silly little things like buying the evening newspaper, going to the English bookshop on Rue de Rivoli and enquiring about a book Milady had ordered, walking Milou again *(don't forget bag to pick up droppings)*. I do hope Milou is a dog, Margo said to herself. She looked up at a huge portrait of Napoleon over the period fireplace. He was sitting on a rearing white horse, his cloak billowing around him, pointing at the dark hills in the distance. *Victory at Marengo 1800* it said on a plaque on the bottom of the gilt frame. 'I suppose you never had to pick up doggie poo,' Margo mumbled. Napoleon stared back at her with an air of superiority in his burning black eyes. 'Remember Waterloo?' Margo asked him. 'Bet you didn't look so snooty when that was all over.'

*

Following consultations with Justine, Margo established that Milou was a bad-tempered, very elderly West Highland terrier who lived in what was called the *arrière cuisine*, a kind of laundry room cum pantry off the main kitchen. He lay in his basket, snoring lightly, on a silk cushion embroidered with his name.

'Hello there, Milou,' Margo cooed, trying to sound like Barbara Woodhouse, 'are you ready for walkies?'

Milou didn't stir. He opened one eye briefly, then closed it again and appeared to go back to sleep.

'Oh, come on,' Margo said, 'you'll love it. Lots of lampposts. We might even meet some lovely girl doggies. Paris is full of poodles, you must know that.' She nudged the basket with her foot. Milou growled softly.

Margo tried to lift him out, but pulled her hand back when he snapped. She stared at the dog, trying to figure out what to do, and he glared back, his eyes like little black buttons. 'You stupid mutt,' she mumbled under her breath. 'You flea-bitten mongrel.'

Milou closed his eyes again.

'What are you doing to the dog?' Justine called from the kitchen.

'Nothing. I can't get him to move.'

'He's lazy,' Justine said. 'Lazy and spoiled.' She walked into the room and glared at the dog. '*Allez, Milou,*' she snapped. 'Behave yourself and get out of there.'

The dog sighed and slowly got out of the basket. Justine clipped his lead onto his collar and handed it to Margo. 'There, take him out for a walk on the Champs de Mars. And don't let him get his own way. Show him who's boss.'

'Right,' Margo said, trying to sound confident.

'Have you got a bag for the *crottes*?' Justine demanded.

'No, I forgot.'

'Here.' Justine handed her a plastic bag with the logo of a well-known shop on it.

Margo laughed. 'That's a very fancy bag to put dog poop in.' She jiggled the lead. 'OK, come on then, Milou.'

Milou sighed again and ambled after Margo as she walked to the front door.

'Have fun,' Justine said with more than a hint of malice in her voice.

*

The Champs de Mars, the big park that forms a wide avenue between the Eiffel Tower and l'ecole Militaire, was situated a stone's throw from the apartment building. Today it was hot and dusty. After walking around the park for a while, Margo dragged the unwilling dog to a bench under a wilting acacia, where he collapsed in the dust and fell asleep. Margo sat down on the bench and wiped her forehead, grateful for the shade and the faint breeze. She leaned her head against the trunk of the tree and looked idly at the long queue of tourists waiting to go up the Eiffel Tower. It was nice to sit here and just let your mind drift, look at the people, the dogs and the flowers and trees. She looked up at the summer sky, where a jet plane left a long vapour trail that slowly dissolved. She could hear the sound of bells jingling nearby and looked around. It was an ice cream van. It parked near the fountain and was at once surrounded by children jostling each other to get first in the queue. Margo suddenly felt parched, but she had no money. Oh well, she thought, I'll have a drink of water when I get back to the apartment. She was about to get up when someone said her name.

'Margo?'

Startled, she looked around. Her eyes widened in shock as she saw who was standing there. Shit, she thought. Rufus. Shit, shit, shit. '*Comment?*' she asked, sitting down again. '*Je crois que tu te trompes.*'

Rufus squinted at her with his small eyes. 'But it *is* Margo,' he insisted. 'You did something to your hair. But your face…I know it's you.'

Margo shook her head. '*Non, pas du tout.*'

'But…' Rufus looked a little unsure of himself. Margo noticed the beginnings of a moustache on his upper lip, even though he was only twelve. He held a dripping ice cream cone in one of his fat hands and there was sweat stains on his T-shirt. 'Why did you turn around when I called your name if you're not Margo, then?' he asked.

'Rufus?' a voice called, and a young woman ran toward them. 'What are you doing here? Come on,' she ordered, 'the rest of the class is getting on the bus.'

Rufus didn't take his eyes off Margo. 'I know it's you,' he said, 'I just know it.'

'He seems to think he knows you,' the teacher said in bad French.

Margo shrugged. 'I don't know why,' she said with a little laugh. 'I have never seen him before in my life.'

'I'm sorry,' the teacher said, 'he's a very difficult child.' She took Rufus by the arm and started to drag him away. 'Come on now. Stop bothering the lady.'

'But…' Rufus said as they walked away, his eyes still on Margo. 'It's…she looked so much like…'

The teacher made some soothing noises and Rufus reluctantly walked with her to the queue of children who were boarding a minibus. Margo could see him staring at her through the grimy rear window as the bus drove off.

*

'Good evening, Marguerite,' Milady said as she swept into the drawing room, where Margo was arranging a big bouquet of roses and freesias in a blue Delft vase. The French windows were wide open and the lace curtains swayed slightly in the cool evening breeze.

'Good evening, Milady.'

'How did your first day go?' Milady asked as she sat down on a gilt chair and took out a cigarette. She had changed into a superbly cut black sleeveless silk shift and matching shoes with stiletto heels. Margo couldn't help noticing that, despite her age, her arms were slim and smooth.

'Very well, I think.'

'You have done all the things I put on the list?'

'Yes.'

'You wrote the invitation cards?'

'Yes, I did.'

'And you included a list of the guests with each one?' Milady asked as she fitted her cigarette into the long black holder.

Margo's hand froze in mid-air. 'I'm sorry?'

'A guest list,' Milady repeated impatiently. 'A list of all the guests and their occupations.'

'Eh, no, I didn't. There didn't seem to be one.'

'But I left a stack of them beside the cards. Surely…'

'I didn't see anything like that.' Margo pricked her finger on a thorn and dropped the rose on the floor.

'Probably because you didn't look for it.' Milady snapped open her gold lighter and lit her cigarette.

'Well, you didn't say,' Margo tried to defend herself while she sucked her finger.

Milady blew out a stream of smoke and flicked ash into a Sèvres ashtray. 'When we invite people to dinner,' she explained with forced patience in her voice, 'we must include information about their fellow guests.'

'Why?' Margo asked despite herself.

'Because that way they don't have to ask questions like "what do you do?" and "is your wife here?" It makes conversations smoother. It also prevents ladies wearing the wrong clothes.'

'How?'

'Can't you guess? Imagine that you are going to a party and you receive a list of the guests.'

'Eh, yes?' Margo bent to retrieve the rose.

'Don't you see?' Milady said impatiently. 'You will know immediately what dress to wear, because last time you met Madame X you wore your blue dress, or whatever, so now you can choose something different and that way you can be absolutely sure that you won't be seen wearing the same outfit twice in a row. Which would be…'

'A fate worse than death?'

'Are you mocking me?'

'No, of course not,' Margo said hurriedly, fitting the last flower into her arrangement. 'It's just, well, that kind of thing doesn't seem terribly important in the scheme of things. If you look at the problems of the world today, I mean.'

'Believe me, it is,' Milady stated. 'You see, my dear, *la politesse* is really about consideration, about making it easier for people to—' She stopped and looked around as the door opened. 'Here he is,' she announced with sudden girlish excitement in her voice.

Margo glanced up from her roses as a shadow fell across the polished parquet floor.

6

'*Bonsoir,*' the man said as he strolled into the room. With the evening sun in her eyes, Margo could only see the outline of his head and shoulders and she squinted at him as he bent to kiss his mother on the cheek.

'*Bonsoir, chéri,*' Milady purred. 'You're home a little early.'

'Yes, I know. One of my meetings was cancelled, so I…' he paused and looked at Margo. 'I'm sorry, I didn't know we had a guest.'

'Oh, no,' Milady said with a little laugh and switched to English. 'Darling, this is Marguerite, my new secretary. Marguerite, this is my son, François Coligny de la Bourdonnière.'

'*Enchanté, mademoiselle,*' the man said and walked closer to Margo. 'How nice to meet you.' He lifted her hand and touched it with his lips in a polite French hand kiss, and, as he turned slightly, she could see him clearly. Of medium height, he looked to be in his early forties and, despite the fact that he had the same dark hair and patrician features as his mother, he had something she lacked – a sweetness of expression. There was real warmth in his brown eyes as he looked at Margo.

'Good evening, Monsieur le Comte,' she said.

'I told you about Marguerite last night,' Milady reminded him. 'Don't tell me you forgot?'

'No, I remember now,' he said. 'I just didn't expect her to be so young and attractive.' He sounded as if he was merely stating a fact and not paying Margo a compliment. 'What a stroke of luck you just happened to walk in like that,' he continued. 'What was it my mother said? Something about a letter?' His English was as fluent as that of his mother but with less of an accent.

'Well, it was a kind of a mix-up, really,' Margo said, picking up a rose petal from the table. 'I was really looking for a job at your château. With the horses. Gráinne, my friend, couldn't take up the position you offered her and I thought as you seemed to be so short handed…'

'I beg your pardon?' The Comte looked a little mystified.

'The event horses,' Margo explained. 'The ones you have to get ready for…' Her voice trailed away. What's the matter with him, she thought, he doesn't look as if he knows what I'm talking about.

The Comte shook his head. 'I'm sorry. This has nothing to do with me. It must be my brother you're talking about.'

'Your brother?' Margo said. 'Oh, I see.'

'Yes,' the Comte said. 'My brother, Jacques. He runs a yard for event horses at our château. He is an excellent rider and trainer, one of the best in France. I am François, the eldest son, and I work at the Department of Justice. I don't know one end of a horse from the other,' he added with a little laugh. '*Maman*,' he chided, 'you should have explained to Marguerite.'

Milady sighed. 'Never mind that. Come here and sit down. Tell me about your day before we change for dinner.'

'How about a drink?' The Comte asked, unbuttoning the top button of his white shirt and loosening the knot of his blue silk tie. 'I could do with one, I have to say.'

'Good idea,' Milady nodded. 'We have plenty of time. I'll have a gin and tonic. What about you?'

'I'll have a scotch,' the Comte said, taking off the jacket of his linen suit and draping it over the back of a chair.

'All right,' Milady said. 'Marguerite?'

'Oh, I don't know. I think I'll have a sweet martini,' Margo said, sitting down on a chair. 'On the rocks, please,' she added. She was quite tired after all the chores and errands and a drink would be lovely.

There was a brief, embarrassed silence during which Milady flared her nostrils and glared at Margo with ill-disguised contempt.

It suddenly dawned on Margo what was going on. 'Oh,' she said, getting up again, her face red. 'I mean, I'll get the—'

'Let me get the drinks,' the Comte interrupted, walking to a cabinet by the big sofa and opening the doors. 'You must be very tired, Mademoiselle Marguerite, you do look a little pale. I'm sure my mother is keeping you *very* busy.'

'François!' Milady snapped. 'What are you doing? This is really not *comme il faut*.'

'What, *Maman*?' the Comte asked as he made a very large gin and tonic. 'You mean offering your secretary a drink? On the contrary, I think it is very nice. Why not celebrate her first day with a drink and wish her welcome?' He handed his mother the glass and quickly made Margo's drink and his own. He held up his glass. 'To Mademoiselle Marguerite. I hope you will enjoy working with my mother.'

'Thank you,' Margo replied, feeling a little foolish as she held up her glass. '*A votre santé*.' She knocked back her martini in one go, the ice cubes rattling against her teeth.

'How about another one?' the Comte offered, taking her glass. 'I don't seem to have put enough in that one.'

'Oh, no,' she stammered, 'that's all right. I have to go and...'

'Please, relax,' he said. 'I'm sure there is nothing really urgent you have to do at this time.' He quickly refilled Margo's glass, handed it to her and sat down in a big leather armchair, crossing his legs as he sipped his drink.

'Well, no, not really,' Margo agreed. 'I have finished for today, unless there is something else Milady wants me to...'

'Milady?' the Comte asked with a little laugh. 'Is that what you call my mother? Hmm, Milady. Yes, I like it. It suits you to a tee, *Maman*. It's like something out of an old English novel.' He smiled fondly at his mother, who looked only slightly mollified.

Margo sipped her drink and felt the alcohol slowly making her feel more confident and at ease. She smiled at the Comte and he returned her smile as he finished his drink. 'So, Mademoiselle,' he started.

'Oh please, call me Marguerite,' Margo said. 'In any case, I'm not—'

'But then you must call me François,' he immediately replied.

'Really!' Milady snorted.

'Why not, *Maman*? Oh, don't be so stuffy! We have entered the twenty-first century, you know. *De haut en bas* is no longer in vogue, I'm happy to say.'

'You speak wonderful English,' Margo said.

'Thank you. I spent some time in London during my student years.'

'Oh? What did you study?' Margo asked, draining the last drops of her martini.

'My son is an ENArque,' Milady said.

'Enarque?' Margo said, putting her glass on the small table by the sofa. 'Is that French for dyslexic?'

'No,' François laughed, 'it means I went to ENA, l'Ecole Nationale d'Administration. It's, well, one of the *Grandes Ecoles*. The great schools of France, where we learn to be...to run this country. Maybe you have heard of them?'

'You mean a kind of training school for higher civil servants?' Margo asked.

'Something like that, yes,' Milady nodded. 'But a lot more. You have to be *very* talented to get in. And then it's very hard work. But François—'

'Enough,' François laughed, 'or you'll have me declared a national monument. I'm not any more illustrious than anybody else in the French public service. You see, Marguerite, it is Jacques who is the real star of this family.'

'Really?' Margo said, intrigued. 'Why is that?'

'He is, as I said before, an excellent rider and trainer,' François explained. 'But, more than that, he has won many medals while on the French show-jumping team. His picture has been in *Paris Match* and even *Time* magazine when he won an Olympic gold medal a few years ago.'

'You might have heard of him,' Milady said with pride in her voice.

'No, I don't think I have,' Margo said. 'But I'm not really into equestrian sports.'

'Women who meet Jacques find themselves suddenly very interested in horses,' François said with a little laugh. 'And when *you* meet him, you'll see why.'

'Oh, but I won't, will I?' Margo said, confused. 'Except if he comes to Paris, of course.'

'But you're coming with us when we go to the country,' Milady stated. 'I'll need you there even more than here in the city.'

'Don't frighten Marguerite, *Maman*,' François laughed. 'I'm sure she's more than busy already.' He got to his feet. 'But now, if you'll excuse me, I have to go and change. A pleasure to meet you, Marguerite. *A bientôt.*' He took his jacket, swung it over his shoulder and walked out of the room.

*

That first evening drink became a daily routine. They didn't really say very much to each other, just made polite conversation about the weather and world events. Margo would not have continued to accept his invitation if wasn't for Milady's obvious disapproval. Margo took a certain wicked pleasure in sitting down in the drawing room with her drink, sensing Milady's seething anger. François didn't seem to notice his mother's annoyance. There was a hint of conspiracy between them as he and Margo chatted, pretending to ignore the chilly silence in which Milady sipped her drink. François always looked at Margo with bland politeness, but she sometimes imagined she saw a little smile deep in his eyes. She loved listening to him when he spoke French, which he did more and more frequently. It was like listening to music. And when he said her name, even that sounded like a compliment. Margo wondered why such a man wasn't married. Maybe he was just very picky? Or maybe *Maman* wouldn't let him go?

What a nice man, she thought one evening as he poured her a drink. Why couldn't I have found someone like him instead of Alan? But no, she said to herself as he gave her the glass and their fingers touched briefly, there is no spark between us, and if

I had met him all those years ago, I wouldn't have fallen for him even then. There is something missing. He's like a beautifully presented dish without spice, a perfect flower with no scent. There's no – she thought for a while – passion, she realised, no interest of that kind, as he looked at her and smiled politely, no glint of sexual attraction in those warm brown eyes. It was as if he merely observed the world and didn't really live in it.

*

The church bells pealed loudly but failed to wake Margo as she slept in the little room in the attic. In her dream, the bells rang as she walked out of the church on the arm of her husband. She looked up at him as they stood on the steps of the church, but the sun was in her eyes and she couldn't see his face. Alan's arm gripped her waist as they greeted friends and family, smiling and kissing everybody on the cheek. Margo caught a glimpse of her parents, pushing through the crowd of well-wishers.

'Oh darling,' her mother whispered in Margo's ear as she finally managed to get through the throng, 'please be happy.'

'Well done,' her father said, 'today you have made me proud. Try not to mess it up.' Her mother started to cry. 'Oh, Margo,' she sobbed. 'Oh, my darling girl.' Alan tightened his arm and, as Margo felt panic rising in her throat, she pulled away from the iron grip around her waist. 'Please,' she begged, 'let me go.'

The bells rang again, even more loudly this time. Margo opened her eyes, the feeling of panic slowly fading. A dream, she thought, it was just a dream. I don't have to get married to anyone ever again. But she could still hear those church bells. Then she remembered – it was Sunday and the bells of all the churches in Paris were ringing. Margo closed her eyes, trying to go back to sleep, but found to her annoyance that she was wide awake. The sun was streaming into the room and it was already becoming hot. I must get something to cover the window instead of that broken blind, and get some ear plugs, she thought, turning the pillow over to the cool side. She lifted her hand and turned her rings round and round on her finger, the thin platinum wedding band and the big square-cut diamond. She thought about the dream and about the wedding, the real one, ten years ago. She had worn such a beautiful dress, made for her by a dressmaker in the little town where she grew up. She remembered Alan's expression as she walked up the aisle toward him, as if he couldn't believe his luck, then the wedding night and, the following morning, sitting in the dining room in the small hotel in Tuscany, waiting for breakfast, looking at her wedding ring on her finger and thinking: I'm married. I'm Mrs Alan Hunter. And she had thought that feeling of perfect bliss would last forever. But this morning she felt it was all so far away, so unreal, as if it had happened to someone else in another century.

On an impulse, Margo took off her rings. I'll put them somewhere safe, she thought and pushed them under her pillow. She yawned and stretched. Sunday. Her day off. She decided to have a lazy morning and then go and have a stroll around the city. Well, it would certainly be different from Sundays in London – breakfast in bed, the Sunday papers, Alan... No. She pushed the thought away and turned her mind to the present, to the week that had just passed. She laughed softly as she remembered her first day and that first evening when she had met François. It was like something out of a French play, she thought.

Suddenly there was a shrill noise from some-where in the room. Confused, Margo sat up. There it was again. Oh God, my mobile, I must have left it on by mistake last night when I was deleting all those messages from Alan. She got out of bed and opened the wardrobe. The ringing stopped. She took the mobile from her bag and looked at it. 'Missed call' it said on the display. Alan again, probably, she thought and checked the number. But the number wasn't his. Then the phone rang again. Without thinking, Margo put the phone to her ear and pressed the button.

'Hello?' Shit, what am I doing, she thought, it will only be Alan. A cold hand clutched her heart at the thought of hearing his voice. But before she could switch off the phone, someone replied.

'Hello? Who's this?' Not Alan's voice, but familiar all the same. Rough, gruff, but so sweet to Margo's ears.

'Gráinne! Oh, Gráinne, it's you!'

'Of course it is. But who the fuck are you?'

'It's me, Marg— Maggie!'

'Who? Oh, holy shit!' Gráinne laughed. 'Jesus, how weird. I was just checking the number of this missed call and here you are. Are you well, love?'

'I'm fine. Very well.'

'You must have been the one who called me then, that day about a week ago. What was it about?'

Her legs suddenly weak, Margo sat down on the bed. 'Nothing, really. I just wanted to say hello.'

'Well, hello to you too. How are you doing? Are you on your way back to London?'

'No, I...'

'Are you OK? You sound a little strange.'

'I'm fine,' Margo said, trying to sound confident. 'Great, really. And I'm still in Paris.'

'Still staying with that friend of yours, then?'

'No. Actually, you won't believe this – I got a job.'

'A job? Really? That's fantastic. What are you doing?'

'I'm a PA. Personal assistant. To this...this woman.'

'PA, eh? Sounds very posh. Some kind of corporate job, is it?'

Margo smiled. 'Well, yes, you could call it that.'

'So what does this woman you're working for do? What kind of business is she in?'

'Fashion,' Margo said without thinking.

'Fashion, eh? Not my bag, really, but I suppose that would be right up your street. So, did you find a place to stay?'

'Oh yes. There's a staff apartment, you see.'

'Really? Is it nice?'

'Lovely.' Margo smiled to herself as she looked around the room. 'It's a penthouse, actually. Fully furnished with a view of the Eiffel Tower.'

'Go away!'

'I swear.'

'Wow.' Gráinne sounded seriously impressed. 'You really did land on your feet. And here I was, thinking you were in some kind of trouble.'

'Trouble? Of course not.' Margo laughed. 'Whatever made you think…' She cleared her throat. 'But what about you? How are you?'

'Me? I'm grand, pet. Same old stuff, but OK. Very busy. Lots of events around the place. Some lovely horses and the *craíc* is really good at the yard.'

'What did you say? The what?'

'The *craíc*,' Gráinne repeated. 'It's Irish for good fun. But hey, it's small potatoes compared to your fancy job and luxury pad. You really have come up in the world since we met.'

'Not really,' Margo said with a little laugh.

'Oh yeah, don't try to pretend. You've become one of those corporate women. And I feel really honoured that you shared a crust with me and slept in my humble truck.'

'Oh, but I really enjoyed it. And my job isn't really that fancy.'

'And she's so modest too,' Gráinne laughed.

'By the way,' Margo said on an impulse, 'do you know someone called Jacques Coligny?'

'Yes, slightly. Why?'

'Oh, no reason. I read something about him in a magazine recently,' Margo lied, 'and I thought you might know him. He seems to be a big star in France.'

'Yeah, he was a champion a few years back. He doesn't ride in competitions any more, but he buys and trains horses for a lot of the international teams,' Gráinne said.

'Do you know him well?'

'Well enough to stay away from him. Great horseman, I'll give him that, one of the best. And very clever. Speaks perfect English, great judge of horseflesh and has a good head for business. And he's amazing with horses. Seems to be able to talk their language or something. And he's very popular. But…' Gráinne stopped.

'But what?'

'Oh, nothing, just not my type of guy. I don't trust him. Good looking, yes, but thinks he's God's gift to women, if you know what I mean. Not that he'd look twice at someone like me, but I've seen some of the damage he's done to others. Loves 'em and leaves 'em, get the picture?'

'Yes, I think I do,' Margo said, surprised by the venom in Gráinne's voice.

'But why are you so interested in him?'

'No reason. The article was interesting, that's all.'

'I see. OK. Well, I better let you go. I'm sure you have more important things to do than talking to me. Now that you've come up in the world, I mean.'

'Actually,' Margo started, intending to tell Gráinne the real story, but was interrupted by a sudden loud beep. 'Oh no! The battery is dying,' Margo shouted. 'Gráinne, don't go – I just wanted to tell you… Please,' she nearly sobbed as the line went dead.

*

It was close to midnight when Margo came back from her stroll around Paris. She hadn't really done very much, but she had enjoyed her day. In the late morning, she had seen people going into a church for mass and she had joined them, thinking she would sit there and listen to the music and have a chance to think. But once inside, she discovered that she wasn't able to think at all. No thoughts of any kind came into her mind and she simply sat there, her mind blank, listening to the sermon, the music and the murmured prayers of the congregation. It was as if a door had closed in her mind and she was suffering from some kind of amnesia. She did, however, feel a kind of peace settle on her as she sat there in the dim light and she emerged from the church into the bright street feeling much calmer and more cheerful. She had gone for a long walk on the banks of the Seine, all the way to Ile St Louis, where she had enjoyed an ice cream while sitting under a willow tree on the water's edge, dangling her feet in the water. Then on to Notre Dame, climbing all the way up one of the towers where there were breathtaking views of the river and the old bridges. Then she had visited La

Sainte Chapelle and stared in awe at the magnificent stained glass windows. After visiting a few museums, she had ended up having dinner in a small *brasserie* on the Left Bank and struck up a conversation with a group of American tourists at the table next to hers. They had invited her to join them for after-dinner drinks at their table but, realising it was getting late, Margo had turned down the invitation and taken the Metro back home.

The lift in the servants' stairs was even slower than the one in the main entrance, and as it creaked its way up, Margo had no thought in her head other than sinking into bed. Except for the sound of the lift, the building was quiet, and Margo looked idly at the different landings as she went up. She noticed that most of them had two or three doors, having been split up into smaller apartments, as Justine had explained. Even so, those apartments would be very big, she thought, but not as big as… She gave a little start as she saw the feet and legs of someone at the kitchen door of Milady's apartment. It was a woman and she seemed to be looking for something in her handbag. One of Milady's friends? No, they would use the main entrance. As the lift rose higher, Margo saw the woman at the door more clearly. She was tall with shoulder-length blonde hair and she wore a red dress. Margo noticed that she was slim and had very good legs. The woman pulled out a key from her handbag and put it in the lock. The lift suddenly creaked loudly and the woman whipped around. For a split second her eyes met Margo's and they stared at each other in the dim light. Margo couldn't see clearly, but she had an impression of huge, dark eyes. The woman turned her back to Margo, quickly twisted the key in the lock, opened the door and disappeared into the dark apartment.

7

The entrance to the Dior headquarters on Avenue Montaigne was very crowded. Hundreds of elegant but bad-tempered women pushed and wrestled with each other in order to get out of the pouring rain and in through the huge double doors without getting their hair and clothes completely soaked.

'People are becoming so horribly rude,' Milady said as she pushed her elbow into the side of a woman in a white suit. '*Excusez-moi, Madame,*' she muttered, poking another woman in the back with her dripping umbrella, '*laissez nous passer, s'il vous plait…*'

Margo couldn't help but admire the way Milady managed to get ahead in the queue and in through the doors by discreetly stepping on toes with her stilettos, poking sides with her elbows while smiling and apologising and looking as if she was simply waiting her turn.

'*Finalement*,' Milady breathed as they started to walk up the wide curving staircase toward the showroom on the first floor. 'It's becoming more and more crowded. They seem to let just anyone in these days. Did you see some of those women? The way they were dressed? So vulgar. After all, this is Dior, not Marks and Spencer.'

Margo smoothed the skirt of her grey linen dress and murmured something soothing in agreement. Milady glanced at her. 'That dress is perfect on you,' she remarked with satisfaction.

'I know,' Margo said. 'All the clothes I found in my room were. I meant to ask you – why, I mean, who—'

'My last personal assistant, of course. That's why I hired you. You're a perfect size thirty-six, just like she was. I spotted that straight away.'

'You mean you hired me for my dress size?' Margo asked incredulously.

'Of course,' Milady said as if it was the most natural thing in the world. 'Here we are,' she continued as they walked into the big room where the autumn/winter collection was about to be shown. Margo forgot her questions as she looked around the huge showroom. Big antique mirrors hung on the walls, the tall French windows were swathed in heavy cream silk curtains and the deep red carpet was crammed with rows and rows of gilt chairs, each one with a programme and a gold pencil on the seat. There were huge vases with spectacular flower arrangements and classical music wafted from the stereo system. Two stick-thin women in black suits turned around and stared as they walked in. 'Marie-Jo!' one of them exclaimed, walking toward them. *'Ma chère, comment ça va?'*

'Très bien, chère amie,' Milady replied, kissing the woman on both cheeks. She gestured towards Margo. 'This is Marguerite, my new personal assistant.'

'Oh,' said the woman, barely looking at Margo. 'I have reserved these two chairs for you in the front row.'

'Thank you, darling,' Milady said.

'Enjoy the show,' the woman said. 'I'll be in the shop downstairs afterwards. Let me know if there is anything you want to try on.'

'Entendu,' Milady nodded.

The room quickly filled with people. Only a few minutes after Milady and Margo sat down, the lights dimmed, the music changed from classical to modern and the show started. Margo stared open mouthed as, illuminated by spotlights, the models, dressed in shimmering garments, glided onto the floor and started to move in time to the pulsating South American beat. Their complexions glowing, their bodies flawless, they moved with catlike suppleness, as if walking on air. It was like a dream, a mirage, and Margo felt her pulse beat faster at the sights and sounds. She couldn't take her eyes off the beautiful creatures and the exquisite clothes, the shapes, colours and textures. Silk, tweed and chiffon in amazing shades twirled in front of her eyes like a kaleidoscope. She glanced briefly at Milady, who, with a business-like air, was taking notes and muttering to herself. '*Non*,' she would mumble, '*pas pour moi*' or '*pas mal, peut être, parfait.*'

As suddenly as it had started, the show came to an end. Margo blinked as the music stopped, the lights came on again and the applause rang out. 'Oh my God,' she said, clapping her hands till they ached, 'that was…'

'Not bad,' Milady said, standing up, 'not bad at all.' She quickly pushed through the crowd with Margo, still mesmerised, at her heels and swiftly descended the stairs, swept through the lobby and pushed the entrance doors open. 'It stopped raining. Thank God.'

'But…' Margo asked as they walked into the street. 'Aren't you going to buy anything?'

Milady stared at her blankly. 'Buy? At those prices? Of course not. I have taken extensive notes. Now I'm going to give them to my *couturière* and she will run the items up in no time at all.' She nodded, looking satisfied. 'Now, apart from accessories, I'm all set up for the *rentrée* and the winter season. We can go to the country.'

'The country?'

'Yes,' Milady said impatiently. 'The country. Our château.'

'Oh, I see.'

'You didn't think I was going to stay in Paris in August?' Milady asked incredulously, as if it was some kind of crime.

'No, I suppose not. So, when…'

'We're leaving as soon as I'm ready. Probably Saturday.'

'We? You mean…?'

'Yes, you too, of course. I need you there. Plenty of things to do. But now I have to go. You must go back to the apartment and start packing.'

'Pack?' Margo laughed. 'That won't take me long.'

'Not for you,' Milady snapped impatiently. 'For me. You have to pack my clothes. Everything I'll need for the country.'

'Right,' Margo said. 'But what…? I mean, how…?'

'There's a list in the drawer of my bedside table. It's stuck into my big leather diary. The suitcases are in the basement. Ask Justine to bring them up.'

'All right, Milady.'

'Good. I'll be home at around six. See you then.' Milady turned around and scanned the street. 'Taxi!' she yelled, raising her arm, and a black cab came to a screeching halt beside her. Milady climbed in, slammed the door shut and stuck her head out the window. 'Don't forget to walk Milou,' she said before the taxi took off.

Margo looked on as the taxi disappeared into the heaving traffic. She turned around and walked straight into someone going in the opposite direction. '*Oh, pardon,*' she said, trying to catch her breath, '*je*—' She stopped as she saw who it was and nearly stopped breathing. 'Fiona,' she whispered as they stared at each other.

'M-M-Margo,' Fiona stammered. 'Oh my God! It *is* you. Then Rufus was right.'

'Rufus?'

'Yes. He said he had seen you. And we thought he was making it up. We thought you had gone back to London. I told Alan…I was sure…' Fiona paused for breath. Without warning, she suddenly grabbed Margo by the arms in a tight grip. 'Christ, Margo, what are you doing here? I couldn't believe it when I spotted you inside. I thought I was dreaming. Then I told myself it was somebody else. But here you are. Where have you been? Where did you go when you ran away? Why were you in there with…with that woman? And what *have* you done to your hair?'

'Please,' Margo said, peeling Fiona's hands away from her arms. 'Stop shouting.'

'I'm not shouting,' Fiona said, 'I'm just in shock, that's all.'

'All right, all right, keep your hair on. Calm down. I'm here, I'm all right, and now I have to go. Goodbye.' Margo backed away from Fiona and started to turn around. But Fiona grabbed her again.

'Don't walk away like that,' she ordered, 'I want an explanation. I want to know…'

'Leave me alone.' Margo tore away from Fiona and started to walk very quickly towards the Metro station. But Fiona pulled Margo by the arm again. 'Stop,' she ordered, 'you owe me an explanation, you know, after what you—'

Margo stopped and glared at Fiona. 'No, I don't,' she said with feeling. 'I don't owe you or anyone else *anything.*'

'Don't be so bloody selfish,' Fiona snapped. 'I don't know what's got into you, but I wish you'd stop and consider what you're doing to everybody.'

'Everybody?'

'Yes. To Alan, for a start. He keeps calling us. He's back in London now, you know, and it's very hard for him to manage without you.'

'I bet.' Margo smiled grimly.

'He's had to hire a temp.'

'Poor baby.'

'You must go back to him, Margo.'

'I can't. I'm not ready.'

'What do you mean?' Fiona asked, looking near tears. 'Please, couldn't you try and…for my sake, at least?'

Margo stared at Fiona. 'For *your* sake? What has all of this got to do with you?'

Fiona turned her head and seemed suddenly very interested in the Dior shop window. 'Nothing, really,' she mumbled, staring at a display of handbags. 'I just…it's just upsetting, that's all.'

'That's very sweet of you, but I wish you'd stop being upset and forget about me. I'm fine, I have a very interesting job and—'

Fiona looked up from the window display. 'Job? You have a job?'

'Yes,' Margo said proudly.

'Doing what?'

'Lap dancing,' Margo said. 'A whole new career.'

'Very funny. Come on, Margo, tell me the truth.' Fiona hitched the strap of her handbag higher on her thin shoulder.

'I'm not going to tell you anything, so you can stop asking all these questions. I'm fine, that's all I'm going to say, absolutely fine.'

'And you won't reconsider…?'

'Not for the moment, no.'

'But you will eventually?'

Margo shrugged. 'Who knows? *Que sera, sera* and all that.'

'But you'll think about it?'

'I might. But not at the moment.'

'OK,' Fiona said, her voice flat. 'I suppose there's no point talking to you then. I'll tell Alan. He'll be relieved to hear you're all right.' Without saying goodbye, she turned and started to walk away.

Margo felt a stab of guilt. 'Fiona,' she called after her, 'I'm sorry. I'll get in touch when…'

But Fiona kept on walking, wobbling slightly on her impossibly high heels.

*

The apartment was quiet as Margo let herself in. She looked around the kitchen and the laundry room, and except for Milou snoring in his basket, there was no sign of life. But when Margo strained her ears, she could hear the faint sound of a radio from behind the closed door of Justine's room just off the kitchen. She must be having her afternoon snooze. Margo consulted her watch. Five o'clock. I'd better have a look at that list, and then I must walk Milou and get the evening paper. Milady wanted me to pick up some stationery for those

112

thank you letters and… Mentally ticking off the list in her head, she went into Milady's bedroom, walked to the bedside table and started to pull out the drawer. It was stuck. She pulled a little harder and suddenly the drawer came unstuck and flew out, crashing to the floor, scattering the contents on the carpet.

'Oh, bloody hell,' Margo muttered as she sank to her knees and began to pick everything up. 'Why does she have to cram everything in like this?' She picked up a fat leather diary with bits of paper stuck between the pages, a small hairbrush, two postcards, a packet of paper handkerchiefs and a stack of letters that had escaped from the blue ribbon that had been tied carelessly around them. Margo glanced briefly at the letter at the top of the pile, which hadn't been put into its envelope. *'Mon amour,'* she read. Oh God, love letters. From the old count, probably. Despite herself, Margo, still sitting on the floor, continued to read the letter, written in a very old-fashioned, precise copper-plate hand.

> *It is only a few hours since we said goodbye but it feels like years, even though I can still feel your lips on mine, your arms around me, your soft breasts against my skin and your long, long legs wrapped around me. I know you were worried we would be discovered, but for me, the risk of discovery only makes our rendezvous more exciting.*

What? Margo thought. The risk of…is that right? She looked at the text again. *Le risque de decouverte* – yes, that's what it means. The risk of discovery. Not her husband then. She must have had a lover. The dirty trollop… But when, and who? Margo looked at the date at the top of the page. April 1969. What age would Milady have been? In her late twenties or very early thirties at the most. And her husband? Fascinated, Margo read on.

> *I know you are worried that our liaison will damage my political career, but I do not think there is any need for concern. We are so very careful and nobody seems to suspect anything when I leave for 'my evening walk' and they all remark on how refreshed I look when I come back. You see, my little one, our love helps me cope with the stress of my position and makes me forget all the problems, if only for a short while. So you are doing a lot for your country without realising it. I adore you even more now than when we first met, and you are even more beautiful.*
>
> *Goodbye for now, mon chou. I kiss your eyes, your mouth, your beautiful breasts. All my love. Vive la France,*
> *Your loving J-J*

All her own problems forgotten, Margo sat on the floor staring at the letter, trying to imagine who

Milady's lover had been. Someone in politics and in high office, obviously. She looked at the other letters, but feeling suddenly guilty about snooping, she stacked them all together, put the letter she had read on the top, retied the ribbon and put everything back into the drawer except the diary. She leafed through it and found the list she had been looking for. She sat down on the antique chaise longue by the window and glanced through the neatly typed list. *Summer wardrobe for the country,* it said. And then a long list. There was everything a well-dressed woman could possibly need for an extended stay at a country house, and Margo smiled to herself as she pictured her own small holdall with just an extra sweater and a change of underwear she brought with her when she stayed at someone's country cottage. But this list was endless. Apart from a lot of different kinds of underwear, Milady seemed to require a small truckload of clothes to see her through a few weeks' stay at her country residence. 'Three suits,' Margo muttered, 'blue linen, cream cotton and green silk, three pairs of casual cotton trousers, two pairs of silk ditto, one black, one white, two bathing suits, one sundress, dinner dresses; the long cream Valentino and two short, the black Chanel and grey silk ditto, the navy Yves St Laurent, the black beaded Galliano...' The list went on and on and Margo groaned to herself as she thought of first finding, then packing it all to be ready by Saturday. It's already Wednesday, she thought. I'll have to get my skates on if... She looked up as the door opened and Milady came in.

'Oh. Marguerite,' she said as she dropped her handbag on the bed and pulled off her gloves. 'You found the list, then.'

'Yes. I'm just going through it. And I was just about to go and ask Justine—'

'Good. Now, if you'll excuse me, I have to shower and change.'

Realising she had been dismissed, Margo rose from the day bed and walked to the door. 'By the way,' she said as an afterthought, 'I meant to ask you…'

Milady turned around. 'Yes?'

'Eh, I know this might not be any of my business, but the other night, when I came back from my day off…' Margo paused, trying to think of how to ask the question without sounding nosy.

Milady looked at her expectantly. 'When you came back…?'

'When I went up in the lift, I saw someone at the front door. No, the back door, I mean. A woman. She went into the apartment. This apartment.'

'A woman? Justine, you mean?'

'No.' Margo shook her head. 'Not Justine. Definitely not. This woman was tall and slim and blonde. She wore a red dress.'

'I really don't know what on earth you're talking about.' Milady sounded bored. 'You must have mixed up the apartments.'

'No, I'm sure I didn't. This floor is the only one with only one front door, and the others—'

'I really don't know what you mean or what you think you saw,' Milady interrupted, a hint of annoyance in her voice. 'And I don't know what it has to do with me. I would prefer if you would do what you're supposed to do instead of standing here asking questions.'

Margo gave up. 'Very well, Milady,' she murmured and left the room.

*

The air was cold and damp and smelled of mildew and rotting leaves. Margo shivered slightly as she followed Justine through the maze of corridors in the basement on their way to the storage room to get Milady's suitcases. 'I was wondering,' she started.

'What?' Justine had come to a stop beside a door and taken out her bunch of keys. 'What were you wondering now?'

'Well, it's about something I saw. Or somebody, to be precise.'

'Somebody?' Justine swung the heavy door open and switched on the light inside the door.

Margo forgot what she was going to ask as she stared in awe at the jumble in the storage room. It looked like a very disorganised antique shop. Old chairs and tables, worn rugs, pictures with broken frames, heaps of old velvet and silk curtains, cots, old toys, trunks, leather suitcases with hotel labels and other assorted items were piled together in ragged heaps, some of the piles nearly toppling over. 'My God,' she said.

'I know. Should all be thrown out if you ask me,' Justine grunted as she squeezed her heavy frame inside. 'But you were saying?'

'Oh, it was nothing really,' Margo mumbled as she fingered a deep red velvet curtain. 'Lovely material.'

'Used to hang in the dining room,' Justine said, pushing further in. 'Where are those suitcases? Could have sworn I put them…here they are.' She started to pull down a leather suitcase from a pile on top of a chest of drawers.

'Here. Let me.' Margo took the suitcase and put it on the floor, watching Justine take down the next one. 'How many do we need?'

'Four. She always takes four when she goes to the country.'

'They are really beautiful,' Margo said as she looked closely at the next one. 'Real leather and such workmanship. Look, they were made by Hermès.'

'So?'

'Well, you know. It's not that common to see this kind of luggage these days.'

'*Ah bon*?' Justine swung the last case down onto the floor. 'We'll take two each. And you might as well take some of the red velvet. Might make nice curtains for your room if you know how to sew.'

'Really?' Margo grabbed the curtain and sneezed as a cloud of dust hit her nose. 'That's really kind. I was just thinking I needed to get something better than that broken blind. I'm not very good at sewing, but…'

'Not much needed. The hooks are still in, see? All you have to do is hook them up on the rail and take them up a little.'

'Oh, I see. Well, that should be—'

'That rug over there might do you as well,' Justine interrupted, lifting up the corner of a worn needlepoint rug in warms hues of red and pink. 'And those tapestry cushions are not really any use to anybody, if you like that sort of thing.'

'Oh, but they're really darling,' Margo said as she admired the faded roses and bluebells on the cushions. 'Thank you. That's so kind, Justine.'

'Hrumph,' Justine grunted. 'Put it all inside the cases, then we can bring it all up in one go.'

'Good idea.' Margo opened one of the suitcases and proceeded to stuff the red velvet inside. 'I'll start on the curtains straight away.'

'Why the rush?' Justine asked. 'Aren't you going to the château in a few days?'

'Yes, I know, but if I improve my room a little bit now, it will be nice to come back to in September.'

'If we're all still alive,' Justine said darkly as she helped Margo stuff the last of the curtain into the suitcase.

Margo looked at her. 'What do you mean, if we're all still alive?'

'I never take anything for granted,' Justine said. 'And the château… It's a strange place.'

'Strange? How?' Margo said with a little laugh. Justine was so melodramatic sometimes.

Justine just shrugged. 'You'll see.'

'Sounds interesting. I'm looking forward to seeing it and meeting the people who work there. Milady told me there's a housekeeper and her husband.'

'Agnès and Bernard,' Justine nodded. 'A very nice couple. You'll like them.'

'And Milady's youngest son, what's he like?'

'Monsieur Jacques?' There was suddenly a dreamy look in Justine's eyes. 'A nice young man. A little spoiled, a little temperamental, but a real gentleman.'

'Charming?' Margo asked mischievously.

Justine coloured slightly. 'A nice boy. Always remembers me at Christmas. And he loves animals. Horses and dogs, you know?'

'He sounds very nice. Can't wait to meet him.'

Justine's expression changed and she looked sternly at Margo. 'You be careful with him, Mademoiselle. He can turn a woman's head and make a real fool out of her.'

'Don't worry,' Margo said. 'I know what men are like. It would be difficult to make a fool out of me.'

'Good. But what was it you said earlier?' Justine asked, folding the rug carefully. 'About seeing somebody?'

'Oh, yes.' Margo looked up from her task. 'I nearly forgot. It was the other night. Sunday night. I was going up in the lift, the servant's lift. And I saw this woman—'

'A woman?' Justine sounded oddly alarmed.

'Yes. She was standing by the kitchen door of the apartment.'

'Our apartment?'

'That's right. She was tall and blonde and quite beautiful, I think. I couldn't see her clearly, but she had huge dark eyes and she wore a red dress.'

'Go on,' Justine urged, her hands still on the rug.

'Well, she took out a key and let herself in.'

'Into the apartment?'

Margo nodded. 'That's right.' She peered at Justine. 'Who was she? Do you know?'

There was suddenly a guarded look in Justine's eyes. 'Must have been another floor. It's very dark in the stairwell. Easy to make the mistake.'

'No,' Margo said. 'I'm sure I'm right.'

Justine looked sternly at Margo. 'There are certain things…' She paused.

Margo stared at the old woman, waiting for her to finish her sentence. But Justine suddenly closed her mouth tightly and her eyes were expressionless again. 'Things are not always what they seem,' she muttered. 'Especially in this family.'

8

The evening sunlight streamed through the open window into the attic room and the light breeze felt cool and pleasant on Margo's face. Pigeons cooed softly on the balcony across the street and two sparrows were fighting over a piece of bread on the windowsill, their loud chirping nearly drowning the faint sounds of oriental music from somewhere nearby. The distant roar of the rush-hour traffic was beginning to ease. Margo struggled with the heavy velvet as she tried to attach the rusty hooks to the curtain rail. Three more to go. Two. One. There. Finally. She smoothed the velvet and stood back to admire her handiwork. What a difference, she thought as she looked first at the view of the rooftops and the tall shape of the Eiffel Tower behind them framed in the soft red velvet, then around the room. The rug on the worn lino and the cushions on the bed made the small room infinitely more inviting, the warm colours enhancing the rich brown mahogany of the bed head and the big old wardrobe. Even the old-fashioned wallpaper with the tiny rosebuds was suddenly more attractive. Now, maybe a print or two and a nice bedspread, and…

A sudden hard knock on the door made her jump. Nobody had ever knocked on her door. Who could it be? Margo wondered if Milady had come home early from her session at the beauty parlour. But she had said she would dine with friends afterwards and then go straight to bed. Margo had packed Milady's four suitcases and they would be setting off early the next morning for the country. No, it couldn't be Milady, she wouldn't come up here herself, she would send Justine, and she, in turn, Margo knew, was busy packing to go on her annual holiday at her cousin's in Tours.

There was another hard knock.

'Who is it?' Margo called. There was no reply, only a faint rustling sound. Margo walked to the door and peered through the spy hole. She could see nothing at first, then the top of someone's head, then an eye squinting at her.

'*Qui est la?*' Margo called, her heart beginning to race in her chest. She felt suddenly nervous and very aware that she was all alone here in this small room, with nobody nearby who would hear, or even care, if she was attacked.

'Jesus Christ, Margo,' a familiar voice shouted, 'will you open the door! There's this strange man staring at me.'

'Fiona,' Margo breathed, at once weak with relief. She unlocked the door and pulled it open. 'Why didn't you tell me it was you?'

'I did,' Fiona panted and nearly fell into the room. 'Please, lock the door, quickly,' she begged as Margo slammed the door shut.

'What's the matter with you?' Margo demanded, looking at Fiona's red face. 'And how on earth did you find me?'

Fiona collapsed on the bed, her hand on her chest. 'I thought...he was...oh God.'

'Who? What?'

'That man out there,' Fiona breathed and gestured vaguely at the door. 'A big dark man with a beard. He was dressed in some kind of, I don't know, caftan or something and he was staring at me and tried to touch my...'

'Your what?'

'My arm. He said something, but I couldn't understand. I was so frightened. Oh Margo, what are you doing here in this...this *ghetto*?'

Margo sat on the bed beside Fiona. 'Stop babbling for a minute. Calm down. Nobody is going to attack you. That was probably my neighbour you saw. I think he's Moroccan or something. He lives in the room next door with his wife and small baby and I imagine that he just wanted to be helpful.'

'Oh. I see.' Fiona breathed deeply, her hand still on her chest. 'Could I have a glass of water?'

'Of course.'

Fiona looked around the room while Margo

filled a glass from the tap. 'So this is where you live now.'

'That's right. How did you manage to find me?' Margo asked, handing Fiona the glass.

'Oh, that was easy,' Fiona said, sounding a little calmer as she sipped the water. 'I just used my head.'

'What do you mean?'

'Well, you said that you were working as some kind of secretary or something.'

'PA.'

'Whatever. Then I remembered that you were at the fashion show with, well, you know.'

'Know what? Stop talking in riddles.'

'Well, you know who she is, don't you?'

'You mean the Comtesse?'

'That's right. Otherwise known as Marie-Jo. Very well-known model in the late nineteen fifties and early sixties. A real fashion icon. But you must know that, of course.'

'Of course,' Margo said, trying not to look surprised.

'And that she married into the French aristocracy and became one of those society hostesses, and, well, all that.' Fiona drew breath. 'Anyway,' she continued when Margo didn't reply, 'I just looked up the address and found the apartment. I called in and asked for you and some old dragon told me you were up here, so, *voilá*, here I am.' Fiona put the empty glass on the bedside table.

'So you are.' Margo folded her arms across her chest. 'And what, if I may be so rude to ask, do you want?'

'Want? I don't want anything. I just thought I'd come and…'

'Spy on me? See if you could persuade me to behave and go back to Alan? Or maybe you just came to gloat?'

Fiona folded her skirt over her knees. 'I don't know what you mean,' she mumbled and flicked an imaginary piece of fluff off the fabric.

There was silence in the small room. Margo didn't know what to say. She wanted Fiona to leave and never come back. She didn't want to be reminded of her life in London, and she didn't want to apologise or explain to anyone for anything.

'This is actually rather nice,' Fiona muttered as if to herself as she looked around the room.

'What?'

'The room. It's sort of quaint. Not that I would like to live here, but it has a rather shabby chic charm.'

'How sweet of you to say so,' Margo said sourly, watching as Fiona walked to the window and looked out.

'Nice view,' Fiona said. She touched the curtain. 'Lovely piece of old velvet.' She walked to the wardrobe and opened the door, fingering the clothes. 'Nice things. Yours?' Without waiting for a reply, she took out the grey dress and peered at the label. 'Chanel. My goodness. And it's one of those classics. How on earth…' Fiona looked at Margo with a touch of envy in her eyes. 'And that shirt you're wearing is definitively a Dior vintage. Is she giving you her old clothes? Got to say, darling, these are the best hand-me-downs I've ever—'

'Stop snooping.' Margo snatched the dress away, hung it back in the wardrobe and slammed the door shut.

'All right. Don't be so bloody jumpy. Look, I just came for a little chat. Just to see, well, to find out...'

'Fiona. Please.' Margo sat down on the bed again, her legs oddly weak. 'I'd like you to leave now. I don't know why you're here, and I don't care. I want to be left alone.'

They looked at each other in silence.

'Why do I have the feeling I have never really known you?' Fiona said, standing in the middle of the room, her hands on her hips. 'I know we've never really been close friends, but I get the impression right now that you have been playing the part of someone else all these years. It really frightens me, you know. How is it possible that someone like you can suddenly just walk away from a life like that to...' she gestured vaguely around the room, 'this?'

'Someone like me?' Margo asked. 'What do you mean?'

'Someone from your background, I mean. I would have thought you would thank your lucky stars to have bagged a man like Alan and hang on to him no matter what...' Fiona's voice trailed away.

'He isn't exactly Prince Charming in private, you know,' Margo said.

'Well, yes, I can see that, but…' Fiona took a deep breath and looked at Margo squarely. 'Just tell me this – if he was so horrible to live with, why on earth did you marry him?'

'Not because I wanted to "bag" a rich husband, in any case,' Margo said hotly. 'We fell in love. It's as simple as that. We got married and…' She paused. 'Well, you know. We were fine. Very happy. And when there were problems, we were able to work it out. Even when—' she stopped.

'When…?' Fiona said.

'I found out I couldn't have a baby,' Margo said flatly. 'I was so upset.' More than upset, she thought as she remembered how the longing to be a mother had been so bad it was like a physical pain. She had felt she had no future if she couldn't have a child, but how could she explain that to Fiona or any woman who had been able to have children?

'It took me a long time to accept that there would never be a baby,' Margo continued. 'And then I was worried that Alan would leave me, try to find someone else who could… But he took it really well. He was so kind and sweet, then. He took care of everything. He was in charge of all the tests so I didn't have to sit in some doctor's office and get the bad news from a stranger. And when he found out that I wasn't a candidate for IVF, he was very good about that too and said that we would try to adopt a baby as soon as his surgery was off the ground and he would have more time to spend with a family. But that never seemed to happen,' she mumbled. 'I don't think he really meant it.'

'I see.' Fiona still stood in the middle of the room, looking slightly uncomfortable.

'Could you please leave now?' Margo whispered. 'I want to be on my own.'

'OK,' Fiona said, looking deflated. 'I'll go.' She retrieved her handbag that had fallen onto the floor by the bed. 'I'm going away in any case. For a holiday, I mean. We're going to spend the month of August in Scotland, as usual. Marcus's parents' house.'

'But you hate it there,' Margo said. 'You always said it was—'

'Cold and boring, I know,' Fiona sighed, closing the zip on her handbag. 'And huge and crumbling and... Well, it's the family seat and all that. And one day it will belong to Marcus and he will be—'

'Sir Marcus,' Margo filled in. 'And you will be Lady Whitney-Jones. And you'll have to live there and freeze for the rest of your—'

'Not if Marcus manages to pull off his diplomatic career,' Fiona interrupted, pulling down the jacket of her suit. 'And that is what I – I mean *we're* – trying to do at the moment. He's doing really well, you know,' she ended proudly. 'So it will all work out according to plan, if you would only – I mean...' She paused. 'Oh God. Shit.'

'What do you mean?'

'Nothing.'

Margo studied Fiona for a moment. She looked tense and worried and there were dark circles under her eyes. 'Are you all right?' Margo asked. 'You seem so stressed.'

'Well, yes, I am a bit stressed,' Fiona said, twisting the strap of her handbag. 'It's hard work running everything; Marcus, his career, Rufus, the nanny, the maid and that huge apartment. You have no idea how difficult it is to deal with the French. They are so snooty and you have to practically beg to get them to come to the tiniest tea party. None of them make the slightest effort to speak English and they look down their bloody noses all the time at everything. I mean, why do we have to do everything according to *their* rules of etiquette?'

'Because this is their country?' Margo said with just a hint of irony in her voice.

'What?' Fiona glared at Margo. 'I should have known you would be no help at all,' she spat. 'You just sit there looking smug and think only of yourself. Well, we can't all be drop-outs. Some of us have to look after our responsibilities. I'm only trying to help, you know. If you had any sense at all, you would get out of here and stay with me for a while. And then, when you're ready, you could go back to Alan.'

'But I don't want to get out of here,' Margo said. 'And going back to Alan is the last thing on earth I would like to do right now.'

'But can't you see that you have created a very difficult situation for him?' Fiona insisted. 'He's had to hire someone else to run the surgery and she is now trying her best to sort out all the patients' records and files and figure out your rather strange filing system, which is making his work very difficult. Not to mention the social embarrassment of having to explain to all his friends and colleagues why you aren't there and why he's having to go to dinner parties on his own. He's had to dream up some sort of family emergency that has forced you to leave London in a hurry.'

'Family emergency?' Margo interrupted. 'Of what kind?'

'He's said that your mother went to Australia to visit her sister.'

'That's right, she did.'

'And that she was taken ill and you had to fly out and join her and he doesn't really know when you'll be back.'

'My God, that's clever,' Margo said with mock admiration in her voice. 'Good old Alan. Always ready with the right explanation. So, in that case, why could we not leave it as it is at the moment? I'm in Australia. Great.'

Fiona took a deep breath. 'OK, I'm going to tell you the real reason I'm here. Alan asked me to tell you that he wants to talk to you himself. He has tried to call you on your mobile, but…'

'I know. I haven't kept it switched on, but I got all his messages.' Margo stood up and walked to the window. 'I can't,' she said, staring out over the rooftops. 'I can't even bear the thought of hearing his voice. It will only end in a row, anyway. In any case, I've taken the SIM card out of my mobile and changed to a French top-up account.' She turned around and stared at Fiona. 'I'm *not* going to give you the number, so don't even ask.'

'All right,' Fiona soothed. 'Don't get yourself into a state. Alan said you're inclined to overreact.'

Margo made a snorting sound. 'Overreact? That's a laugh.'

'What am I going to tell him, then?'

'You don't have to tell him anything, do you?'

'Oh, yes I do. He knows I was coming to see you today, and I promised I would get you to go back to London to at least talk to him.'

'You promised? How could you promise such a thing?' Margo said. 'Did you tell him you knew where to find me?'

'Yes,' Fiona murmured, looking a little guilty. 'But don't worry. He won't rush over here. He can't. He's too busy.'

'Of course,' Margo said ironically. 'Too busy to worry about a little detail like his wife and his marriage.'

'*You* left *him*, remember?'

'Oh, I remember all right,' Margo said bitterly. 'I remember every word. Every insult. It will take me a long time to forget. A very long time.'

They stared at each other, Fiona standing in the middle of the room as if rooted to the spot and Margo sitting on the bed again, willing her to leave.

'Just one more thing,' Fiona said.

'Please,' Margo pleaded. 'No more. Just leave me alone.'

'But what about your, well, your assets?' Fiona insisted without paying attention to the exasperation in Margo's voice. 'I mean, your lovely house, your personal possessions, your jewellery. Can you really leave all that behind? Just like that? If you're not careful, you'll lose everything you have in London. Alan could sue you for desertion, you know. He said…' Fiona paused, suddenly looking very uncomfortable.

'What? What else did he say? Spit it out. I want to hear everything.'

'He said that you were unstable. That you had some problems with your mental health in the past and that you have had psychiatric help.'

Margo suddenly felt the ice in her chest melt and turn into red-hot lava. '*What?*' she almost shouted. 'He what?' Then she remembered. 'Oh no,' she gasped, 'he wouldn't use that…'

'Use what?'

'I did see a psychiatrist once,' Margo whispered, looking down at her hands. 'Years ago. That time when we found out about my not being able to conceive. I was so upset and Alan said I needed counselling. But I only went once to this woman. A friend of Alan's, of course. I didn't feel it helped me at all. I didn't think someone I didn't know could… Oh, I can't believe it.' Margo looked up at Fiona. 'Is that what he's planning?' she demanded. 'Is that why you're here? To give me this ultimatum? That if I don't come back and behave myself he will declare me insane and take all I – *we* – own together? Are you running his errands, is that it? Have you offered your services as his solicitor? Is all of this your idea?'

'No!' Fiona exclaimed, looking horrified.

'Absolutely not. I want – I *need* you – to get back together again.'

'Why?'

'Because I think you're so great together,' Fiona said feebly.

'We're great together.' Margo looked at Fiona, trying to figure out if she was being honest or just pretending.

'Yes, you are. And Alan is really desperate. He's so lonely without you, I can really feel it when he's talking about you.'

'He's got a strange way of showing it, I must say.'

'He's just trying everything he can to get you back.'

'I bet. Look, Fiona, I don't want to even think about this at the moment. I want to be left alone. I want to just have some space, I suppose. So you can tell Alan from me that I'm not coming back for the moment. I'm not going to talk to him until I'm ready.'

'All this because of a silly little row?' Fiona said. 'I find this very strange, to be honest. I mean, Marcus can be a real shit sometimes, but, well, I don't usually take it seriously.'

'It wasn't really because of *one* row,' Margo said. 'That incident on the motorway was the last straw because of the way he's been speaking to me for quite a long time now. Every time he loses his temper, every time something doesn't go his way, he treats me the way no man should treat a woman. Or a dog,' she added. 'It hurts to be treated like that.'

'So that's it, then? You're not going back? That's your answer?'

'Yes.'

They looked at each other in silence for a moment until, with a little sob, Fiona stumbled to the door, pulled it open and left as suddenly as she had arrived.

Margo stared at the door that had just slammed shut. What was going on? Was Fiona heading for some kind of breakdown? She had always been very tense, but now she was positively unhinged. But she seemed to have got the message all the same and with a bit of luck she wouldn't appear again. I'm on my own, Margo thought and, for the first time since her escape from Alan, felt it was true. She shivered, suddenly a little frightened. My possessions, she thought, our lovely house in Chelsea; the drawing room with the blue silk curtains and Regency furniture, the cosy kitchen and little courtyard outside with my herb garden. My Flora Danica dinner service, my Georgian silver and the Venetian glass chandelier. I wonder if Alan has remembered to water the plants, she thought, the yucca in the hall and the big azalea in the conservatory... Bits of memories flashed through Margo's mind as she sat there in the hot little room, memories of her marriage; good times and bad, everyday things, scenes, arguments. It was all so wonderful at first, she thought, when we lived in that small flat near the hospital and we came back to it after work and cooked dinner in the tiny kitchen, drank wine and made love. And then we bought the house, that gorgeous old house, and we spent the weekends painting it. And little by little, Alan started to make money and we could afford to buy beautiful antiques and Persian rugs and silk curtains. What happened to us, she wondered, when did that sour note creep in? Did we become too busy to enjoy it, too used to being able to buy whatever we wanted, taking it all for granted? We were so happy in the early days, Margo thought, when having success and money was only a dream. Before Alan became the big-shot consultant, before we knew there would be no babies and long before he started taking out his frustrations on me. She heard Alan's voice in her head, asking questions, demanding, insisting, controlling, and suddenly overcome with a feeling of sadness, tears welled up in her eyes and she lay down on the bed, staring out the window without really seeing the view. Outside, the sparrows took off, one after the other, and she followed their flight over the rooftops until they were tiny specks against the darkening sky.

*

'Shoes,' Milady said the following morning as they stood on the hot pavement beside the Jaguar, ready to board for the trip to the country. 'I don't think I have all my shoes.'

'But I packed all the ones on the list,' Margo said. 'And put shoe trees in every one and wrapped them in tissue paper and put them into the shoe bags.'

'Even the black evening sandals?'

'Yes,' Margo said, beginning to feel frustrated. She looked at François for help, but he sat in the driver's seat, the door open, reading the morning paper with an air of resignation.

'And the red slingbacks?' Milady continued.

'Yes,' Margo said, unable to stop herself sighing.

'And my green Wellingtons?'

'What?' Margo stared at her. 'Green Wellingtons? But they weren't on the list.'

'Weren't they?' Milady glared at Margo. 'But you should have known. One simply cannot go to the country without green Wellingtons. I thought you would know that, being English and everything.'

There was a strange sound from François. Margo glanced at him, but he was turning the page of the newspaper, his face expressionless.

'You have to go back up and get them,' Milady ordered. 'They're in the hall cupboard.'

'Is there anything else?' Margo asked. 'I could get that at the same time.'

'No. Go on,' Milady urged, 'hurry up. We have to get out of Paris before eleven o'clock, or we'll get caught in the worst of the traffic.'

Margo had to go back up to the apartment three times for assorted items that Milady had neglected to put on her list, and it was ten to twelve by the time François started the engine and pulled the heavily loaded car into the busy traffic. Milady sat in the passenger seat, smoking and giving François instructions on which route to take in order to avoid the worst of the traffic jams. Margo leaned her head against the back window, exhausted. Milou crawled from his cushion and settled his body across Margo's legs. She tried to push him back onto the cushion, but he growled menacingly.

'He likes to sit on someone's lap in the car,' Milady announced as she glanced back at Margo. 'Try not to move too much, or he'll be sick.'

Margo squirmed, her thighs sticking to the leather upholstery, and tried to get used to Milou's hot body. She regretted her decision to wear black trousers as she knew they would be covered in white dog hair in no time at all. Oh well, Margo thought, what did it matter? Who would notice how she looked? She put her arms around Milou and closed her eyes, as the motion of the car made her feel a little sleepy. For the next hour or so, she listened idly to snatches of conversation in French from the front seat; a good-natured discussion about politics, something about family matters and a slight argument about where they would stop for lunch.

'Chartres,' Milady said. 'We should stop there. There's a very good restaurant just off the main square.'

'But that's a huge detour,' François protested. 'We won't arrive until late, and I'll miss the evening news on television. Why can't we have a sandwich in one of the motorway stations?'

'A sandwich?' Milady asked as if François had suggested she take a dose of strychnine. 'In one of those…those…places? How could you possibly suggest such a thing?'

'Sorry, *Maman*,' François mumbled.

'And we could pop into the cathedral afterwards,' Milady suggested, sounding satisfied. 'I love walking around in that peaceful place. And the windows are superb.' She turned her head and looked at Margo. 'Have you ever been to the cathedral in Chartres, Marguerite?'

'No, I haven't,' Margo mumbled.

'There,' Milady said to François. 'See? We have to show it to Marguerite.'

'Very well,' François said with a resigned little sigh and turned the car into the exit for Chartres.

The little restaurant in the town was lovely, and Margo enjoyed sitting there, admiring the exquisite décor and the view of the street from their table. Milady took a very long time to pore over the menu and finally ordered filet mignon for all of them, despite François's protests, which Milady waved away. 'And a bottle of this excellent Bordeaux,' she added, pointing at the menu. 'And we want the steaks blue, of course.'

'Of course,' the waiter agreed, looking respectfully at Milady.

'And please,' she added, giving Milou, who was lying on one of the chairs, a little pat, 'could we have a bowl of water for my dog?'

'Right away.'

'*Bleu*?' Margo asked. 'I heard you say blue, what does that mean?'

'It means rare,' Milady said. 'The only way to eat good-quality fillet steak.'

'It means more than rare,' François added. 'It means that instead of cooking the steaks, they just wave it briefly over the frying pan.'

'Oh.' Margo suddenly didn't feel very hungry. 'Excuse me,' she said to the waiter, who was just about to walk away, 'could you change my order to a tomato salad?'

'*Bien, Madame,*' he nodded and left.

'Not very hungry,' Margo said sheepishly to Milady, who just shrugged.

'I hope you realise that you and Marguerite will have to drink that wine by yourselves,' François said as the waiter came back with a bottle. 'As you know, I never drink and drive.'

'You really are such a sissy,' Milady said. 'A glass of wine never harmed anyone. It's not as if I'm asking you to drink alcohol, is it?'

'My mother,' François said conspiratorially to Margo, 'like a lot of French people of her generation, does not think wine contains any alcohol at all. "Alcohol" to them means hard liquor. Wine is like mother's milk.'

Margo laughed, but Milady shrugged and sipped her wine that had just been served. 'Your generation is just too soft,' she remarked. 'This wine is superb. Try it, Marguerite.'

Margo sipped the wine and had to agree it was indeed excellent. By the time the food arrived, she was a little tipsy, but Milady, who had already had two glasses, appeared perfectly sober. She devoured her steak and washed it down with more wine. 'I think I will just have a nice piece of Camembert and then chocolate mousse,' she said. 'That should keep me going until dinner. Marguerite?'

Margo, who thought it might keep anyone going until next week, finished the last of her tomato salad. 'I'm all right, thank you,' she murmured. 'I'll just have a cup of coffee.'

'Fine. François?'

'What?' François muttered from behind a copy of *Le Monde* he had found on a nearby table.

'What will you have to follow?'

'Nothing, *Maman*, thank you,' he said, putting down the newspaper. 'And I think we'll have to go and visit the cathedral now, if you want to arrive before midnight.'

'As you wish,' Milady sighed and waved at the waiter, who almost ran up to their table. '*Trois cafés et l'addition, s'il vous plaît*,' she said in her haughty French.

'*Tout de suite, Madame.*'

They entered the cathedral and Margo wandered around in the cool dark interior for a while, wondering why this was supposed to be such a marvel, when François told her to look up. She did, and gasped as she saw the pillars soaring above them and the huge stained glass windows, glowing like hundreds of jewels in all the colours of the rainbow. The beams of light shimmered through the darkness, illuminating the cathedral in an eerie, iridescent glow. 'Twelfth century,' François whispered. 'Amazing, no?'

'Oh, yes,' Margo whispered back, 'absolutely breathtaking.' She felt at once dizzy, awestruck and very small. She craned her neck and could not take her eyes off the wonderful sight. She heard the sound of monks singing Gregorian chant in the distance. The air smelled of incense and candles and she felt as if she had suddenly been transported hundreds of years back in time. Nine hundred years, she thought and shivered suddenly, tightening her cardigan around her shoulders.

'Cold?' François asked.

'No, just someone walking over my grave.'

'I know the feeling,' François murmured. 'But now, we have to get back on the road. I'm going to the car to make sure we don't end up with a parking ticket. Could you find my mother and tell her?'

'Of course.' Margo nodded. 'I'll see you in a minute.' The cathedral was so dark it was difficult to see anyone from afar, and Margo walked slowly around, peering at tourists looking up at the windows, but Milady was not among them. Margo continued up one of the side aisles and finally spotted Milady in a little side chapel devoted to the Virgin Mary. Margo stared at the slim figure of the Comtesse, kneeling at the altar, deep in prayer, and backed away, not wanting to intrude. Milady suddenly turned around and Margo was startled by the expression of immense sadness in her eyes.

'Oh,' Milady mumbled, crossing herself. 'Time to go.' She rose, straightened her shoulders as if to shake off her sorrows, and walked down the aisle with her usual confident stride.

*

It was nearly nine o'clock in the evening when the car swept trough the tall black gates and drove up the long tree-lined avenue that led to Château la Bourdonnière. Margo stared out through the window at the fields and paddocks, where horses wandered through the lush, green grass under huge oaks, with a feeling of relief. It had been a very long day. A journey which, according to Margo's calculations, should have taken around four hours had stretched into nearly eight. As the car neared the château, Margo could see a low, long building that must be the stables and a big stone-faced barn. Absorbed by the view through the window, she only half-listened to the exchange in French between Milady and François.

'I hope Jacques is ready to dine,' Milady said, 'it is such a bore having to wait until he has fed the horses and done all those chores.'

'I rang yesterday,' François said from the driver's seat. 'He said he was looking forward to seeing us for dinner and then he will show us all the things he has done during the winter months.'

'I should really have been here earlier in the year,' Milady said, 'but there was so much going on in Paris…'

'And I have been so busy at the ministry,' François filled in, 'I haven't had a chance to come down for a long time.'

'But Jacques manages the estate so well,' Milady said. 'And runs his yard at the same time. I don't know how he does it.'

'He's amazing, really,' François said. 'But he loves the place, you know.'

'Yes,' Milady sighed, 'he does. Oh, look,' she continued, pointing at something ahead, 'he's cut down the ivy on the cottage. And those flowerbeds have been replanted. It looks really nice. See, François, Jacques has really been working hard.'

'The gardener, you mean,' François said. 'But the place looks quite nice, I have to say. He must have managed to sort out all the problems he was complaining about last winter without all the money he said it was going to cost. Marguerite,' he continued, 'we're coming up to the main building now. Look at the setting sun to the west, over those hills. It shines straight into the drawing room windows and it always looks as if the whole place is on fire.'

Margo turned her head to look. There it was – Château la Bourdonnière, an early nineteenth-century castle built of sandstone with a tower at each end. The sunset was indeed reflected in the many windows on the side facing the park, and it really did look as if the ground floor of the château was in flames. 'It's magnificent,' she said and suddenly realised she had been here before. The towers of the castle, the hills behind it and the stream… It had to be the place she had been to with Gráinne that night. Why hadn't she realised it from the start? Of course. That letter must have been…

'And there is Jacques,' Milady exclaimed.

Margo looked up at the figure standing at the top of the steps.

9

Those eyes. Margo saw them in her mind's eye as she went to sleep. A tall man, with wide shoulders. Black hair that fell onto his forehead, a rather big nose that looked as if it had been broken at some stage, a wide mouth with slightly uneven, very white teeth, dark stubble on a square chin. He wore his faded jeans and worn polo shirt with a casual elegance that made the perfect grooming of his older brother seem faintly over the top. And the eyes. Blue – not like Alan's watery blue that turned to ice when he was annoyed or irritated, but a deep azure blue, under black brows and lashes. She had taken it all in as she looked up from the back seat of the car, Milou scrabbling to get out, Milady opening the door on her side, calling to Jacques to help her, François pulling the hand brake and then the sudden commotion as two enormous black dogs rushed toward Milou, who had escaped from Margo's grip and jumped out of the half-open window.

The ensuing shouting and barking was suddenly silenced by a loud command from the man on the steps, and the dogs stopped and slunk behind their master. Milou continued to bark from the safety of Milady's arms, but changed to a whimper as she told him to be quiet.

Feeling slightly wobbly, Margo slowly got out of the car as Milady climbed the steps and greeted her son and François started to take the luggage out of the boot. 'Here is your bag,' he said and handed Margo the tote bag. 'Was that all you had?'

'That's it, thanks,' she said, taking the bag. She hadn't brought much, as the clothes in her room in Paris weren't really suitable for the country, just the T-shirt and linen trousers she was wearing, a swimsuit, a pair of jeans and two cotton summer dresses she had picked up at the market.

'My personal assistant,' she could hear Milady say. 'We call her Marguerite.'

'Oh,' the man said and glanced at Margo from above. '*Bonsoir.*' Their eyes met for a second and Margo thought she saw a flash of recognition in those blue eyes.

'*Bonsoir,*' she replied, not knowing quite what to do. Should she go up the steps and shake his hand? His disinterest in her was bordering on rude, making her think she had imagined that brief flash of interest, and she stood there holding her bag, looking at him as he turned his broad back to her and resumed talking to his mother.

'*Chéri*,' she could hear Milady say, 'everything looks marvellous. And you had the roof done.' She turned to François. 'Look, darling, Jacques had the roof repaired. And you said it would cost a fortune.'

Margo turned around as she heard steps on the gravel. A stocky, grey-haired man wearing a blue apron had just appeared. '*Bonsoir, Monsieur le Comte*,' he said, picking up two of the suitcases and, as an afterthought, '*bonsoir, Mademoiselle*.'

'*Bonsoir*, Bernard,' François replied. 'This is Marguerite, my mother's—'

'I know,' the man grunted. 'Monsieur Jacques told me.' He started to put the luggage on a handcart.

'Marguerite,' François said, 'this is Bernard. Our butler, gardener, caretaker…well, everything really. His wife Agnès is our housekeeper.'

'Oh. *Bonsoir*, Bernard,' Margo mumbled, holding out her hand, but drawing it back when she realised that Bernard was neither able nor willing to shake it.

'Go with Bernard,' François said. 'He'll introduce you to Agnès and she will show you to your room. Have a nice evening and I'll see you in the morning.'

'Oh, eh, right,' Margo said, suddenly feeling her stomach rumble. What about dinner, she wondered, regretting her decision to have a very light lunch earlier. But François seemed to have forgotten her existence as he bounded up the steps and shook hands with his brother and they all disappeared into the château through heavy oak doors.

Margo trudged after Bernard, who was pulling the handcart with the suitcases across the gravel, around the corner, through an archway, into a cobbled courtyard and stopped in front of a door. 'In there, Mademoiselle,' he said, opening the door. 'My wife will take care of you.'

Margo stepped into a small room which looked like an old scullery, through a second door into a huge kitchen, where a diminutive black-haired woman was taking a leg of lamb out of an Aga cooker. There was a delicious smell of roast lamb, rosemary and garlic, and Margo felt her stomach rumble so loudly she was sure it was echoing around the kitchen.

The woman turned around. 'Oh,' she exclaimed. 'I thought it was Bernard. You must be the new girl.' She put the roasting tin on the big pine table, wiped her hand on her apron and held it out to Margo. 'I'm Agnès,' she said. 'The wife of Bernard.'

'My name is Marguerite.' Margo shook the small strong hand.

'Nice to meet you,' Agnès said. 'But you have to excuse me. I'm just about to serve dinner. Monsieur Jacques said they would be hungry and Madame likes the *gigot* rare, and it's just about perfect, so I have to carve it straight away. The gratin of garlic potatoes and the beans are all ready too.' Her French was so rapid, Margo had to concentrate to keep up. 'Maybe you could give me a hand and take it all to the dining room?' Agnès added.

'Yes.' Margo felt her mouth water. 'Of course.'

It was exquisite agony to bring the meal into the dining room and place the dishes on the big sideboard. Margo barely noticed the beautiful room, the big oil paintings of innumerable ancestors or the huge tapestry that covered the wall opposite the French windows. She clenched her teeth as she carefully placed the silver dish with the meat on the heating tray and swallowed furiously as Agnès placed the other dish with the potatoes and green beans beside it, trying not to breathe in the garlic and herbs, or notice the brown crust on top of the rich, creamy potatoes.

'There.' Agnès wiped the edge of the potato dish with her apron. 'I'll just go and tell them it's ready and then we can go down and get you something to eat too, if you are hungry.'

'A little,' Margo admitted and smiled weakly, again bitterly regretting having had such a light lunch.

'Well, there isn't much. Bernard and I ate earlier, but there's some bread and cheese, I think.'

'That'll be fine,' Margo lied, taking a last, longing look at the meal on the sideboard. She wiped her mouth with her hand just to make sure she wasn't actually drooling and left the dining room.

'But first we have to go and unpack the luggage of Madame la Comtesse,' Agnès said as she led the way down a corridor and into a huge hall with a stone-flagged floor where the mounted heads of deer and wild boar competed for space on the oak-panelled walls. She started to ascend a curved staircase with ornately carved banisters. Margo looked up at yet more Coligny ancestors, staring haughtily at her through hooded eyes. She could hear the voices of Milady and her sons as they filed into the dining room below, then a door closed and, except for the creaking of the stairs, there was silence. Margo trudged after Agnès up the staircase and onto a landing. They padded silently on Persian rugs through a long corridor lined with many doors, turned a corner and went in through an open door. Margo looked around the big, bright room. 'It's lovely,' she said without thinking. 'Really beautiful.'

Agnès turned around from the pile of suitcases in the middle of the faded Aubusson rug. 'Yes, it's a very nice room. The furniture is *Directoire*, early nineteenth century.'

'Oh?' Margo said, looking at the mahogany headboard of the double bed. 'That's what we call Regency in England.'

'The wallpaper is original as well,' Agnès volunteered. 'And the curtains. Restored, of course, but it looks nearly exactly the way it would have looked then.'

'Exquisite,' Margo mumbled, carefully touching the green silk with the delicate embroidery of tiny pink rosebuds. She glanced out the French window at the garden below. In the fading daylight, she could just make out immaculate lawns, lined with beds of red roses and clipped shrubs, yet more roses spilling over old walls, tubs of hydrangeas and geraniums and the glint of a swimming pool further away. 'Lovely garden,' she said.

'Yes. Bernard's pride and joy,' Agnès nodded. 'But we better start unpacking, Mademoiselle, if you don't mind. There are a lot of clothes here and I need to take whatever there is to be ironed.'

They worked silently for about half an hour, hanging the clothes in a big double wardrobe, arranging shoes on shelves below them, sorting out underwear and nightgowns and putting them into the chest of drawers between the windows.

'There,' Agnès said when they were finished. 'All done. And there was nothing that needed to be ironed for the moment. Bernard will take the empty suitcases. Now we can go and tidy up after dinner and Bernard will serve coffee on the terrace.'

'Oh, yes,' Margo said, a surge of hope lifting her flagging spirits. Leftovers, she thought. There was enough on that leg of lamb to feed ten people. I'll be able to have some cold lamb and maybe a little bit of that potato...

But the dishes were empty. Margo stared in disbelief at the pool of meat juice on the serving dish. 'What about the leftover meat and the... bone?'

'They must have given it all to the dogs,' Agnès replied as she took the dishes off the heating tray. 'And what was left of the potatoes too. Could you take the big platter and I will take these two.'

Back in the kitchen, Margo sank down on a chair by the table, past caring whether she was polite or not. There was a dry knot of hunger in her stomach and she was beginning to feel weak. Agnès loaded the dishes into a dishwasher under the big old-fashioned sink, slammed the door shut and twisted a knob. '*Et voilà*,' she shouted over the noise of the machine. 'All done. I can put my feet up now, as soon as I've shown you your room.'

'But,' Margo called, trying to make herself heard over the din, 'what about my supper?'

'Oh, *oui*.' Agnès smiled apologetically. 'I totally forgot.' She went in through a door which seemed to lead to a large pantry and came back with a plate and half a stick of bread. 'Here. Some salad from our lunch and a piece of Camembert. A bit tired, but that's all there is tonight. I think there are some apples in the *arriere cuisine*.'

'Never mind,' Margo said and took the piece of bread. 'This is fine.' She cut a wedge of Camembert with a knife that was lying on the table, broke off a piece of bread, put the cheese on top and crammed it all into her mouth. 'Delicious,' she muttered through her mouthful, feeling instantly better. The bread was tough and the cheese a little too ripe for her taste, but beggars can't be choosers, she thought, suddenly realising how it would feel to actually be a beggar.

'I'm sorry about the food tonight, but we didn't know you were coming until the last minute,' Agnès said as she poured Margo a glass of wine. 'You'll take your meals with Bernard and me while you're here, Monsieur Jacques said. I hope you like vegetables. Bernard is a strict vegetarian, you see, and I can't eat anything rich as I have a problem with my digestion, so we eat very simply, not at all the rich food of *Les Comtes,*' she continued with a toss of her head in the direction of the dining room. 'And we never eat anything fried either.'

'Oh,' Margo said, trying to swallow a big piece of bread. 'Sounds healthy.' She sipped the wine and watched as Agnès tidied the kitchen.

'Monsieur Jacques was very concerned that you be comfortable,' Agnès said as she wiped the top of the Aga. 'He's a very considerate man. Nice to work for, if you see what I mean.'

'I've heard a lot about him,' Margo said, breaking off a piece of bread. 'A lot of different things, actually. It's difficult to form an opinion about him, really.'

'Oh? Why is that?'

'Well, some people seem to love him and others seem to loathe him,' Margo said, remembering what Gráinne had said.

'I don't know what you've heard,' Agnès said, her voice full of disapproval, 'but around here Monsieur Jacques is both loved and respected. He is a decent man, even if—' She stopped.

'If?'

'If he sometimes has a problem with…' Agnès stopped again. 'Women throw themselves at him, you see, and that is not his fault. Sometimes he takes advantage of it – he's only human, after all – and serves them right, I always say. You have to make a man guess, you know, make him think you don't care, and… But what am I thinking? I shouldn't be talking like this. Forget what I said, Mademoiselle.'

'Of course,' Margo said. 'It's forgotten.'

'Good.' Agnès resumed polishing the Aga, her mouth pinched shut.

Margo watched her work, her thoughts on the man she had just glimpsed. Interesting, she thought. I wonder if I'll like him or loathe him? But I'll probably never get a chance to find out.

'Finally,' Agnès sighed, untying her apron. 'All done. And tomorrow is Sunday. Our day off. I'm looking forward to it, I have to say. The next few weeks won't be easy.'

'Oh? Why?'

'Well, August is always very busy, you see, with all the family here and all the parties. But I'm so glad you're here.' Agnès sat down opposite Margo and poured herself a glass of wine. 'Last year I had nobody to help and I nearly collapsed with fatigue. I said to Monsieur Jacques that if I didn't get some help this year, I would quit. Not that I would, of course,' she continued, winking at Margo, 'but it doesn't hurt to threaten to from time to time. Keeps them on their toes, if you know what I mean.'

Agnès finished her wine and got up from her chair. 'It's getting late. If I don't get going, I'll miss my television programme. I'll just take you to your room. Follow me.'

*

The room was high up in one of the towers, a big, bright room with white walls and antique pine furniture and, on the floorboards, a large blue rug that matched the bedspread and curtains. 'It's the old nursery,' Agnès said, 'or part of the nursery suite, I should say. This was the nanny's room. Monsieur Jacques told me to put you here, because it has its own bathroom and toilet and it's separate from the rest of the house. And you can get to the kitchen very easily by the back stairs. It's not very modern, freezing in the wintertime, but quite comfortable in the summer. Nice and cool because it faces east and you don't have the evening sun making it too hot to sleep.'

'It's fine,' Margo murmured, putting her bag on the bed and walking to the window to look out. It was dusk, but she could still see the whole garden and beyond – the paddocks, stables and the stream. And a little further away, the weir and the hay barn and meadow where she had slept in Gráinne's truck that night. It seemed so long ago.

'Close the shutters and leave the windows open when you want to sleep,' Agnès prattled on, 'and the bathroom is through that door there.'

'All right,' Margo murmured, looking down at the back terrace. There was a glint of light as a door opened and someone came out. A man. He looked up, and Margo pulled back.

'I'll close the shutters for you,' Agnès said, coming forward, 'they're a little tricky. You have to lean out and grab the edge like this, and then close them with this hook here, see?' The shutters banged as they came together and the room was plunged into darkness. 'I'll just switch on the light,' Agnès laughed. She turned a switch by the bed and a small bedside light illuminated the room in a soft pink glow. 'There. I made the bed earlier. *Bonne nuit*, Marguerite.'

'*Bonne nuit*, Agnès. And thank you so much.'

'*De rien*,' Agnès smiled. '*A Lundi*.' She walked out of the room and softly closed the door.

When she had found the bathroom and had a quick shower, standing in the old chipped enamel bath trying not to look at a big spider in the high ceiling, Margo crawled in between the cool lavender-scented sheets. She stared into the darkness, trying to get used to the feel and smell of the room. It was very dark, unlike her room in Paris, where the streetlights would cast a faint glow through the window. And no traffic noise, she realised, no noise at all, just the curious impression of the sound of silence. There was a sudden cry from an owl outside, then silence again, and a sliver of moonlight shone through a crack in the shutters. Margo closed her eyes and tried to empty her mind and go to sleep. The floor suddenly creaked, making her sit bolt upright and stare into the darkness, her heart pounding. Mice. Or rats, she thought, are there rats up here? Stop it, she said to herself. The floorboards are just cooling down. These old places always creak. She lay down again, forcing herself to relax. She took a deep breath and then breathed out very slowly, feeling calmer. Those eyes, she suddenly thought, such blue... No, calm down. Breathe slowly. In...and out. That's it. But as she breathed in again, she could just distinguish the smell of a Gauloise being smoked somewhere close by.

10

Margo peered through her window at the terrace below. Where was everybody? It was nearly eleven o'clock, but there wasn't a sound. She could see a round table under a blue and white striped umbrella with a litter of cups, saucers and a big coffee pot, and bees buzzing around what must be a pot of jam. She looked across the sunlit garden to the swimming pool, but it was quiet and empty, the blue-green water undisturbed, the deck chairs unoccupied. There was no sound of voices or any kind of life at all, only birdsong, the cawing of crows in the big trees and the distant, soft whinnying of a horse. The room felt airless and oppressive, and Margo realised it was going to be a very hot day. She dressed quickly, putting on a sundress and sandals, and made her way to the kitchen. There was nobody there except a large black cat who looked at her with suspicion as it cleaned its face and body with a pink tongue.

'Hello there, pussy cat,' Margo said, 'nice to meet you.'

The cat yawned and jumped onto the windowsill, where it lay down in the sun and closed its eyes.

Margo went to the pantry to look for something to eat. She found some bread, half a croissant, two peaches and a pot of apricot jam. The coffee machine on the counter was still switched on, and she poured herself a cup and sat down at the kitchen table. At least I got some breakfast, she thought, but only by accident. As Margo slowly spread jam on a piece of croissant, she realised what was going on, why there was nobody about. It was Sunday and the Coligny family were all doing what they normally did on a Sunday, whatever that was. Margo, like all servants since the beginning of time, had, to them, simply ceased to exist. As she began to understand how little Milady or anyone else in the family cared about her when she wasn't doing her job, a feeling of desperate loneliness washed over her as she sat there in the empty kitchen. Oh God, she said to herself, what am I doing here in this God-forsaken place with these weird people? And what am I going to do next? Stay here and continue being part of the furniture? Or just get up and leave? Go to Paris, then on to London, have it out with Alan and sort out my life. Get some kind of job, rent a flat… She wrapped her arms around herself and stared into space. I'm a failure, she thought, a thirty-seven-year-old bloody failure. I can't even decide what to do with my life. And I have nobody to blame but myself. Tears suddenly welled up in Margo's eyes as she gave in to feelings of utter despair and self-pity. I'm all alone in the world, she thought, nobody on this planet gives a shit about me. She started to cry uncontrollably, the tears running unchecked down her face and onto the table. Her desperate sobs echoed around the big old kitchen, changing into a kind of keening that came from the very bottom of her soul. The cat jumped down from the windowsill and slunk out into the courtyard as Margo's sobs became louder and louder. She squeezed her arms tighter around herself, wailing, unable to stop. As the tears finally ebbed and the sobs became softer, she sat there, slumped, utterly spent, her mind blank.

*

'*Bonsoir.*'

Margo looked up from her meal. '*Bonsoir*,' she replied casually.

Jacques looked at her with a puzzled expression in his blue eyes. 'What are you doing here?' he asked in English.

'What does it look like?' she replied. It angered her that he seemed to think she had no right to sit on the terrace, as if she was a lowly servant who belonged in the kitchen.

'It looks like you're having dinner,' he replied, taking in the plate, the food and the bottle of wine. 'And that's a very good wine, if I'm not mistaken.'

His English startled Margo. Not the fluency, but the accent which, with French undertones, was vaguely familiar.

'That's right,' she said archly. 'It is. Excellent.

And just out of curiosity, do you normally let people who work for you go hungry, or is that just reserved for the English help? I'm not surprised you were so short of staff in the stables. What happened? Did they have enough energy to crawl away, or did they simply starve to death?'

There was no reply. Jacques just stood there and looked at her plate. 'Any more of that beef?' he asked as if he hadn't heard what she had said.

Margo sipped her wine. She looked at the glass thoughtfully, studying the ruby liquid and the streaks of glycerine on the sides of the glass. 'There was,' she said. 'Rather a big piece, actually.'

'Good, maybe then—'

'But I gave it to the cat.' She put down her glass and looked at him innocently. 'He loved it. Fillet of beef, you see. Very juicy.'

'*Merde*,' Jacques mumbled.

'Oh, were you hungry?' Margo purred. 'How terrible for you. I mean, it would be all right for me, a lowly servant, to have nothing to eat all day, but not for the master. Not for Monsieur Jacques, oh no, not at all. *That* would be a scandal.'

'I don't know what you're going on about,' Jacques said in an aggrieved voice, running his hand through his thick black hair. 'I have been out breaking my arse off all day and had to come back to feed the horses, and—'

'Oh, so you feed *them*, do you?' Margo lifted one eyebrow. 'Interesting. And I'm really impressed with your knowledge of the lower forms of English. Actually, you sound very much like a friend of mine, or acquaintance, I should say.'

He didn't reply, but took a chair and, straddling it, his arms across the back, studied her intently. 'And what have *you* been doing all day?' he asked.

'Me?' Margo asked, her anger slowly disappearing as he smiled at her. He didn't seem to think she didn't matter or that she was not his equal. He had the air of a man who knew he was more than handsome and very pleasing to women, but she liked the friendly way he spoke to her. And she wanted him to like her. His smiled broadened, and she glanced down, feeling a sudden urge to check that all the buttons on her dress were done up.

'Yes, you, Mademoiselle Marguerite,' he said. 'I would like to know how you spent your day.'

'Well.' Margo thought for a moment, trying to return Jacques's gaze without blushing. 'First I had a shower and then I went downstairs,' she started. 'And had my breakfast,' she ended feebly, thinking it was a good thing he hadn't been there to witness her outbreak.

'Oh? And after breakfast?' Jacques asked, as if her every movement that day was of intense interest to him.

'I walked around for a bit,' Margo said, thinking that the day had improved immensely since breakfast. When she had finally calmed down she had felt oddly at peace with herself, as if the crying fit had released some kind of tension that had been building up for weeks.

'You walked. Where? In the garden?' he asked.

'Yes.' As soon as she had felt a little stronger, she had left the kitchen and walked into the garden, down the path to the swimming pool. It was really hot by then, and Margo had sat down in the shade of an umbrella to escape the burning sun.

'And then?' Jacques enquired. 'No, let me guess. You went for a swim, yes? I would have.'

'Yes, I did.' The blue-green water had looked so cool and inviting and, after having quickly glanced back up the path, she had taken off her dress and slipped into the water. She had swum a couple of laps, then sat in the shallow end, her face to the sun, and just enjoyed the sensation of the cool water on her body.

'And when you had finished swimming?'

'Then I...' Margo's thoughts returned to the afternoon. When she'd had enough of the pool and the day turned even hotter, she had walked back into the cool interior of the château, and started to wander around, idly looking at paintings and furniture, her interest growing as she walked around the big rooms. 'I decided to go for a little tour of the château,' she told Jacques. She had peered at family photographs in what appeared to be a kind of study, looked at the titles of the leather-bound books in the library, studied the faces of the ancestors of the paintings in the hall. The air smelled of rose petals and lavender and Margo felt as if she was in some kind of time warp and that some crinolined lady would come through a door and ask what she was doing there. There was so much to see in the château, so many corridors and hidden corners, that Margo lost track of time. The daughter of an antique dealer, she had always loved old buildings, and this one was a gem. She was looking at the paintings in the dining room with great interest when suddenly, an old clock on a mantelpiece chimed. Margo had looked at the spindly roman numerals and realised it was seven o'clock. It's late, she had thought, have I really spent the entire day here? She had walked back into the kitchen to try to find something for supper.

'I'm afraid I snooped around a little,' Margo said. 'All over the house, actually.'

'Everywhere?'

'Well, yes, I suppose.'

'Shit.'

'What?'

'I did not tidy my room.'

'You mean your room was the one full of smelly socks?'

'No, that's François.'

Margo laughed, feeling the tension between them easing. 'I didn't really go into any of the bedrooms,' she said. 'I just explored all the rooms on the ground floor. There are some amazing antiques and paintings here.'

'You like old things?'

'Oh, yes, I do. I love old houses like this that haven't really been touched by the modern world. It's as if time has stood still for hundreds of years here. It's very…' she paused, trying to find words to describe her feelings. 'Very reassuring, somehow,' she ended, drinking the last of the wine in her glass, letting it rest in her mouth for a while to savour the rich taste of blackberry mingled with a hint of liquorice. 'This wine is delicious,' she murmured as it slid down her throat like velvet.

'It should be. It's a *grand cru classé*. Reserved for visiting royalty. And English staff, of course,' he added with a throaty laugh.

'Oh,' Margo said. 'I see. Well, in that case, I forgive you all.'

'Good.' Jacques rose from his chair. 'I'm going to get a glass from the dining room. Don't move, I'll be back in a second.'

Margo pushed back her plate and relaxed in her chair, looking up at the sky that was still a light blue. The evening breeze cooled her face and bare arms and she felt suddenly quite content and happy with the world. 'I was wondering,' she said when Jacques came back with a glass.

'Yes?' he poured himself some wine, turned the chair around and sat down opposite Margo.

'That painting in the library? The one over the fireplace. It's of a very beautiful woman in a blue dress. I was intrigued by her. Who is she?'

'That woman?' Jacques said, looking at Margo over the rim of his glass with a strange look in his eyes. 'That's the first Comtesse Coligny de la Bourdonnière. Née Mademoiselle Louise de la Bourdonnière.'

'Really? But how come...' Margo paused. 'How come she was née de la...'

'Bourdonnière? Well, back then the Colignys were not aristocrats.'

'They weren't? But how did they get their title, then?'

'From Napoleon. You see, he was deeply grateful to the Coligny family. It was thanks to them that there was anything left of La Grande Armée after their retreat from Moscow.'

'Why was that?'

'Because of the sausage.'

'I'm sorry?' Margo said, startled. 'What did you say?'

'The Coligny sausage,' Jacques said. 'The Colignys were butchers and they supplied the army with this special sausage that was so nutritious and so well preserved that it could keep a man alive for months. An army marches on its stomach, you must have heard that saying. Even the emperor himself survived on it when there was nothing else to eat.'

'Really? How interesting.'

'Oh yes. It would have been the end of Napoleon but for the sausage. Anyway, when he came back from Moscow,' Jacques continued, 'he made Edgar Coligny, the then head of the family, a count. He also suggested he marry Louise de la Bourdonnière and add her name to his. She was the daughter of a count of the *ancien régime*, the owner of this castle. A very old and illustrious family. This castle was built by them sometime in the Middle Ages. And the last count, Louise's father, was beheaded during the Revolution.'

'Oh, that was very sad.'

'Oh, yes. Very sad. But she knew how to survive. She was one of the ladies in the coterie around Madame Tallien. They were a very fast crowd and Louise was one of the most popular of the *grande horisontales*.' Jacques smiled at Margo. 'That means—'

'I know what it means.'

'Really? You are very well educated, Mademoiselle Marguerite. Anyway, Louise, who had been rumoured to have slept with Napoleon himself, did not mind marrying the handsome Edgar, especially as she was with child.'

'With child? You mean by...'

Jacques lifted one eyebrow. 'Who knows? Maybe by the emperor himself?'

'You're joking.'

'No, I'm not. It's absolutely true,' Jacques declared with an innocent air. 'It all happened exactly as I've told you. Louise and Edgar moved into the castle and Edgar used some of his vast fortune to restore it. Louise gave birth to a son, and after that they had seven more children.'

'I see.'

'So now you know the story of this family. And this house.'

'Fascinating.' Margo looked at him thought-fully.

'It is, isn't it?' he said, sounding very proud.

'Yes. The most fascinating load of rubbish I've ever heard.'

Jacques looked stunned. Then he threw back his head and laughed. 'How did you know?'

'Well, first of all, the lady in the painting is wearing a dress in the style of Napoleon III. That style of dress was made fashionable by the Empress

Eugenie around 1850 or so. And this château is not medieval. Built in the beginning of the nineteenth century, I think. And apart from all that, the whole story seemed so off the wall it just couldn't be true. I might have believed the first part, but when you started telling me about the sausage...' Margo snorted a little laugh.

Jacques shrugged and smiled ruefully. 'What a pity. Girls are usually fascinated by the history of my family.'

'I'm not a girl.'

'No, you're a woman.'

'Yes,' Margo said, feeling herself blush at the look in his eyes.

'The idea that there is a little bit of Napoleon in me turns women on, I have found,' he added.

'Maybe there is a little bit of Napoleon in all men.'

'What a very profound observation,' he said, nodding slowly in mock admiration. 'I begin to realise that you are not just a pretty face.'

'I should hope not.'

Jacques sipped his wine without taking his eyes off her face.

Margo ran her finger around the rim of her glass. 'Tell me,' she said to break the silence that was threatening to become a little heavy. 'What's the real story of your family?'

'Oh,' Jacques shrugged. 'It's all very dull. Edgar Coligny was a court official. Napoleon gave him the title of count and he added on the name la Bourdonnière when he decided to build the château here, because that is the name of the village.'

'And Louise?'

'The daughter of a businessman who became rich from trading in the West Indies. Not beautiful at all, but I suppose the money made up for that.'

'And the lady in the portrait?'

Jacques smiled. 'Nobody knows. My father bought that painting to add to his art collection years ago.'

'Lovely painting. He must have been a good judge of fine art.'

'He was.' Jacques poured himself some more wine. 'It's difficult, you know,' he said, his voice more serious.

'What is?'

'Keeping a big house like this. I mean, maintaining it,' he continued.

'It must cost a fortune to keep it in good condition,' Margo said.

'Yes, and it is very difficult to get people to do the work.'

'So you have to look after the upkeep and the farm as well as running your yard?'

'Well, my brother is supposed to help me with the house, but…' Jacques stopped, looking glum.

'But he doesn't?'

'He is never around when he is needed. He spends very little time here, really. He says that I'm doing such a good job and he doesn't really have the same touch, or some nonsense like that. He's just lazy. And I don't think he loves it like…'

'Like you do?' Margo asked softly, touched by the expression in his eyes.

'Something like that, yes,' Jacques said and looked away. 'Even though he owns the land, the house and everything in it.' He shrugged and there was a bitter line around his mouth.

As the shadows deepened and the terrace grew darker, Margo got up and started to tidy away the remnants of her meal.

'Where are you going?' Jacques asked.

'It's late. I'm just going to clean the dishes.'

'Would you mind…' Jacques paused. 'Do you think you could make me something to eat?'

Margo hesitated. 'I don't know.'

He smiled at her, his teeth white against his dark tan. '*Allez*,' he urged. 'I know you can swim. Let's see if you can cook too.'

11

'*Et voilá*,' Agnès said, wiping her brow. 'That's it for today, thank goodness. Thirty people for lunch on such a hot day is hard work, I have to say.'

'I agree,' Margo said as she put the last of the serving dishes into the sideboard in the dining room. 'I can't understand how they managed to eat all that food in this weather.'

'*C'est vrai*,' Agnès sighed. 'It was thirty degrees at ten o'clock this morning, and now it must be at least thirty-five. Well, I'm taking the rest of the day off, and so should you, Marguerite.'

'Are you sure that's all right?'

'Yes, of course,' Agnès nodded. 'Most of the guests have gone, except for one or two who are cooling off in the pool. The Comtesse is gone to her room for her siesta and will not appear until later and then she is going out for the evening.'

'I suppose I can relax, then,' Margo said. 'And I'll keep my mobile switched on in case she wants anything.' She walked out of the room toward the kitchen and the back stairs. 'Have a nice rest,' she said to Agnès.

'And you. Come down to supper around eight.'

'Very well,' Margo said. More boiled food, she thought as she slowly walked up the long flight of stairs to her room.

It was nearly two weeks since that first Sunday that had ended in such a strange way. She had cooked Jacques what was left of the steak and he had kissed her hand to thank her. She hadn't seen him since, except for the odd brief encounter when she was with Milady or helping out at a party. She liked him, but she decided to avoid him as much as possible. He made her feel strangely giddy and she didn't want to rock the boat. Things had to stay the way they were for the moment. But there was little time to worry about anything at all, as Milady kept her very busy. House guests came and went, replaced by more guests. There were lunch parties, dinners, pool-side drinks, afternoon teas and other occasions when people just seemed to drop in and require attention. Margo was expected to do anything from serving drinks to making up beds, working side by side with Agnès as well as doing various secretarial duties for Milady. 'You're looking a little tired,' Jacques had said one evening as he came into the kitchen. 'My mother is very demanding sometimes. Don't let her take over your personal life.'

'That's not possible,' Margo had replied levelly. 'I haven't got one.' But she found, once she accepted her place as a member of staff, that she

171

enjoyed most of the work, being part of the life of the château and this family, mixing with the people of the region; other château owners and family members who made up what she supposed was the cream of society in these parts. She found it fascinating to study the way they dressed and spoke, the way they were trying to cling to a way of life that was dying out very fast, and how they valiantly carried on with their social engagements despite the searing heat, trying their best not to show a drop of sweat or a red face.

The weather continued to be hot and sunny and, as the temperature soared, the pace slowed down and the socialising took on a more sedate pace. The heat made everyone languid and Margo found herself doing everything very slowly, following Milady's example of a long siesta in the middle of the day. 'The hottest summer here for more than one hundred years,' Agnès had told her. 'A lot of old people have actually died in Paris. Some people just leave their old relatives behind in the city when they go on holiday. Horrible, no?'

'Awful,' Margo agreed and wondered if she would have survived in that attic room in nearly forty-degree heat if she had been left behind. It was lucky I was needed in the country, she thought, or the heat would have driven me back to England. But it was nearly as hot in London, she had seen on the weather map on the television in the little staff sitting room beside the kitchen. Here in the country it was a little fresher, despite the baking heat. There was always a breeze in the

172

evening and the interior of the château remained fairly cool most of the day. Her own room high up in the tower was sometimes very warm, but if she closed the shutters and windows in the morning she managed to keep it comfortable, even if the nights were sometimes hot and sticky.

*

When Margo came into her room, she found it unbearably stuffy. She knew she wouldn't be able to sleep and she changed into linen trousers and a top and walked slowly down the stairs again. I'll go to the stream, she thought, it will be cool under the trees and I can paddle in the water. Maybe I can nip into the library and take a book with me? She tiptoed across the hall into the dim interior of the library. She looked in awe at the bookcases filled from floor to ceiling with leather-bound volumes and peered at the titles. Most of the books were French classics, from Balzac to Stendahl, mixed with plays by Moliere, the collected works of the best-known French poets of the past two centuries and the odd paperback pushed in between the volumes – Agatha Christie, Ed McBain and, surprisingly, Barbara Cartland. Margo pulled out a slim volume.

'Looking for something to read?'

Margo nearly dropped the book. She twirled around and realised there was someone sitting in one of the deep armchairs by the window.

'You startled me. I didn't know there was anyone in here.'

Jacques's smile was slow and lazy. 'I was half asleep. Didn't notice you come in and then I opened my eyes, and there you were. But maybe I'm dreaming?'

'I could pinch your arm, if you like.'

'No thanks. I feel suddenly wide awake. What have you got there?'

'I don't know. I pulled it out at random.' She looked at the title. '*Toi et Moi*. Paul Geraldy.'

'Poetry. Was that what you wanted?'

'No, I...'

'*Si tu m'aimais, et si je t'aimais,*' Jacques quoted, still sprawled in the chair, '*comme je t'aimerais!* If you loved me and if I loved you, how I would love you! That's what it means.'

'Yes, I did get that.'

'Very romantic.'

'Yes.' Margo looked down at the book and, realising there was a very explicit picture of a naked woman on the cover, quickly pushed it back into the bookcase again. 'I just took it out by accident. I was looking for a novel to read in the garden.'

Jacques rose from the chair and walked slowly toward Margo. 'In that case,' he said, 'how about a nice, romantic novel from the beginning of the last century? Have you read *Le Grand Meaulnes* by Alain Fournier?'

'No, I haven't.'

'Don't look so suspicious. I wasn't going to give you anything risqué.' He scanned the row of books. 'Now where...oh yes, here it is.' Jacques took out a worn paperback. 'Not in very good condition, I'm afraid.' He leafed through the book. 'Some of the pages have come loose.'

'I'll be careful.'

Jacques handed her the book. 'The French is very easy. You'll like it.'

'How do you know?'

'Because everyone does. It's one of the most-loved novels of French literature. The author only wrote that one. Then he was killed in the First World War.'

'Oh.' Margo opened the book. *Jacques Coligny* it said in a childish hand on the flyleaf.

'So, of course it makes it extra melancholic,' he said.

'I suppose. This is your book?'

'Yes. I read it for the first time when I was sixteen. And I loved it. I was a very impressionable and romantic young man.'

'Hard to believe.'

'Why do you say that? Isn't everyone impression-able and romantic in their youth? I bet you were.'

'Maybe,' Margo murmured, remembering reading *Wuthering Heights*, *Jane Eyre* and positively devouring *Vanity Fair*, dreaming about young ladies in empire gowns being wooed by romantic heroes in tight trousers.

'And now?'

Margo looked up at Jacques. His intense gaze made her face feel hot and she looked away, pretending to be interested in the books. 'No, not at all. I'm much more realistic. We all have to grow up.'

'How sad.' He kept looking at her in a way that made her face feel even hotter. 'Are you finding it difficult to cope with the heat?'

'A little.' Margo slowly backed away from him, clutching the book.

'Would you like some iced tea? Agnès just brought me a huge pitcher. Really good on a hot day.'

'Yes, why not?'

Jacques walked to the table by the sofa and poured Margo a glass, the ice cubes rattling. 'Here,' he said, handing her the drink, 'this will quench your thirst and cool that flushed face.'

'You sound like an advertisement,' Margo said with a laugh as she lifted the glass to her lips. The cold liquid was wonderful and she drank thirstily until she had drained the glass.

'Good?' Jacques enquired.

'Lovely,' she said, slightly breathless from drinking so fast. 'Thanks a lot. I do find the heat really bad sometimes, I have to admit. It kind of drains you.'

'I know,' he nodded. 'But sit down. Have another glass of iced tea. Take a break from all your chores.'

Margo sank down on a chair, still holding the book. 'I was going to go for a walk in the woods,' she said. 'But it's very hot, so I might wait until later, when the sun is lower.'

'Good idea,' Jacques said, settling back into the chair he had vacated earlier. They were quiet for a while. Margo looked down at the book she was holding, tracing the letters with her finger, not knowing quite what to say.

'*Un ange passe,*' Jacques said softly.

'What?'

'An angel is passing through. That's what we say in France when there is this kind of silence that is full of unspoken words.'

'Oh.'

'Where were you going to walk?'

'Oh, I don't know. The woods, maybe. I thought I might go and sit by the stream and read.'

'That's my favourite place, the woods by the stream,' Jacques said. 'There is a lot of wildlife there, have you noticed?'

'Not really. What kind of wildlife?'

'There are a lot of birds nesting there,' Jacques said, 'rare birds you don't see in other parts of France. This area has no industries nearby, and the motorway is quite far away. If you go there late in the evening or early morning, you will see the birds feeding. Early May is the best time, of course, because they are nesting then, but even now they are quite easy to spot if you know what to look for.'

'And what's that?' Margo asked, intrigued.

'There is a pair of kingfishers that have been there for years. If you stay still and try not to make a sound, you will see a flash of brilliant blue when the birds fly along the river. They follow the line of the water, looking for small fish, and their flight is like a fighter plane; straight, silent and very fast. It is a beautiful sight.'

'I must look out for that. Thank you for telling me.'

'Most people walk around completely blind to the magic of nature, you know,' Jacques said with slight regret in his voice. 'If they could learn to open their eyes and see all the wonderful things there are, the world might be a better place.'

'Maybe it would. But most people never get a chance to get away from their city lives.'

'I know. I'm very lucky in that respect, I suppose. You know,' Jacques said with a far-away look in his eyes, 'early in the morning when the sun has just risen and I go out to check the stock. That's the best part of my day.'

'I can imagine.'

'Yes.'

They were quiet once more. Margo cleared her throat.

Jacques's eyes focused on her again. He looked at her as if he had momentarily forgotten her presence and was surprised to see her there. 'Would you like to come with me some morning?' he asked. 'To ride out and check the cattle and ride along the stream and watch the birds?'

'Ride? I don't know,' Margo said. 'I haven't sat on a horse since I was a child. And then it was only a pony.'

'I have an old mare. Very quiet. I could put my grandmother on her – if I had a grandmother,' he added with a little laugh. 'So how about it? Will you come with me?'

'Maybe.'

'Tomorrow morning?'

'Why not?' Margo said, touched by the enthusiasm in his voice. 'What time?'

'Six o'clock. I'll wait for you at the stables.'

'If I manage to wake up,' Margo said with a smile.

'I'm sure you will. And I'll make sure you're back in plenty of time before my mother wakes up.'

'All right.' Margo got to her feet. 'But now, I think I'll be going. I'd better get out while I can, or I won't have time to do anything before your mother needs me again. Please,' she added as Jacques rose politely, 'don't get up.'

'I'm sorry,' he said with an apologetic smile. 'Can't sit while a lady is standing. It's the way I was brought up. It's second nature.'

'Then I will leave quickly so you can sit down again.'

'Thank you. *A demain matin, Mademoiselle Marguerite.*'

*

'What have you got yourself into?' Margo muttered to herself as she walked down the path. 'You should stay away from him, you fool. He seems so harmless, but I know he's trouble. Pull yourself together and act your age,' she ordered herself. Still muttering under her breath, she walked on, through the woods and down the hill toward the weir. There wasn't a breath of wind and nothing moved, not even the tiniest blade of grass. It was as if the whole landscape was holding its breath, pressed down by the relentless sun. Margo shaded her eyes with her hand and looked toward the weir. The water level was lower, and the gushing of the stream had slowed to a soft gurgle. The grass was yellow rather than green and there were even bare patches in the meadow. Then she spotted something bright green between two pine trees. A tent. Someone was camping by the weir. Intrigued, Margo walked closer. I wonder who is camping here, she thought, padding softly toward the tent. The flap was open and there was no one about. Margo walked up to the tent and peered inside. 'Hello?' she said. But there was no answer. Whoever was camping there had left for the moment. Margo could see a sleeping bag, a rucksack and a few items of clothing. She was about to turn away, but suddenly something poked her in the back. 'Don't move,' a gruff voice said in English. 'This is a shotgun. It's loaded and I'll use it if I have to.'

12

Margo froze momentarily. But then she suddenly realised who it must be and turned around to face the owner of the voice (and the gun) who was standing there, stark naked and dripping wet. 'Oh, I don't believe it!' she exclaimed. 'Gráinne!'

Gráinne lowered the gun. 'Shit, if it isn't Maggie! Jesus, you gave me a hell of a fright.'

'What do you mean?' Margo demanded. 'I thought you were going to blow my head off. Where do you think you are, the Wild West?'

'The world is full of creeps. You have to be able to defend yourself these days,' Gráinne replied.

'Well, you're asking for it, walking around with nothing on.'

Gráinne looked down at herself as if she had just noticed her lack of clothing. 'Yeah, right,' she muttered. 'I'll throw something on.' She sidled into the tent, closed the flap and, after having rustled around for a bit, came out moments later dressed in a T-shirt and shorts. She towelled her hair dry, sat down on a tree stump and stuck a cigarette in her mouth. Smiling at Margo, she lit the cigarette shakily. 'Sorry, but you did scare the shit out of me. I didn't recognise you with that hairdo.'

Margo sank down on the ground beside her. 'I didn't mean to frighten you. What's with the gun?'

'I always carry it with me when I'm alone. Just to be on the safe side, know what I mean? A woman alone is an easy target for all kinds of creeps. Sorry about sticking you up like that.'

'But you don't really have anything that anyone would like to steal, do you?' Margo said. 'And I was only looking into your tent to see who was there. Just out of curiosity, you know?'

'Well, you know what curiosity did to the cat,' Gráinne mumbled, blowing out a plume of smoke. 'And it wouldn't be money he would be after.'

'He? Who?'

Gráinne shrugged. 'Anyone. Any man on the prowl. They're all the same. If they find you alone and vulnerable, they'll just…well, you know.'

'Oh,' Margo said as it dawned on her what Gráinne meant. 'I see. Well, I suppose you're right. Women get attacked all the time these days. But you seemed ready to shoot and ask questions later. Aren't you afraid you might hurt someone, or even kill them?'

'No. That's not what I would be afraid of,' Gráinne said grimly. 'And if anyone even tried it, I'd shoot his balls off. They deserve nothing better, the bastards.' Her voice was full of venom as she stubbed out the cigarette.

'Where did you learn to use a shotgun?'

'My brother. I grew up on a farm and it comes in handy sometimes to be able to shoot. Crows, rabbits, pheasants, stuff like that. And now I always bring the gun with me in the truck. Camping on your own is not really safe any more. Especially around here.'

'Around here?'

'Yeah. I know that pervert from the castle likes to prowl around and take a peep when I'm not looking.'

'Who are you talking about? Jacques?'

'Yeah, Jacques. Don't tell me you didn't notice he was sneaking around when we were here last? Didn't you get the stink of those French fags?'

'Oh,' Margo mumbled. 'Yes, well, I suppose I did. But I mean, he wouldn't really… And in that case, you shouldn't be walking around in the buff.'

'Yeah, I know. I usually only take a dip in the dark. But today, as *he* has no idea I'm here, and it was so hot, I just thought I might get away with it if I just had a quick splash.'

'I see.'

'You better be careful too, love,' Gráinne said. 'You're quite good looking, even if you're a bit skinny. Very good looking, actually.'

'No, I'm not,' Margo protested.

'No, really. You are. Great tits and ass.'

'Oh, eh, thanks.' Margo moved a little further away.

Gráinne lit another cigarette. 'But what the fuck are you doing here? I thought you were swanning around being the assistant to some rich and famous executive. I thought you'd be in the Bahamas or wherever those people go in the summer.'

Margo wrapped her arms around her knees. 'Well, I have to admit I told you a fib or two.'

Gráinne stared at her. 'You didn't get yourself that job then?'

'No. I mean yes, I did. I got a job, but it wasn't as fancy as I told you on the phone. And it was you who got me the job, actually.'

'Me? What are you raving about now?'

'Well you see, I, well, I found myself completely alone and without any money and I didn't know what to do. And then, as if by some kind of miracle, I found this letter in my bag. A letter from, eh, Jacques Coligny de la Bourdonnière offering you a job here.'

'Me? What? In your bag?'

'Yes, it was that bit of paper with your number you gave me, remember?'

'Oh. I didn't realise… I remember that letter all right. But I thought I had thrown it away. I didn't want that job. I wasn't going to work for that… Go on.'

'Well, to cut a long story short, I went to their apartment in Paris and pretended to be you and said I would like to take the position.'

'Jesus, you didn't!' Gráinne squealed. 'You pretended to be me! You told them you were a dab hand with horses as well? I bet they thought that was a real laugh.'

'No they didn't, because they had never met you. Jacques wasn't in Paris. It was his mother who received me.'

'Yeah? She received you? How bloody posh. What's she like?'

'She's, well, I'm not sure you would ever have met anyone like her, actually.'

'An old dragon, is she?'

'No, not really, just a little, well, a real lady, and very…'

'Stuck up?'

'A bit, maybe. Anyway,' Margo breezed on, 'she saw through my little game at once, but that didn't knock a stir out of her. She offered me this job as personal assistant instead. And a room in the attic.'

'So there was no penthouse apartment?'

'Well, no. I'm sorry to disappoint you. But the room is very nice actually, not what you would call luxurious, but kind of cute.'

Gráinne smoked the last of her cigarette in silence, looking very thoughtful. 'That's a shame,' she said after a while.

'What is?'

'Well, here I was thinking you had this great job and the luxury pad. It was cheering me up, thinking about you. And now you turn out to be a skivvy just like the rest of us.'

'Sorry about that,' Margo said with a little laugh.

'Weird,' Gráinne said, 'really weird.'

They were quiet for a while, each lost in thought while the stream gurgled softly over the rocks and the shadows lengthened across the meadow.

'But what about you?' Margo suddenly asked. 'What are you doing here? Are you bringing a load of horses somewhere?'

'Me? Oh, I'm on my way to pick up two horses down south. My boss has just bought two young show jumpers. So I thought I'd spend the night here and then head off early tomorrow morning. I have a new truck,' Gráinne said proudly. 'It's parked over by the barn. You'd like it. Brand new with air-conditioning and a jacks and everything.'

'Sounds great. Your boss must be very nice.'

'Nice?' Gráinne laughed raucously. 'You think he got it for me? Nah, it was for these fancy French horses. They're used to being pampered. My boss wouldn't give a shit if I was dying of the heat. He even told me not to waste fuel by having the air-conditioning on when I'm on my own. That's why I'm sleeping in the tent. Thought it would be cooler here under the trees.'

'I see.'

'But I'm feeling a bit hungry,' Gráinne announced. 'I'm going over to the truck to get my tea. Want to join me? I have pork chops and potatoes and some great soda bread. And I put a couple of cans of lager into the stream to cool earlier.'

'Sounds fabulous,' Margo replied, thinking it seemed a lot more inviting than Agnès and Bernard's boiled food. 'But I better go back to the château and see if I'm needed first. I'll be back in about half an hour or so. I could bring back some raspberry tart that was left over from lunch. I saw a big piece in the fridge.' She got to her feet, brushed off the back of her trousers and picked up the book from the ground. 'See you in a little while, then?'

'Make it an hour,' Gráinne said. 'It'll be a bit cooler then and I'll have had a chance to tidy up and get the stove going.'

'Right.' Margo walked back the way she had come with a feeling of happy anticipation. But as she was nearly at the château, she heard a sound that made her forget all about Gráinne and the evening ahead. She stopped dead and listened. Could it be? Yes, sirens. The fire brigade? Was the château on fire? But there was no sign of smoke. She looked down the long tree-lined avenue and within seconds two police cars came into view, driving at top speed, lights flashing, sirens blaring, shattering the peace of the summer evening.

*

'*Voleurs!*' Milady cried. 'Thieves! Here in my house while I was sleeping! *Mon Dieu, c'est scandaleux!*' She was standing in the middle of her bedroom, which looked as if it had been hit by a bomb. Clothes, shoes and jewellery were spread over the bed, chairs and floor. Milady looked equally dishevelled, her hair messy and her dressing gown wrinkled. Two policemen were walking around the room, as if trying to assess the damage.

'Are you all right, Milady?' Margo asked as she stepped into the room.

'All right?' Milady exclaimed. 'How can you ask such a thing? I've been broken into, can't you see?' Despite the imperious tone, she looked suddenly old and frightened.

'Yes, of course I can see that,' Margo soothed, taking Milady's arm and leading her to a chair. 'But why don't you sit here and try to calm down. I'll get you a cup of tea and—'

'Tea?' Milady screeched. 'How can you talk of tea at a time like this?'

'I just thought...'

Milady shook off Margo's hand. 'I won't be calm until they have found the thieves who did this.'

'What happened, Madame?' one of the policemen asked. 'When did you discover...' he gestured around the room, 'this?'

'This?' Milady stared at him, her eyes wide. 'What do you mean, *this*?'

'This...this disorder,' the policeman explained. 'There seems to have been a terrible struggle here.'

'*Maman*? Are you all right?' Jacques arrived, breathless, at the door. 'I heard the sirens and I rushed over from the stables.' He paused as he saw the state of the room. '*Merde*,' he whispered. 'What happened here? Who did this? Who tore your room apart?'

'Why are you all so hung up on the state of the room?' Milady demanded. 'I was robbed, do you hear? At first I thought I was mistaken, that I had

188

mislaid it and I would find it, so I had to pull everything out, that's why there's a bit of disorder here.'

'You did this yourself?' the policeman asked.

'Yes, yes!' Milady snapped. 'I did. I had to go through everything to make sure.'

'Why don't you start from the beginning,' Jacques suggested. 'But I think we should go down to the library and have a drink while you tell us what happened.' He put his arm around his mother and led her out of the room, followed by the policemen and Margo.

'*Alors, Madame,*' the policeman said when they had settled Milady in an armchair in the library and given her a large cognac, 'could you please tell us what has been stolen. Is it money? Jewellery? Or, perhaps, a work of art?'

'Yes, that's it,' Milady said, 'a work of art. An original. Worth over ten thousand euros.'

'Not that little Chagall drawing,' Jacques exclaimed. 'I told you not to keep it in the bedroom!'

'No, not that,' Milady snapped. 'This is a lot more serious. It's the Galliano.'

There was a brief puzzled silence.

'I don't think I've heard of this particular artist,' one of the policemen said. 'But if you could describe the item to me?'

'It's black,' Milady started, 'and it has tiny seed pearls around the neckline. Pure silk, of course. I was going to wear it tonight. A bit extravagant, I know, but it's a special occasion, so—'

'Hold on,' Jacques interrupted. 'You were going to *wear* it? Are we talking about a dress?'

'Yes, of course,' Milady said impatiently, 'I told you. A Galliano from this year's collection. It was in my wardrobe yesterday, but when I looked for it after my shower it was not there any more. I couldn't find it anywhere. There are only two like it in the world. So you can imagine how—'

The policeman snapped his notebook shut and looked sternly at Milady. 'I'm sorry, Madame la Comtesse,' he said, his voice cold, 'but I really don't think this is a matter for the police. We do not usually deal with missing, eh, items of clothing. When you called you said this was a matter of utmost urgency. A very serious crime, you said. As this is the home of the Comte Coligny de la Bourdonnière, we thought …'

'By the way, where is François?' Jacques suddenly asked. 'Why isn't he here to sort this out?'

'Because he is in Paris,' Milady said. 'He left early this afternoon for some emergency at the ministry. He'll be back at the weekend.'

'Right,' Jacques mumbled. He turned to the policemen. 'I'm really sorry, *Messieurs*. My mother made a mistake. I hope you can forgive her and not press charges for this little incident. It's the heat and, well, you know. My mother is a little…' He pointed at his head behind Milady's back.

'Little incident?' Milady snapped. 'A dress of great value has been stolen from my room. If that's not a major crime, I don't know what is.'

But the policemen were leaving without taking any notice. They bowed and mumbled their farewells, looking at Milady with a hint of pity in their eyes.

'But wait,' Milady exclaimed. 'You are leaving? What about my dress?'

'I'm sorry, Madame,' the policeman said, 'but we cannot.' He backed out of the room. Apologising again, Jacques went out to see them off.

Milady sighed and took another large gulp of cognac. She looked across the room and suddenly noticed Margo. 'You!' she exclaimed in English. 'Where were you when this happened? What have you been doing all afternoon?'

'I…I went for a walk,' Margo stammered. 'You said you didn't need me, so I…'

'You should have been here in the house. If you had, this would not have happened.'

'I'm sorry,' Margo said hotly, 'but I really think that is a little unfair. I had worked very hard helping out with your lunch party. I felt I had earned some time off, actually, and I—' She was interrupted by Jacques coming back into the room, his face white and his eyes flashing. 'Never mind,' he snapped at Margo, 'you can whine later. I have to speak to my mother.'

'Whine?' Margo demanded. 'What do you mean? I was accused of—'

'I mean shut up,' he snapped. 'Mind your own business.' Without waiting for a reply, he turned to Milady, who looked at him coolly over the rim of her brandy snifter. '*Et toi,*' he snarled, '*tu vas m'ecouter, d'accord?*'

'Why are you shouting?' Milady said. 'And why are you so angry? I have lost some very valuable property.'

'Yes, I know,' Jacques said. 'Ten thousand euros' worth of a dress. First of all, I can't *believe* you spent that amount of money on a dress!'

'No,' Milady said coolly, draining her glass. 'I didn't.'

'What?' Breathing hard, Jacques stared at his mother. 'You mean you were lying? To the police?'

'No,' Milady replied in an exasperated voice, 'I told them the truth. The dress *is* worth ten thousand. But I didn't pay for it. It was a gift. From Monsieur Galliano himself. He gave it to me to wear at the fashion gala last spring, and then he told me I could keep it.'

'*Merde!*' Jacques exclaimed. 'Can you not see what you have done? What are they going to think?' Jacques towered over his mother, his fists clenched. Margo felt a strong urge to run out of the room, but decided to stay in case he was going to attack his mother.

But Milady didn't seem frightened at all. She looked up at her son with a puzzled look in her eyes. 'I don't know what you mean,' she said, putting the now empty brandy glass on the table beside her chair and taking a cigarette from an inlayed box.

'But don't you see?' Jacques continued his tirade. 'We have an awful lot of things in this house that are very valuable. Paintings, furniture, silver. Not to mention my horses and all the equipment in the stables. If we were to have a real emergency and needed the police, they will think twice about coming here next time we call them. They might decide not to turn up at all. Plus,' he continued, 'they are probably telling this story to anyone who cares to listen. We will be the laughing stock of this whole village.'

'Laughing stock?' Milady said, lighting her cigarette. 'Of course not. Who is going to dare?'

'*Nom d'un chien,*' Jacques moaned, staring up at the ceiling. 'Why do I bother? Why do I have to listen to this stupid—'

'Oh, put a sock in it,' Margo snapped in English. 'Can't you see your mother is very upset? She has had a bad shock. You seem to forget that her dress was stolen, which means there is a thief in this house. Someone who wanted to steal a very valuable designer dress. I think that's a very serious matter.'

'I think that is a very serious matter,' Jacques mimicked in a squeaky voice. 'Somebody stole a dress. Big deal. Maybe it was Agnès? She might have wanted to impress her relatives at that wedding she's going to next Saturday. Or maybe it was you? Did you want to wear it when you're out with your boyfriend when you go back to Paris?'

'I don't have a—' Margo stopped. She wanted to hit him. 'You're a shit,' she said.

'And you're a prissy old maid,' he retorted. 'And I'm wasting time standing here talking rubbish with women.' He turned and started to walk out of the room.

'Oh Jacques,' Milady said in a sad voice, 'you're becoming more like your father every day.'

Jacques stopped and turned to look at his mother. 'Which one?' he asked.

His words startled Margo, but not as much as the bitterness in his voice.

*

'Are you serious?' Gráinne exclaimed as she handed Margo a plate of food in the cabin of the truck. 'She called the police because she couldn't find a *dress*? Is she a bit of a fruitcake?'

'No,' Margo said, suddenly regretting she had told Gráinne the whole story. 'You don't understand. Fashion is her life. A dress like that is worth a lot more than just the money to her, it's a statement. It's telling the world she is still to be reckoned with, that she's still young and attractive.'

'But she isn't?' Gráinne sat down on the seat opposite Margo and picked up a pork chop with her fingers.

'Not young, no. I think she must be around sixty, but she is very elegant and well preserved. And she has great guts. She went out to that dinner party tonight despite the fright she must have had. I suggested she go to bed and that I would bring her a nice cup of tea, but she snapped at me not to be silly and ordered me to tidy up her room and help her get ready.'

'No sign of the missing dress?'

Margo shrugged. 'No. I have no idea what happened to it. I know it was in the wardrobe, because I put it there myself when I unpacked Milady's luggage. But maybe she lost it. Took it out and then put it away somewhere and forgot about it. It's such a huge place that it could easily happen. But she was really upset. White as a sheet and shaking like a leaf until she got that cognac into her. I felt really sorry for her.'

'But she pulled herself together?'

'Oh, yes. She put on another dress, did her hair and make-up and then off she went to the party like a ship in full sail in Bernard's old jalopy.' Margo smiled. 'She is a real trouper, I have to say. And the way she changed from frightened old woman to elegant society lady in just a few minutes was amazing.'

'But why did she have to go in an old jalopy?' Gráinne bit a chunk of meat off her chop.

'Because Jacques's car is too messy and smells of dogs. And François had taken the Jaguar to Paris.'

'The other son?' Gráinne mumbled, her mouth full of meat.

'That's right.' Margo sawed at the chop on her plate.

'What's he like? Just as big a bastard as his brother?' Gráinne asked, taking a slug of beer from her can. 'Go on, pick it up with your fingers, this isn't Buckingham Palace, you know.'

'OK.' Margo gnawed at her chop. 'This is good,' she added, 'really nice, Gráinne.'

'Glad you like it. Not like some of that fancy French stuff you must be used to, but quite tasty, even though I say so myself. But go on, what about the brother?'

'François?' Margo stopped eating. 'Oh, he's a real gentleman. Very considerate. Good looking, too. And so well dressed. Always perfectly turned out.'

'A bit of a hothouse flower?'

'I suppose you could call him that. But he is a real Parisian and very intelligent and well educated.'

'Just your kind of guy?' Gráinne enquired.

'No. I mean…' Margo paused and picked up the pork chop again. She laughed suddenly, thinking how wrong Gráinne was. François simply wasn't a man you could be attracted to in that way. 'He's a total contrast to his brother.'

'I'm sure he is. I hope you stay out of his way. Jacques, I mean.'

'Oh I will, don't you worry,' Margo said hotly, sipping the beer Gráinne had poured into a glass for her. 'I thought he was quite nice, but I have just seen him treat his mother like shit. You have no idea how mean he was.'

'Must have been if he makes Goody Two Shoes say things like "shit",' Gráinne laughed.

Margo smiled back at her and turned her attention to her food. They ate in silence until they had both cleared their plates.

'This was lovely,' Margo sighed, licking her fingers. 'A real treat.'

'Yeah, the pork wasn't bad.'

'The black pudding was very good too.'

'Should be. It's from Clonakilty. They make the best black pudding in the world there. So how do you like the new truck, then? A bit of all right, don't you think?'

'Fantastic,' Margo agreed, looking around the cabin. 'And the little kitchen is great. Stove, microwave, fridge.' She burped loudly. 'Excuse me. Not used to drinking all that beer.'

'I know. Kind of recurs on you.'

'You have everything anyone could possibly want in here,' Margo said.

'Want to try the jacks?'

'No thanks, I don't really need to.'

'OK. But when you do.'

'Looking forward to it,' Margo said, thinking that beer was a little strong. 'Anyway, it's a great truck.'

'Yeah. You could go around the world in this.' Gráinne looked at Margo with a sudden glint in her eyes. 'Hey, why don't we do just that?'

'What?' Margo stared at Gráinne.

'Why don't we take off, just the two of us? Go down south, all the way to Italy. Wouldn't that be fun?'

'Then what?' Margo laughed. 'We'll get arrested for stealing this thing. It must be worth a lot of money. We wouldn't get far before your boss would get word you hadn't arrived to pick up those horses, and then…'

'Yeah, yeah,' Gráinne sighed, 'I know. It was fun just thinking about it for a while. It would be a laugh, wouldn't it?' She looked wistfully at Margo.

'I suppose it would for a while,' Margo agreed. 'To just drive around and see the sights and have a holiday. But then we would run out of money.'

'You're so sensible,' Gráinne said with a tinge of criticism in her voice. 'I bet you never did anything really wild in your whole life.'

'Wild? How do you mean?'

'Like something totally off the wall, something really cracked, you know?'

Margo looked at Gráinne and wondered what she would say if she found out that Margo had walked out on her husband right in the middle of the motorway. But it probably wouldn't rate as terribly 'wild' in Gráinne's book. She might even consider it sensible. 'Did you?' Margo asked. 'Do something wild, I mean.'

'God yes, all the time,' Gráinne laughed. 'But you won't, you're not the type.'

'How do you know?' Margo asked, suddenly annoyed. 'How do you know what I'm capable of? I might just surprise you one day.'

'Doing what?'

'I don't know. But I'll think of something.'

'Yeah, right,' Gráinne said.

13

'Marguerite,' Milady called from the terrace, 'where are you?'

'Right here, Milady,' Margo replied as she mounted the steps from the garden.

'Where have you been?' Milady demanded, closing her newspaper. 'It's ten o'clock already and I thought I told you to be here.'

'At ten o'clock,' Margo filled in with a big smile. 'And here I am, right on time.'

'So you are.' Milady looked at Margo for a moment through her huge sunglasses. 'You're smiling,' she remarked in a voice that suggested it wasn't quite *comme il faut*. 'I have never seen you smile before. It makes you look…happy.'

'Yes, I feel happy today,' Margo said. 'It's such a lovely day, why wouldn't that make me happy?' But it wasn't really the weather that had lifted her spirits, it was her early morning outing with Jacques. She had decided not to go after his ugly mood the day before, but then she had woken up at daybreak and, looking at her watch, realised she would be able to make their date in plenty of time. Why not, she thought, washing quickly and putting on jeans and a T-shirt, I'll go and see. If he's obnoxious I'll just leave.

*

'*Bonjour*,' Jacques said as she rounded the corner of the stables. 'Right on time. The horses are ready. Lovely morning, isn't it?'

'Sublime,' Margo said, looking up at the blue, cloudless sky. 'And so fresh still.' She shrank back as the two big Labradors trotted forward with lolling tongues and started sniffing at her legs.

'Don't worry,' Jacques said. 'They won't hurt you.'

'Are they coming on the ride?'

'Not today. They will jump into the river and frighten the birds. You weren't thinking of riding in those shoes, were you?' Jacques continued, looking at her feet.

'No, but that's all I have. I though there might be a pair of wellies or something.'

'Let's go and have a look in the tack room. I think there's a pair of my mother's old boots somewhere. And her riding hat too.'

Half an hour later, Margo, wearing a pair of scuffed leather boots and a riding hat covered in worn black velvet, was sitting on top of an old grey mare, trying her best to stay on. Jacques, riding a frisky chestnut gelding that looked as if it was ready to burst out of its skin, studied her critically. 'Just relax,' he said. 'Let old Sophie do what she wants.'

'What if she wants to throw me off?' Margo said nervously.

'She won't. She is as quiet as a lamb.'

'Really? Oh!' Margo squealed as the horse skipped suddenly. 'What's she doing now?'

'Just kicking at a fly.'

'But... Oh no! What was that?'

'She swished her tail. They do that sometimes,' Jacques said with a broad smile.

Margo tightened her hands, sweaty with nervousness, on the reins. 'I don't know if this is such a good idea,' she said in a shaky voice.

Jacques rode up alongside her and put his hand on hers. 'Try to relax,' he said. 'If you're tense, the horse can feel it.' The chestnut jumped suddenly and skipped sideways, but Jacques didn't seem to notice. He just tightened his legs and the horse settled again. 'See? He's just a little fresh. But I didn't take any notice and he calmed down. Now sit down deeper in the saddle and relax your shoulders. Try not to grip so hard with your legs. That's it,' Jacques said when Margo tried to do as she was told. 'See? Sophie is much happier now.'

'How can you tell?' Margo said, suppressing a gasp as Sophie swished her tail again.

'Her ears are pointing forward and she's walking quietly along,' Jacques said as his own horse suddenly jumped sideways again. 'But this one is a little impatient, so we'd better trot now.'

'Trot?' Margo asked with more than a hint of panic in her voice. 'I can't trot!'

'Of course you can,' Jacques said as he rode out in front of her down the path from the stables. 'Just loosen the reins and leave Sophie alone. Let yourself go.'

Jacques's horse broke into a trot in front of Margo, and as she relaxed her tight grip on the reins, Sophie started to trot slowly behind the prancing young horse. Margo found herself bouncing uncomfortably, her bottom hitting the saddle painfully at each step. Jacques glanced over his shoulder. 'All right?' he asked.

'Y-y-e-e-s,' Margo said, trying desperately to stay on, but feeling very much like a lump of butter on a hot potato. She gripped hard with her legs, but felt herself sliding sideways with each painful step. Jacques was far ahead now, his horse bouncing and shying, fighting to break into canter, and Margo could hear him swear in French. This will end very badly, she thought, I will fall off and break something, my neck probably. Oh God, please help me. But God seemed busy with other things. Margo felt she was going to fall painfully to the ground when she suddenly remembered something from a long time ago, a phrase that had been repeated again and again. *Rising trot*, someone seemed to whisper in her ear, and at once, she knew what to do. *Meet the horse's movements*, she said to herself, *get into rhythm*. She tried to remember what she had been taught all those years ago at pony camp and she started to stand up and sit as the horse trotted on. It was like a kind of dance and the music was the movements of the horse. As she got used to the rhythm, she began to enjoy the feeling and her tension eased. Sophie had a lovely, elastic gait and it was quite easy to follow her movements. This is fun, Margo thought a few minutes later, feeling proud of herself as Sophie trotted on down the path. Jacques and his horse were still having arguments far away in the distance, but Jacques seemed to be winning, and he managed to slow the horse down and wait for Margo. He turned around and smiled at her as she came closer. '*Ça va?*' he asked. 'Everything all right?'

'Lovely.' Margo pulled on the reins and they slowed to an easy walk along the fence toward the first gate, which led to a field where a herd of cattle were contentedly chewing grass and flapping away the flies with their ears.

'We're going in here to check this herd,' Jacques said. 'Then we trot up the hill to the next one and then we can ride along the stream down to the river.'

'Great.'

'But we'll take it easy. I don't want you to be too sore tomorrow.'

They walked the horses among the cattle and Jacques counted them to make sure they were all there and none of the calves were missing. 'They can easily get into trouble,' he explained to Margo, 'get stuck in a bush and choke or wander off and get themselves tangled up in barbed wire.'

'This is a big herd.'

'There are sixty head in this one, and fifty-two in the one in the next field.'

'Do you look after all this on your own?' Margo asked.

Jacques shook his head. 'Oh no, I couldn't manage this farm on my own. I have two Lithuanian boys working for me. At the moment we have to do our best to keep the cattle in good condition, and in this drought it's quite hard work.'

'How do you manage?'

'By moving the herds around and using the fields by the river, where there is still some good grass. We were lucky to have taken in two crops of silage this year as well.'

'I see,' Margo said, trying to look interested. 'Seems like you're managing very well.'

'Fascinating, isn't it?' Jacques said with a broad smile.

'Oh yes.'

'No, it isn't. I can see you're getting both hot and bored.' He turned his horse around. 'Come on, let's go and look at the other herd and then we can ride down the stream to the river.'

It became increasingly hotter as the morning wore on, and by the time they were walking the horses along the river, Margo felt both sweaty and sore in every muscle. But she forgot her discomfort as Jacques suddenly grabbed her arm. 'Look,' he said, 'there, the kingfisher, can you see it?'

Margo looked along the river and, suddenly, there was a flash of brilliant blue as a small bird flew swiftly just a few inches above the water's surface. Another flash, and it was gone. 'Oh,' Margo sighed. 'How wonderful. So fast and so…so beautiful.'

'Yes.' Jacques shaded his eyes with his hand and scanned the river. 'He's gone. I think he went into those trees over there. If we sit quietly, we might see him again.'

But the kingfisher didn't reappear. Instead, they saw a pair of swans with five tiny cygnets. Margo watched in delight as the babies scrambled onto their mother's back and the whole family slowly glided down the river.

The horses shied suddenly as a heron flapped its wings on the opposite bank and rose gracefully above the trees. Margo followed its flight as the huge bird sailed away in the distance until it was a tiny dot against the blue sky.

'OK?' Jacques asked, still steadying his horse.

'What?' Margo turned. 'Oh, sorry. I was looking at the heron. It's such a graceful bird in flight.'

'Sophie behaving herself?'

'Beautifully,' Margo said, patting the horse's neck.

'Time to go back,' Jacques announced and turned his horse around.

As they rode slowly home, Margo secretly studied Jacques, thinking he was so different from the night before, when he had lost his temper with his mother. This morning, he looked perfectly calm and there was an expression of contentment in his eyes that had been there all morning. She admired the ease with which he rode the hot-tempered young horse, and realised she was in the presence of a superb horseman. She wanted to say something, tell him how much she had enjoyed the morning, thank him for inviting her to ride with him, but found herself strangely tongue-tied. Jacques suddenly turned his head and met her gaze. They looked at each other for only a split second, but Margo felt they said more to each other than if they had exchanged a thousand words.

*

'They are forecasting thunder for this afternoon,' Milady said in a gloomy voice from her deck chair. 'And I know they are right. I can feel my migraine coming on.'

'How was the dinner last night?' Margo enquired, thinking it might cheer Milady up to talk about the party.

Milady shrugged. 'Rather ghastly, really.' She took a cigarette from the gold case on the table and slowly lit it. She inhaled deeply, but then started to cough violently, her thin shoulders shaking and her chest heaving.

Margo poured a glass of water from the carafe on the table and held it out. 'Here, Milady, have some of this.'

Milady took a sip. 'Thank you.' She held the

cigarette out to Margo. 'Please, put this out. I shouldn't have lit it. I don't really feel like smoking right now.'

Margo stubbed the cigarette out in the crystal ashtray. 'So,' she said in a bright voice, 'what do you want me to do today? What's on the agenda?'

'Please, Marguerite, sit down,' Milady said. 'And try not to sound so jolly. It's very wearing.'

'All right.' Margo sank down on the chair opposite Milady's sun lounger and tried to arrange her features into a more serious expression, but she couldn't help smiling to herself as she thought of the morning. It was magic, she thought, like being in another world. She couldn't remember when she had ever felt so carefree. Jacques was very relaxing company when he was in a good mood. She had looked for Gráinne as they had ridden by the stream, glanced at the spot where the tent had been, but it was gone, a flat area of grass the only sign she had been there at all, which was just as well, Margo thought. Gráinne might not approve of my spending time with Jacques.

'Awful *ensemble*,' Milady said, cutting into Margo's daydream, 'quite the wrong colour for that sallow complexion. And she has put on a lot of weight. Somebody should tell her not to wear things that show up that big *derrière*.'

'I suppose,' Margo said dreamily.

'Now, the newspaper.' Milady held it out to Margo. 'My eyes seem very tired today. In fact, they are tired all the time these days. I can't see very well close up, even with my reading glasses.

Everything is blurred when I try to concentrate. I don't know what's wrong with them.'

'Could be cataracts,' Margo said, opening the newspaper. 'What do you want me to start with? The main news? The heat wave is the top story still, I see.'

'I beg your pardon? What did you say?'

'The heat wave.'

'No, before that. About my eyes.'

'Cataracts,' Margo repeated. 'I thought that might be what's wrong with your eyes.'

'But that only happens to very old people.'

'Not really. My mother had her cataracts done when she was in her late fifties.'

'Done?' Milady said.

'Yes, she had an operation to remove them about ten years ago. It was a huge success. She says she hasn't seen so well since she was a young girl. She went on to do an art history course afterwards. And now she's in Australia to visit her sister.'

'Oh. And the operation? Was it what they call major surgery?'

'Not at all. These days it's done with laser and you are in and out the same day.' Margo suddenly laughed. 'You know the difference between major and minor surgery?'

'No. But I'm sure you are going to tell me.'

'Well, minor surgery is on someone else and major surgery is when it is on you. On oneself, I mean.'

Milady smiled wanly and lay back in the sun lounger. 'I see. A medical joke?'

'Yes. It was a doctor friend of mine, who…' She paused.

'A man?' Milady asked with more interest in her voice.

'Yes, and a very dear friend.'

'A boyfriend?'

'No. Just a friend.'

'I see.'

'So, on to the news of today,' Margo said breezily and turned her attention to *Le Figaro*. 'It says here that the hot weather is due to continue. The hospitals in Paris are full of sick people, most of them elderly.' Margo read on, turning the pages, and it seemed as if Milady was drifting off to sleep. She read more gently, her voice a soft murmur, checking the inert form of Milady now and then for signs of life. *'Bad forest fires in Provence,'* she read, her voice a near whisper, *'thousands of acres of pine forest destroyed near St Maxime.'* There was a slight snoring sound from Milady. *The home of Jean Jacques Gengoux, former president of France,'* Margo droned on, *'was threatened by fire and the former president suffered…'*

'What?' Milady gasped, sitting bolt upright. 'What did you say?'

'I was reading about the forest fires in Provence. It's been declared a national emergency and the army—'

'No, not that!' Milady snapped, tearing off her sunglasses and looking wildly at Margo. 'That name – what was it about?'

Margo scanned the page. 'Jean Jacques Gengoux?'

'That's it. What has happened to – I mean, go on, read it again.'

'*The home of Jean Jacques Gengoux, former president of France, was threatened by fire, but was saved by a huge effort of the fire fighters. M Gengoux, who suffered a mild heart attack as a result, is now out of danger. He told reporters that he was feeling much better and was looking forward to enjoying the rest of the summer with his wife at the villa. "I am not going to run away," he said and he has even offered accommodation to his neighbours who were not as lucky and have lost their homes.*' Margo drew breath and turned the page. 'Now, here is a story about a robbery in Bordeaux…'

'Is there a photo?' Milady asked, staring at the newspaper.

'Of the robbery?'

'No! Of the president.'

Margo turned back to the previous page. 'Yes, there is. M Gengoux with his arm around his wife on the steps of the villa.'

'Give it to me,' Milady snapped and snatched the newspaper from Margo. She put on a pair of reading glasses that lay on the table and peered at the photograph.

'He looks very nice,' Margo said. 'I remember him. He was president of France about thirty years ago, is that right?'

Milady did not reply, but kept studying the photo in the newspaper.

'He was a very good-looking man,' Margo

continued. 'I've seen pictures of him when he was president.'

'Mmm,' Milady mumbled, her eyes on the photo.

'But his wife was no beauty, that's for sure,' Margo said. 'A very homely woman, as far as I can remember. Not at all as glamorous as her husband. No wonder he had all those affairs.'

Milady looked up at Margo. 'What do you mean?' she said, her voice cold.

'I read that somewhere. He is supposed to have had a lot of mistresses.'

'Nonsense,' Milady said sternly. 'He was very faithful.'

'Must have been some other president I read about,' Margo said, realising that she had committed some kind of *faux pas*. Milady would probably never admit that a president of France could misbehave in any way. 'And in any case, M Gengoux and his wife look very happy in that picture. He is still so attractive, even though he must be at least…'

'Seventy-nine,' Milady said. 'Not old at all, really.'

'Of course not,' Margo soothed.

'How old are you?' Milady suddenly asked.

'Me?' Margo stared at her. 'I'm thirty-seven. But why…'

'Oh. Thirty-seven. Young enough. Tell me, what does your father do for a living?'

'What?' Margo asked. 'My father? He was an antique dealer. He had an antique shop in a small town in Dorset. That's where I grew up. The shop was on the ground floor of our house and we lived on the top two floors.'

'Big house?'

'Well, no, not really. A Victorian semi,' Margo replied, still mystified.

'Semi?'

'Semi-detached.'

'I see. And your parents are still alive?'

'No, my father died about five years ago. But my mother is.'

'In Australia?'

'That's right.'

'Brothers and sisters?'

'Two brothers.'

'And they are…?'

'Well, my eldest brother took over my father's business for a while. Then he sold it and now he is working for Sotheby's in London as one of their art experts. He lives in Oxford. And my younger brother is an engineer and is at the moment working in Japan on a big contract.'

'And you? Why did you not follow in your father's footsteps? Go into the antique business?'

'Oh.' Margo shrugged. 'I was quite interested in it for a while. But I wanted to do something else. My mother is a nurse, you see, and I shared her interest in health and medicine.'

'You wanted to become a doctor?'

'No, not really. I was quite squeamish when it came to blood. And nursing seemed too hard. So I took up physiotherapy.'

'Did you find that interesting?'

'Very. I especially liked treating injuries from accidents. I found it so wonderful to see patients recovering their mobility and regaining their fitness after serious accidents. It's amazing how the human body—'

'I see,' Milady interrupted, obviously not interested in the human body. 'But you told me you were a medical secretary, I seem to remember?'

'Yes, well. I gave up physiotherapy because...' Margo stopped. 'It's a long story. But why are you asking me all these questions all of a sudden?'

'No reason,' Milady said airily. 'I just felt I should know a little more about you. About your background, I mean.'

'I see.'

They were quiet for a moment while Margo squirmed under Milady's gaze. Then Milady seemed to lose interest, put her sunglasses on and lay back in the sun lounger. 'What about your husband?' she asked after a while, as if an afterthought. 'The surgeon. What happened to him? Are you still married?'

'We're separated.'

'Marriage a bit of a mistake?'

'You could say that.'

'Ah, yes,' Milady murmured, *'le marriage...pas toujours facile...'* She suddenly looked very sad. 'It's hard to lose someone you love, you know. Very hard. When it's over, all you have are the memories. But they are not enough.'

'No, I can imagine. I'm sure you miss him a great deal.'

'Oh yes, I do.'

'He must have been such a nice man.'

'Who?' Milady asked, looking puzzled.

'Your husband, I mean. I'm sure you miss him.'

Milady sat up and took off her sunglasses. 'My husband? Oh, no, I don't miss *him* at all.'

*

'Then the first gorilla said to the second gorilla…'

'What?' Margo asked. 'What are you talking about?'

'Haven't you been listening?' Gráinne said. 'I was telling you this joke and I'm about to come to the punchline.'

'OK, go on.' Margo leaned across the kitchen table and looked expectantly at Gráinne who, on her way back to Ireland, had stopped off with the new horses.

'The first gorilla said to the…' Gráinne stopped. 'Shit, I forgot what I was going to say. It was so funny when Seamus told it to me last week.'

'Maybe you've had too much wine?' Margo suggested.

'Yeah. Maybe. I'm not used to drinking wine. I don't usually like it, but this was really great.'

'Who is Seamus?'

'The vet's assistant back home. Tells a good joke. Any more of that stuff?'

Margo held up the bottle and peered at it. 'Enough for a glass each. Nice of François to give it to us.'

'Yeah. Must say he's OK for a guy. I hope you said thank you.'

'Oh yes. But he said that was the least he could do after all your work.'

'Ah, sure, it was nothing.'

'No, it was a great deal. I couldn't possibly have carried that heavy trunk and the rest of the boxes all the way from his car to the attic. You're very strong. François couldn't even lift the trunk.'

'Bit of a wimp, your Mr Fancy Pants,' Gráinne said, flexing her biceps.

'Stop. He's not my anything.'

'OK. Good looking though, I give you that. But a bit too pretty for my taste. Not that I have any taste at all when it comes to men.' Gráinne cleaned her plate with a piece of bread. 'Thanks for inviting me to tea. I've never eaten in a real château before. And you're quite a cook.'

'Oh, thank you. Agnès had to go home early, but she told me I could cook whatever I liked from what I could find in the larder. This was all I could come up with, I'm afraid.'

'Cauliflower cheese happens to be one of my favourites.' Gráinne sipped her wine.

'I've got some stewed apple to follow,' Margo said, getting up from the table. 'With custard, but I think it went a bit lumpy. It's probably this hot weather, it seems to curdle the milk or something.'

'Yeah, it's a real stinker today. I was so glad to get out of the truck and turn out the horses at last. I've been on the road all day. But give us the custard, I don't mind a few lumps.'

Margo handed her a plate, but nearly dropped it as the kitchen door flew open and Jacques burst in, looking furious.

'So, here you are,' he snarled, glaring at Gráinne. 'Having a nice supper while those fine horses are running around loose outside.'

'What?' Gráinne exclaimed, her face suddenly white, and got up so fast she knocked the plate out of Margo's hand.

'Yes, they seemed to have escaped from the paddock,' Jacques said grimly. 'Someone was in too much of a hurry to lock the gate properly.'

'Jesus,' Gráinne said, running to the door.

'It's OK,' Jacques said before she had a chance to open it. 'I caught them and put them back in. *And* I locked the gate.'

'Oh.' Gráinne sighed and pushed her hair back. She sank down on her chair again. 'Thanks,' she mumbled.

'Aren't you getting a little careless?' Jacques asked. 'Those horses are worth a fucking fortune, don't you know that?'

'Of course I do, I'm not an eejit,' Gráinne snapped. 'And I'm quite sure I locked the gate. I remember thinking that they could escape if they rattled it. That bay gelding is a right bastard to get out. Maybe someone opened it to make trouble for me?'

'Maybe you were in too much of hurry to make sure they were locked in?' Jacques suggested nastily. 'Maybe you were distracted by the lovely Mademoiselle Marguerite here?'

'It was François,' Margo said, trying to ignore his tone. 'He had just arrived with a lot of luggage from Paris and he asked us to give him a hand...'

She stopped, feeling foolish, prattling on like a five-year-old.

'Never mind,' Gráinne said. 'Everything is OK now, right?'

'And you are very cosy here together,' Jacques said, looking at the table. 'Food, wine. That's a *very* good Chablis.'

'François gave it to us to thank us for the help,' Margo said. 'And yes, it was very nice.'

'Must have gone well with that…' Jacques made a face as he looked at the dish on the table, 'yellow stuff.'

'Very well,' Margo said. 'And we thought the rest of it would go beautifully with the dessert.'

'Except for what ended up on the floor thanks to you,' Gráinne remarked, picking up the plate.

'There's plenty more,' Margo said, heaping another dish full of stewed apple. 'Would you like some? I made the custard myself.'

'No, thank you,' Jacques said, more politely. 'Yellow is not my favourite colour.' He looked at Margo apologetically. 'Sorry. I seem to have forgotten my manners. How are you, Marguerite? Not too stiff and sore?'

'I was a bit stiff, I have to admit,' Margo said. 'But not too bad. And I so enjoyed the other morning.'

'So did I. Sophie is a little lame at the moment, but when she's better we might go out again?'

'I'd love to,' Margo said.

'Good.' Jacques walked over to the pantry. 'I'm going to get some Calvados. Bernard keeps a bottle here. My mother likes a glass with her coffee.' He emerged seconds later with a bottle. 'Would you like some?'

'No thanks,' Margo said, 'I'll just finish the wine, I think.'

'And I don't drink turpentine,' Gráinne cut in.

'Very well.' He made a little bow. 'I wish you a pleasant evening, ladies.'

'Shit,' Gráinne said when Jacques had left, 'I better go and have a look at the horses. I don't trust that bastard.'

'The bay gelding?'

'No, Jacques.' Gráinne looked at Margo, her eyes narrowing. 'What was that about the other morning? Who's Sophie?'

'A lovely old mare.'

'You went riding? With that creep? I don't believe it!'

'It's really none of your business,' Margo said sternly.

'You better be careful or you'll end up like all his other women.'

'How did they end up?'

'Laid,' Gráinne said, getting up. 'Better go. Are you coming? We could get the truck and go into the village when I've made sure everything is OK.'

'The village?'

'Yeah, it's a group of houses with a street, a square, a church and a couple of shops.'

'I know *that*,' Margo laughed. 'It's just that I haven't been anywhere since I came here two weeks ago.'

'You mean they're keeping you here against your will?'

'No, of course not. I just haven't had either the time or the inclination to go anywhere else. It just didn't enter my mind.'

'Well incline yourself and come on,' Gráinne said, lighting a cigarette. 'It isn't much of a village, but there's a bar there with a nice terrace overlooking the river. We could have a couple of beers and chat up the locals.'

'Why not?' Margo said. 'You go and check the horses and I'll tidy up here. I'll meet you at the truck in about twenty minutes?'

'Got ya,' Gráinne said and left.

Margo had just finished tidying up the kitchen when she spotted something on the table. A packet of cigarettes. Gráinne must have left it behind, she thought and picked it up. No, these are Gauloises. They must belong to Jacques. I'll give them to him right now. And I might as well tell Milady I'm going out. They'll all still be on the terrace.

But the only person sitting there was Jacques, who was sipping a glass of Calvados and reading the newspaper in the fading light.

'Oh,' Margo said.

'Oh what?' he said, lowering the newspaper and getting up from his chair. 'What can I do for you?'

'Nothing. I was just going to tell your mother that I was going out. And give you these.' She held out the packet of cigarettes.

'Cigarettes? Why?'

'But they are yours, aren't they?'

'No.'

'I'm sure they are,' Margo insisted. 'This is the brand you smoke, isn't it?'

'Certainly not.'

'What do you mean?' Margo stared at him.

'I don't smoke,' Jacques said.

14

'He doesn't smoke?' Gráinne asked incredulously.

'That's what he said.' Margo picked up the cold glass of beer and brought it to her lips. It was delicious. Funny how I never knew how nice a glass of ice-cold beer is on a hot day, she thought as she felt the cold liquid slip down her throat. They were sitting on the terrace of the small café that overlooked the river in the village. Two ducks swam by, ducking their heads into the water from time to time. 'I like the look of the locals,' Margo added, putting down her glass.

Gráinne looked around the deserted terrace. 'It's a bit quiet, I know. But it might be early yet. This is dinner time in France, still, isn't it?'

'I suppose. But I don't care. It's nice and quiet, the beer is good, and look what a beautiful sunset.'

'Yeah, it's great,' Gráinne agreed. 'And what do we need more people for? Don't we have each other?'

'We do.'

'Isn't it great the way the French make their riversides look so beautiful? We have lovely rivers in Ireland, but nobody seems to notice. They chuck their rubbish into them instead.'

'Seems a pity.'

'Sure is. But what was it we were talking about? Oh yeah, Jacques. He said he doesn't smoke? What a liar.'

'But maybe he's telling the truth? Have you actually seen him smoke?'

Gráinne thought for a moment. 'No, but... Oh come on, I have smelled those awful French fags every time I've been at the weir. He's been watching me while I was stripping.'

'Maybe it's not him?' Margo suggested.

'Of course it is,' Gráinne said hotly. 'He's a holy terror when it comes to women. I've seen him in action at events and shows. He's always chatting up those sexy girl grooms.'

'But is that proof that he's a peeping Tom? I mean, just because he likes to flirt doesn't make him one.'

'Of course it does. And I bet he does more than flirt with those girls.'

'So he likes women, what's wrong with that?' Margo asked, thinking Gráinne was exaggerating. Of course Jacques would have had lots of women. With his looks, his charm and sense of humour, he would be quite irresistible. Well, to other women, Margo thought, women who could put up with that violent temper. But had he taken any of them riding early in the morning?

'I've noticed the way he looks at you as well,' Gráinne said, her voice cutting into Margo's thoughts. 'Like he wants to eat you without salt.'

'Me?' Margo's face suddenly felt hot. She turned toward the river to catch the faint breeze, avoiding Gráinne's probing eyes. 'I don't know what you mean.'

'He has the hots for you, no doubt about it.' Gráinne nodded wisely and lit a cigarette. 'But I can't say I blame him. You're a hell of a looker. Especially with that hair. Makes you look the spit of David Bowie.'

Margo laughed. 'So he's into guys as well, then?' She leaned forward and looked at Gráinne sternly. 'Jacques is not your peeping Tom. All right, so he's a womaniser and has been sleeping around, but I think that's quite normal, actually. He's very good looking and very passionate. And French, of course,' she added.

'And we all know what they're like,' Gráinne stated. 'OK, it probably isn't him. But then there's some other man lurking in the bushes. I just know it. So you better be careful, love.'

'I will,' Margo said, more to humour Gráinne than anything else. 'But maybe that's all he does. Peep, I mean. Those men are usually quite harmless.'

Gráinne shrugged. 'Who knows? I'm not going near that stream until I know what's going on. But let's forget about that for now. Let's have another beer.'

'Aren't you driving back to the farm?'

'Yeah, but this stuff isn't that strong and we won't be going home for ages. Anyway, there's never anyone on that road. Don't be such a fucking nun. Chill out, have some fun for a change.'

They ordered more beer and continued sitting on the terrace, enjoying the sunset and the soft breeze on their faces, watching the ducks and talking, at first about trivial things, but then, as the evening wore on, about themselves.

'Bad luck,' Gráinne said when Margo started telling her about Alan. 'Bad luck to meet such a creep. Can't see why you married him.'

Margo looked at her thoughtfully. Why did I marry him, she wondered. He was good looking, yes, and I was flattered by his attention. Every nurse in the hospital fancied Dr Alan Hunter. But he wanted *me*. And then I fell in love. He had too, she knew he had. And he needed her, she had realised very shortly after their marriage. He was surprisingly insecure for someone so talented, always looking for praise and reassurance. She had found his vulnerability so touching at first.

*

'I want you to be there,' Alan said. 'I really need you, Margo.'

'But why?' she protested. 'It's only a little speech to some students. Surely you can do that by yourself. And I have to read up on my notes. I'm trying to figure out the best way to treat that new patient I told you about. He has pins and needles in his arm and I have to find a way to get some more flexibility in his shoulder. The rotator cuff is such a difficult muscle to get to.'

Alan took the book away from her and pulled her out of the sofa. 'Darling,' he said, taking her by the shoulders and looking deep into her eyes. 'I really want you to come tonight. Am I not more important than some patient?' He kissed her lightly on the lips. 'When you're there I'm not nervous, you see. I feel much more confident when I see you sitting there, listening.'

Margo laughed softly and returned his kiss. 'All right,' she soothed. 'I'll come. But we have to come straight home afterwards so I can catch up.'

But they had ended up going on for drinks and then dinner, during which they went through every word of his speech and Margo complimented him, remarked on the apparent admiration of the students and kept reassuring him that he had been interesting, informative and intelligent.

'And that joke at the end, it was quite clever, don't you think?' he asked like a little boy.

'Oh yes,' Margo nodded, touched by his need for her approval. 'It really ended it beautifully.'

'Good.' Alan took her hand. 'Thank you for coming tonight. Your support is so important to me.' He paused, playing with her fingers. 'I've been thinking, darling…'

'Yes?'

'You're working so hard. I thought maybe you'd like a change?'

'A change? How do you mean?'

'Well, you know my secretary is leaving at the end of the month…'

'So?'

'I had this idea that maybe you could take over from her? Chuck in that job at the hospital and start working with me?'

Margo stared at him. 'Give up my job? But you know I love it. It's hard work sometimes, that's true. And the hours can be long if I have a lot of patients, but…'

'But you'll have to give it up anyway when we start a family,' Alan said. 'And I thought running my surgery might be the best job for you in the meantime. Good hours, interesting job and the boss is quite a decent chap, they say.'

Margo laughed. 'I thought he was a bit of a slave driver, actually.'

Alan smiled briefly. 'Seriously, darling, I think it would be a great idea. My patients will love you and we'll be together all the time.'

'But I…oh, I don't know…'

'OK, let's do it this way,' Alan said, sounding suddenly business like. 'You come and work for me for two months. And if you don't like it, you can go back to physiotherapy. I'll even help you set up your own practice, if you like. And if – I mean, when – that baby has arrived, you could work part time or something like that. Whatever you want.'

'Whatever I want?'

'Absolutely.'

Margo had agreed and started running Alan's surgery, a job that was a lot more demanding than she had imagined at first. As Alan's career blossomed, Margo found herself working even longer hours than while she was a physiotherapist.

She missed her old job at the hospital, her patients and the satisfaction of helping an injured person recover, but came to discover that Alan couldn't really manage without her and that his success was partly due to her support and enthusiasm and the way she ran the surgery. She did, however, get to use her skills as a physiotherapist quite often. Alan's back was sometimes very bad and she would give him a massage that seemed to ease his pain and relax him when he was becoming tense. He would groan with pleasure as she kneaded his stiff muscles. His need for her, however, so beguiling at first, had with time begun to feel like a burden, his bad-tempered outbursts became more and more abusive, and her longing for a child, which he didn't seem to understand, grew into a constant, nagging pain.

*

'I don't know why any woman wants to be married, to be honest.'

'What?' Margo asked as Gráinne's voice jolted her back to the present.

'Hello? Are you asleep? I asked why women want to get married.'

'I don't know. Because they're in love?'

'Yes, but you have to like the guy too,' Gráinne said. 'Because if you don't, there's nothing left when that first romance is gone.'

Margo looked at Gráinne thoughtfully. 'You might be onto something there,' she said. 'But then there are the children. Most women want to have a family. I know I did, in any case. I really wanted children.'

'Kids?' Gráinne said. 'What for?'

'I suppose I wanted someone to love,' Margo said.

'Maybe you wanted someone to love *you*,' Gráinne suggested. 'I think that's why a lot of women have them.'

'Maybe you're right,' Margo said. 'I never thought about it that way. Have you never wanted to have a baby?'

'Not me. I can't stand kids. Noisy little buggers. Always bawling and wetting their pants. Why not have a dog instead? Dogs never let you down. They love you no matter what and you only have to take them for a walk and feed them once a day. I have a lovely dog at home. A red setter called Rory. Now that's a real gent. Loves me to bits and I love him right back.' Gráinne smiled fondly. 'Dogs are better than men or kids, that's for sure.'

'You don't seem to be too fond of men,' Margo said.

'Dead right. No man ever did me any favours. I never had anything but trouble from them. I make sure they don't come too close.' She paused and looked away.

Margo looked at Gráinne, concerned by her obvious distress. 'Did something bad happen to you?' she asked softly.

'Yeah, that's right.' Gráinne looked back at Margo. 'This bugger raped me when I was fifteen.'

'Oh God. How awful.'

'Yeah. It wasn't very nice, I'll tell you that.'

'But how…what…' Margo stopped. 'I'm sorry. I didn't mean to pry. You don't have to tell me if you don't want to talk about it.'

'No, it's OK.' Gráinne leaned across the table and took Margo's hand. 'I want to tell you. You're such a good person to talk to. And you are one of them…therapists. Isn't that what you said?'

'What? No, I was—'

'Whatever.' Gráinne took a deep breath. 'Anyway, like I said, it happened when I was fifteen. At the farm. It was during the summer holidays and I was in the kitchen getting my breakfast. Everyone was out taking in the silage. I could hear the tractors working away in the field across the road. As I thought I was alone and it was very hot, I didn't bother to put on my dressing gown. Just as I had finished making myself a cup of tea, the door opened and Mick came in.'

'Mick?'

'Yeah, Mick Flannery, one of the lads helping out with the silage. Big spotty guy. Went to school with my brother Liam. Fancied himself big time. Anyway, he just stood there leering at me. I asked what the fuck he was looking at and he said "your tits".' Gráinne paused. 'I felt suddenly so…dirty, you know?' Her eyes glistened with tears as she looked at Margo. 'I didn't know what to say back. Then…he…he said he always thought I looked like a guy and hadn't realised I had tits or how big they were, but now, as I was standing against the light he could see them clearly.' Gráinne wiped away a tear. 'He looked at me in such a filthy way and I didn't...I couldn't...I was kind of frozen to the spot. And then...' Gráinne paused again.

'And then?' Margo whispered, still holding Gráinne's hand.

Gráinne swallowed. 'Then he said he would like to feel them, and before I could do anything, he came up to me and put his hand down the front of my pyjamas. I told him to fuck off, but he took no notice and started to feel me up all over. I tried to fight him, but he was a lot stronger than me. He slammed me up against the wall and put one of his hairy hands between my legs and said he knew I was dying for it.' Gráinne stopped, her face white. 'The rest isn't very pretty. Want me to go on?'

'Only if you want to tell me.'

'Yeah. OK. Well. Then he started fumbling with his trousers and I was scared shitless. I've never been so scared in all my life. I thought, here it comes. But then...'

'Then?' Margo whispered.

'Then I got mad. Oh, Jesus, I don't remember ever being so mad. I brought my knee up as hard as I could and he...he screamed his head off and grabbed his balls. "You fucking bitch!" he yelled. Then I took a shotgun that just happened to be hanging on the wall and pointed it at his groin and told him if he didn't get out of there fast, I would make sure he walked funny the rest of his life.'

'What happened?'

'He got out of there faster than a bat out of hell. Of course, the shotgun wasn't loaded, but he didn't know that.' Gráinne drew breath and looked at Margo. 'So that's it. That's my story. I'm sure you haven't heard anything as bad as that, ever.'

Margo tried desperately to keep her face straight. 'No, I haven't.'

'But as one of them psychotherapists, you must have.'

'I was a *physio*therapist,' Margo corrected.

'Yeah? So?'

'That means I was looking after people with physical injuries. Broken limbs, bad backs, you know.'

'Oh.' Gráinne suddenly laughed and let go of Margo's hand. 'Jesus, you must think I'm really thick. And here I was, pouring my heart out about…the rape and everything.'

'You weren't really raped, Gráinne.'

Gráinne stared at her. 'Oh. Well, you see, the creep went around telling everyone we had…he had…you know, with me, so I started to believe it myself. It felt as if I had been. It *felt* like rape. But you're right, of course. I wasn't '

'No, but it was awful all the same.'

'Yeah. And all the time I was thinking of my dad.'

'Your dad?'

'Yes.' Gráinne's eyes filled with tears again. 'It was about six months after he died, you see. I was thinking that he would have been so upset if he had been alive and seen what Mick thought of me. Like I was some kind of slut or something. You see, my dad thought the world of me.'

'But Gráinne, sweetheart,' Margo said gently, 'don't you think your father would have been proud of the way you defended yourself? It wasn't your fault that you were attacked, was it?'

Gráinne looked thoughtfully at Margo. 'No, I suppose it wasn't.' She suddenly smiled. 'You're right. Oh God, I feel so much better now. Better than ever before, actually. I only wish…'

'What?'

'That the shotgun had been loaded.'

*

'Someone has to go to Paris,' Milady announced the following afternoon when Margo brought some iced tea up to the terrace.

'Oh? Why?'

'Because of the Lalique bowl.'

'Lalique? The one you brought with you for that sixtieth birthday party?'

'Yes. I opened the box this morning to make sure it wasn't damaged, and then I realised it was the wrong one. I had picked out one in a very classical style, but they seemed to have mixed up my order and packed a very vulgar modern one with a fluting around the edge. It won't do at all. The party is tomorrow evening and I have to have the bowl before I go.'

'But would Lalique not send you a replacement?'

'I called them and they said they couldn't guarantee that it would be here in time.'

'What about François? Didn't he drive back to Paris yesterday?'

232

'I don't know where he is. I have tried both the apartment and his mobile but got no answer. Then I called his office, but they said they couldn't reveal his whereabouts to anyone.' Milady looked irritated. 'How dare they? I'm his mother, after all.'

'Didn't you tell them that?'

'But of course. But they said they needed proof of identity or some such nonsense.'

'I see.' Margo returned Milady's expectant gaze. 'I suppose you would like me to go?'

'Yes, of course. I have worked it all out. You will take the train from Tours this evening and get to Paris around ten o'clock. Take a taxi to the apartment and spend the night there, I'll give you the key. You'll sleep in the small guest room as the attic will be far too hot. Then, tomorrow morning, you'll take a taxi to Lalique on Avénue de l'Opéra and exchange the bowl for the right one and continue on to the train station and catch the mid-morning train back. Bernard will pick you up and bring you back here.' Milady looked at Margo with a satisfied air. 'Won't take more than twenty-four hours in all. Very neat, don't you think?'

'Very.'

'So there is no time to lose. Bernard is expecting you to be ready to go in about twenty minutes.'

'But what about dinner?' Margo asked, wondering if she would have time to eat before leaving, or maybe it would be possible to eat on the train.

'Well, we'll have to manage without you. But there are only eight for dinner tonight, so Agnès will cope.' Milady put on her reading glasses and turned back to her copy of *Vogue*.

Realising that her own dinner was of minor importance and that it would be pointless to argue, Margo left to put a few things together in an overnight bag.

*

The train pulled out of the station and gathered speed. Margo looked out the grimy window as the town became countryside and fields and trees whizzed by faster and faster until the train had reached cruising speed. She picked up the magazine she had bought at the station, but put it down and looked out the window again. Thanks to the air-conditioning, the carriage was relatively cool, but the compartment was empty, probably because very few people would feel like going to Paris in the middle of August during the heat wave of the century. I must be mad, Margo thought. Why did I agree to go?

As the train made its way further north and Margo looked out at dry fields where the grass had died and the earth had turned to dust, she realised that the heat wave had made the countryside a near desert. If it doesn't rain soon, there will be a disaster, she thought, wondering how Jacques managed to feed and water his horses in this drought. Gráinne had said that she would try to get back to Ireland with the new horses as quickly as possible, as feed in France was becoming so scarce and expensive. She had left in the truck at dawn. She'll be really tired, Margo thought, after that late night. But it had been fun.

*

It was dark by the time the train finally arrived at Gare St Lazare. The platform was nearly deserted and it was so hot Margo felt as if she was stepping straight into a sauna. By the time she had got a taxi, her dress was soaked with perspiration and she felt as if she was going to faint. She mumbled the address to the taxi driver and slumped into her seat, wiping her brow. 'Could you switch on the air-conditioning, please?' she asked the driver.

'It's on,' he grunted. 'It usually works well, but it doesn't seem to be able to cope with these temperatures. It's still thirty degrees, you know. At eleven o'clock! *Incroyable*! And the humidity, *infernal*.'

'I agree.' Margo looked out the window. She had never seen Paris so empty. Most of the restaurants were closed and even the bars seemed deserted. There was an eerie hush about the streets, a feeling of impending doom.

'Terrible, this *canicule*,' the taxi driver volunteered. 'It has driven a lot of people out of the city. But here we are.' The taxi pulled up outside the apartment building. Margo paid the driver and looked up at the building. Apart from the odd light here and there, the building was dark. She saw that Milady's apartment was completely without light. She had been hoping François would be home so that she wouldn't have to spend the night on her own in the huge apartment. But no such luck.

'Will you be all right, Mademoiselle?' the driver asked.

'Oh, yes, fine,' Margo said, rummaging around in her bag for the key. What a nice man, she thought.

'I'll stay here until you're inside, just in case.'

'Oh, that's not necessary.' Margo found the key and paid the driver. She was just about to put the key into the lock when the door swung open and a slim figure dashed past and got into the taxi. Margo stared in shock as it pulled away from the curb. The smell of perfume was still hanging in the air. But it wasn't the woman's perfume that had startled Margo. It was what she was wearing.

15

'I'm telling you,' Margo said to François, who had miraculously appeared in the kitchen the following morning with a bag of fresh rolls and croissants, 'she was wearing the dress. The Galliano that was stolen from your mother's wardrobe.'

'How could you be so sure?' François said as he poured Margo a cup of coffee. 'Hot milk?'

'Yes, please.' Margo put two lumps of sugar into her cup. 'I'm very sure. I know that dress. I have handled it enough to be certain. You know how you notice minute details sometimes when you're stressed? I saw the hand beading around the neckline clearly. And I found two seed pearls on the floor of the lift. I put them into the bowl on the hall table, if you want to see them. And I could smell her perfume. It was Joy de Patou. That very expensive one, you know? My mother got a present of a tiny bottle of it once, and I still remember the smell. She used to put it on when she was going to a party. You know how smells can bring you right back?' She stared at François as he sat down opposite her.

'Hmm,' he said, smearing apricot jam on a piece of bread.

'What do you mean, "hmm"? Don't you believe me?'

'Yes. I believe you *think* you saw this woman in that dress, but...'

'But what? You think I'm deranged or something?' Margo blew aside a lock of hair that was falling into her eyes.

'No, of course not. It's just a little difficult to believe.'

'Yes, I find it hard to believe myself.'

'It seems to be worrying you. Maybe you should try to forget about it.'

'How can I? The whole thing is so weird, it's driving me crazy. I have seen that woman several times now, and this last time she looked at me as if she knew me.'

François frowned. 'I think there is probably an explanation to all this, and when you realise what it is, you will feel a little silly. Sometimes the mind plays tricks on you, especially in moments of great stress. You have probably been thinking about the dress a lot, wondering what happened to it, and since it's on your mind, you see it everywhere.'

Margo looked at him thoughtfully. 'Maybe you're right.' She picked up her cup. 'Thanks for making breakfast. And for going out to get bread.'

'I knew you'd like fresh croissants for breakfast.'

'How did you know I was here?'

'I saw your bag in the hall late last night. You must have just gone to bed when I came in.'

'I was exhausted. The trip was terrible.'

'And now you have to go back again.'

'But first I have to go and exchange the bowl.' Margo sighed and blew on her hair again.

'Your hair is growing out.'

'I know,' Margo said and pushed away the lock of hair that wouldn't stay put. 'I should really have a trim, but I don't have the time. And I doubt if I'll be able to find the same hairdresser again.'

François looked at his watch. 'It's only seven-thirty. If you like, you could try and see if you can have it done somewhere else. The colour needs to be retouched at the roots.'

'Does it?'

'Yes. It's not that noticeable, but it could do with a little work.'

Margo shrugged. 'What does it matter? Who's going to look at me anyway?'

'I'll tell you what,' François said, looking as if he just had a brilliant idea. 'There is a hairdresser near the Lalique shop. Their salon is air-conditioned and I know they open very early. My mother is one of their best customers. They might help you. You could have your hair cut and then go and get the bowl and continue to the station in plenty of time to catch the train. Why don't I give them a call and see if they can fit you in?'

'Well, that's very kind. I mean, if you don't mind. If they aren't too expensive.'

'It's on the house. On me, I mean.' François smiled at her fondly. 'That's the least I can do after all you've done for my mother.'

'Oh, but I haven't really done anything.'

'Oh yes. You're very kind to her.' François looked at her, his eyes warm.

'I'm glad you think so.'

'And I know a visit to the hairdresser will be just the thing for you. A little pampering is so good for one from time to time.' He took out his mobile. 'I'll give them a call right now. And why don't you have a manicure and a facial while you're there? I'll tell them to really spoil you.'

'Oooh,' Margo sighed, 'that sounds wonderful. Thank you so much.'

François dialled the number. 'I'll tell them you're a very special friend of the family,' he said and winked at her. 'They'll treat you like royalty, I just know it.'

'You're very kind.'

Françoise smiled as he waited for a reply. '*Allo? Monsieur Claude? François Coligny ici…*'

'They're expecting you at nine o'clock,' François said after having finished the call.

'That's great. Thank you so much.'

'I couldn't let you go back without having your hair seen to. That style really suits you. It makes you look a little like Isabelle Huppert.'

'Really?'

'Yes. She is very beautiful, don't you think? And when she wears her hair short like yours, she looks rather boyish, but in a very attractive way.'

Margo tilted her head and smiled at him. 'Is that the kind of woman you like? The boyish type?'

François picked up his half-empty coffee cup. 'I don't really have a type as such. I admire all women who are beautiful. Especially those who look after their appearance.'

'I'm a little careless about the grooming bit,' Margo admitted.

'You don't really need to do all that much.' François studied her critically for a moment. 'All you need is that haircut and you'll look fine again. With that gamine face and those big green eyes, you're charming even without make-up.'

'That's a relief.' Margo smiled at him, thinking how easy he was to talk to. Frenchmen are much closer to their feminine side than Englishmen, she thought. She couldn't imagine having this kind of conversation with the Englishmen she knew, and especially not Alan. She suddenly laughed as she tried to imagine it.

'What's the joke?' François asked.

'Oh, nothing. I was just thinking about someone.'

'Someone in your past?'

'Mmm.' Margo picked up a piece of bread and put it in her mouth, chewing slowly.

'I presume it's a man. Do you want to tell me about him?'

'No, not really,' Margo said, trying to keep her voice friendly.

'I didn't mean to pry,' François said apologetically. 'It's just that you look so troubled sometimes, and I was wondering if you'd like someone to talk to. Someone who would just listen and try to help you solve whatever it is that worries you so.'

'Oh.' Margo looked into her cup and sighed a sigh so deep it felt as if came from the bottom of her stomach. 'It's not something that would be easy to solve. And now is not really a good moment.'

François reached across the cups and plates and put his hand over Margo's. 'I understand. But if you feel you want to talk, I'm here. I'm a very good listener.'

'Thank you.' Margo smiled. 'It's nice to have a friend.'

'Things are not so easy for you.'

'How do you mean?'

'I know my mother is very, shall we say, tricky?' François said, removing his hand.

Margo shrugged. 'She has her moments.'

'Be careful with her, or she'll swallow you up.' His voice was suddenly serious.

'How do you mean?'

'I mean don't let her take over your life. Don't let her…' He stopped.

'Let her what?' Margo asked with a little laugh. 'You make her sound quite dangerous.'

'Oh, never mind. Forget what I said.' François closed his mouth, looking suddenly as if he had regretted his words. He looked away, and for a fleeting second Margo saw a strange expression in his eyes. But his features quickly resumed their usual blandly polite air and she thought she had imagined it.

'Maybe you need a friend too?' she asked softly, just in case.

'Me?' François's laugh sounded a little forced. 'I don't know what you mean.' He rose and collected the coffee cups. 'Time to go. I have a very early meeting and then I have a luncheon appointment.'

Margo got up and helped him put the dishes in the dishwasher. 'You work very hard,' she said. 'Don't you go on holidays in August like everyone else?'

'In my job it's impossible to take long holidays. I can take a few days off here and there, but not more than a week at a time.'

'Must be hard. Especially now, when it's so hot.'

François shrugged. '*C'es't la vie.*'

'I'd better get dressed,' Margo said. 'I suppose I'll see you at the château at the weekend?'

'I hope so.' François stepped a little closer and kissed her warmly on both cheeks. '*Au revoir* Marguerite, *chère amie*,' he murmured softly into her ear. He smelled faintly of something strangely familiar, and as he walked out of the kitchen, Margo realised what it was.

*

The journey back was uneventful, if rather tiring. But Margo was happy she had managed to both get her hair coloured and styled, and exchange the bowl. Milady looked at her with approval as she handed over the package. 'Your hair looks nice. The cut is much better than before.'

'Thank you. It was François who thought I should have it done.'

'He has a good eye,' Milady said proudly. 'Now, where is the box from Lalique?'

Margo handed her the box and Milady looked satisfied as she unpacked it. 'That's the right one, finally,' she said. 'Now all that remains is to gift wrap it, and then I'll have to get ready. It's going to be a very elegant party. Everyone will be there.'

The next hours were taken up with gift wrapping the parcel to Milady's satisfaction ('No, not gold paper, silver, I said. Please unwrap it and do it again.') and selecting a dress suitable for such a glittering occasion ('I said the cream Chanel, not the red one. And the skirt needs to be pressed.'). Then there was a heated argument between Milady and Jacques which made Margo feel both embarrassed and angry and, finally, the pair departed in a taxi. Feeling exhausted, Margo had a simple supper with Agnès and Bernard and then went into the library to find a book to bring to bed. She scanned the shelves until she spotted a book about medieval art that looked interesting. She settled in the big sofa and started to leaf through it, but found her eyes closing. God, I'm tired, Margo thought, and lay back against the soft cushions. I'll just have a little nap and then I'll...

'Hello, anybody there?'

Margo's eyes flew open. She blinked and stared at Jacques, who, dressed in a dinner jacket, was standing in the door of the library, looking at her with an amused expression. 'I must have fallen asleep,' she mumbled.

Jacques walked into the room, took off his dinner jacket and threw it on a chair. He sat down beside Margo, loosened the black bow tie and unbuttoned the top button of his white shirt. 'Can't stand black tie in this heat.'

'What time is it?' she asked. 'Is the party over?'

'No, I left early. I couldn't stand any more of the crap. So, when I had wished the birthday girl many happy returns and kissed all the old bags on the cheek, I snuck off.'

'And your mother?'

'Still there, having a good time. She won't notice I'm gone until it's time to go, and then I'll miraculously appear at her side, ready to escort her home. That way I can relax here at home, have dinner, watch the news and avoid being bored to death. Clever, eh?' He grinned, showing his uneven, almost wolfish white teeth.

'You're a genius,' Margo said flatly, trying to unravel her legs, which seemed to have gone to sleep under her.

'You seem in a bad mood. Still tired?'

'No, I'm fine.' Margo had managed to get her legs free and her feet on the floor.

'You don't seem fine to me. You look as if you were…a little annoyed with me?' He looked at her thoughtfully for a moment. 'Was it that little argument you walked into earlier?'

'OK.' Margo looked at him coolly. She was still upset after having witnessed Jacques raving and ranting at his mother just before they were due to leave for the party. It had upset her to see again this childish streak in him, which, in turn, frightened her because of her growing attraction to him.

'I know this isn't any of my business, but I think you were horrible to your mother,' Margo said sternly. 'She was very upset, even though she did her best not to show it.'

'You're right. It *isn't* your business.'

'Fine.' Margo started to get up.

'No,' Jacques's tone was serious. He put a hand on her arm. 'Just a minute. I want to explain. I don't want you to think I...' He paused.

'Think what?' Margo sat down again and turned to look at him.

'I don't want to be cast in the role of some kind of monster.'

'I don't think you're a monster,' Margo said archly, 'I just think you behaved like a bad-tempered two-year-old. There is no excuse to speak to your mother the way you did. Just because you didn't want to go to a family party? If that is the way you behave every time things don't go your way, I feel deeply sorry for her.'

'Deeply sorry?' He gave a little snort. 'There is no need to feel the slightest bit sorry for her.'

'How do you mean?' Margo said, puzzled by his expression.

Jacques shook his head. 'Never mind,' he murmured. 'It is, as you said, none of your business.'

'Exactly.' Margo looked at him coldly. 'I'd prefer to forget the whole thing, to be honest. Maybe it was my own fault for being in the wrong place at the wrong time.'

'I have a terrible temper,' Jacques said. 'And sometimes I can't control it.'

'Maybe you need therapy?' Margo suggested, touched by the contrition in his voice.

'Are you volunteering?' Jacques asked, his voice lighter.

'I wouldn't know where to start.'

'It would take a long time to straighten me out.'

'I'm sure it would.'

'But it might be a lot of fun.' Jacques laughed softly and sat back in the sofa, his arm draped along the back of it. He looked at Margo intently with an expression in his eyes she couldn't quite interpret.

'I doubt it.'

'Maybe not.' Jacques sighed. 'So,' he continued, 'what happened to your girlfriend? The butch one from Ireland?'

'Gráinne? She's gone to—' Margo stopped and stared at him, surprised by his tone. 'Butch? What do you mean?'

'You know.'

'No, I don't.'

'You must. Everyone knows what she is.'

'Everyone?'

'People talk, you know,' Jacques said, looking smug. 'The horse world is very small. Everyone knows everyone else. There is a lot of talk all the time.' He folded his arms across his chest and looked at her, his eyes narrow. 'They talk. About that girl. That she is not a real woman. That she likes other girls, I mean.'

'Are you saying that people think Gráinne is gay?'

'That's it. I know I'm right. And I thought maybe you and she...'

'Hold on a minute,' Margo said. 'Just a second here.'

'Yes?'

'What business is this of yours?' she demanded. 'So what if Gráinne is gay? Isn't that her affair?'

'Eh…'

'And if she and I are having a relationship, what does that have to do with you? Why would that make you so angry?'

'Well, I…because…' Jacques's voice faltered.

'Scares you, does it? The idea of two women, well, you know. Makes you feel a little inadequate?' Margo couldn't help feeling a certain vicious satisfaction. He looked suddenly so foolish.

The expression in Jacques's eyes changed and he seemed to recover his poise. 'Oh,' he said coolly, resuming his position and putting his arm along the back of the sofa again, lightly touching Margo's shoulder with his hand. 'It's just that I think it would be a shame. A waste of a beautiful woman.'

Margo sat up straighter to avoid his touch. 'Why would it be a waste? If I was gay and had a relationship with another woman and we really loved each other, why would that be wasteful? Don't you believe that love between two people, whatever their…inclinations, is always beautiful?' What am I saying, she asked herself. Why don't I just walk out of here? 'Isn't it love that's important, not the gender thing?' She ended with more passion in her voice than she had intended, but she felt suddenly disappointed that he was so narrow-minded.

'*Ah, oui, l'amour,*' he murmured, lightly touching the back of her neck with his fingers, making her shiver. 'I don't really care,' he continued. 'I have never felt that strongly about it. Until now.'

'Why now?' Margo asked, even though she knew what he was going to say. It was as if she suddenly had a compulsion to feed him his lines.

'Because I am interested in *you*, Mademoiselle Marguerite.' His arm was now lightly around her shoulder, but she didn't move, didn't try to get away from his touch. 'If you are, well, that way inclined,' he continued, 'I would like to know, so…'

'So you won't waste your time flirting with me?' Margo said, turning to look at him. Their faces were so close their lips nearly met, and she pulled away slightly.

I'm a married woman, she said to herself, but it didn't seem real somehow, as if she was another person, not Margo, Alan's wife, but Marguerite, young and free and available. That was what she felt at that moment, with Jacques's arm around her and his warm breath tickling her neck. She glanced at his mouth, wondering what it would feel like to kiss him, and looked away, afraid he would guess what she was thinking.

'That's right,' he said with a little laugh. 'I don't like wasting time. Life is far too short for that. Don't you agree?'

'I suppose,' she murmured, looking away from his burning eyes. She felt trapped, but couldn't get away – didn't really want to, if she was honest with herself.

'You smell nice,' he said, leaning forward, touching her neck with his nose. 'What is that perfume?'

'No perfume,' she said, her voice oddly hoarse, 'just soap. Lily of the valley.'

'And the scent of your skin,' he said, turning her face and kissing her so suddenly she jumped. She could smell his aftershave and feel his hot, slightly damp skin through the thin fabric of his dress shirt. Unable to stop herself, she slid her arms around his neck. His arms came around her waist and he held her gently while he kissed her again, this time sliding his tongue into her mouth, which made her gasp with shock mixed with pleasure. He kissed her again and again with such skill she could not help being carried away, not wanting him to stop. What am I doing, she thought, I must be mad. She had never been kissed like this before, never felt like this in any man's arms, not even Alan's. The thought of her husband made her stiffen slightly and Jacques pulled away, looking searchingly into her eyes. Unable to speak, Margo leaned her head against his shoulder, trying to catch her breath and still her racing heart.

'Marguerite,' he murmured, '*mon amour.*' He started to kiss her again, her face, her eyes and her neck. As his mouth travelled further down, she felt her pulse quicken and her body respond in a way she hadn't thought possible. He murmured something in French and started to undo the buttons of her dress, his fingers brushing her nipples. Margo lifted her hand weakly to stop him, but then let her hands fall and allowed him to continue. She closed her eyes as she felt his lips on her breasts.

A phone rang somewhere in the house. 'Oh God,' she murmured and, momentarily coming to her senses, pulled his hands away. 'No, please. Stop.'

'Why?'

'The phone,' she said. 'It's ringing.'

'So? Let it ring.'

She tried to push him away. 'We can't...we mustn't.'

He sat up. 'You're right. Not here. We can't do it here.'

'Not anywhere,' Margo said buttoning her dress. 'This is crazy.'

'What's crazy about it? Didn't you just say that when two people love each other...'

'Love?' Margo said. 'We hardly know each other. This is not love. And I'm a...' The phone started ringing again. Margo lifted her head and listened. It stopped and then, after a few minutes, rang again. She looked at Jacques. 'It's late. Your mother...the party.'

'*Merde*, you're right.' He pulled away from her and glanced out the window. 'It's dark. What time is it?' As if answering his question, the ormolu clock on the mantelpiece chimed. 'Oh God, it's one o'clock,' he said, getting up. 'She'll be spitting nails by now.'

Margo stood up and pulled up the straps of her dress. 'Well, we can't stay here all night in any case.'

'No, Mademoiselle Marguerite, we can't,' Jacques minced. He put his arms around her. 'Will I see you later? When I have picked up my mother and...'

'No, please,' Margo said, pulling out of his arms. 'Please don't. I—'

The phone rang again.

'My mother is getting impatient,' Jacques said. 'I'd better go.'

'Be nice to her.'

'I'll do my best.'

'Do better,' she ordered.

'I'll be back,' Jacques said, putting on his jacket and retying his bow tie. He kissed his fingers to her and left.

Margo slowly buttoned up her dress. She looked at her reflection in the antique mirror above the sofa and laughed suddenly at her dishevelled appearance. 'Margo Hunter, you're a slut,' she told her reflection. She thought she could hear faint laughter in the room and turned around to meet the mischievous eyes of the woman in the blue dress, smiling at her from the portrait above the fireplace.

16

Margo was in the kitchen making a cup of tea when she heard footsteps on the gravel outside. He's back, she thought, pure joy flooding through her. Will I wait for him to come here, or should I just go to him right now? No, what am I thinking? This must not continue. Despite herself, she smiled mischievously as the door opened. But it wasn't Jacques.

'François? You're back,' Margo said, trying to compose herself.

'Yes, I just arrived.'

'But I thought you were going to stay in Paris until…'

'I know. I wasn't going to drive down until the weekend, but then I managed to take care of things at the ministry and get some time off. I didn't know I would until quite late, otherwise you could have driven down with me. But never mind that.'

François wiped his normally cool forehead with a big white handkerchief. 'There is…' he started. 'Something terrible has just happened.'

Margo stared at him. 'What?'

'Someone has died. My mother—'

'Your mother?' Margo gasped. 'Good God, no.'

'No, not my mother. But she's very upset. She was there, you see, when he died. He just dropped dead suddenly. Oh, my poor *Maman*…'

Margo felt herself go ice cold and the colour drained from her face. 'Jacques?' she whispered. 'Jacques is…?'

'No, don't be silly.' François pulled out a chair and sat down. 'I had better explain. My mother was attending that party.'

'The sixtieth birthday party?'

'Yes. It was a very big event. Lots of prominent people, some of whom had interrupted their holidays and flown in from their various villas on the Riviera. One of them was Jean-Jacques Gengoux, former president of France. Do you know who I mean?'

'Yes, of course. I read about him in *Le Figaro* only the other day.'

'Well, he was there with his wife. He seemed to have recovered very well from his slight heart problem and I'm told he looked to be in very good form. But after dinner, as he was talking to my mother on the terrace, he suddenly collapsed. His wife rushed to his side and then, within minutes, he died in her arms.'

'In your mother's?'

'No, in the arms of his wife, of course. Poor *Maman*.' François shook his head.

'It must have been a horrible shock to witness it all,' Margo said.

'Yes, she is very shaken. Jacques brought her home and I had just driven up when they arrived. She was nearly hysterical. I've called the doctor and he'll be here soon.'

'Good. Is she in bed?'

'No, not yet. Jacques brought her upstairs, but he's not able to handle her at all. He's too rough. So, Marguerite, I'm asking you if you could possibly go upstairs and see if you can.'

'But I don't see what I could do,' Margo protested. 'This is really a family matter.'

'She trusts you. You're very gentle and kind. See if you can calm her until the doctor comes.'

'All right. I'll go and see if I can do anything,' Margo said.

'Thank you so much.'

They made their way together through the hall and up the big staircase, walking quickly toward Milady's bedroom. Margo was about to knock on the door when it burst open and Jacques came out. His face white, he looked at them as if he had never seen them before. '*Toi?*' he snapped, glaring at François. '*Que'est-que tu fais là?*'

'I brought Marguerite to see if she could help *Maman*,' François explained. 'Get her into bed before the doctor arrives.'

'Well, you can try. I have had no luck at all with her. But…' he stopped and breathed deeply. 'She has just told me something that I...that I find impossible to accept.'

'What?' Margo asked, putting a hand on his shoulder. 'What's the matter?'

But he shook her hand off. 'I'm sorry, but I can't.' He stumbled past them.

François looked at his brother's figure as he rushed down the corridor. 'Poor Jacques,' he mumbled. 'Poor bastard.'

'François?' Milady called weakly from the bedroom. 'Is that you, *mon chéri*?'

'Yes,' François called back, 'and I brought Marguerite.'

They walked into the room, finding Milady sitting on the bed trying to undo the tiny mother of pearl buttons of her cream silk jacket. Her hands were shaking and her face was the colour of putty. She looked up at them with eyes so full of despair Margo felt tears welling up in her own eyes. 'I can't,' Milady whispered. 'The buttons. Please help me.'

Margo flew to her side. 'Of course, my dear Milady,' she exclaimed. 'I'll help you. Don't fret, we'll soon have you comfortable. The doctor is on his way.'

'Doctor?' Milady said bitterly. 'What good is a doctor? Can he heal a broken heart? Can he make the dead come alive? Of course not. Nobody can. Nobody can ever undo the hurt or stop the pain.'

Margo undid the buttons, removed the rest of Milady's clothes and got her into her nightgown. With François's help, she managed to get the agitated woman into bed, propped some pillows under her head and tucked the light cotton cover around her. There was a faint crunch on the gravel below. François turned his head and listened. 'That'll be the doctor,' he said. 'I'll go and show him up. Stay with my mother, Marguerite.'

'Of course,' Margo said, taking the hanger with the cream silk suit and opening the wardrobe. As she pushed the clothes aside to hang it up, she spotted something eerily familiar. The black silk dress. Margo peered at it, wondering if she was mistaken, but no, there it was. She lifted the hem and sniffed it. Yes, a slight touch of perfume still lingered on the fabric. Of course, she thought, suddenly realising what had been going on. The last piece of the jigsaw fell into place. How stupid of me not to understand it at once. But never mind. Let's leave it for now. She hung up the suit and quickly closed the wardrobe.

'François?' Milady said weakly. 'Where is he gone?'

'To show the doctor up,' Margo said, smoothing the hair from Milady's forehead. 'He won't be a minute. Try to rest now.'

Milady's hands shook as she plucked at the lace on the sheet. 'He died in *her* arms,' she muttered, 'in the arms of that…that prune-faced bitch. Dressed in the most horrible outfit. And her hair…' She stopped and looked up at Margo with eyes full of pain. 'I loved him,' she whispered, 'oh God, how I loved him. I just wanted him to know…to know about…'

'Shh,' Margo whispered. 'Try to relax.'

'Relax?' Milady's voice was shrill. 'My heart is broken. My poor love is dead, and you're telling me to *relax*?'

At that moment, the doctor walked into the room, followed by François.

'*Chère Madame,* so sorry to hear we are not well,' the doctor boomed. 'Let's have a look at you and see what we can do to make you feel more comfortable.'

The doctor gave Milady a shot and she seemed instantly calmer, lying limply against the pillows, her eyes half-closed. François left with the doctor and Margo was about to tiptoe out when Milady said something.

'What?' Margo walked closer to the big bed.

'Close the shutters. The light...it's too bright.'

'But it's dark outside.'

'I want them closed. I want all the shutters in the whole house closed. As a sign of mourning. Of respect.'

'Of course. I'll tell François.'

'Good. But don't go yet. Sit here with me for a little while.'

'All right.' Margo sat on a Louis XV chair beside the bed.

'Hold my hand.'

Margo took the thin, cold hand in hers. The skin felt as fragile as tissue paper. 'There. All right?'

'Yes.'

'Try to sleep,' Margo said softly.

'Yes,' Milady muttered, 'sleep. I will dream of him. I will pretend we are together.'

*

Je vous salue Marie, pleine de grace…

Margo woke slowly from an uneasy sleep. She sat up in the chair and straightened her stiff back. The murmuring continued, accompanied by a soft clicking noise. In the faint light of the bedside lamp, Margo peered at the dim figure in the bed. The prayer continued, Milady's hand moving the beads of the rosary. The sound was oddly soothing, like a mantra, the words repeated over and over again, until Margo knew it by heart and started to join in. As she recited the ancient prayer, she felt a calm come over her, and she had an odd feeling that they were not alone, that there was something or someone watching over them. It was a comforting and at the same time very calming thought somehow. Finally, Milady stopped praying and, still clutching the rosary, turned her head toward Margo.

'Marguerite?'

'Yes, Milady.'

'You are still here? What time is it?'

'I don't know. Late. It's still dark.' Margo rose from the chair. 'If you feel a little better, maybe I could…'

'No!' The voice was full of despair. 'Don't go. I don't want to be alone.'

'But maybe François or Jacques could…'

'No, don't disturb them. They need their sleep, poor boys.'

Margo sat down again. 'OK. I'll stay for a while longer.'

'Thank you.' Milady sighed and shifted in the bed. 'I'm wide awake now. Whatever the doctor gave me has worn off. I need something stronger. Could you call him?'

'But it's the middle of the night.'

'He's a doctor. It's his job to look after me. Even in the middle of the night.'

'Yes, but…' Margo didn't feel like calling the doctor. Milady didn't seem that bad. Sad, yes, but not as badly shaken as earlier. 'I'll get you a drink,' she said. 'Some hot milk with a little whiskey. I have always found that very good.'

'Well, we could try.' Milady didn't sound too convinced.

When Margo came back with the hot milk into which she had splashed a considerable amount of scotch, Milady was sitting up in bed looking at a photograph in a silver frame. She showed it to Margo.

'This is the only picture I have. Look, wasn't he handsome?'

Margo put the steaming mug on the bedside table and took the photograph. She peered in the dim light at the attractive man smiling broadly into the camera, and thought he looked just a little too conceited for her taste. He also seemed vaguely familiar; someone she knew looked a little like this, but she couldn't think of who it was. She looked at the man again, at his white teeth and thick dark hair. Too sure of his good looks and effect on women, she thought and handed the picture back. 'Very handsome,' she agreed.

'Yes,' Milady sighed. 'And he loved me. Only me.'

'Yes, of course he did,' Margo soothed. 'Drink your milk now.'

Milady slowly sipped the milk. 'Tastes odd. Bitter and sweet at the same time. Like my life.' She drained the last drops, gave the mug to Margo and laid back against the pillows again. 'Sit with me for a while.'

Margo sat down on the hard chair again.

'I feel,' Milady said, 'as if I'm trapped in some kind of nightmare. As if I will wake up any minute and everything will be as it was before. But then I look around the room and all the things in it and I know I'm not dreaming. I look at you and your tired face and everything comes rushing back.'

'It must be so horrible,' Margo said.

'It is.' Milady was quiet for a while. She looked at Margo. 'Have you ever been through this kind of thing? Have you ever lost someone you loved more than your own life?'

'No,' Margo said, suddenly realising it was true. She had never loved anyone like that.

'But you lost your father…'

'My father? Yes, he died about five years ago. Of course I was sad, but we were never really close.'

'Tell me about him.'

Margo felt as if a cold hand clutched at her stomach. 'He was…strict,' she said, as memories she had tried to force out of her mind came flooding back. 'Distant,' she added. 'And critical. I never felt I quite measured up to his expectations. I remember thinking, when I was very young, that he didn't really love me.'

'I'm sure you were wrong,' Milady murmured. 'I'm sure he must have loved you in his own way.'

'Maybe he did. He just never showed it. And he didn't really give me any praise or tell me he was proud of me. He only complained about my bad behaviour and poor marks at school. I sometimes lied and said I was at the top of my class, but when he found me out he was furious. And then I really made an effort and eventually got very good results in the end, but by then he had lost interest. He was only pleased with me once in my entire life.'

'When was that?'

'When I got married. He was very proud of the fact that I married such a successful man.'

'Maybe he thought it would make you happy.'

'No, he thought it would be good for business.'

'You sound bitter.'

'Do I?' Margo shrugged. 'What does it matter now? He's dead.'

'What about your marriage?' Milady asked with more interest. 'Is it over?'

'I don't know. It depends. Maybe we just need to be away from each other for a while.'

'But there is nobody else, is there? No other man in your life?'

Margo was grateful for the dim light. 'No,' she said.

'Good. That would cloud the issue. Make you feel confused, I mean. You have to make up your mind about your marriage first. There is nothing worse than being torn between two men.'

'Like you?'

'Me? No, I wasn't torn at all. I only ever loved one man.' Milady sighed deeply. 'Only him. We were lovers for many years. Then we broke up, and we didn't see each other for a long time. Years. But then we met, about twenty years ago, and we started seeing each other again. My husband had just died. Jacques was fourteen and François twenty-two and going to university. I thought that we would eventually marry, now that my husband was dead and his political career was coming to and end, but he couldn't leave his wife. She had the money, you see. And she threatened to expose him if he left. He wanted to protect his image as this charismatic man with a big heart and a happy marriage.'

'I suppose he didn't want to upset his children,' Margo suggested.

'He had no children. In his marriage, I mean. He did have a son, but he didn't know about him until tonight.'

'Oh? How come?'

'Because I told him.' Milady clapped her hand to her mouth and tears started to course down her cheeks. 'I hadn't seen Jean-Jacques for nearly twenty years,' she sobbed. 'Twenty long years since he told me we couldn't go on seeing each other, that he would never leave his wife. I didn't know he would be there tonight, and when our eyes met, I thought I was going to faint. Then I saw his wife. That cow! I was furious, both with him and her. I had never told him about the baby, you see. The baby that was born as a result of our love affair. I thought I should leave well enough alone, not upset anyone. But then, tonight, when we met on the terrace, I wanted…I felt so angry with him, so I told him everything. We had a terrible argument and then…oh God, he just sank down in front of me. His face – it was contorted with shock and rage. Then that woman rushed to his side and…' Milady covered her face with her hands. 'He died. Right there in front of me; died hating me, in the arms of his wife.' Milady's shoulders shook. 'I closed his eyelids and whispered "*adieu mon amour*" in his ear, but he was already gone. I can't get it out of my head,' she wept. 'The scene is playing in my mind like a film, over and over again.'

Horrified, Margo stared at Milady. 'Oh you poor thing,' she murmured, sitting down on the edge of the bed, putting her arms around the weeping woman. 'I am so sorry. So terribly, terribly sorry.'

Milady suddenly clutched Margo's hands and looked up at her with mournful eyes. 'Look after him,' she begged. 'Promise me you will.'

'Who?' Margo asked.

'Jacques. Look after Jacques.'

17

'Mademoiselle Marguerite?'

'*Oui?*' Margo said, standing by the phone on the small table in the hall. 'Who is this?'

'I'm sorry to call so late.' The woman's voice was slightly hoarse and her English heavily accented and very affected. 'I hope I'm not disturbing you.'

'No, not really. But if you were hoping to speak to the Comtesse, I'm afraid she is not available at the moment.'

'How is dear Marie-Jo? Not too shaken after what happened yesterday?'

'Yes she was, actually. Very shaken. She has been resting all day and now I think – I hope – she's asleep.'

'Of course. It was horrible. Quite, quite horrible.'

'If you give me your name, I'll tell her to call you tomorrow?'

'No. Yes.' The woman hesitated. 'I really called to speak to *you*, Mademoiselle.'

'Me?' Margo said, mystified.

'Let me explain. My name is Rose du Jardin. We have met several times. Last time when you accompanied the Comtesse to that garden party, and—'

'Yes, I remember you,' Margo interrupted, the image of a heavily made-up, overweight woman springing into her mind. 'Used to be a call girl,' Milady had whispered in Margo's ear. 'Married to that vulgar Georges du Jardin. *Bought* his château and thinks he can buy his way into society as well. She sells information to the gossip columns of those awful magazines. Don't know how she managed to get invited.'

'I just wondered,' the woman continued, 'if dear Marie-Jo has said anything to you about what happened. Or about her long, ahem, friendship with the late president?'

'No.'

'I would be very grateful if you could give me any kind of information. I might consider a generous reward for—'

'Madame du Jardin,' Margo interrupted, 'what makes you think I would betray the confidence of my employer to you? That I would tell you even if I did know anything? Which I don't,' she added.

'Not even for fifteen hundred euros?'

'I beg your pardon?'

'All right, make it two thousand, but that is my final offer. A little more if you had photographs.

I'm sure there might be some of the two of them together, lying around in the house somewhere. And letters, or—'

'I don't know what you're talking about,' Margo snapped.

'I think you should consider it,' Madame du Jardin insisted. 'You don't have to make up your mind right now. You could call me back later.'

'My mind is made up,' Margo said. 'And the answer is no.'

'You'll find my number on the Minitel if you change your mind.'

'Goodbye.' Margo banged the phone down and it rang again almost immediately.

Margo picked up the receiver. 'The answer is still no,' she said.

'No to what, pet?'

'Gráinne! Is that you?'

'Sure is, love.'

'Where are you? Why are you calling this number?'

'I'm in Ireland. I was trying to get in touch with Jacques. Is he around?'

'No. I haven't seen him since…' Since he stormed out of his mother's bedroom last night, Margo thought.

'Well, could you give him this message then?'

'I'll do my best. What's the message?'

'My boss wants to know if he still wants to buy that horse. Someone else has his eye on him and if Jacques could make up his mind, we could do a deal, one way or another.'

'OK. I'll tell him.'

'Yeah, and sooner rather than later.'

'I'll do my best.'

'Thanks, love. See ya. Bye.'

Margo hung up, smiling to herself. It always cheered her up to hear Gráinne's voice. She started to walk across the hall and bumped into someone coming the other way.

'Ooops,' Margo laughed, 'sorry.' The smile died on her lips as she looked at François. 'Oh, it's you,' she said. 'You look awful. No sleep?'

He stood there looking at her for a while, his face serious and his eyes bleak. 'Who was that on the phone?'

'It was Gráinne,' Margo said. 'Asking about a horse. Jacques has to let them know...' She stopped.

François took her hand. 'Marguerite. Could I ask you to do something for me?'

'Yes, of course.'

'Could you talk to Jacques?'

'About what?'

'Could you tell him that, well, that things haven't really changed. That he's still my brother and I want him to stay and carry on like before.'

'Why can't you tell him yourself?'

'I have tried, I really have. But he wouldn't listen to me. He won't even open his door. I'm sure if you...' François paused, looking slightly uncomfortable. He cleared his throat. 'Marguerite, I know it's not fair to drag you into our family business like this, but you're my only hope. If Jacques leaves, we're finished.'

'How do you mean?' Margo asked, alarmed.

'I mean us, this family, the château, the property. This has been a disastrous year for farming all over France because of the weather – the drought, I mean. Farmers are killing their cattle because they can't feed them. You must have seen how bad it was when you went on that train journey. Most of the farmland around here is like a desert.'

'Yes, I did see that.'

'But Jacques has done much better than most farmers. The cattle seem to be surviving thanks to whatever it is that Jacques is doing. We will be able to sell good-quality cattle at the end of this year and make a handsome profit. If Jacques stays, that is. But if he decides to leave…' François's voice trailed away. 'I won't know what to do, nor will anyone else. It will mean the end of the farm and that very important income. I might even have to sell.'

'The château?' Margo said, horrified.

'Well, not the house. But some of the land. And we will have to tighten our belts considerably. Auction off some of the art and furniture. And our lifestyle will be seriously compromised. We might even have to open the house to the public, eventually.'

'Oh God, no,' Margo whispered, imagining Milady serving tea to tourists wearing chain-store clothes. The image made her laugh suddenly.

'You find this amusing?' François asked, looking appalled.

'No, I'm sorry. Just nerves, I suppose.'

'It would mean that your job would go too, of course.'

'I realised that,' Margo said, even though this was just dawning on her.

'So,' François said, 'will you do this for us? For me? Talk to Jacques. Explain what I just said? Try to make him stay?'

'I don't think I have the slightest chance. But OK, I'll have a go.'

'Thank you. I'm sure Jacques will listen to you. Sometimes an outsider can be better than a family member in this kind of situation. No emotional involvement, if you see what I mean.'

'No emotional involvement,' Margo repeated. 'Of course.'

*

Jacques's room was in the tower opposite Margo's. As she walked up the two flights of stairs, she repeated the words to herself like a mantra: *no emotional involvement. Don't get involved, don't get carried away, don't even think about letting him touch you again. Just deliver the message, then leave.* OK, she thought as she stood in front of the door, this is it. She took a deep breath and tried to still the butter-flies in her stomach. Another deep breath and she lifted her hand and knocked on the door. There was no reply. She knocked again, harder this time. Again, no reply; no footsteps on the other side of the door, no voice asking who it was, just silence and the thumping of her heartbeat in her ears.

'Jacques?' Margo called. 'Are you there?'

No reply. He must be out, Margo thought, turning the handle and pushing the door, expecting it to be locked. But it swung silently open. 'Jacques?' Margo said, peering in. 'Are you there?' She walked into the empty room and looked around. So this is his room, she thought, his own private space. It was simply furnished – a huge bed, a tall bookcase crammed with books, a leather armchair, a worn Indian carpet on the floor. There was a desk near the window with a pile of papers and a laptop computer. It was a nice room, a room for relaxing and reading, a room for getting away from the rest of the house. Margo glanced out the window. The view was only slightly different from her own. From here, she could see the stables and the horses in the paddock, the dogs walking around, and just glimpse the woods, the stream and the river beyond. She walked away from the window, across the carpet to the bookcase. She looked at the titles, wondering what sort of books Jacques liked to read. Among the paperback titles of detective stories, political thrillers and biographies there were a number of books about horses and wildlife. She took one out and flicked through it, admiring the stunning photographs.

'What are you doing here?'

Margo twirled around and dropped the book. 'Oh. It's you,' she stammered.

'Who else did you expect?' Jacques closed the door behind him. 'This is my room, after all.'

'I know.'

He stood for a moment looking at her, puzzled. 'Why are you here? And don't tell me it's because you wanted to borrow a book.'

Margo picked up the book and put it back on the shelf. 'No,' she said, 'I came because François asked me.'

'Why? What did he want you to do?' Jacques gestured toward the leather chair. 'Sit down.'

Margo sank down on the chair and Jacques walked to the bed and sat down too, all the while looking at her with curiosity.

'Go on,' he said. 'Tell me what you were asked to say.'

'François wants you to stay,' Margo said, grateful for the distance between them. 'He wants everything to be the way it was before. Before the, well, you know what…before last night.'

'Last night?'

'When you found out about…your mother and…your father. The real one, I mean.'

'I see.'

'I came to tell you François is worried you'll leave, you see, and he won't know how to run the farm and he'll lose a lot of money. And then he'll have to sell the land and the furniture and open the château to the public,' Margo babbled on. 'And your mother will have to wear cheap cardigans and serve tea to Japanese tourists, and…' She stopped for breath, realising that she had probably blown it. She looked at Jacques, who was still sitting there, now looking very angry.

Margo got up. 'Sorry. I didn't put that very well.'

'Oh no, you put it exceptionally well,' Jacques said, slowly getting off the bed.

'And Gráinne wants to know if you're buying that horse from Ireland,' Margo added and quickly walked to the door. 'That was all I came to say.' She struggled with the door handle, but Jacques put a hand on hers to stop her. 'Are you leaving already?' he said softly into her ear.

'Yes, I have to go now.' Margo tried to pull her hand out of his grip.

'Marguerite, don't go,' Jacques said, pulling her across the room toward the bed. 'Stay here with me for a while.'

'All right,' Margo sighed, sitting down awkwardly on the bed. 'But only for a minute. And it would be a great help if you didn't touch me.'

Jacques laughed and held up his hands. 'All right. No touching.'

'Good.' They looked at each other and, at that moment, Margo regretted her last request. There was deep despair in his eyes that belied the light-hearted tone in his voice, and every fibre in her cried out to touch him, to put her arms around him and comfort him.

'I like your room,' she said.

'And I like you,' he said. 'I really like you, Marguerite.' There was a kind of hunger in his eyes that had nothing to do with sex. He took both her hands in his and kept looking at her. Then he put his arms around her. 'I'm sorry,' he said, holding her close, 'I know I promised not to, but this is what I want to do right now, just hold you like this.' He seemed to draw comfort from their physical contact and he held her close for a long time without speaking or moving.

'I'm so sorry,' Margo whispered. 'It must be so hard for you.'

'Not really,' Jacques said gently, his cheek against her hair. 'It's something I have suspected for a long time. Now that I know, it's a kind of relief.' He pulled back and looked at her with a far-away look in his eyes. 'I didn't want to believe it, but the doubt was always there.'

'Why?' Margo asked, looking into his troubled eyes. 'Was it…her husband? Wasn't he kind to you?'

Jacques let her go and just sat on the bed, his shoulders slumped. 'He wasn't anything. He didn't really have any contact with his children, neither François nor me. Of course, he was a lot older than my mother. At least twenty years. I didn't think much about it when I was a small boy. It was when I was a teenager that I started thinking, wondering.'

'That must have been terrible for you,' Margo said, putting her hand on his shoulder. Jacques pulled away and lay back on the bed, staring at the ceiling. 'I seemed so different, you know? Like a square peg trying to fit into a round hole. I have always loved animals, horses especially. I love living in the country, can't stand cities. François is the complete opposite, so like my father…I mean, *his* father. Elegant, *intello*. And of course, looking at us, any fool would know we aren't brothers. I look like my real father, I must have been blind not to notice. He had the same build and the same eyes. Great horseman too.' Jacques sighed and turned his head to look at Margo. 'Why didn't she tell me?'

'Maybe she was afraid you would be hurt,' Margo said softly. 'Maybe she thought it would be best to leave well enough alone, if you were happy. She must have been so unhappy herself all these years. She really loved your father, you know. He was the love of her life. And she was his.'

'How do you know this?'

'She told me. I have been sitting with her all night.'

'You sat all night in her room?'

'Yes, she was so upset. I couldn't leave her.'

'Oh. That must have been exhausting.'

'I was happy to help in some small way. It helped her to talk, I think. She told me how hard it was, how she loved him all these years, even though they didn't meet for many years.'

'But Marguerite,' Jacques said, sounding like a child, 'if they loved each other so much, why didn't they do something about it? Why didn't they run away together or something?'

'I don't know,' Margo replied. 'Maybe they didn't have the courage?'

'*She* would have,' Jacques said with feeling. 'But he? What a wimp. I'm sorry he is my father. I feel ashamed.' Jacques sighed and wrapped his arms around his chest as if trying to stop himself from feeling the pain. 'Can you understand,' he asked, 'what it's been like for me? To work here at this château, thinking it was somehow mine, that I had a part of it? I love this place,' he said passionately. 'I knew, of course, that it belonged to François, the eldest son, but he has no real interest in it, other than coming here for a holiday. He has left it all to me for the past ten years. All the problems, the upkeep, the farm, everything. I thought…I was hoping he would let me have it one day, or that we would come to some kind of agreement. But now…now that I know who I am…what I am…' He paused.

'But François doesn't want you to leave, I just told you that. He can't run the place like you do. And he's worried that it will all go if you leave.'

'That's not true, and he knows it,' Jacques exclaimed. 'He just doesn't want to get his hands dirty. There's enough money to keep this property going for quite a few years.'

'But why did he…?'

'He's very stingy, you know. Last winter, when there was a problem with the roof and a lot of other things too, I asked him to let me have some money from the trust fund my fa— I mean, *his* father, set up for the running of the château. But he let it drag on until I had to raise the money in another way. He is just lazy and he wants me to go on doing everything so that he can carry on with his precious lifestyle.'

'So there is no problem then?'

'No, not with money in any case. Or with me. I don't want to leave. I love this place, it has been my home all my life and, despite what I have just found out, I still want to work here. I can't think of anything I'd rather do. So you can stop worrying about my mother.'

'Good. I think it would kill her if she had to change her life.'

'No, it wouldn't,' Jacques murmured bitterly. 'She would survive anything. I think it would serve her right if she lost all her money. But she would get used to it and turn it to her own advantage, somehow. It would suddenly be chic to wear polyester and work in the tourist industry.'

'I know what you mean,' Margo said with a little laugh.

'My mother,' Jacques said bitterly, 'has no feelings.'

'Is that why you're so angry with her all the time? Why you yell at the top of your voice?'

'That's right. I keep trying to get a reaction out of her, to get her to *feel* something. But she just sits there, smoking her cigarettes.'

Margo started to laugh. 'She is really brave, I have to say.'

Jacques looked at her for a moment, and then suddenly joined in her laughter. 'It's a game, you know,' he said. 'A silly game between the two of us.'

'Pretty violent, though,' Margo said.

'Oh God, Marguerite, I'm sorry.'

'For what?'

'For involving you in all this.'

'I don't mind. If it helps you to talk about it…'

He reached out and gently touched her hair. 'You're so lovely,' he whispered. 'Like a flower.'

She took his hand and held it, then turned it and stroked his palm, running her finger along the calluses. 'Rough hands,' she murmured, suddenly not daring to look at him.

Gently, he put his hand under her chin and turned her face up, and she met his gaze, feeling shy and uncertain. Then she sighed and closed her eyes, not wanting to look into his eyes any more. She knew what he wanted, and she wanted it too, but she felt afraid. She had only ever slept with one man in her life, and that man was her husband. Even though she now knew her love for him was dead, she still felt it would be a kind of betrayal to sleep with someone else. And she also worried about what sex with Jacques would be like, what he would want from her. He had had so many women, done all kinds of things, whereas she and Alan, like most married couples, had got into a routine in their love-making and settled into a cosy and comfortable relationship, even if the sex had lately turned into something quite joyless.

'It's all right,' Jacques said softly.

She opened her eyes and looked into his, now so tender. 'I know,' she said, 'but I just don't know what to do. Or say, or…' Her voice trailed away.

'We're just two people. A man and a woman.'

'No,' Margo said in a small voice, pulling away from him. 'It's too late. Too late for me. We met at the wrong time.' Tears stung her eyes as she tried to get a grip on her feelings.

'I don't agree,' Jacques said hotly. 'What's in your past doesn't matter. Or mine. There is only now, and you and me.' He took her hand. 'But if you feel that you can't...' He stopped.

Touched by the look in his eyes, Margo leaned forward and kissed him lightly on the lips. 'I'm sorry,' she said. She was going to pull back and get off the bed, walk away, leave the room, but, as if he could sense a longing in her that had not been there before, he pulled her close to him. 'Marguerite,' he whispered, 'do not be afraid. I would never hurt you.'

'I'm not afraid of you,' Margo murmured into his chest. 'It's me.'

'Shh. Don't talk.'

She gave up the struggle. What was the use anyway? Alan was far away. She would not, could not go back to him and their formal parting was only a matter of time. This was real now, much more real than her feelings for Alan. Jacques was here beside her, wanting her, making her feel special and beautiful and loved.

'Marguerite?' he whispered, starting to touch her in her most private places. '*Mon amour*...may I...can we?'

'Yes,' she whispered back, feeling all her inhibitions and doubts disappear, 'Yes...please.'

*

'What's the matter with you?' Gráinne said, looking searchingly at Margo. 'You look strange. Spaced out.' They were sitting on the terrace of the café yet again, drinking beer and looking at the ducks swimming past on the still black water of the river. Gráinne had arrived in the horse truck

279

that morning, bringing with her the horse Jacques had bought from her boss in Ireland. 'Has something happened while I was away?' she asked.

Margo sighed and picked up her glass. 'Yes. No. I don't want to talk about it.' She didn't feel like discussing what had happened with anyone. It was her secret, hers and Jacques's.

*

'My darling,' he had said as he was getting ready to go out to the farm early the following morning, 'what happened between us last night was so special, so precious to me. But I feel that you…that there is something you have to work out before we can go any further. Am I right?'

'Yes,' she mumbled, pulling the sheet up to her chin, a little shy under his probing gaze. Jacques sat down on the bed. He pulled the sheet away from her hands. 'Please,' he said, 'don't be shy. I have seen every inch of you, why do you feel you have to hide now?' He ran his hand down her body from her neck to her hip. 'So lovely,' he whispered, 'like a painting by Degas.'

'Oh, Jacques.' Margo put her arms around his neck and pressed her breasts against his bare chest that was peeping out through his half-opened shirt.

'Marguerite, *mon trésor*,' he mumbled, *Je t'aime.* As if surprised by his own words, he pulled back and looked into her eyes. 'My God, that's the first time I've…'

'What?' Margo said incredulously. 'You never told any girl you loved her?'

'Oh, I've *said* it,' he laughed. 'I always *say* it. That's what women want to hear. But I've never meant it. But this time I do, I really do. I want you to believe that.'

'Oh Jacques, I don't know,' Margo said, feeling suddenly frightened by the intensity in his voice. 'Love is such a big word. I don't know if I want to say things like that yet. I don't think I want to even think about it.'

'All right.' He kissed her on the mouth. 'We'll take it nice and slow. No pressure.'

'Thank you,' she sighed, relieved.

'But I want you to know that I have never felt... No woman has ever touched me like you have.' Jacques looked at Margo, and she could see sadness in his eyes. 'I have had a lot of affairs, I'm sure you know that.'

'Yes,' she said softly, 'I know.'

'But it has always ended in tears. Theirs, not mine,' he added wryly. 'Not because I'm heartless or mean, or...' He stopped and looked away. 'I seemed to be looking for something. Someone.' He looked back at her again and now there was a veiled look in his blue eyes. 'It never worked out and I have always been left with a feeling of having been let down. My fault, probably. I'm not telling you this because I'm looking for pity. I just didn't want you to be put off by my past.'

'Oh, I don't care about all that,' Margo said. 'It has nothing to do with me. It all happened before we met. But...' She paused, wondering how to go on.

'But what?'

'It's that temper of yours. I find it very frightening. You see, I...' Now it was Margo's turn to hesitate. 'I once lived with a very abusive man,' she murmured against Jacques's chest.

He pulled away and looked at her. 'Abusive? You mean he hit you?'

'No. He wasn't abusive physically, only verbally. He called me names. Told me I was stupid and...' Margo looked away, tears pricking her eyes. 'I don't really want to talk about it.'

Jacques was quiet for a long time while he stroked her hair. 'What a bastard,' he said finally. 'But a lot of men are like that. Angry when they can't control people or the world. I'm not. I just blow up from time to time and, well, it's mostly with my mother. I was so angry with her. I've told you all that. But I'm not angry with her any more. And I feel more at peace now that it's all out in the open. Please, my darling Marguerite, do not be afraid of me. Even when I blow off steam. It's just the way I am.'

'OK,' Margo sighed, trying her best to believe him. 'At least you're aware of it.'

'Yes, of course. But I'm sorry, my darling,' Jacques continued, getting up from the bed, 'I have to go and see to the farm and the horses.'

'I know. And I have to get up and get your mother's breakfast and see what else there is to be done.'

'But it's only six o'clock. Why don't you stay and rest here for a while? We didn't get much sleep last night,' he said, grinning at her.

'No, we didn't.' Margo smiled back, remembering the night. 'Every muscle in my body feels tender.'

'I should be the one to complain,' Jacques said. 'You were like a wild thing. I didn't expect such passion from a prim English girl.'

'You turned me on,' Margo said, lying back against the pillows, looking at him as he moved around the room. She loved watching him. He moved with such grace, surprising for a big man. And the way he had made love to her… Margo smiled. She had known he would be an accomplished lover, but she had been amazed by his generosity and the fact that he seemed more concerned about her pleasure than his own. She had surprised herself with the intensity of her own passion and how she had not felt the slightest embarrassment with him.

Jacques walked softly to the door, opened it a crack and peered out. 'Nobody there,' he said and walked through. 'Got to go. *A bientôt, mon amour.*'

*

'Is it Jacques?' Gráinne asked, her voice sharp.

'Is what Jacques?' Margo said, startled out of her thoughts.

'That half-witted look on your face. Is it because of him? Has he made a pass at you?'

'Never mind.' Margo looked at the ducks.

'He did, didn't he? Oh Jesus, I knew it. What did you do? I hope you told him where to get off.'

'I haven't seen Jacques for over a week,' Margo said, 'so could you please get off my case?'

'Hmm.' Gráinne looked thoughtfully at Margo. 'Not for a week, you said?'

'That's right. He has been very busy with the farm and then he had to go to this show jumping thing in Lyon.'

'You seem to know a lot about his movements.'

'Not really.'

'He's coming back tomorrow, did you know that? He'll have to take care of the horse I brought, see?'

'Yes, I understand.'

'Is it the brother, then? I thought you really fancied him. Is he the one that has you looking like a…'

'François? Good God, no.' Margo drank some beer. 'I'm really annoyed with him, to tell you the truth. He's been a little dishonest with me. He's not the gentleman I thought he was. And in any case, he has a girlfriend.'

'Oh? When did he tell you that?'

'He didn't. I figured it out for myself.' Margo leaned across the table. 'You see, it was the dress. You know the one that was missing?'

'The Googlie-thing?'

'Galliano. That's right. I know what happened to it.'

'Really? How?'

Margo smiled, proud of herself. 'I just put all the pieces together and then, bingo! It all seemed to fit.'

'This sounds weird. But go on.'

'Well, I had seen this woman coming out of the apartment late at night a couple of times.'

'The blonde bombshell you were telling me about?'

'That's right. Then the dress went missing and it happened on the same day François left for Paris.'

'Aha!' Gráinne exclaimed.

'That's right. Then, when I was in Paris, I spotted the woman again, coming out of the building wearing—'

'The dress!' Gráinne said triumphantly.

'How did you know?'

'You told me.'

'Anyway, the last piece of the jigsaw was the reappearance of the very same dress in Milady's wardrobe the night François came back. Plus,' Margo added, touching her nose, 'I smelled the perfume. The perfume that woman was wearing still lingered on François the next morning. And there was a faint whiff of it on the dress when it magically reappeared in the château.'

'Really? Are you sure?'

'Absolutely. Joy de Patou, I know it well.'

'But,' Gráinne said, looking puzzled, 'you said the woman was *leaving* the building wearing the dress. Where was she going? And where was François?'

'They were going to a party. He told me he had been at a do somewhere in the neighbourhood and came home very late. My guess is that he was working late and told her he would meet her there and then they went home together. Or something,' Margo added vaguely.

'Hmm,' Gráinne said. 'I suppose that all makes sense. Except…'

'What?'

'Well, why the mystery? Why does he need to make such a song and dance about the fact that he has a girlfriend?'

'You don't know his mother. She would not approve of just anyone. This woman may not have the right pedigree. She might be working class or a foreigner or something. She does look rather exotic, with those dark eyes and the blonde hair.'

'Hmm,' Gráinne said again. 'I find all of this hard to believe.'

'Why?'

'I always thought that guy was a fruit.'

'He's not,' Margo said indignantly.

'Why not? All the signs are there.'

'Stop it, Gráinne.'

'Oh, *sorreee*,' Gráinne said. 'Didn't know you felt like that. I thought you just told me you didn't have any feelings for the guy. That you were pissed off with him.'

'I don't have "feelings", as you call it, for him,' Margo said indignantly. 'I never have. It was all in your mind. Please, can we talk about something else?' Margo drained her glass. 'I came out tonight to relax and forget about work and that family for a while. It has been a very difficult week.'

'I can tell. You look really shaken. Not your usual self at all.'

'I just feel totally drained. But enough about me. What have you been up to?'

'Nothing much. Very busy at the yard. We had

a lot of young horses to school and then this transport came up because we sold Stan.'

'Stan?' Margo said, her eyes lighting up. 'You mean that lovely horse you had the first time we met? You sold him to Jacques?'

'That's the one. Very talented event horse. Cost a bomb. Don't know how you-know-who could afford him.'

'Jacques?'

'Yeah. He must be loaded.'

Margo shrugged. 'Must be.' Her thoughts drifted while Gráinne chatted on. It's the end of August, she thought, we'll be going back to Paris soon. What about Jacques? How can I keep seeing him? Maybe he'll come to the city? We'll be going back to the château for weekends in any case. Milady seems a little better, even though she is very sad. But she seems to be able to put up a brave front and carry on as before. Back to Paris, Margo thought. I'll have to decide what to do next…

'…was amazing. He stitched up the wound and the horse improved within days,' Gráinne said, cutting into Margo's daydream.

'What? Who?'

'Seamus. The trainee vet. I told you about him. Great friend of mine and a great vet. Or will be when he's qualified,' Gráinne said proudly.

'Oh.'

'Yeah.' Gráinne looked at Margo. 'Listen, there is something I wanted to ask you.'

'What?'

'I want you to be completely honest. No bullshit, OK?'

'Right.' Margo waited while Gráinne looked suddenly very shy.

'Do you find me attractive?' Gráinne finally blurted out, her face red.

Taken aback, Margo stared at Gráinne. 'Well, I...'

'You don't,' Gráinne said flatly, looking close to tears.

'I like you a lot, you know,' Margo said. 'But...only as a friend. But don't worry,' she continued when Gráinne looked suddenly upset, 'I have absolutely no prejudices against people like you. I think everyone has a right to be whatever they are. It's nobody's business but their own. It's just that you have to know that I'm not...you know...that way.'

'Of course you're not. You're normal. Not a freak like me,' Gráinne said bitterly. 'The reason I am the way I am is that nobody could possibly be attracted to a butt-ugly woman like me.'

'Ugly?' Margo said. 'You're not. You're very nice looking, really.'

'I am?'

'Oh yes.' Margo studied Gráinne for a minute. 'You have a nice face and a lovely smile.'

'My eyes are small and too close together.'

'But you have amazingly long eyelashes.'

'And I'm fat and squat,' Gráinne said without listening.

'You're just a little chubby, but it suits you. And you have...'

'Huge boobs.'

'No. Well, you do have a big bust, but if you wore a better bra, it would look very good.'

'It would?' Gráinne squinted down at her chest.

'Oh yes. And listen, Gráinne, the most important thing of all is that you're very good company and great fun.' Margo smiled fondly at her. 'You'll find that special person one day.'

'I already did,' Gráinne said. 'Don't you see? I *have* found someone I really like.'

'You have? Then what's the problem?'

'The problem is me,' Gráinne said glumly. 'I can't bring myself to tell him.'

'Him?' Margo said, suddenly feeling an odd sense of relief. 'It's a man?'

'Yeah, what did you think it was, a fucking monkey?'

'No...eh...'

'How can I tell him?' Gráinne asked. 'What's he going to say? He couldn't possibly be interested in a twenty-seven–year-old...' She stopped. 'I can't even say it myself.'

'Oh, come on, say it,' Margo urged. 'Try to pretend I'm him, and just say it.'

'Oh, OK. I'll give it a go.' Gráinne looked intently at Margo. 'Seamus,' she said. 'There is something I have to tell you. Promise not to laugh. Oh God, no, I can't.'

'Gráinne,' Margo said sternly. 'If he really cares for you, it won't matter. I'm sure he won't give a damn what you've been up to before you met him. Maybe it will even make him more interested in you.'

'Do you think so?'

'Men are strange. The weirdest things turn them on. Go on now, have a go. If you say it once, it won't be so hard the next time.'

'OK.' Gráinne swallowed, looked down at the table and muttered something.

'What?' Margo asked. 'Speak up.'

Gráinne looked up, her face pale. 'Oh, Maggie,' she whispered, 'I'm still a virgin.'

*

'Have you finished packing?' François asked, coming into Milady's bedroom.

'Nearly,' Margo replied, closing the biggest of the suitcases. 'Agnès is ironing the last of the blouses and putting them into tissue paper.'

'Good. In that case, why don't you leave it for a while and come and have a drink on the terrace? It's such a lovely evening.'

'Yes, it is. Much cooler, too. And I'd love a drink.' Margo followed François out of the room and down the corridor.

'There is a real feel of autumn in the air,' François said as they made their way down the stairs. 'Makes one a little melancholy, don't you think?'

'But I like the autumn,' Margo said. 'I love the crisp air and the bright colours of the leaves. And that smell of burning wood and the brightness of the sky.' She suddenly felt very homesick for Dorset and the small town she had grown up in. She thought of picking apples and coming home to their cosy house on cold evenings, the fire burning in the grate in the living room. Of her mother making apple and blackberry crumble and walking through autumn leaves on Sunday walks. She sighed. 'Makes me think of my childhood in England.'

'But the autumn is lovely here too,' François said, opening the door to the terrace and stepping back to let her pass. 'You should see the park and all the trees in their glorious colours. And you will, of course. My mother will be coming here for weekends until the beginning of November.'

'I know.'

'There you are,' Milady said. She was sitting at the table near the end of the terrace, sipping a glass of champagne. 'And Marguerite. Sit down. I asked Bernard to open a bottle of champagne.'

'What's the occasion?' François asked.

'No occasion, really, except to say goodbye to summer.' Milady put her glass on the table and smiled at them. 'Pour Marguerite a glass, François. Let's enjoy the last warm summer's evening. They are forecasting a break in the weather tomorrow. I have asked Agnès to serve dinner in half an hour.'

'You must eat with us, Marguerite,' François said.

Margo glanced at Milady. 'Well, thank you, but...'

'Yes, do,' Milady said graciously. 'Why not? Just this once.'

'Thank you, that's very kind.' Margo took a sip from the glass François had just offered her. 'Will Jacques be joining us?' she enquired casually. She didn't know where he was, but he had said he would come to her room later and they would finally be able to be together. The last week had been torture, Margo thought, as she had been consumed with longing for him and knowing he was so near, yet not able to take any time off because of pressures with running the property and trying to cope with the drought. Every time they had planned to meet, there had been some kind of emergency and Jacques had been forced to rush off to deal with it. And then, just as Margo thought she would have a chance to be with him, he had to go to Lyon.

'I thought he would be here already,' François said. 'He came back from Lyon this morning. Is he not dining with us?'

'No, he ate earlier,' Milady said. 'Said something about the vet coming to check the new horse. He had an upset stomach, I think. The horse,' she added with a laugh, 'not the vet.'

Margo joined in the laughter, feeling relieved that she wouldn't have to talk to Jacques in front of his family and pretend there was nothing going on between them, and pleased that Milady seemed so much better. The first few days after the death of her elderly lover, she had stayed in bed and hadn't touched any of the food Margo had brought up. The day of the state funeral, she had locked herself in her room, refusing to talk to anyone, not even François. But now, except for a lack of appetite and an increased number of cigarette butts in her ashtray, she seemed to have recovered some of her old drive.

Margo drank more champagne and enjoyed the evening air, which was still warm, but not as uncomfortably hot as before. A huge harvest moon rose above the trees and the sky slowly turned a velvety blue.

'*Madame est servie*,' Agnès announced from the door of the dining room, and they slowly rose and made their way inside.

'This is such a beautiful room,' Margo said as she sat down on the chair François pulled out for her. 'The paintings, the old oak panelling.'

'I suppose you must know quite a lot about furniture and old paintings, being the daughter of an antique dealer,' Milady said, putting her napkin in her lap.

'I'm no expert,' Margo said modestly, 'but yes, I learned quite a lot over the years. I used to love going to auctions with my father and my brothers. And my father taught us the tricks of the trade, so to speak, how to spot a bargain, tell a fake from the real thing and so on,' Margo explained, remembering how she had tried her best to soak up everything in a futile attempt to win her father's approval. She sighed and helped herself to a slice of roast chicken from the dish Milady passed her.

'There is a lot of very valuable furniture in this house,' François said. 'Some of it very old.'

'Yes, I noticed,' Margo said, picking up her wine glass. 'I was amazed to see it all. The drawing room furniture is remarkable. That inlayed table beside the sofa is exquisite. Eighteenth century, isn't it?'

'That's right.'

'And the cupboard against the far wall,' Margo continued, 'seventeenth-century Dutch. A very fine piece.'

'You are very knowledgeable,' Milady said, sounding impressed. 'François, *Chéri*, more wine.'

'What about paintings?' François asked, refilling his mother's glass. 'Do you know anything about them?'

'Yes, a little,' Margo replied. 'No, a lot, actually. My brother specialises in old paintings. You have some really important works here. I love the portrait of the woman in the blue dress in the library. An early Manet, isn't it?'

'That's correct,' François said and smiled. 'How clever of you. Maybe we should ask you to help out with the cataloguing we are planning to do later this year. What do you think, *Maman*?'

'Good idea,' Milady nodded. 'Boring work, but it has to be done. For the insurance, you see. Would you feel like doing a little of that, Marguerite?'

'Of course,' Margo said. 'I would love to. I like old things.'

'This room has always been my favourite,' Milady said. 'And I have always thought it was so clever to put the best paintings in here.'

'And even more clever to replace them with such excellent copies,' Margo added brightly.

There was a sudden, stunned silence. Milady turned very pale.

'I beg your pardon?' François said, staring at

her, his eyes huge with shock. 'Are you saying that some of these paintings are…fake?'

'No,' Margo replied, putting down her wine glass. 'That's not what I meant.'

'Of course not,' Milady said, the colour coming back to her cheeks.

'Not *some* of the paintings,' Margo said, gesturing with her fork around the room. 'They all are.'

18

At first, Margo tried her best to smooth over her enormous *faux pas* as Milady and François stared at each other in wordless horror. 'But they are excellent copies,' she said. 'Nobody would guess, really.'

'*You* did,' François muttered.

'Yes, but I know what to look for. My brother is a renowned art expert, and...' She paused, thinking about how her brother had been so pleased with the way she had been able to pick up even the slightest flaws. 'These copies must have been done by the very best,' she continued with an encouraging smile. 'I mean, some of the paintings are actually *better* than the original. You know how Rembrandt couldn't do hands? But in that little study of the old lady, the hands are...' She paused again when there was no reply. Nobody seemed to have heard her feeble attempt at looking on the bright side.

'*Mon Dieu,*' Milady whispered, staring at François, 'what are we going to do?'

'Nothing for the moment,' François said, switching to French, his voice icily determined. 'Until we find out who has been…' He paused. 'I have a feeling we don't have to look too far.'

'You mean…' Milady said.

'Yes,' François said. 'I think it's quite obvious, don't you?'

'But…' Milady's shoulders slumped. 'Yes, you're right. There can't be any other explanation.' She suddenly started to sob. 'The shame,' she wept, 'the embarrassment. What will people say?'

'Nothing,' François soothed, putting an arm around her shoulders. 'Nobody will find out, I'll make sure of that. We'll carry on as before.'

'We will? But how? We have to tell the police, the insurance company.'

'Not at all,' he assured her. 'We won't say anything to anyone. Except,' he continued, his voice cold, 'I have a few things to say to…' He stopped and glanced at Margo as if he had only then realised she was there, but wished she wasn't.

She rose from her chair. '*Excusez moi, mais je crois que je vais,*' she mumbled. They didn't seem to hear her, but continued to talk to each other in a near whisper as she silently left the room.

*

Margo was packing her few items of clothing into her tote bag and generally tidying up her room. It was late, and although she was very tired she was looking forward to seeing Jacques again. He had written her a note, telling her how much he was longing to be with her and would try to finish with the vet and the horses so they could spend this last night together. *It's sad to part, but we'll have the weekends,* he had written. *I'm looking forward to showing you how lovely the park and the woods are in the autumn.* As soon as I go back to Paris I will try to get in touch with Alan, Margo thought as she packed. Tell him it's all over and we'll have to get the divorce proceedings going. She froze, suddenly frightened by the word 'divorce'. She had never really thought of it like that before, never said the word to herself even in her thoughts, as if it was something that didn't really apply to her, something that happened to other people. Being 'separated' didn't seem so bad, it wasn't final; it left the door open. She felt a sense of guilt about her affair with Jacques and she knew she wouldn't be thinking like this if it wasn't for him, but he had given her the final push to close the chapter with Alan. She also knew she would have to tell Jacques about her marriage. They had agreed that their individual pasts weren't really important, but a marriage of ten years wasn't something you could airbrush out of your life. I have no idea at all where I'm going with Jacques, she thought. It might just end in tears, probably mine. But right now it's so lovely. And I will tell him about Alan. Soon.

Margo finished her packing and looked around the room, thinking how much she was going to miss it and the château. It's like a time warp here, she thought, like going back in time. A place of peace and tranquillity in a sea of noise and confusion that is the modern world. How lucky they are to have this place. But all was not well tonight, she said to herself, laughing suddenly as she remembered the scene in the dining room earlier. It had been a little ridiculous, she thought as the faces of François and Milady, frozen in shock, danced before her eyes. She had regretted her words as soon as they came out of her mouth. But she had, in all fairness, been convinced they knew, that it had been part of some insurance ploy.

Margo sighed as she closed her bag. Why did I have to go and tell them? she asked herself for the thousandth time.

The door suddenly flew open. Startled, Margo looked up from her task as Jacques burst into the room.

'So, here you are,' he snapped.

'Jacques,' Margo said as her whole body flooded with happiness. She walked over to embrace him, but recoiled as she saw the look on his face. 'What's the matter?'

'How can you ask?' Jacques looked at her so coldly Margo felt the colour drain from her face.

'What do you mean?' she demanded. 'Why are you looking at me like that?'

'Why did you have to tell them? Why did you have to open your big mouth?'

'About what?'

'What do you think? The paintings, of course.'

'The paintings?' Margo looked at him in confusion. Then it suddenly dawned on her what he was talking about and, her knees oddly weak, she sank down on the bed. 'Oh no,' she mumbled. 'Oh God. It was you. *You* stole them. But why?'

Jacques walked to the window and stared out at the park below. 'I'm not a thief,' he said. 'I want you to know that. I didn't really steal them. Perhaps in a way, but for a very good cause.'

'What kind of cause?'

'This place.' Jacques turned and looked at Margo. 'Last winter, there was terrible storm and half the roof fell in. It had to be replaced in a hurry, or the rain would have destroyed the house. I got a builder to come and have a look and give me a quote. When he finally arrived, he had a look at the rest of the house and found a lot of other problems that needed to be dealt with as well. Dry rot in the cellar, wood worm in the rafters and so on. The quote came to over a million euros.'

'My God.'

'So I called François and asked him if I could have some money from the special account. But he said he couldn't believe the problem was that big, and he would come down and see for himself. But he never came and the rain started again. I didn't know what to do,' Jacques sighed.

'So what happened?' Margo asked.

'I have a friend in Amsterdam who is an art dealer. I asked him if he could sell one or two of the paintings and he came here and had a look. He said that he could take care of it in such a way that nobody would know. And nobody would have if you hadn't stuck your nose where it doesn't belong. Those copies are excellent and, of course, had to be paid for too.'

'Yes, but you must have got a small fortune for those paintings,' Margo said. 'That Holbein is worth well over a million, for a start.'

'You don't get the full price when you sell them in that way, you must know that.'

'Yes, of course.'

'I was only going to sell one, but then the bills started to come in and, little by little, they all went.'

'And the money was used only to fix the château?'

'Most of it, yes.'

'Most of it?'

'I bought a couple of horses. But I knew I would get that money back, because I was going to sell them on as soon as I had schooled them.'

'I see,' Margo said.

'It was so easy,' Jacques said, looking at her with pain in his eyes. 'I couldn't see that anyone would suffer. Nobody noticed and the house was saved. François was so pleased. He didn't even ask where I got the money. Everyone was happy. Until you had to go and show off about being such an art expert.'

Margo jumped up from the bed. She took his hands and squeezed them hard. 'Oh Jacques, I'm so sorry. I really didn't know. I just made an idle remark. I thought everyone knew those paintings were fakes. I thought they had been copied to protect against theft or something. I had no idea. If I had, I wouldn't have…' Her voice trailed away.

'I see.' Jacques pulled away from her. 'Well, whatever you meant to do, the damage is done. I have never seen François angry, but tonight, believe me, he was. Not screaming and raging, but ice cold, as cold as only a real Coligny can be. I've seen my father – I mean, the man I thought was my father – like that only once. And then I was so frightened I ran away and hid in the woods for two days. I was only seven years old, but I'll never forget it.' Jacques looked at Margo, his eyes full of pain. 'He hates me,' he said, his voice a rasping sob. 'My own brother hates me. My mother won't speak to me. And that is all your fault.'

'No,' Margo said, suddenly furious. 'That is *not* my fault. *You* did it. *You* stole the paintings, *you* tried to cover it up and now you're in the shits because of all that. If I hadn't said anything, someone else would have, sooner or later. Don't blame me for what's happening to you! You're responsible your own actions, nobody else.' Margo drew breath and looked at him, daring him to argue.

They stared at each other in silence for a long time. Jacques looked at her as if he expected her to say something.

Margo shook her head. 'I'm not going to say I'm sorry if that's what you're waiting for,' she said defiantly. 'Because I'm not.'

'But I am.' Jacques clenched his jaw. 'I'm sorry I met you,' he said bitterly. 'I'm sorry you came here and started stirring up trouble. And I'm sorry I thought you were different from the rest.'

'And I'm sorry we're standing here like this, hating each other,' Margo whispered.

'Yes, well, you should have thought of that before you tried to be clever,' Jacques muttered. Without another word, he turned on his heel and walked to the door. Poised to leave, the door open, he looked at Margo with such anger in his eyes she shivered. Then he walked out, slamming the door shut behind him.

*

The garden was shrouded in mist as Margo made her way down the gravel path. It had become hot again during the night, and even though both the windows and the shutters had been open, she had only managed to get a few hours' sleep. When the pale light of dawn brightened the sky, she had left her bed and walked outside to seek relief from the stuffiness of her room. The weir, she thought, cool water on my hot skin. The idea of sinking into the silky water was so tempting she walked faster, her sandals making a crunching sound on the gravel. Margo jumped as an owl suddenly screeched nearby and a flutter of wings swept past. She had an eerie feeling of being watched as she walked through the woods, but told herself sternly not to be silly. It's six o'clock in the morning, she said to herself, nobody is up yet. She suddenly thought of Gráinne as she reached the spot where the tent had been pitched that night, and smiled to herself as she remembered the last evening at the café. What a night, she thought, what a summer it's been. She felt a stab of sadness as she thought of Jacques, and wondered where he was, what he was doing. He'll never want to speak to me again, she thought. And Gráinne, will I ever see her again?

As Margo walked on, she could hear the gurgle of the stream and see the dark water falling over the edge of the weir. With a sigh of pleasure she stripped off her top and jeans and sank into the water, swimming slowly across to the other side and turning to float on her back. She looked up at the sky, where a weak sun was beginning to penetrate the mist. It was going to be another warm day. Margo felt a pang of regret at having to leave. She suddenly understood Jacques and his love for this beautiful, peaceful place and the devastation he must feel now. It's all my fault, she thought. If it hadn't been for me, everything would be all right. How he must hate me. Tears pricked her eyes as she swam towards the shore, and she fleetingly wondered how it would feel to just give up, to sink to the bottom of the weir and disappear, not to have to worry about anything any more, just slip away into the next world. But as her feet touched the bottom, she pushed the thoughts away and told herself not to be so morbid.

As the sun rose higher, so did Margo's spirits, and walking back toward the château, she started to feel better. I have to move on, she thought, leave this place, this family. Sort out my life and start again. But oh, Jacques… She was so absorbed in her thoughts she didn't notice the figure disappearing behind the trees, or smell, again, the strong acrid smoke of a cigarette.

19

'I'm leaving.'

'What?' Margo whispered, staring at Jacques, who had just appeared before her in the courtyard outside the kitchen like a ghost, or a shadowy figure in a dream. 'Leaving? Why?' She looked into his eyes, ready for the anger and pain that had been there last night. But his eyes were calm, determined and sad.

'I had another row with François,' Jacques said. 'I went back and tried to reason with him, but he was still so angry. He said some things. That I was a bastard, that I didn't belong here.'

'Oh God, how horrible. But I'm sure he didn't mean it.'

'He tried to take it all back when he realised what I was going to do, but I couldn't just forget it all, and anyway, it made me think. Made me realise that I can't stay and be his servant any more. I have to go.'

'What are you going to do?'

'I'm going to sell the horses and then I will look for something else, something I can do that will be just for me and nobody else.' He took her hand. 'I'm sorry,' he said softly, kissing her fingers, 'I didn't mean all the things I said last night.'

'It's all right,' Margo said, afraid to move in case she broke the spell. 'You were upset.'

'I've had time to think since then. I've spent all night thinking.' Jacques took her hands in both of his, holding them so tight it hurt.

'And?' Margo whispered.

'I'm going. As soon as I have packed the things I want to take with me.'

'But how can you leave everything just like that?' Margo stammered. 'The farm and the livestock – who is going to look after them? François?'

Jacques let go of her hands and laughed ironically. '*Ah, oui, c'est ça.* François is going to turn into a farmer. That would be an interesting sight.' He shook his head. 'No. I've spent the last few hours sorting everything out and I think it's all under control. I'm leaving the two Lithuanian boys to run the place for now. They are very good and know exactly what to do. And I'll ask the farm manger from the neighbouring property to help out with the sales. That takes care of the farm for the moment. François will have to find someone to take over eventually, of course, but things will be ticking over for a while. He'll have to look after the house and grounds himself, though. Then he'll find out what happens when the roof falls in.'

'What about the horses?'

'I'm taking them to the French equestrian team headquarters in Saumur. They're looking for good horses and will give me a fair price. I'm leaving old Sophie here, but the farm hands will make sure she's OK.'

'So everything is under control, then,' Margo said bitterly. 'You have it all sewn up beautifully and now you can just go off into the world and do your own thing, is that it?'

'More or less, yes,' Jacques said, looking puzzled. 'What's wrong with that?'

'But what about me?' Margo asked, feeling tears well up in her eyes. 'What about…us? Don't I mean anything to you? Are you so angry with me you don't want to see me again?'

'Of course not.' Jacques stepped forward and took her hands again, looking at her sadly. 'I don't know how I feel about you,' he mumbled. 'I don't know how I feel about anything at the moment. But I do know I have to get away, to start again. This is all I know right now.'

'You said you loved me,' Margo whispered.

'I meant it. Then. I was blown away by your beauty, by your charm and gentleness. And if we'd had a little more time…'

'It's my fault you're leaving,' Margo said. 'If I hadn't said anything about the paintings, this wouldn't be happening.'

'I think it was a good thing you did,' Jacques said. 'I know I lost my temper last night, and I lashed out at you, which was very unfair. But now

I realise you did me a favour. I needed something to push me out of here. So I'm really grateful to you, Marguerite. But I have to put some distance between us for now. Please tell me you understand. Tell me you'll wait.'

Margo didn't know what to say. She was afraid to speak in case she said something to frighten him away. He looked suddenly so fragile, so unsure of himself, and she realised that his confidence and belief in himself had been seriously damaged by whatever had been said between him and François. 'Go then,' she said gently. 'I wish you luck, I really do. You deserve it.'

Jacques held her hands tight again. ' 'I'm sorry,' he said. 'I didn't mean you any harm. I would never want to hurt you. We'll be together again when the time is right.'

'Maybe,' Margo said, fighting to stay calm. 'But right now you need space and time to start over.'

'Thank you,' he said, letting go of her hands. He leaned forward and touched her lips with his in a kiss as light as a butterfly. 'Thank you for understanding, Marguerite.' He stood for a moment looking at her. '*Au revoir*,' he said softly before turning around and walking down the path out of sight toward the stables.

Margo wrapped her arms tightly around herself. She felt too sad to move, or even cry. 'Come back to me,' she whispered. 'Please, come back.'

*

'He's gone,' Milady said, sitting in her bed with her untouched breakfast tray on her lap. 'Jacques has left. And it's all my fault.'

Margo was packing the last of the dresses into the biggest of the suitcases, but she stopped in her tracks and stared at Milady. 'Your fault? Why?'

'I was too angry. Too unforgiving. I wouldn't speak to him, even when he came to say goodbye.'

Margo stood up and walked to the bed. She took Milady's hand and gently stroked the back of it. 'But he must have understood how upset you were. What a shock it was to find out about the paintings. Your husband's art collection that he must have been so proud of.'

'Oh yes,' Milady said, a bitter little note in her voice. 'He was more proud of that than of his own children. He would spend so much time going to auctions and art galleries trying to find the best paintings, the best investments. And when he was here, he would go around looking at them, showing them off to his friends. He used to travel to museums all over the world when they were on loan, just to see the sign that said "on loan from the Coligny collection". He would to say that it was his legacy, something the family would be proud of when he was gone. "The Coligny collection will be famous all over the world for centuries," he used to say.' Milady sighed deeply. 'I believed him. I was proud of it too. It was my security, part of my image. But now it's gone, ruined, because of what Jacques did.'

'He did it to save the house,' Margo said, still rubbing Milady's hand. 'What good would the collection be if the house had fallen down?'

Milady looked up at Margo, her eyes clouded with sorrow. 'Yes,' she said. 'Yes, you're right. And what do a few paintings matter, after all? Why could I not have told him that just now? Maybe he wouldn't have left if...'

Margo sank down on the bed. 'He had to leave,' she said. 'He has to go away and find himself, to stand on his own and not lean on anybody. He has to grow up at last,' she ended a little nervously.

'I don't understand,' Milady said in an aggrieved voice. 'Why does he have to go away from me, his mother? He knows I love him and that I need him to be here, by my side. To run the property, to keep up the standards we have always maintained. François understands it, why doesn't Jacques?'

Margo looked at the older woman, and felt a strong urge to tell her how preposterous it was for her to expect her sons to live only for her and not have their own lives, but Milady looked so sad and tired, Margo decided against it. What would be the point? Milady was convinced that her children owed her this kind of servility and nothing Margo said would convince her otherwise. 'Jacques will come back,' she soothed. 'He won't stay away forever. And when he returns, he'll be much stronger and happier.'

'Do you really think so?'

'I know he will.' Margo got up from the bed. 'Now let's get organised,' she said in a cheery voice that belied her own mood. 'I'll finish the packing while you have your breakfast. And then I'll draw you a bath and when you're dressed we'll be ready to leave for Paris.' She walked to the wardrobe and took out the last of the clothes. 'These summer dresses…'

Milady looked up. 'Yes?'

'Do you have to bring them back to Paris? I mean, it will be autumn soon and you won't need summer clothes.'

'Pack everything,' Milady ordered, her voice resuming its imperious tone. 'I might go on a cruise in the Caribbean in January.'

'Oh really? That would be nice.'

'Yes,' Milady said, sounding happier, 'and Jacques will have returned by then. And he'll take up his old job and everything will be back to normal again.'

*

'*Au revoir*, Agnès,' Margo said as she stuck her head in the kitchen door. 'We're off to Paris in a few minutes.'

Agnès looked up from a big pile of laundry. 'Oh, Marguerite,' she said, rushing up to Margo and taking her hand in both of her own. '*Au revoir*, and thank you for all your help.' Agnès looked at Margo with affection in her brown eyes. 'I don't know how I could have managed without you,' she continued. 'Or how *they* would have managed either.' She squeezed Margo's hand and gave it a little shake. 'Look after yourself now, and be careful.'

'Careful?' Margo said with a little laugh. 'What do you mean?'

'Paris is a very dangerous place. I don't know why anyone would want to live there.'

'It's no worse than any big city,' Margo said.

'Murderers, thieves, rapists,' Agnès declared. 'The whole city is full of them. It's all those immigrants, you know. I don't know why the government lets them into our country.' She shook her head disapprovingly.

'I'll be careful,' Margo promised. 'And I hope I'll see you again very soon.'

'You'll be coming for the weekends with Madame, I suppose?'

'That's right.'

'Oh, good. The weekends in the autumn are very nice. Much calmer than the summer season. Not too many parties, just suppers with family and friends. You'll see, it will be very pleasant.'

'I'm looking forward to that.'

'I'd better start the ironing. Goodbye again,' Agnès said, 'and *bon voyage*.'

'Marguerite,' François said, walking into the kitchen, nearly bumping into Agnès as she left, 'there you are.'

'Yes, I was just saying goodbye to Agnès, and now I'm ready to leave.'

'But that was what I came in here to tell you.' François looked both annoyed and oddly deflated. 'I can't leave just yet. I have to stay here for a bit and sort some things out. I'm afraid I'm going to have to put you and my mother on the train. She won't like it, but I have no choice.'

'What's happened?'

'It's Jacques. He's gone. He's left for good.'

'I know,' Margo said dully.

'You knew? But why didn't you…?' François stopped. 'Never mind. It's not your fault, it's mine.' He looked at her for a moment, as if he was trying to decide what to say next. Then he took a deep breath. 'You might as well know,' he continued. 'Jacques stole the paintings.'

'I know that too.'

'How?'

'He told me,' Margo said, feeling suddenly annoyed as she looked at François's immaculate appearance – his smooth hair, his perfectly pressed linen jacket, white shirt and blue silk tie, the spotless beige chinos and gleaming Italian shoes. She folded her arms across her chest and kept looking at François, her annoyance turning into blazing anger. 'He told me everything.'

'Everything?' François asked, looking slightly unsure of himself.

'Yes.'

'I see.'

'You're a miserable, spoiled little wimp, do you know that?'

'What?' He flinched, looking every bit as stunned as if she had hit him in the face with a frying pan.

'You heard.' Margo dug her nails into her arms, barely feeling the pain. 'You think you own everybody, don't you? You think that you're so superior, that everyone in this world owes you a living. You think that you should be allowed to go through life without having to make an effort and you can just snap your fingers and everything is done for you. Snap,' Margo clicked her fingers in the air, 'the farm is taken care of, and snap,' she clicked her fingers again, 'the roof is fixed and all the dry rot gone, and snap—'

'Yes, yes, I get the picture,' François said, taking her hand. 'Stop doing that, you're making me nervous.'

'Oh, I'm *so* sorry, I didn't mean to frighten you.' Margo took a deep breath, trying to still her anger, but failed. 'Jesus *Christ*,' she almost shouted, 'how can you treat someone like that? Your own brother!'

'Like what?' François stammered.

'Like a bloody servant! Jacques has worked his heart out for you, don't you see that? He has been looking after this place, this lovely house, the grounds, the land, everything, knowing he wouldn't get anything in return. Simply because he loved it and thought he had a part in it. And when he found about his real father, he *still* went on working as before. And all for you.'

'For me? How do you mean?'

'Yes, you, his brother. And his mother. He felt you were still a family, that he should do all he could to make sure you could continue your lovely, privileged lifestyle as before. And by the way, you lied to me,' Margo added, wanting to heap every-thing that she had been annoyed about on top of him while she was at it. 'You told me you were in real financial trouble.'

'I know,' François muttered, looking guilty. 'You're absolutely right, of course.'

'You would have to sell—' Margo stopped. 'What?'

François pulled out a chair and sat down at the table. 'You're right,' he repeated, pushing his hand through his hair.

Her anger suddenly dissipated, Margo sank down on a chair opposite him. 'I am?'

'Of course.' François nodded. 'I'm not stupid. And I'm not the ogre you take me for. I know this whole mess is my fault. I know Jacques did what he did to save the château. I should have listened to him when he asked me to come down, I should have taken over the responsibility of the house and looked at all the quotes he sent me. But I was too caught up in…something else. It was also my mother. She needed me. Her secretary had just left suddenly and the winter season was in full swing with all the parties and so on.'

'Parties,' Margo snorted.

'I know. It sounds so trite. But it's my mother's life. Without her social circle, she has nothing. You, more than anyone, must know that.'

'I suppose,' Margo muttered.

'It's the way she was brought up, the way she has lived all her life.'

'But it seems so useless, somehow,' Margo said.

'Of course it is. Completely useless. But it makes her happy and keeps her out of my hair.'

Margo looked at him, feeling a little puzzled. 'I see. But why do you have to keep her out of your hair at all? I've been asking myself this all along. Why do you still live with your mother at your age?'

'It's not really like that,' François protested. 'She is living with *me*. The apartment belongs to me, you see, and the château too, of course. I could have told her to leave, to get her own apartment, but it didn't seem necessary. In any case, I'm planning to modernise the apartment and split it into two. I have had the plans drawn up and some builders lined up, but...'

'You haven't got around to it yet?' Margo said ironically.

'I'm going to do up the room in the attic,' François said, sounding suddenly angry. 'I'm going to turn it into a studio and sell it. That could be done very quickly. And my mother might be able to do without a secretary if she cuts down on her social obligations.'

'I see. You want to fire me.' Margo shrugged. 'Go ahead. I think it's time for me to move on, in any case. This job was just a pit stop for me, actually.'

'Oh God,' François sighed. 'I don't know what I'm saying.' He reached across the table and took Margo's hand, squeezing it hard. 'I'm sorry. Please, Marguerite, don't even think of leaving right now. We can't manage without you.'

'Rubbish,' Margo snorted, pulling her hand away. 'Of course you can. You just don't want to.

You don't want to have to deal with your mother and you want me to try to get Jacques to come back so that everything will fall back into place.'

'Do you think you could?' François asked, a glimmer of hope in his eyes.

'Get Jacques to come back? Certainly not. I don't think he should, to be honest. He must go away now, and start afresh; get a new life on his terms and nobody else's. It's the only way for him to be happy.'

'What about me?'

'I'm sorry?'

'How can I be happy?'

'You?' Margo asked, surprised at the question. 'I don't know you, François. I know nothing about your life, so how could I know what you should do with it?' She thought for a moment. 'Maybe you could start by cutting the cord?'

'The cord?' François looked mystified.

'Yes. The umbilical one, I meant.'

'Oh. That.'

'Yes,' Margo said, feeling reckless. 'Take the thumb out of your mouth, throw away the teddy bear and the security blanket and go out there and take your chances. The world is a great place, you know. Maybe not so pretty, and it might ruffle your hair and mess up your clothes.' She stopped and studied him critically. 'It might make you less…bland. Less like a mannequin in a shop window. A very elegant shop, of course,' she added to take the sting out of her words.

He looked at her without replying.

'Oh, come on, François,' Margo said, trying to suppress an urge to grab him by the shoulders and shake him. '*Do* something with your life. Tell your mother to take a jump and do something dangerous. I bet that in your whole life, you've never really misbehaved.' She suddenly laughed for no particular reason, only because it was such a relief to say exactly what was on her mind and because she had had the courage to do so. It was a heady feeling, making her almost dizzy. She looked at François defiantly, expecting him to be shocked at her outburst.

François didn't look shocked, but made a sound that was halfway between a chuckle and a laugh.

Margo stared at him in astonishment as a slow, wicked grin transformed his face. 'That, my darling Marguerite,' he said in a deep voice, so different from his normal way of speaking, 'is because you don't know me. You don't know me at all.'

He looked and sounded, at that moment, so like Jacques it took her breath away.

20

'So, Mademoiselle, are you happy to be back in Paris?'

Margo looked up from the silver teapot she was polishing. It was so unusual for Justine to initiate a conversation for no reason, and they had been cleaning silver in the kitchen for more than an hour with only the radio breaking the silence, each lost in her own thoughts. Margo looked from Justine to the kitchen window, where the rain was making dirty streaks on the glass. It had been raining for the best part of a week now, and even though the rain was welcome after the terrible drought, it was beginning to feel very dreary. Margo pondered the question for a moment while the last bars of Edith Piaf singing 'La Vie en Rose' died away. 'I don't know,' she said. 'It's certainly different. What about you? Do you prefer Paris to Tours?'

Justine shrugged. 'It's all the same to me. Life is life, wherever you are.'

'What do you mean?'

'Every place has its ups and its downs,' Justine said, looking as if she was regretting taking the initiative to talk.

'Yes, but there are some places where it's easier to deal with the downs.'

'Like the château, you mean?'

'Yes, I suppose that's what I meant. It's a beautiful place.'

'Knew you'd like it,' Justine muttered, rubbing a particularly dirty silver dish. 'Just your kind of place.'

'How do you mean?'

'Romantic,' Justine grunted, as if the word was making her choke.

'Yes, I suppose it is,' Margo said, turning her attention back to the teapot. 'I think we're running out of polish.'

'Here, there's some left in this tin,' Justine said, pushing it across the table. 'And there's another one in the pantry. We have to get this done before Madame is back. She wants the tea service this afternoon and the big silver dishes for the dinner party tomorrow.'

'We'd better speed it up, then,' Margo said, giving the teapot a last rub and putting it with the cleaned silver at the end of the table.

'How many for dinner tomorrow?' Justine asked.

'Ten. Milady has invited nine guests, and as François is gone down to the château for a few days, that makes it ten all together.'

'That's a bad business,' Justine mumbled, 'very bad indeed.'

'What is?'

'What happened at the château. Monsieur Jacques leaving like that, and Monsieur François having to take over.' Justine looked suspiciously at Margo over the edge of a big silver dish with ornate decorations on the rim. 'I have a feeling you know a lot more about it than you let on.'

'Me?' Margo looked at Justine, her eyes wide.

'Yes, you, Mademoiselle. I knew you'd cause trouble the minute you walked in that door.'

'I don't know what you mean,' Margo said. But she did. She knew exactly what Justine meant. The relatively calm life of the Coligny family had been turned upside down because of her. As the result of an innocent remark from me, Margo thought, Jacques is gone, François is left looking after the property and Milady has to spend her evenings alone or in the company of guests. It reminded her of how, once when she was a little girl, she had poked an anthill with a stick and watched the ants running around, trying desperately to put their nest back together again. She had gone back the next day to see if they had managed to build it up again and found that they had, even though their home was not as perfect as before.

'Monsieur François has changed,' Justine said glumly. 'He looks different. Younger. Happier.'

'I know,' Margo said with a little laugh. It was true, she thought. Ever since that argument in the kitchen, François had changed. The difference was very subtle, but he seemed a lot more carefree, and despite the fact that he had to both hold down his job at the ministry and keep an eye on the property in the country, he seemed more relaxed and at ease than ever before.

'But you don't,' Justine said. 'You look worse.'

'I have been feeling a little under the weather since I came back,' Margo admitted. 'Probably just the change of air or something. And of course, it's been pretty hectic around here lately.' But it was more than that, she thought, I'm so tired and listless. She slept well, but it seemed as if she couldn't get enough sleep, and she dragged herself out of bed every morning without enthusiasm for the day ahead. There had been no word from Jacques, and although Margo tried her best to put him out of her mind, she missed him so much it was like a constant pain in her chest. Maybe it's just that, she thought, maybe I'm simply lovesick. It will probably go away in time. One day I will be over him. In about fifty years or so.

'Madame is frantic,' Justine said. 'I have never seen her so restless.'

'She's just trying to get back into the swing of things,' Margo said, even though she thought that Milady's behaviour was bordering on the hysterical. Previously very selective about the invitations she accepted, she now went to every single social event she was invited to, often going from lunch to cocktail party then on to dinner, only popping back to the apartment to quickly change into a different outfit.

'She is behaving really strangely,' Justine argued. 'She even went to a pop concert last week.'

'And a cat show yesterday,' Margo said with a laugh. 'She said she was thinking of getting one, that a Siamese might match her new Chanel twin set. And then, last week, she wanted to go to Euro Disney for the afternoon, but I had to explain to her that a flyer with 'come to Euro Disney' was not a personal invitation, just junk mail. And now I have to check her post before I give it to her.'

'Madness,' Justine said, shaking her head. 'Maybe we should tell Monsieur François to talk to her doctor?'

'I don't think it's any of our business,' Margo said sternly.

'Yes, but if she's ill…' Justine looked worried and Margo suddenly realised how much the old woman cared about the Comtesse. But Margo also thought she knew the reason for Milady's behaviour – she was trying to stop herself from thinking. Her grief for her dead lover must still be very real, and this was the only way Milady could deal with it.

'I'm sure she'll calm down soon,' Margo soothed. 'And we're going down to the country at the weekend. That should help her relax for a bit.'

'If only Monsieur Jacques would at least write,' Justine sighed. 'I think Madame is very upset about the way he left.'

'Yes, maybe,' Margo muttered, bending her head over the silver sugar bowl she was cleaning. Why doesn't he write to *me*, she thought.

'*Attention*, Mademoiselle,' Justine suddenly warned. 'You've made a big mistake.'

'What?' Margo snapped her head up so fast it made her neck hurt.

'You have put scouring cream on the silver,' Justine mumbled, gently taking the bowl from Margo.

*

'Isn't it strange how life keeps changing?'

'How do you mean?' Margo asked, looking at François as he walked beside her through the park, where the autumn leaves were falling around them and heavy drops slowly fell from the bare branches of the big trees.

'When I was younger, I thought my life would always be the same,' François explained, putting up the fur collar of his suede jacket. 'I thought I would always be the way I was; work at the ministry, come here for my weekends. Jacques would be looking after everything for us, my mother would run our social life. I thought that maybe one day I would get married, but that wouldn't change things really. I would just do the same things, only with a family. But now…' He stopped.

'Now?'

'Now things have changed. And I have changed. And I want to go on changing. Give up my job and do something completely different.'

'Like what?'

'I can't tell you that yet,' François said, sounding oddly elated, 'only that it is something new and exciting and a little risky at the same time.'

'Really?' Margo asked, mystified. 'Risky? How?'

'I can't talk about it just yet. But I can tell you this – I used to be afraid of taking risks. But now I'm not afraid any more, only happy and excited.'

'Well, that's good.'

'How about you?'

'What do you mean?'

'Did you not think your life would always be the same?'

'Yes, you're right, I did,' Margo said, putting her hands into the pockets of the old waxed jacket she had found in the cloak room. 'I thought when I got married, it would be forever. That I would always live in London.' Her voice trailed away and she suddenly shivered.

François looked at her and put his arm through hers. 'Cold?'

'Not really. It's a little damp, but the air is nice.'

'It will be dark soon.'

'I know.'

'Let's continue walking for a bit.' François pulled Margo along and she fell into step beside him. They walked in companionable silence for a while, kicking the leaves, until François suddenly stopped and turned to face her. 'Marguerite?' he said softly. 'What's the matter? You seem so down. Is something troubling you?'

Margo looked away, blinking furiously. 'No, I'm all right,' she said, trying to sound calm. 'Just feeling a little…'

'What?' François put his hand under her chin and looked into her eyes. 'You look terrible,' he said. 'What's wrong?'

The gentle concern in his voice was too much for Margo. She leaned her forehead against his chest and let her tears run. 'It's nothing,' she sobbed, 'I'm just going through some…stuff, that's all.'

'Stuff? How do you mean?'

'Oh, just my life and how it's slowly sliding into the toilet,' she said bitterly. 'How I don't seem to be able to do anything right. How I've hurt a lot of people, including myself. And how I don't know what the *fuck* I'm going to do now.'

'You must be very upset,' François said with a little laugh. 'I've never heard you use that word before.'

Margo lifted her head. 'Not a word I'd use normally. But I've learned what a great word it is when you're really pissed off.'

'And right now, you are, eh, pissed off?'

'Yes.' Margo nodded. 'Mostly with myself.'

'Why?'

'Don't you see?' Margo exclaimed, thumping François in the chest so hard he had to take a step backwards. 'I've ruined everybody's life. Milady's, Jacques's, yours.'

'Not mine,' François protested. 'Not at all.'

But Margo didn't listen. 'You were perfectly happy and then I come along and just—' She stopped and looked at François. 'What?'

'I said you haven't ruined my life. In fact,' he continued, 'you have saved it.'

'What do you mean?' Margo sniffed, rummaging around in her pocket for a tissue.

'Here.' François handed her a crisp white handkerchief. 'Blow your nose and cheer up. Nobody is miserable except you.'

Margo blew her nose noisily. 'That's a great help. You know,' she continued, 'I'm one of those people who put things together and look at the instructions later, and then only if it doesn't work. The thing I was trying to make, I mean.' She handed François back the hanky, but he shook his head and she stuffed into her own pocket. 'Do you know what I'm talking about?'

'Of course,' François mumbled with the air of someone who was trying to humour a lunatic.

'I mean I'm like that with my life too. I just jump in with my two big feet and do what comes into my mind without looking at the instructions.' She drew breath.

'Life doesn't come with instructions,' François said with a soft little laugh.

'I know. Pity.' Margo sighed deeply. 'I could have done with some from time to time. But that's my problem and nobody else's, so why should I expect you to care?'

'But I do,' François said, taking Margo gently by the shoulders. 'I care enormously. I was going to say a while ago that you have been really good for us, for this family. You gave us the wake-up call we all needed. And I have to tell you that even though I have to work a lot harder now, I have never felt better. You see, my dear Marguerite, you gave me the courage to be myself and not worry about what anybody thinks. I have the most amazing life in Paris, and now I'm on the threshold of something.' He stopped and cleared his throat. 'Maybe one day I will tell you about it. And this place,' he made a big sweep with his arm to include the château, the garden and the park, 'is unique. I didn't realise how important it was to me until now, or how much I love it.'

'Even the farm?'

François laughed. 'Well, no, not the farm. I'm no good at that. I don't like mud and manure. Not my thing at all. But I know what I'm going to do with it.'

'You do? What?'

'I'm going to sell the stock and let the land to another farmer. It won't bring in the same income, but it will still pay some of the bills.'

'Jacques won't like that.'

'It's none of his concern any more, is it? He's gone.'

'I know,' Margo said, her voice bleak.

'And I'm glad he went,' François declared without noticing the look in Margo's eyes. 'It was very painful for him, I know. But it was the best thing for him in the end. It wasn't right for him to stay here.'

'Do you know where he is?' Margo asked, trying to sound casual.

François sighed, picked up a stick from the ground and flung it away into the darkness. 'No. But I'm sure he'll be in touch eventually. I know Jacques. He won't stay away from the family forever. He'll come back. But not until he's ready. So you see, Jacques will also be very happy in the end, thanks to you.'

'Thanks to me,' Margo muttered. 'Great.'

'That's right.' François put his arm around her shoulders and they continued walking, the gravel crunching under their feet.

'But what about your mother?' Margo asked. 'She's in a terrible state. I'm really worried about her, to be honest. When she's in Paris she's like a whirligig. And when she's here, well, you know what's she's like. Listless and apathetic. She just sits there with that smelly old Milou in her lap, staring into space.'

'I know. But she's grieving. Not your fault.'

'Jacques leaving didn't help,' Margo sighed.

'She'll get over it. She's very strong.'

'I suppose you're right. It just makes me sad to see her like that.'

François stopped and looked into her eyes. 'You're very kind, Marguerite. You really care about people. But maybe you shouldn't try to carry everybody's burden like this. And you shouldn't feel guilty about what happened to us. Life changes. It would have happened anyway. But,' he added, squeezing her shoulder, 'we are lucky you are here to help us. That day you walked into our lives was a lucky one indeed.'

Margo opened her mouth to protest, to tell him what a fraud she was instead of the kind, caring person he imagined, that she was a woman capable of walking out on her husband of ten years and then cheat on him with another man, who happened to be François's own brother. That she had 'forgotten' to mention the small detail of a ten-year marriage on the rocks. And, if she had the chance to sleep with Jacques again, she would. In a heartbeat. But as she looked through the gloom at François's sweet face and saw the concern in his eyes, she changed her mind. It wouldn't be fair to shatter his illusions. He already had enough to cope with – and it was quite nice, if she was honest with herself, to be cast in the role of an angel.

'I suppose I shouldn't worry about it,' she murmured.

'No. Absolutely not. Feeling better now?'

'Yes. A little.'

'Good.' François smiled and let go of her. 'I'm glad we sorted that out.' He felt in his pocket. 'You don't mind if I smoke?'

Margo stared at him as he took out a cigarette and lit it with one of his mother's gold lighters. 'I didn't know you smoked,' she said, shocked, as the acrid smell of the Gauloise stirred something at the back of her mind. Oh my God, she thought, is it really possible? François?

'Only occasionally,' François blew out a plume of smoke that hung in the still, cold air like a small cloud. 'I stole this one from a packet I found in the study. I think it belongs to Bernard. He's not supposed to smoke because of his bad chest, but he has one now and then when he thinks Agnès isn't looking. He goes out and smokes one on the sly in the woods from time to time. He's been at it all summer.'

'Bernard?' Margo said, both relieved and alarmed. 'Oh my God. So that's...' She stopped and suddenly giggled, imagining what Gráinne would say when she heard.

'What so funny?'

'Nothing.' The laughter died on Margo's lips as she decided not to tell François that Bernard was guilty of a lot more than smoking. She didn't feel like stirring up more trouble. What good would it do? Poor Agnès. How would she cope? Let's leave it for now, Margo thought. In any case, it's too cold for skinny dipping in the weir.

'Come on, let's go in,' François said with a shiver in his voice. 'It's really cold now. I asked Bernard to light a fire in my study. We'll have a hot whiskey to warm up.'

'Mmm. Lovely.'

They walked back through the gloom toward the château, where the soft light from the study lit up the darkness. As they walked up the steps to the terrace, they could see the fire flickering in the fireplace, illuminating the oak-panelled room in a warm glow.

'It looks so lovely,' Margo said. 'Like a fairytale. As if nothing bad could ever happen there.'

'And nothing will,' François said, throwing away his cigarette, making a shower of sparks in the darkness.

Margo watched as the cigarette butt glowed and died on the wet tiles of the terrace. 'I hope so,' she whispered, breathing in the last faint wisps of smoke.

21

'Sorry I'm so late,' Fiona panted as she arrived at the table in the small fish restaurant on the Left Bank. 'I couldn't get a taxi.'

Margo looked at Fiona's flustered face and wondered why she had agreed to 'do lunch' as Fiona had suggested when she had called the day before. The call had come out of the blue on a very dull Monday at the beginning of November and Margo had agreed, partly because she was feeling a little lonely and also because she felt she needed to get out of the apartment. 'My treat,' Fiona had said, sounding very eager to meet.

'Why didn't you take the Metro?' Margo asked. 'It's much more reliable.'

'The Metro?' Fiona stared at Margo as if she had just suggested a trip down the sewers.

'Yes. It's an underground railway system. Not unlike the Tube in London.'

'I know what it is,' Fiona snapped. 'But I never use it, if I can help it. It stinks of garlic and there is always a nasty kind of draught that ruins my hair and makes my eyes water.' She looked at Margo for a moment. 'How are you?' she continued. 'You look marvellous. What do you call that look? Bohemian chic?'

'It's just clothes,' Margo said. 'A skirt and jacket. Why does everything have to be a "look" with you?'

'It's Paris,' Fiona said. 'You just get into the habit of thinking that way. And you seem to be having the run of the best wardrobe in town.'

Margo shrugged. 'I get the odd hand-me-down. No big deal.'

'Lucky you,' Fiona sighed. 'I'm sorry I haven't been in touch until now, but September was such a pain with all the school stuff for Rufus and then getting back into the swing of entertaining and all that. How was your stay at the château?'

'Not bad. Rather nice, actually. Most of it, anyway. How was Scotland?'

Fiona shrugged. 'It was a nightmare in hell, if you must know. It rained most of the time, the roof leaked and the garden flooded. I got a fungus infection in my feet from wearing wellies all the time, and to cap it all, Rufus caught the chicken pox and nobody with children wanted to come near us for over a fortnight. Then it was the bloody "glorious twelfth" and we had to spend days on end on the moors shooting grouse wearing those stupid Barbours. You have no idea how glad I am to be back in Paris.'

'I can imagine.' Margo opened the menu a waiter had just handed her.

'What would you like?' Fiona asked. 'The oysters are marvellous here.'

Margo swallowed, the thought of the slimy molluscs making her feel more than a little sick. The fatigue that had started when she got back to Paris had not gone away. She didn't sleep well and often felt both exhausted and weepy. In the last week or so, she had also started to feel nauseous. At first she had thought she had eaten something that didn't agree with her, but when the nausea and fatigue didn't go away, she was beginning to suspect that it was some kind of virus and she just had to wait until it cleared up. She had felt a lot better today, though, and was hoping she was beginning to improve, but when Fiona had started talking about oysters…

'I don't like oysters,' Margo said, trying to push down the bile that was rising in her throat.

'Oh?' Fiona said from behind her menu. 'Try the scallops then. They do them in this lovely buttery sauce with cream and leeks.' She looked up as Margo suddenly rose from her chair. 'Where are you going?'

'I just have to…not feeling very well,' Margo said as she stumbled toward the ladies'. Once inside the pink tiled interior, she staggered into one of the cubicles and neatly threw up her entire breakfast into the toilet bowl. Gasping for breath, she wiped her face with some soft pink toilet paper and leaned against the wall until she felt a little better. When she had rinsed her face, brushed her hair and applied a little blusher to her pale cheeks, she went back into the restaurant and sat down on her chair again. 'Sorry,' she said to Fiona, 'I was just feeling a little…off.'

'Off?' Fiona stared at her. 'You look bloody awful.'

'A moment ago you said I looked marvellous.'

'I was just being polite. You look like shit, to be honest, darling.'

'I'm OK, really.' Margo smiled reassuringly and took a sip of water. 'It's just, well, I've been feeling a little strange lately. Some kind of virus, I think.'

'Have you seen a doctor?'

'No. But I'm sure that's not really necessary. I'm beginning to feel better.'

'*Mesdames? Vous avez choisi?*' A waiter had materialised at their table, pad and pen at the ready.

'Not yet,' Fiona snapped with a wave of her hand as if she was swatting a fly.

'But I have,' Margo said and picked up the menu. 'I'll have the marinated salmon, followed by breaded sole with asparagus and new potatoes.'

'What?' Fiona stared at Margo. 'But I thought you weren't feeling well?'

'I'm starving now,' Margo beamed. 'I told you I'm not that bad.'

'*Et vous Madame?*' the waiter said, glaring a Fiona.

'A dozen oysters,' Fiona said, her eyes still on Margo. 'And half a bottle of Chablis.'

'Just water for me,' Margo said. 'I have to go back to work, remember.'

'So,' Fiona said when the waiter had gone, 'you're suddenly feeling better?'

'Oh, yes. It's very strange, but this virus seems to hit my stomach all of a sudden like that, and when I've, eh, been sick, I'm starving again.'

'Very peculiar,' Fiona said, breaking a piece of the bread roll on her side plate. 'What other symptoms have you been having?'

'Nothing, really. I just feel very tired all the time. Kind of drained, you know?'

'Hmm,' Fiona said. 'I really think you should see a doctor. Have some blood tests. You could be suffering from mononucleosis. I had that last year and it took me ages to get better. I felt totally drained all the time. Even getting dressed was an effort.'

'Glandular fever? But I don't have swollen glands.'

'Neither did I. My doctor didn't know what was wrong until the results came back. But it could be something else. Toxoplasmosis or listeria. You get those from eating French food. All that raw meat and mouldy cheese.' Fiona shuddered. 'You must have some tests.' She picked up her handbag and, after having rummaged around in it, pulled out a card. 'Here. This is the address of my doctor. He runs this marvellous clinic for women on Avenue Montaigne. You can have everything examined, from top to toe. You can even have a mammogram and all those gynaecological tests, and heart and lungs and so on. You go in the morning and a doctor has a look at you and decides what you need to have done. They take blood and urine and do an EKG test.'

'Hold on,' Margo interrupted, 'a private clinic? I can't afford that.'

'Look Margo, you really have to do this. I'll pay. No, don't look at me like that. I insist. You look really ill, you know. You *have* to find out what's wrong with you.'

'OK, I will,' Margo said, suddenly touched by the concern in Fiona's voice. 'Thanks. You're very kind.' Margo put the card in her bag.

'No problem,' Fiona said, putting a piece of bread in her mouth. 'Alan is coming to Paris,' she said through her mouthful.

'Who?' Margo stared at her for a moment, as if the name had awakened an unpleasant and very distant memory.

'Alan. Your husband, darling, remember him?'

'Oh. Well, yes. Vaguely.'

'I'm so glad you haven't totally erased him from your mind,' Fiona said ironically. 'Even if you seem to have completely forgotten about this conference he's going to.'

'No,' Margo said very slowly. 'I remember. I booked the hotel and everything myself last spring. Seems like a hundred years ago now.'

'Marcus said that Alan is hoping to see you, and that he has decided to leave you alone until then. He said he would be willing to forgive you and start again.'

'How very big of him,' Margo said, lifting her knife and fork, ready to dig into the plate of salmon the surly waiter had just brought. 'This looks divine.'

'Glad to see your appetite is back,' Fiona said, picking at an oyster.

'I'm absolutely starving,' Margo said, putting a huge piece of salmon in her mouth.

'So you will see him, then?'

Margo looked up from her plate. 'See who?'

'Alan! You will see him when he comes to Paris? I think you should,' Fiona said without waiting for an answer. 'And maybe by then you'll feel differently. You might even…'

'Go back to him?' Margo filled in.

'Yes.' Fiona looked down at her plate and picked up one of the oysters. 'You can't possibly want to continue working like some kind of maid forever,' she said, putting an oyster into her mouth and swallowing quickly. 'I understand that you wanted to get away, that you wanted to be free and do your own thing for a while – God knows we all need to do that. But for goodness' sake, Margo, think about it! Alan is a perfectly nice man and you had a life most women would give their eye teeth for. Don't tell me you're not tempted to go back!' Fiona's huge dark eyes bored into Margo's as she looked across the table.

Margo thought for a moment. 'No,' she said. 'I'm not going to tell you that. Of course it's very tempting to go back and pick up my life again, to have the comfortable lifestyle. But I hadn't really thought about all this for a while, and that has been a great relief. I have been so caught up with the Coligny family and all their problems that my own situation hasn't really seemed very important. I suppose I've been running away from my own life and now I have to confront it. But there is one small problem.'

'What's that?'

'Alan. I can't remember what he looks like.'

Fiona stared at Margo, her mouth half open as if she had momentarily lost the power of speech.

'His face is a blank,' Margo said. 'I have tried and tried, but it won't come to me.'

Fiona took a deep breath, and suddenly she was able to speak again – very rapidly. 'You stood in front of a minister once,' she said, pointing at Margo with her fork, 'and in front of a lot of people publicly declared your love for each other. You *swore* to love Alan for better or worse, in sickness and in health until death did you part.' She put down her fork, leaned back in her chair and looked triumphantly at Margo. 'You can't deny *that*, can you?'

'I didn't know you were so hung up on marriage vows,' Margo said.

'Well, I truly believe…'

'Rubbish.'

'What?'

'Rubbish,' Margo said again. 'It's just a last, desperate attempt to get me back with what's his name. What *is* his name? I forgot.'

'Alan.' Fiona said flatly. 'And you didn't forget.'

'I'm trying my best. And I really don't want to talk about this now.'

'Why not? You have to come to a decision sometime.'

Margo put down her knife and fork with a bang. 'Listen, Fiona, leave this alone. You're like a dog with a bone. This is nobody's business but mine and Alan's. And to be honest, I have to tell you that these past few months I have come to realise that freedom is worth a lot more than comfort, or money, or' – she waved her fork vaguely – 'doing lunch in an expensive restaurant. Before I left Alan, I had a feeling that life was passing me by, that I had made all the wrong choices and was stuck with them. Do you know what I mean?'

'No,' Fiona said.

'You do know. I can tell by the look in your eyes. All married women feel like that some time or another. Stuck. We're all stuck.'

'Not me. And I think you have some nerve to talk like this, Margo, I really do. You have to make up your mind, you know. It's not fair to carry on like this.'

Margo looked at Fiona across the table as she started to reply and, suddenly, it was as if Fiona had shrunk and Margo was looking at her through the wrong end of a telescope. Fiona's mouth moved, but Margo couldn't quite make out the words, as if Fiona was speaking a language that was impossible to understand. Suddenly, as if hit by lightning, she understood what had happened to her that day when she walked out on Alan. She had stepped out of her normal life into a kind of bubble or vacuum, where a metamorphosis had taken place and she had become something other than the woman she was then. Now she was no longer Margo, but Marguerite, a free spirit, a woman who knew her own mind and had the courage to do what she wanted, not what other people thought she should. Fiona's mouth was still moving and Margo was beginning to hear her again.

'It can't go on much longer,' Fiona said.

Margo shook her head to clear her mind. 'What did you say?'

'You have to decide what to do,' Fiona said very slowly, as if she was talking to a child.

'I have,' Margo said. 'Just now, this very minute.'

*

Plaisirs d'amour,' the voice sang, '*ne durent qu'un moment. Chagrin d'amour, dure toute la vie.*'

How true, Margo thought as she listened to the old song a woman's voice was singing somewhere nearby – the pleasure of love lasts only a moment, the sorrow of love lasts your whole life. Will my sorrow last the rest of my life? Margo sighed and went back to her work. It was very late and she was in the dining room, tidying up the debris from a dinner party that had continued into the early hours of the morning. We only knew each other a few short weeks, Margo thought as she brushed the crumbs off the table, but it feels like a lifetime. And my marriage to Alan like a journey that started well but ended badly. But it was another time, another life, and now I have to keep going, keep living. She sighed and turned her attention back to her chores. It had been a nice evening; the guests seemed very close friends of Milady's and the conversation had been lively and friendly. But who *is* singing that song? She walked to the window she had opened to let out the smoke from many cigarettes and leaned out to find out where the voice was coming from. Somewhere in the street, a car radio maybe? But the street was dark and empty, tyres occasionally swishing on the wet tarmac the only sound. The song ended. What a lovely voice, Margo thought, deep, yet feminine and very sexy. Where had it come from? Somebody's CD player in the apartment next door? Funny how noise in these old buildings carries through walls and floors like this. She closed the window and pulled the heavy brocade curtains across it.

'Are you still up?' François looked in through the half-opened door of the dining room.

'Just finishing tidying up,' Margo replied.

'Good party?' François said as he strolled into the room.

'Very good,' Margo said, piling the linen napkins on a chair. 'I think your mother went to bed happy, for a change.'

'*Formidable.*' François went to the mahogany sideboard and picked up a bottle of cognac. He looked at her and held up the bottle, but Margo shook her head.

'Are you feeling all right?' François suddenly asked. 'You have been looking really tired and pale lately.'

'No, I'm not a hundred per cent,' Margo replied. 'I've been feeling quite ill, I have to tell you. I don't know what the matter is, some kind of bug, I think.'

'Have you seen a doctor?'

'No, but I'm going to if this doesn't clear up.'

'Yes, I think you should. And you shouldn't work this late if you're not feeling well.'

'You're up very late yourself,' Margo said, studying him critically, having suddenly noticed his appearance. He was dressed in navy velvet trousers and an open pink shirt, and he wore his hair longer than before, which made him look younger but less masculine, somehow.

'I've been out with some friends,' François said, swirling the cognac around in the Baccarat brandy snifter. He put his nose into the glass. 'Mmm. Lovely stuff.' He took a sip, then looked at Margo. 'I had a pretty good night. Very enjoyable.'

'Did you? That's nice.' Margo yawned. 'I'd better go to bed. I'll just put the dirty linen away.'

'I'll take care of it,' François offered. 'And I'll stack the dishwasher. You go off to bed.'

'Thanks.' Margo switched off the big floor lamp. 'Oh, by the way, did you hear that voice just now? That woman singing "Plaisirs d'Amour"?'

'No.'

'Lovely voice,' Margo said dreamily. 'Like dark, rich velvet. Don't know where it came from. Maybe someone's CD?'

'You think it was good enough to be on a CD?' François asked, looking curiously excited.

'Definitely,' Margo nodded. 'And if I could find out who the singer is, I'd buy a copy.'

'You would? That's very interesting,' François said as if to himself. 'Very interesting indeed.'

*

'*Bonjour, Madame,*' the white-coated receptionist said.

'*Bonjour,*' Margo replied. 'I have an appointment with Doctor Marchand at nine o'clock.'

The woman scanned a huge diary on the desk. '*Ah, oui, Madame…*?'

'Hunter.'

'Yes, that's right,' the receptionist nodded. 'I see your appointment here. Take a seat in the waiting room through there, and a nurse will come and get you for the blood test. You have been fasting since last night?'

'Yes.'

'And you brought a urine sample?'

'Yes,' Margo said, 'I have it right here.' She handed the receptionist the small plastic container and went across the polished parquet floor through the double doors into the very elegant waiting room and sat down on a chair upholstered in cream silk. A Mozart sonata played softly from a hi-fi system and the green silk curtains swayed in the gentle breeze from the half-open window. The hustle and bustle of Paris seemed so far away here in this genteel environment, and it was difficult to imagine that this place had anything at all to do with illness. Margo took a copy of *Vogue* from the pile of magazines on the glass table and idly leafed through it, feeling more than a little apprehensive. She was nearly regretting having made the appointment, and wouldn't be there if she hadn't been feeling so ill. The nausea and fatigue hadn't improved in the two weeks since she had seen Fiona and, out of a feeling of desperation, Margo had finally taken the card out of her handbag and rung the clinic. They said there had been a cancellation and she could come the following day. Margo tried to stop herself feeling nervous as she flicked through the pages of the magazine and stared absentmindedly at the latest fashions. *This season's look is ladylike*, she read, *tweed mixed with silk, twin sets and pearls*. Margo flicked through the pages with pictures of stick-thin models dressed in tweedy rags with pearls dripping down their fronts, her mind drifting. She was worried about the tests and what they might reveal. Maybe I have something really serious, she thought, something even fatal? No, of course not, I don't feel that bad. Oh God, what if it's something I picked up from Jacques! How stupid I was, I should have...oh no, what if... Margo swallowed, panic rising in her chest. She jumped and dropped the magazine as the door opened and a nurse stuck her head in.

'Madame Hunter?'

'Yes?'

'It's time for your blood test.'

*

Four hours, two blood tests, a mammogram, a bone scan and several examinations by various doctors later, Margo was sitting on a cold examining table dressed in a hospital gown made of paper waiting for the final verdict. The doctor came through the curtain, a bland expression on his face.

'Well, Madame, that's it. We're finished.'

'Oh, good,' Margo said, desperately trying to clasp the gown together at the back. 'So,' she started, 'what have you…I mean, can you tell me…?'

'Why don't you get dressed and we'll talk in my office,' the doctor suggested.

'No!' Margo exclaimed and grabbed the front of his white coat, forgetting the gown. 'Tell me now. I have to know. It's bad, isn't it?'

The doctor lifted her hands gently from his coat and stepped back. 'Now, calm down, *chère Madame*, what I have to tell you is serious, yes, but not in any way—'

'Is it Aids?' Margo whispered. 'Don't try to hide anything from me, I have to know the truth.'

The doctor folded his arms across his chest and looked levelly at Margo. 'But my dear girl,' he said with a little smile, 'you must know what it is. Most women would.'

'Cancer,' Margo whispered. 'Oh God, I knew it.' She put a hand on her lower abdomen. 'There is a tumour here, isn't there?' She looked up at the doctor with huge tearful eyes.

The doctor laughed. 'Don't be melodramatic. The news is very good and I think you will be delighted when I tell you.'

'Oh. It's benign,' Margo sighed, feeling limp with relief.

'It's a baby,' the doctor beamed.

'I'm sorry?' Margo stared at him. Was she hearing right? Had he just said… 'A b-baby?' she stammered. 'But that can't be!'

'But it is,' the doctor said, putting his hand on her shoulder. 'Congratulations, Madame Hunter, you're pregnant.'

22

Margo didn't know how she got back, couldn't even remember going up in the lift. She just suddenly seemed to have been catapulted into her small attic room and was sitting on her bed, her hand on her stomach. A baby, she thought. There is a baby in there. I can't believe it. I must be dreaming and I'll wake up and it will be gone. But she knew it was true. It all fell into place – the nausea, the fatigue and the mood swings. Pregnant! She lay back on her bed, staring up at the cracks in the ceiling, trying to take it all in.

Margo had felt a little embarrassed about seeming so stupid when talking to the doctor. But then she had explained that she had thought it was impossible for her to ever get pregnant, that she had been told there would never be the slightest chance. The doctor had shaken his head. 'I don't know who told you this,' he said. 'There is nothing at all wrong with you. And I have to say that, on the contrary, you are very fertile and one of those women who will have no problems conceiving in years to come. In fact,' he added with a little smile, 'I would say that you will have to be very careful about birth control in the future.' He went on to tell her she was at least ten weeks pregnant, if not more – it was difficult to tell, as her periods were so irregular. An ultrasound scan in a few weeks would establish the exact date of birth. But she knew, of course she knew. Jacques, she thought. Oh, Jacques. What would he say? How would he react when she told him? I don't care, she thought. It's my baby. It became clear to her that Alan had lied to her all these years and that it must be his fault they hadn't been able to conceive a child. But it didn't make her angry because she knew now that she didn't owe him anything any more and she was finally free of all obligations toward him. 'I'm having a baby,' she said to herself again. 'It's mine, all mine, to care for and love and watch grow up. I'll never be alone again.' She suddenly laughed, a happy, joyous laugh, feeling at the same time that she had been given a wonderful gift, and that life would never be the same again.

*

'Milady?'

'Yes, Marguerite?' Milady looked up from the book she was reading on the chaise longue in her bedroom.

'I'm sorry to disturb you.'

'Is this important? I was hoping to have a little siesta after lunch so I'm rested before this evening. You know I have a cocktail and then a dinner.'

'Yes, I know,' Margo said, walking into the room, 'but I have to speak to you.'

Milady sighed, took off her glasses and put down her book. 'All right, then, if it's not too long winded.'

'No, I'll try to make it brief.' Margo stood in front of her, trying to think of how to break the news.

'Sit down,' Milady ordered, indicating an embroidered stool beside her. 'You're making me nervous standing there twisting your hands.'

'All right.' Margo sank down on the stool. 'There is a bit of a problem I want to discuss with you.'

Milady's' head shot up. 'Are you trying to tell me you're leaving?'

'No, it's not that.' Margo twisted her hands in her lap.

'Good. That would be terrible. The autumn season is very busy and I can't manage without you for even a minute.'

'I know.'

'So what is it then? I thought you were going to hand in your notice, but as you're not, I can't think of anything else that would cause a problem.'

'I'm pregnant,' Margo blurted out.

'You're what?' Milady exclaimed in shrill voice. 'What did you say?'

'I didn't know,' Margo stammered. 'I thought I couldn't…but it seems that…well, that I am….'

'Pregnant?'

'That's right.'

Milady sat up fully and swung her legs over the edge of the chaise longue. 'And now you're going back to your husband?'

'No.'

'No? But I don't understand.'

'It's not his baby.'

'Oh.' Milady stared silently at Margo. 'Do you know who the father is?'

'Of course I know,' Margo snapped. 'What do you take me for?'

'Please,' Milady soothed. 'I don't think anything at all. I just assume that you have had an affair and now you are pregnant as a result. So you must tell the man who is the real father about the baby. Come and sit here next to me,' Milady said, patting the chaise longue. 'That stool is very hard.'

Margo got up from the stool and sat down beside Milady.

'You must tell him,' Milady said.

Margo sighed. 'I can't.'

'But you have to,' Milady exclaimed passionately. She looked at Margo with sad eyes. 'You must not make the mistake I made. You must tell him. You must!'

'But I don't know where he is.'

'Where who is?'

'Jacques,' Margo said before she could stop herself.

Milady gasped and stared in shock at Margo. 'Jacques?' She said. 'Jacques is the father of your baby?'

'Yes, Milady,' Margo mumbled.

There was silence in the room while Milady tried to come to terms with this latest revelation. She put her hand on Margo's and squeezed it. They looked at each other and, in that moment, all they had learned about each other that summer, their sadness and disappointments, their deepest feelings, seemed to pass wordlessly between them.

'So, how do you feel about this?' Milady finally asked softly.

'I don't know,' Margo said. 'I'm still trying to get used to it.'

'Of course.'

'It's wonderful, though, isn't it?' Margo said without thinking.

Milady nodded. 'It's a miracle.'

*

'Hello?' Margo pressed the receiver closer to her ear. 'I can't hear you. The line is very bad.'

'Maggie?' she heard a familiar voice say through the crackling. 'Finally! I've tried to phone your mobile several times, but...' More crackling.

'Gráinne? Is that you? I can hardly hear you. I've lost my mobile. Where are you?'

'On the ferry,' Gráinne was shouting. 'Nearly out of range...on my way to...'

'Where?' Margo shouted. 'You're on the way to where?'

'Paris!'

'That's great! When are you—' But the line went dead. Margo smiled and hung up. She had wanted to tell Gráinne her news. But now she was coming here. She would know soon. Margo looked at herself in the hall mirror and put a hand on her stomach. 'Gráinne is coming,' she said, turning sideways to look at her figure. There was a tiny bump under her sweater, but except to the very discerning eye, she didn't really look pregnant yet. 'We'll carry on as normal,' Milady had said. 'What else is there to do? I have tried to get in touch with Jacques, but I haven't really had much luck. François is putting all his resources at the ministry on the case, and I'm sure we'll have word soon. I'm not going to tell anyone about this until we get to Jacques, except for François, of course. What do you think?'

Margo had agreed. 'I want to keep going as before, until…' Until when, she didn't quite know. She was still trying to get used to it all, to the idea of the baby and motherhood. She knew she would have to make arrangements for the birth, to decide what to do with the rest of her life, but right now, she just wanted life to continue without any more excitements. Milady had insisted she move down to the apartment, into a guest room with a big bathroom across the corridor all to herself. Reluctant to give up her independence, Margo had agreed only because the room was near the hall and the front door, and she could come and go as she pleased. But she missed the little attic room with the old-fashioned wallpaper, the old mahogany bed, the faded rug, the alcove where she would sit and look out the window at the rooftops and the

Eiffel Tower. She even missed the sparrows on her windowsill. She missed her independence too, and had come to think of that little room as her home. She sometimes went up there and sat on the bed, looking out the window, simply enjoying being alone. Justine hadn't approved of the new arrangement and had grunted under her breath about 'staff getting ideas above their station'.

'The charity lunch at the George V,' Milady said, coming through the front door, 'is on the fifteenth of November.' She took off her fur-trimmed cashmere coat and hung it up on the hall stand.

'The day after tomorrow?' Margo said.

'Yes, that's right.' Milady looked into the mirror, smoothed her hair into place and straightened the bow on her blue silk shirt. 'You had not forgotten?'

'No, of course not. And the list of guests is on your desk in the study. Almost everybody accepted.'

'Good. We're hoping to raise a lot of money for the orphanage in Bosnia. Last year we made over eighty thousand euros. I hope it will be as successful this year.' She handed her gloves and scarf to Margo.

'I'm sure it will be,' Margo said and put the items away.

'And you think you'd be well enough to attend?'

'Of course. It won't be too tiring.'

'No. All you have to do is take care of the donations and then bring the cheques and money to the bank and lodge them in the special account.'

'I'm sure I can handle that,' Margo assured her. 'By the way,' she added as an afterthought, 'I don't seem to be able to find my mobile phone. You haven't seen it anywhere, have you?'

Milady shook her head. 'No.' She looked sternly at Margo. 'But never mind the phone. What are you doing here? Aren't you supposed to be having your nap?'

'I'm not tired.'

'But you have to lie down. You have to make sure you get some rest in the middle of the day. Have you had lunch?'

'Yes, I ate with Justine earlier.'

'Did you remember to drink your milk and take all your vitamins?'

'Yes, don't worry.' Margo sighed. Ever since she had announced her pregnancy, Milady had been more clucky than a mother hen and become obsessive with Margo's health and well-being. She was feeling much better now, the nausea and fatigue nearly gone, and the ultrasound scan had revealed that the baby would be born around the end of April. When she had shown her the fuzzy picture of the baby in her womb, Milady had looked at it with great interest. 'Is it...could they see if it's a girl?' she had asked and been very disappointed when Margo had said that it was too early to see that yet.

'You go right back to your room and lie down,' Milady ordered.

'All right,' Margo said meekly and walked down the corridor into her room with Milady at her heels. When she was lying on the big bed, Milady put a rug over her legs and propped another lace-trimmed pillow under her head.

'There,' she said. 'Try to sleep now.'

But Margo had never felt more wide awake. Milady sitting there staring at her as if she was some kind of scientific experiment was unnerving, to say the least. 'Has François had any luck yet?' she asked.

'With what, my dear?'

'With finding Jacques.'

'Oh.' Milady shrugged. 'I don't know. He's so busy these days, I don't want to bother him.'

An alarm bell went off somewhere in Margo's head. 'You did ask him, didn't you?' she said, trying to appear calm.

'Ask him what?' Milady looked at Margo absentmindedly.

'To find Jacques.'

Milady patted Margo's leg. 'But my dear girl, we don't want Jacques right now. We don't need him hanging around making trouble. You'll see,' she said dreamily. 'We're going to be so happy. Just you, me, François and the baby.'

*

The lunch at the George V went off without a hitch. The fashion show had been spectacular, the speeches interesting and the short film about the orphanage so moving that many of the elegant guests had handed Margo cheques with very generous donations. Margo looked at the top table, where Milady was still entertaining the VIPs, and wondered if she could slip away quietly. She was feeling quite tired and the big room was very stuffy. Coffee had just been served and the guests were chatting amicably, but some of the ladies were already getting ready to leave. Margo straightened her back and put her hand on her stomach, something she seemed to do without thinking lately, as if to make sure it was true, and to check that the baby was growing bigger each day. She was looking forward to looking really pregnant, to putting on some of the lovely maternity wear Milady had bought for her, to show the world she was, at last, becoming a mother. But it was time to go. Margo gathered the cheques and put them into her bag. She would take them to the bank on the way home. She rose slowly, trying not to attract attention, but stepping back from the table, she bumped into someone.

'Oh, sorry.'

'Margo!' It was Fiona, reeking of wine and perfume, wearing a tweed suit, rows of heavy gold chains around her neck and a fur coat thrown over her shoulders. 'Hello, darling. Great lunch, don't you think? Thought I might bump into you here, as your boss is one of the organisers. You look...' She stopped as her eyes travelled down Margo's body. 'Is that...oh my God,' she whispered, and Margo felt as if her small bump had suddenly grown to the size of Mount Everest.

'What's the matter?'

Fiona's eyes bulged. 'You're...oh shit. You're not, are you?'

'What?' Margo asked airily.

'Pregnant,' Fiona hissed in her ear.

'That's right,' Margo whispered back. 'I am.'

Fiona put her hand over her mouth as if to stop herself laughing out loud. 'That's...oh God, that is *so* fabulous.'

'It is?'

'Yes.' Fiona laughed again. 'I can't wait to see his face when I tell him.'

'Tell who?' Margo asked, mystified.

'The big shit, of course. Won't he be surprised! God, this is priceless.' Her eyes sparkling, Fiona took Margo by the shoulders. 'You're off the hook, don't you see? And so am I. What a relief. What a great, big shagging block off my shoulders.'

'Off the hook? What do you mean?' Margo asked, bewildered both by Fiona's behaviour and her words.

But Fiona had turned around and was already walking toward the exit. Margo watched, bemused, as Fiona hurried away, and she slowly realised what had been going on. Her stomach tightened into a nervous knot as she knew she couldn't put it off any longer. The time had come to confront Alan.

*

'*Memories are made of this...*' Dean Martin sang from the loudspeaker. Poor Dean, Margo thought on her way to the tenth floor of the Meridian

Hotel, how sad to end up as elevator music. And why does he have to sing about memories right now? The lift came smoothly to a stop and the doors slid open. Margo stepped out onto the thick carpet and padded silently down the wide corridor, her knees shaking and her armpits clammy with cold sweat. What will he say when he sees me? What will he do when he finds out? The old feeling of dread came back like a recurring nightmare, and she wanted to turn around, walk back down the corridor, press the button and step into the lift again, run through the lobby, down the street and back to the apartment. But she knew she had no choice. She had to face him. Here's the door now, she thought, her heart beating so loudly in her chest she thought the sound would echo down the silent corridor. She lifted her hand to knock, but before her knuckles made contact with the door, it flew open and Alan's eyes met hers. They stared at each other for what seemed like an eternity. He looks the same, she thought, just as tall and imposing and slightly pompous, and those pale blue eyes. He looked calm and composed, but Margo could see the corner of his left eye twitch slightly as it did when he was tense or unsure of himself. She noticed his shirt was as crisp as always and wondered idly who did his laundry now.

Alan finally spoke. 'Margo,' he said pleasantly, as if she was someone he barely knew. 'There you are. Come in.'

She walked in and Alan closed the door behind her, making her feel suddenly trapped.

She looked at the elegant surroundings. 'Lovely room.'

'It's a suite,' Alan said, walking toward two easy chairs by the window. 'Sit down.'

'Lovely suite,' Margo said, sinking down among the cushions. 'I bet you can see the whole city from up here.'

'Most of it, yes.' Alan sat in the chair opposite and crossed his legs, his Gucci loafers gleaming in the late afternoon sun. 'Don't you want to take off your coat?'

'No, I'm fine. The curtains are really nice. Not like hotel curtains at all.'

'Yes, that's true,' he said in a disinterested voice while studying her so intently she squirmed. 'You cut your hair.'

'Yes,' Margo said brightly, touching her curls. 'Do you like it?'

'No. But I'm sure you didn't come here to show me your new hairdo. Or to admire the curtains,' he added dryly.

'No.' Suddenly hot, she started to unbutton her coat.

'I was surprised to hear your voice on the phone.'

'You were?'

'Yes. And pleased, of course. I've been...' He paused and cleared his throat. 'It's been a difficult few months.'

'Yes.'

'For me, I mean.'

'I suppose,' Margo said flatly. Oh God, she thought, why do I feel guilty? Why does he always manage to make me feel as if I'm at fault? But the guilt turned to anger as he sat there with a long-suffering expression on his face, as if he was some kind of martyr who was trying to come to terms with a huge pain inflicted by Margo. 'Oh, Alan,' she said in a low voice, 'have you no idea? No idea at all?'

'How do you mean?'

'Why it happened, I mean, why I left you like that?' Suddenly, the words poured out of her like an unstoppable stream. 'I couldn't take it any more,' she said. 'I couldn't stand being called a moron and a stupid bitch and all the other things you said I was. I thought I would go mad if I stayed with you. Maybe I should have left a long time ago, when you started to change.'

'Change?' Alan asked, looking both hurt and puzzled. 'What do you mean? I didn't change, it was you who—'

'No!' Margo almost shouted. 'It wasn't me! *You* did! You became sneary and superior, you started to lose your temper when you were stressed, you picked on me every time something went wrong. And I took it, I took the blame and the abuse.'

'Abuse?' Alan snorted. 'I think you exaggerate just a little, darling.'

'It *was* abuse,' Margo whispered. 'Verbal abuse. You made me feel as if I was worth nothing.'

'Hold on,' Alan snapped. 'Calm down. You make me sound like a real heel.' He paused and looked at her with that superior little smile he used when he wanted to intimidate her. 'OK, so I flew off the handle. I got a little annoyed. But it was a hot day and my back was really beginning to hurt. I was nervous about the conference and the speech, you must have known that. I know I gave you a hard time, but I think you overreacted there, you know. Why didn't you wait for me to calm down? I would have, you know I would.'

'Yes. I suppose you would have. Until the next time.'

'What do you mean?' he asked, no longer pretending to be aloof. 'How could you do what you did, Margo? How could you just walk away like that?' He stopped. 'Can you not try to imagine what I went through? I thought something terrible had happened to you. I thought you were dead, until Fiona told me you had turned up at her place. Can you not understand how frightened I was?'

'Yes,' Margo replied. 'It must have been very worrying. And I'm sorry I put you through that, I really am. But I felt I had no choice, I felt I had to go, to save myself from...'

'From what?' Alan demanded.

'From dying,' Margo said in a small voice.

'Oh, Christ, that's so over the top,' Alan said. 'Like pop psychology from some kind of soap opera.'

'That's how I felt.'

'OK,' Alan soothed, humouring her now. 'So you needed a break. Space, I think you told Fiona.'

'Yes, I did.'

'Right. And now? What have you come here to tell me, exactly? Are you ready to come back? Is that it?'

'No.'

'In that case, I have to tell you—' He stopped, looking startled. 'What?'

'I said, no,' Margo said calmly. 'I'm not going back to you, Alan.'

'What do you mean?' Alan sighed, looking impatient. 'I see. You're still angry, aren't you? Oh, OK, I know I've been a little bad tempered, and I know it must have hurt you. And...' He paused. 'All right, I'm sorry.'

Margo didn't reply. She looked at him and wondered how it was possible that she could have loved him once.

'For God's sake, Margo!' Alan said, sounding exasperated. 'You can't be serious about leaving for good. Think of all we have, the practice, the house, our life together. You can't seriously mean that you're going to give it all up, just because you can't put up with my temper?'

'No,' Margo said, 'that's not the reason.'

'What?'

'I said, that's not the reason. I mean, the whole story. Your behaviour is one of the reasons, but there's a lot more.'

'More?' he said, sounding irritated. 'How do you mean? What else do you think you have to complain about?'

'You lied to me,' Margo said.

'I lied to you? About what, for God's sake?'

'You said I couldn't get pregnant, remember? You said it was my fault we couldn't have a child.'

'Yes? So?' The confusion in Alan's eyes was suddenly mixed with a growing fear.

'Well,' Margo said. 'I have just found out I can.'

'Found out you can what?' Alan whispered, although Margo could tell he knew the answer. 'You mean...'

'Yes, that's right,' Margo said as she saw the expression in his eyes. 'I'm pregnant.'

'Oh my God.'

'Amazing, isn't it? Such a miracle, don't you think?'

Alan didn't reply. He seemed to have suddenly discovered that his shoes were very interesting. They were both quiet for a while.

Alan looked at Margo again. 'You've had an affair? Who was it? Some French creep?'

'It's none of your business,' Margo said. 'Nothing to do with you.'

'Nothing to do with me? My wife has an affair and it has nothing to do with me? And here you are pregnant, for God's sake.'

'I wouldn't be if you hadn't lied,' Margo said, wondering how she was managing to stay so calm. 'If I had known...' She stopped. 'Oh God, if you hadn't lied to me, how different everything would be, can't you see that? If I had known that there was something wrong with you, we could have...'

'How do you know it was my fault?' Alan demanded. 'How do you know there wasn't something wrong with *you*, something that somehow...'

'Got better?' Margo lifted one eyebrow. 'Do you seriously expect me to believe that?'

'No,' Alan mumbled.

'And why are you suddenly so shocked to find out I've been with someone else, when you've had some kind of fling with Fiona?'

'What? Fiona? How did you…has she…'

'She hasn't said a word,' Margo said. 'It was just a hunch, really. She has been behaving so strangely. And she has been desperate to get us back together again. It seemed like a matter of life and death to her. So I put one and two together.'

'One and two?'

'One, you had an affair,' Margo stated. 'Two, you have been threatening to tell Marcus about it if she didn't manage to get me to go back to you. Am I right? Yes, I see that I am. You did. When did you have that little fling then?'

'It was a long time ago,' Alan said impatiently, as if she was fussing over nothing. 'Just a few times, really.'

'Oh.'

'It was around the time when we were trying to have a child,' Alan continued. 'When I found out…I was upset. I couldn't face you. I needed someone who didn't judge me, who I didn't really care much about. Just straight sex, no strings, you know what I mean?' He looked at her as if he was willing her to understand, to agree that it had been very important for him to forget his troubles by sleeping around.

'I see.' Margo was quiet again. As she was trying to digest what he had just told her, she felt suddenly very sad. 'You were so sweet at that time,' she whispered, 'so caring and gentle. I loved you more than any other time then, because I thought you were so kind. You seemed to really understand what I was going through. And of course you did,' she added bitterly. 'You knew what it felt like to know you would never have a child of your own.'

Margo rose from her chair with all the dignity she could muster. 'I have to go,' she said. 'I can't stay here with you any longer.'

'But I'm...' Alan protested. 'I want to tell you... we have to...'

'No,' Margo said, buttoning up her coat and walking to the door. 'There's nothing more to say. Except...'

'What?' Alan asked, his voice a hoarse whisper.

'Goodbye,' Margo said softly and walked out.

23

Dean Martin was still singing in the lift, but Margo didn't hear him this time. She rode down to the ground floor, feeling utterly exhausted, so exhausted she had to sit down in one of the leather chairs by the reception desk and catch her breath.

'Are you feeling all right, Madame?' the young female receptionist asked, looking at Margo's pale face with concern. 'Can I get you a glass of water, perhaps?'

'Yes, thank you, that would be lovely.'

Margo gratefully sipped the water when it arrived, trying to gather enough strength to get going again. She was surprised at how deeply sad she felt, as if someone had died. But it wasn't the death of a person, only the end of a marriage, she thought. The end of Alan and Margo, a couple, a life; a part of her gone forever. She didn't want to think about the way they had parted, didn't feel triumphant about having exposed his lies and his affair with Fiona. And although she was now vindicated, Alan's last words of apology still ringing in her ears, she didn't have a sense of victory, only a certain tired satisfaction. And pity for Alan. How miserable, she thought, to have lived a lie all these years.

'Are you feeling better, Madame?' the receptionist asked, now looking as if Margo's presence was beginning to annoy her. 'Maybe I could call you a taxi?'

I'd better go, Margo thought, they probably don't want sickly looking pregnant women lowering the tone of their establishment. 'Yes please,' she said. 'Get me a taxi.' She had suddenly remembered she had promised to meet Gráinne for a drink in her hotel around seven. Now I have to tell *her* about this, Margo thought as she walked into the busy street. What on earth is she going to say?

*

Gráinne stared at Margo. 'Well, I'll be fucked,' she said. 'Sorry, didn't mean to sound rough, but you really took me by surprise.' They were sitting in a brasserie near Gráinne's hotel and Margo had just broken the news. 'Jesus, Mary and Joseph,' Gráinne continued, 'you really know how to startle a girl.'

'I was pretty startled myself when I found out,' Margo said with a little smile.

'I bet you were. But being pregnant is one thing. What caused it is even freakier.'

'Freaky? What do you mean?'

'Well, you and what's-his-name. I never thought you would want to do it with someone like that. Not that he isn't great looking,' Gráinne added when she saw the expression in Margo's eyes, 'but he's such a…' She stopped. 'OK, I won't go into it. You did it and here you are. Pregnant.' Gráinne looked at Margo disapprovingly. 'What were you thinking? You must have known about babies and how they're made and all that.'

'But you see, I thought I couldn't get pregnant. My husband and I had tried for years and then he told me that…well, that I would never be able to have a baby. He made me think it was because there was something wrong with *me*, when all the time…'

'He was shooting blanks?' Gráinne shook her head in disgust. 'What a fucking creep. And look at the trouble it caused. But he probably never thought you would try it with someone else.'

'No, I suppose not.'

'Have you told him?'

'Alan? Yes, I—'

'Not him, you dope, Jacques. Have you told him he's going to be a daddy? I'd love to have been a fly on the wall when you broke that particular piece of news.'

'I haven't told him yet,' Margo said bleakly. 'I don't know where he is.'

'What?' Gráinne stared incredulously at Margo. 'He's done a bunk?'

'No, not really. He had to leave the château after, well, a family row. Long before I knew about…' Margo gestured at her stomach. 'And nobody seems to know where he is. Not that they've been trying very hard,' she added.

'Why wouldn't they? Haven't you told them yet?'

'Well, yes. I told Milady.'

'Bet that made her sit up and take notice.'

'She was really shocked at first,' Margo said. 'But then, when she was used to the idea, she seemed delighted. A bit too delighted, actually.'

'How do you mean?'

'She has become obsessed with me and the baby. And she seems to think I'm going to live with her forever or something. It's getting really scary, to tell you the truth. She has bought piles of baby clothes from Baby Dior, and only in pink. She says she knows it's going to be a girl and that we'll call her Josephine after her.'

'Hmm,' Gráinne said, looking thoughtful. 'I've seen that a lot. An older mare getting possessive about the foal of a younger mare. And if it's a filly…'

'What are you going on about now?' Margo laughed. 'I'm not a horse. Oh, shut up. Let's talk about something else. Let's talk about you.'

'Me? But I'm not half as interesting.'

'Of course you are. I want to know what you're doing in Paris.'

'OK, just a minute. I just wanted to say one more thing. About him. The daddy to be. I know—'

'No, not another word,' Margo interrupted. 'I don't want to hear what you think of him.'

'But I—'

'No,' Margo said. 'Stop it or I'm leaving.'

'OK, keep your hair on. What was it you wanted to know about me?'

'I want to know,' Margo said, leaning forward, staring at Gráinne, 'what you are doing here and how come you look so well and so happy.'

'I look well?' Gráinne smiled. 'Really?'

'Yes. You've lost weight and your hair is a bit longer and you look...' Margo studied Gráinne for a while. 'Softer,' she ended. 'Prettier. Happier.'

Gráinne blushed. 'I stopped smoking,' she said. 'And, well, it's Seamus.'

'Oooh,' Margo said, nodding. 'I see. You're in love.'

Gráinne blushed even more, until her face was crimson. 'Yeah, well, you know.' She cleared her throat. 'And I'm here in Paris with him, you see. We were at this international show jumping competition in England. I was there as groom and he was the vet to the Irish team. And when the competition was over, he said why not jump on the ferry and go to Paris for a few days? He wanted to see the sights and stay in a nice hotel and he asked me.' Gráinne looked into her coffee cup.

'Aha, a romantic weekend. And where is this wonderful man now? I'd love to meet him.'

'He went to see some war museum,' Gráinne said. 'Invalids, or something.'

'Les Invalides,' Margo said. 'That's a great museum. Very interesting.'

'Yeah, but I'm not really into that sort of thing, so I told him I wanted to see you and he said of course, off you go and see you later. You see, that's what's so great about Seamus.'

'What is?'

'He lets me do my own thing. He actually pushes me to go off and do things on my own. He doesn't like women who are doormats, he says, and he doesn't think I should be his slave.'

'Seems like a great guy,' Margo said.

'Oh yes, he is.' Gráinne looked at her watch. 'He should be back soon. Do you want to go back to the hotel and wait for him? I know you'll like him.'

'I'm sorry, I have to go,' Margo said, getting up. 'I promised Milady I would be back for early supper.'

'So you're leaving now?'

'Yes. But maybe we can get together before you go back?'

'OK. But if you're leaving anyway, I'm going to tell you what I was about to a while ago.'

'What?' Margo sighed. 'Go on then, tell me. Tell me he's a bastard...'

'No, that wasn't it,' Gráinne protested. 'Not that I wouldn't say that too.'

'Yes, go on then,' Margo urged, poised to walk out. 'Spit it out.'

'I know where he is,' Gráinne said. 'I spoke to him two days ago.'

*

'Good evening.'

'Oh, good evening, François,' Margo replied, putting down the newly filled crystal jug on the kitchen table. 'Dinner is nearly ready. I brought the chicken casserole into the dining room and the potatoes too. I just have to bring in the water, and then we're ready to eat. Could you tell Milady dinner is served?'

'No, I can't,' François said, a hint of laughter in his voice.

'Why?' Margo turned around, expecting to see him dressed in the more casual clothes he had begun to change into when he came home from the ministry, but tonight he was still in a dark suit, crisp white shirt and discreet silk tie, his hair neatly brushed.

'Because my mother won't be home in time for dinner. She just called and said she was stuck in a meeting with the Red Cross. They're doing a report on that lunch the other day. She asked me to keep you company tonight.' He took the jug. 'I'll bring this in. Is there anything else?'

'No, just the bread. I'll take that.'

'Fine. Where's Justine?'

'She has the evening off. She made the casserole before she left. But if there's just the two of us, we can eat in the kitchen,' Margo suggested.

'The dining room is much nicer,' François said.

'Of course.' Margo followed him down the corridor.

In the dining room, François lifted the lid of the casserole dish. 'This smells nice.'

'Mmm, yes,' Margo said, sitting down at the round mahogany table. 'Justine is a very good cook.'

François took a bottle of red wine from the rack on the sideboard. 'How are you feeling these days?' he asked, pulling the cork out of the bottle.

'I'm feeling fine. Amazingly well, actually.'

'Good. And you're sleeping well?' François sniffed the cork and poured a small amount of wine into a glass.

'Like the proverbial log. Do you want me to serve you some chicken?'

'Yes please. I'm glad you're feeling so well.' He stuck his nose into the glass, then twirled it around and examined the ruby red liquid critically before taking a mouthful and swirling it around in his mouth.

'Is it all right?' Margo asked, putting a plate of food at his place.

'Excellent.' François poured more wine into the glass and, bringing glass and bottle with him, sat down at the table with a satisfied look. He held out the bottle toward Margo. 'Would you like a glass?'

'I shouldn't really,' Margo said, helping herself to some chicken.

'Because of the baby?' François looked at her with a little smile.

'Oh. She told you.' Margo blushed slightly.

François put down the bottle and put his hand over one of hers and gave it a little squeeze. 'Congratulations,' he said gently. 'I'm really very pleased.'

'Thank you. I'm glad you know.'

'Well, it would be a little difficult to keep it a secret for much longer.' He held up the bottle again. 'How about a little wine to celebrate? Just a small glass?'

'I've been told I have to stay off any alcohol.'

François raised an eyebrow. 'Oh? By whom? My mother?'

'Well, yes. And I'm sure she's right. Drinking would not be good for the baby.'

'Half a glass of this really superb wine couldn't do you or him any harm, I'm sure.'

'Or her,' Margo said with a little smile. 'All right, half a glass, then.'

'That's the spirit,' François said and poured the required amount into Margo's glass.

Margo sipped the wine, looking at him thoughtfully. He seemed ill at ease tonight, or was he nervous? 'This is indeed very good.'

'Should be. A *grand cru classé* of the very best Bordeaux. We might as well enjoy it, as my mother would never allow me to open such a bottle in the middle of the week.' He drank from his glass with the air of someone enjoying some extremely forbidden fruit. 'Ah, that is truly excellent,' he sighed. He looked at her, his eyes warm. 'There is nothing better than good wine, good food and good company. And here I am enjoying all three.'

'Me too,' Margo nodded.

'That's very kind of you.'

'Not at all. I really enjoy your company, you know.'

'Yes, we get on so well together, you and I,' François said, pouring himself yet another glass of wine. He held the bottle toward Margo, but she shook her head. 'Wise,' he said, 'very wise.' He drank deeply from his glass.

As the meal progressed, Margo watched with apprehension as François finished the bottle and proceeded to open another one. 'Just to go with the cheese,' he said, noticing Margo's expression.

'There isn't any,' Margo said. 'Justine forgot to buy cheese today. There's just a little bit of the apple tart left over from Sunday.'

'Well, then, the wine will go just as well with that,' François remarked. 'Bring it in, and we'll see if I'm right.'

Margo fetched the apple tart from the kitchen and François declared it and the wine a truly excellent combination. She looked at his slightly flushed face and thought he looked like a little boy bunking off school. Then he looked at her across the table and, as their eyes met, his expression changed.

'Marguerite,' he said softly, 'may I ask you a question?'

'Yes, of course. What's the question?'

He put his hand on hers again. 'Marguerite, I was wondering...if Jacques doesn't come back and you find yourself alone when the baby comes, would you consider...marrying me?'

Margo stared at his kind face and, for just one second, toyed with the idea of marrying François and enjoying all the perks that would come with it. Then she came to her senses. 'Oh, François,' she said, 'that is so sweet of you.' She put her other hand over his. 'I like you a lot, I really do. But...'

'You don't find me attractive?'

'Oh, no,' she exclaimed. 'I do. You're a very handsome man, you really are. And so elegant and well dressed. And I'm sure you'd be a marvellous husband and we'd get on really well, but...'

He pulled his hand away. 'I see.'

'Please don't be hurt,' Margo said. 'I know that a lot of women would jump at the chance of marrying you. It's just that I think you and I...well, it wouldn't work.'

'No, I suppose you're right.' François sighed, looking both resigned and, to Margo's surprise, relieved. 'All right, there we are. No harm in asking.'

'Of course not. It was sweet of you.' Something suddenly occurred to Margo. 'But what about your girlfriend? Why are you asking me to marry you when you're already in love with someone else?'

'In love?' François looked at her, alarmed. 'What do you mean?'

'Please, don't pretend,' Margo begged. 'I know all about her. I've seen her several times.'

François looked down at his plate, then back at Margo. 'All right then. I know you've seen each other. She told me.'

'She's very beautiful.'

'Beautiful?' François asked, sounding strangely pleased. 'Do you really think so?'

'Oh yes,' Margo assured him. 'I've only seen her briefly, but I noticed her lovely figure, her blonde hair and those legs. God, they're fabulous.'

'That's very kind,' François said, looking a little shy.

'But why the secrecy? Is it because your mother wouldn't approve of her?

'She certainly would not.'

'Why?'

François hesitated. 'You see, Paquita, my… girlfriend, is not at all the kind of girl my mother would like me to be associated with. She's Brazilian, and sings in a nightclub.'

'I see. But if your mother met Paquita, and got to know her, don't you think she would learn to accept her in time?'

'No, that's impossible,' François said flatly. 'I don't want to even imagine what she would do if she knew what was going on.'

'You think she might try to have Paquita deported?' Margo asked.

'Maybe.'

'But why don't you just do it? Marry Paquita and tell your mother to get lost? It's not as if you're a minor or something. You can do what you want, surely?'

'Marry her?' François said, suddenly making a noise that sounded strangely like a giggle.

'Yes,' Margo said. 'Why not?'

François shook his head. 'No, that is not possible, believe me.'

'I'm sorry. That's really sad for you, François.

'You have no idea how sad it is,' François sighed and poured himself some more wine. 'And I'm really sorry you don't want to marry me. It would have solved a lot of problems. My mother would be so happy if…'

'She put you up to it, didn't she?' Margo said, feeling suddenly angry.

'I'm sorry?'

'Milady told you to propose to me,' Margo said, nodding slowly. 'I can see in your eyes that it's true. And she stayed out tonight to give us a chance to be alone.'

'Yes, you're right,' François said, looking slightly shamefaced. 'She said it would make her so happy. We would be this perfect family. My mother, the glamorous grandmother, you, me and Josephine.'

'Josephine,' Margo whispered. 'Oh God.'

'The baby girl.'

'I know.' Margo jumped as the front door slammed.

'Hellooo?' Milady sang from the hall as François and Margo stared at each other across the table. 'Anybody home?'

*

Later that evening, Margo was getting into bed, looking forward to a good night's sleep for once, when there was a gentle knock on the door.

'Who is it?' she called.

'It's me,' François murmured.

'Oh all right, just a minute.' Margo sighed, got out of bed, threw on her dressing gown and opened the door. 'What's the matter?' she asked as François tiptoed through the door and closed it softly behind him.

'Shh,' he whispered, 'she's still on the prowl.'

'Who? What are you talking about?' Margo asked, feeling both tired and irritated.

'My mother, of course,' François said and walked closer to Margo. 'I have something to tell you.'

'What? I thought we had finished our talk. And your mother didn't seem too worried when we told her I was going to think about it. About marrying you, I mean.'

'No, she accepted my explanation,' François nodded. 'We'll have plenty of time to get her used to the idea there will be no wedding. Between you and me, I mean,' he added, making a vague gesture.

'Good. So what's the problem, then? Why are you here?'

'To tell you something very important.' François looked around the room. 'May I sit down?'

'Of course,' Margo said, showing him the chair in front of the dressing table. 'Why don't you sit there?' She sank down on the bed and looked at François as he made himself comfortable on the spindly chair.

Once he was sitting down, François leaned forward and stared at Margo. 'I have come to tell you,' he said, 'that you have to get away from my mother.'

'Why?' Margo asked, mystified both by his words and his demeanour.

'Because she is dangerous,' François whispered. 'She will eat you alive like a black widow spider and then steal your baby.'

Margo sat up. 'You drank too much wine at dinner.'

'No, please listen to me,' François insisted. 'Maybe I have drunk a little too much, but it gives me the courage to speak to you like this. My mother is…a little mad, I think. She is becoming obsessed with the baby.'

Margo started to say something, but François held up a hand to stop her. 'Let me explain,' he said. 'Please, just listen to me for a moment.'

'All right,' Margo said, her heart beating a little faster.

'My mother thinks that this is her last link with her…lover. Your baby, I mean. She thinks that the baby will be a girl and that she will be the daughter they never had.'

'That's why she wants me to marry you?'

'But of course. She begged me to ask you, and I agreed just to humour her, you see. But I knew deep down you would say no. And you did, and I was rather relieved, I have to say. I don't really want to marry anyone.'

'Not even Paquita?' Margo asked.

'Especially not her. Oh Marguerite,' he exclaimed, 'I'm so sorry. I really like you, and if, well, if things hadn't happened the way they have, maybe…who knows?' He pushed his hand through his hair, making it stand on end.

'But,' Margo stammered, trying to take it in – that Milady was obsessive and dangerous. 'Are you sure? I mean, she's been so kind, so concerned and supportive. She treats me as if I was made of glass. I had a feeling we were getting so close and that she really cares about me.'

'She is really good at that,' François nodded. He leaned his elbow on the dressing table, slipping slightly sideways. 'Don't you see?' he whispered in an exaggerated way. 'You are only the vesh…the wish…the vessel. It's what's inside you she's really intresh…interush…that she really wants. Once she gets her hands on her…'

'Or him.'

'Or…what?' François looked a little confused. Then he nodded. 'Or him, yes, then she will no longer care about you. She will drive you away and keep the baby.'

'I think you're exaggerating,' Margo said. 'And I think the wine has gone to your head.'

'Oh Marguerite, you don't know my mother. Just think about it for a while. Haven't you noticed how she hovers around you all the time?'

'Well, yes, but she's just being kind.'

'And I'm sure you've also noticed that she is very careful never to leave you on your own during the day.'

Margo thought for a moment. 'Yes,' she nodded, 'you're right. She's always around, and wants me to go with her most of the time. And the other day, when I went to meet Gráinne and I came back a little late, she was in such a state. And,' Margo continued, a feeling of dread washing over her, 'I can't find my mobile phone.'

François nodded wordlessly.

'And she hasn't made any attempt at all to contact Jacques, has she?' Margo mumbled. 'I told her Gráinne had met him at an international show jumping competition in England and...' Margo put a hand to her mouth as the whole picture became clear. 'She said she would get in touch with the French team, but...oh God.'

'She won't, of course,' François filled in. 'She doesn't want you and Jacques together, because she knows you would go away with him. Now do you see what I mean?'

'Yes,' Margo whispered.

'You must go. I will help you. And there's no problem about money. I have prepared a little gift for you.'

'A gift?'

'Yes. Something that you will really like. I thought, in the event of you refusing my proposal, you would need some kind of insurance, a nest egg, if you like.' He paused. 'But not a word to my mother, promise?'

'Yes, I promise,' Margo murmured, feeling as if she was having a particularly strange dream.

'I will give it to you and then you must leave. Go to...to...' He stopped, as if he had lost his train of thought. 'To England. As soon as you can. Is there anyone you could...?'

'Yes,' Margo said. 'Duncan. My brother in Oxford. I can go to him. He won't be delighted, but...' She stopped and listened. 'I think I can hear her coming down the corridor.'

'Go,' François whispered as the clicking of Milady's heels came closer. 'Make the arrangements and then let me know when you're leaving.' He pressed something into Margo's hand and walked to the door, opened it a crack and peered out. 'The coast is clear,' he whispered. 'She went to the kitchen. I'll be off then.' He gave her an encouraging little smile and left. Margo looked at the object in her hand. It was a mobile phone.

*

'Duncan? Is that you?' Margo murmured into the phone, trying to keep her voice as low as possible. She had waited until, at one o'clock, the apartment had become silent and she was sure Milady was in bed.

'It's me, Margo,' she said. 'I'm fine, Dunc, really well. Sorry to call this late, but... Yes, I know. I haven't been in touch for ages... Who? Alan? Not very well, I hope,' Margo said. 'We're separated, you see.' She laughed happily as she listened to her brother's voice, realising how much she had missed him. 'That's right. We split up,' she said. 'I finally left him... All right, all right, there's no need to sound so bloody ecstatic. I knew you never liked the man, but...' She tried to think of how to explain her situation and decided it was better not to say anything until she arrived. 'Well,' Margo continued, 'I'm in Paris, actually... No, no, Duncan, never mind that. It's not important now... Yes, I promise. I'll get a good solicitor and he'll get what he deserves... But listen,' Margo murmured into the phone, 'I need a place to stay for a while. I thought you might put me up for a few weeks until...' There was a soft noise by the door. She paused and looked at it, her heart beating faster, as the door handle moved. 'Got to go,' she whispered into the mobile, 'I'll be leaving as soon as I…' Margo froze as the door started to open very slowly.

'Marguerite?' Jacques was standing in the doorway.

24

Margo dropped the phone. Unable to speak, she stared at him, at his tall frame, his black hair and deep blue eyes. She noticed he was dressed in a long dark coat that was open to reveal a white shirt, blue sweater with the French team logo, jeans and riding boots. She was wondering if she was dreaming, or going mad. She had thought of this moment for weeks, wondered if she would ever see him again, and fantasised that he would arrive exactly like this. 'Is it really you?' she asked.

'Yes, it's me,' Jacques replied, walking into the room, taking off his coat and dropping it on a chair. 'I've just arrived from the ferry.'

'Hello,' Margo said, suddenly nervous. 'How are you?' She looked into his eyes, trying desperately to think of something clever to say. 'Nice to see you again,' she prattled on. 'It's been a long...' Oh shut up, she told herself. He looks so tired, she thought. And sad and worried. She wanted to push that heavy lock of hair out of his eyes and put her arms around him and…

He walked swiftly across the floor and took her suddenly ice cold hand. 'Oh Marguerite, I came as soon as I heard. She told me. She was so angry.'

'Who? Your mother?'

'My mother? I haven't spoken to her for nearly two months. No, it was that friend of yours. Groan, Grey, Grainia, whatever her bloody name is.'

'Gráinne?'

'That's right. Gráinne. What a name. She got me on my mobile and called me all sorts of names. My God, I have never heard anyone swear like she does, and I have hung around stables all my life.'

'I know,' Margo said and laughed. 'Gráinne knows how to express her feelings.'

'She made me feel like a right shit. Even though I didn't know about…' Jacques looked at Margo's waist. 'The baby.' He took a step forward. 'My baby.'

'No, it's mine, actually,' Margo said, backing away and pulling her dressing gown tighter around her. 'All mine.'

'What do you mean?' His eyes changed from blue to black and his thick eyebrows came together in an angry frown.

'I mean that it's my baby and it only belongs to me, nobody else. I don't know why you're here, but…'

'I came to tell you that I know I'm the father and I'm willing to take the responsibility for—'

'That's very big of you,' Margo interrupted. 'How very admirable, I must say.' She walked over to the other side of the bed so that there would be something solid between them. 'So, are you offering to take over here?' she asked. 'I mean, in case you think your bit was too easy, those fun few minutes back in August that you have probably forgotten about?'

'No,' Jacques said softly. 'I haven't forgotten.'

Margo opened her mouth to say something scathing, to pay him back for leaving her like that, for not getting in touch, for the pain and sadness she had felt the past few months. But the look in his eyes stopped her. 'Oh Jacques,' was all she managed to say. Then anger got the better of her. 'You big *shit*!' she suddenly shouted. 'Where have you been? Why have you not been in touch? Why did you leave me to cope on my own?'

'Please,' Jacques said in a hushed voice. 'Keep your voice down. You'll wake everyone.'

'Don't worry,' Margo said. 'Your mother is asleep in her bedroom which is half a block away and François drank enough wine to floor an elephant. So I can shout as loud as I want.'

'I don't understand why you're so angry,' Jacques said. 'I'm here. I'll do anything you want. I'll even marry you.'

'Wow!' Margo shouted. 'You'll *even* marry me! Christ, that is so saintly of you! So utterly, utterly wonderful.'

Jacques grabbed one of the bedposts so hard his knuckles whitened. 'You are the most stubborn, infuriating woman I have ever met,' he snapped. 'I came here to tell you how much I've missed you and that the reason I haven't been in touch is because I didn't want to come back until I was ready – until I knew who I was and what I was doing. Until I had something to offer you.'

'And now you do?'

'No, not quite. I have some plans. I was going to see if I could start something new, and once that was off the ground, I would…but then I heard about the baby. I had to come back sooner.'

'I see.' Margo looked at him, waiting for him to continue.

'I didn't get in touch with you earlier because I was trying to come to terms with everything,' he said, his eyes willing her to understand. 'With my past and my parents and…you. And what you did to me.'

'I'm sorry?' Margo said. 'What was that you said? What *I* did to *you*? Are you referring to the fact that you stole those paintings? I had nothing to do with that.'

'Oh, shut up about that,' Jacques snapped. 'That's not important now. I don't know why you had to bring it up.'

'I brought it up?' Margo asked incredulously. 'But it was you who said—'

I didn't mean *that*,' Jacques said, sounding exasperated. 'I meant what you did to my feelings. How you made me fall in love with you, made me think of only you and how I would come back to you and ask you—'

'So it wasn't about the paintings?' Margo interrupted.

'No, of course not. I don't blame you for that. You made an innocent remark which forced me to leave, but I have forgiven you.'

'Oh, good,' Margo said ironically. 'There you go again, being a saint and forgiving me. How can I possibly resist you now? Even though you left and haven't been in touch by so much as a postcard.'

'But when I left, you said to me that you thought I needed to go away,' Jacques reminded her.

'And you said you'd be back.' Margo stopped. They looked at each other in silence, the air thick with emotion.

'Will you marry me?' Jacques suddenly said, standing there holding onto the bedpost as if he was afraid to move closer.

Margo stared at him. 'What did you say?'

'I asked you to marry me.'

'That's what I thought you said. Oh God.' Margo sat down on the bed, her back to Jacques. 'I can't,' she murmured.

'Why not?'

'Because I'm already married.' Margo wrapped her arms tightly around herself.

Jacques made a strange sound. 'You're what? You're *married*?' he repeated as if he couldn't believe it.

'Yes.'

'And…your husband? Where is he?'

'At this moment?' Margo paused. 'He's in Paris, actually. At a medical conference.' She turned around and looked at Jacques. 'I left him months ago. And I'm not going back to him, if that's what you're worried about.'

'I'm not worried.' Jacques shook his head. 'I didn't realise. Why didn't you tell me?'

'I didn't want to think about it,' Margo said, feeling ashamed. 'And when you and I…when we…I forgot all about him when I was with you.' She sighed and put her head in her hands. 'I'm not very proud of all this, you know,' she mumbled into her hands, not looking up when Jacques came around the bed and sat down, putting his arm around her. 'I've done a lot of things I shouldn't have.'

'It doesn't matter,' he whispered, holding her close.

'I was so happy when I found out about the baby,' Margo said, turning her head into his shoulder and breathing in that smell that was so particular to him – soap, freshly laundered cotton and just a hint of horse. 'I had been trying for years to have a baby. Oh, you have no idea how happy I was. I'm so happy,' she said again into his chest.

'Are you also happy the baby is mine?' Jacques asked softly.

'Yes,' Margo sat up. 'But it wouldn't have mattered if it was the postman. I'm finally having a child, my own child.'

'I see.'

'But of course I'd prefer it to be yours,' Margo added hastily. 'The postman is not as good looking, and he's very short. Oh, what am I saying?'

'I don't know,' Jacques said softly, stroking the short blonde curls away from her face. 'Tell me, do you think you might marry me once you've sorted out your divorce?'

'No.' Margo shook her head to emphasise her words.

'Why not?' Jacques demanded.

'Because getting married was the biggest mistake I've ever made. And I'm not going there again.'

'But where are you going?' Jacques asked, his voice calmer. 'What are you going to do?'

'I'm going home,' Margo said, pulling away from him and sitting up straighter. 'Back to England. I'm going to stay with my brother for a while.'

'Then what? How are you going to support yourself and the baby?'

'I'm going to go back to my old job. I'm a trained physiotherapist, you know,' she said proudly.

'And then you'll live happily ever after,' Jacques said harshly, 'you and the baby. You have certainly worked it all out to your own advantage, haven't you?'

'And why not? Why shouldn't I think of myself first? I've spent these past long weeks thinking hard, you know. At first, I was going to stay here, have the baby and then decide what to do. Your mother was so kind. It was so lovely to just be taken care of, not to have to worry about anything. But then…' She suddenly laughed.

'Then what happened?'

'François asked me to marry him.'

'What?' Jacques looked at her, dumbstruck. 'He asked you to…'

'Yes, he did. I thought that was very sweet of him, actually.'

'Oh yes,' Jacques said. 'And how convenient.'

'What do you mean?'

'François, my darling,' Jacques said, taking her hand, 'is not the kind of man who will ever marry or have a child. He knows that and my mother, I suspect, knows it too. But this way, he would have a baby and a lovely wife. The Coligny family would rise again.'

'I don't know what you mean,' Margo said, confused, looking into Jacques's face for clues.

'Oh, never mind. It doesn't matter. Except if you were thinking of accepting his proposal, of course.'

'No, of course not. I told him I couldn't.' Margo sighed. 'It would have been nice, though. To be a countess and live in a château and waltz around wearing designer clothes.'

'And you do wear Chanel so beautifully, darling,' Jacques said in a voice that was eerily like François's.

Margo laughed. 'You idiot.'

'But you're right,' Jacques said, his voice more serious. 'You can't stay here.'

'No. Especially after what he told me tonight.'

'What do you mean?'

'I was talking to François and he told me I had to get away from her. Your mother, I mean. He told me some weird story that I don't really believe, but it made me think. And I realised that I have to make my own way, to support myself and be independent. And I suddenly felt such a great wish to do just that. To stop hiding and go out there and earn my own living, to raise this child. So I thought I would go back home and organise my life. I was just talking to my brother when you came in.' Margo picked up the phone from the floor and held it to her ear. 'He hung up. I'll call him in a minute and tell him when I'll be arriving.'

'Or that you won't be coming at all now that I'm here,' Jacques said in a determined voice.

'What do you mean? I don't know if I…oh my God,' Margo suddenly gasped, putting a hand on her stomach.

'What?' Jacques cried. 'What's the matter?'

Margo looked at him, her face white and her eyes shining. 'He moved,' she whispered. 'The baby just moved. Right here, inside me.'

'Oh,' Jacques whispered and put his hand on her stomach. 'Can I?'

The baby kicked again and they looked at each other without speaking while Margo's stomach heaved once more and then was still. 'It stopped,' she said. 'He must have gone to sleep.'

Jacques took his hand away and put his arm around her. 'Thank you,' he said softly. Without speaking, they lay down on the bed, their arms around each other. Jacques kicked off his boots and Margo switched off the light. 'It would be so easy,' she whispered into the darkness, more to herself than to him. 'To marry you and just let you take over. But I can't, I just can't. I want to be in charge of my own life, I want to be the one who decides where to go, what to do and where to live. I know it won't be easy, but…' She sighed, tightening her arms around him. 'Maybe, if we waited a few years,' she continued, 'until I've got my career going again, we could review the situation? Maybe then, we would be better able to decide whether we can live together, when we're completely equal? What do you think?'

There was no reply.

*

The baby moved again in the night, waking Margo. She moved away from Jacques and tried to get comfortable, but he pulled her close to him again. 'What time is it?' he mumbled.

'I don't know. Four or something. I thought I heard the clock in the drawing room strike a while ago.'

'Oh.'

'What's that noise?' Margo said, suddenly wide awake.

'What noise?'

'That creaking. Sounds like someone opening the front door very slowly.'

'But I thought you said everyone was home.'

'Yes, but maybe François went out again,' Margo whispered. 'Maybe he had a date with his girlfriend?'

'His what?'

'His girlfriend. He told me about her when we had dinner. She's a Brazilian nightclub singer and she was probably working late.'

Jacques laughed softly. 'What did you say? A Brazilian?' He laughed again.

'Why is that so funny?' Margo asked, still whispering. 'He's really in love with her, you know. And it's so sad that they have to sneak around like that.'

'And why do they have to sneak around?' Jacques asked, sounding amused.

'Shh, not so loud. I can hear the door closing. It's because of your mother,' Margo continued into Jacques's ear. 'She wouldn't approve, you see.'

'You bet she wouldn't,' Jacques said.

'I can hear footsteps,' Margo said. 'High heels on the parquet. He must have brought her home.'

'This I have to see,' Jacques declared and got out of bed.

'Where are you going?'

'I'm going out to meet what's her name.'

'Paquita,' Margo said, tiptoeing after Jacques. 'But wait, are you sure we should? I mean, maybe we shouldn't disturb them?'

Jacques didn't reply but slowly opened the door and looked out into the dimly lit corridor. Margo craned her neck to see beyond him into the shadows and caught sight of the shape of someone walking carefully down the corridor. 'There,' Margo whispered, 'she's walking toward François's room.'

Jacques stepped out into the corridor and walked swiftly and silently on stocking feet behind the woman. Margo padded behind him, trying to catch up. When Jacques was nearly at touching distance, the woman suddenly whirled around, stared at Jacques for a moment, gave a little gasp and then ran as fast as her high heels would allow towards the door of François's bedroom. But Jacques was faster. He put out a hand and grabbed the woman by the shoulder.

'Paquita,' Margo stammered, 'Wait! Jacques, what are you doing? Don't pull her hair!'

But Jacques was already holding in his hand the shining blonde head of hair that Margo had so much admired. 'It's a wig, you dummy,' he said and turned the woman roughly around to face to her. Margo gasped.

'Meet Miss Brazil,' Jacques laughed triumphantly.

25

Margo stared in horror at the woman, then at the blonde wig in Jacques's hand, then back at the woman again. 'François!' she whispered, clutching her throat. 'Oh my God!'

François, dressed in a silk dress and his brown eyes heavily made up, looked slightly grotesque without the blonde wig. 'Oh Marguerite,' he sighed. 'I should have told you. I should have explained.'

Margo turned to Jacques. 'You knew,' she said angrily. 'All this time you knew and you didn't tell me.'

'Would you have believed me?' Jacques asked.

'No, probably not,' Margo said. 'But I really didn't need to know at all, did I? Why didn't you leave well enough alone? Why did you have to do this?'

She looked back at François, who seemed to have recovered some of his cool and was now shaking out the wig, looking at it with great concern. 'Don't worry, I won't tell anyone,' she assured him. 'It doesn't matter at all. I have always felt that people should be allowed to…to be whatever they are. And being gay is nothing to be ashamed of.'

François looked up. 'Gay? I don't know, to be honest.'

'What?' Margo looked at him, confused. 'But what's all this then?' she asked, gesturing at the dress, a light blue Chanel vintage, and the wig.

'It's…I'm…' François stopped. 'How can I explain?'

'I need a drink,' Jacques said. 'Let's go to the study and have something to calm ourselves down.'

'I'll make some tea,' Margo said.

'And I'll go and slip into something a little more comfortable,' François suggested. 'These heels are killing me.'

A little later, they sat in the study, looking at each other without saying anything.

François, the make-up washed off and dressed in a silk dressing gown, was the first to break the silence. 'I'm not gay,' he said to Margo. 'Well, not completely anyway.'

'What are you then? A cross-dresser?'

'That's right. I like women, and I like the clothes even more.'

'You don't like men?' Margo asked, trying to understand.

'I don't know,' François said with a sigh. 'I am, and have always been, confused about who I am. It used to make me so unhappy.' He stopped and looked at Margo. 'I shouldn't burden you with all this, I suppose.'

'*Bien sur que non*,' Jacques murmured.

'No, François,' Margo protested, 'don't worry. If it helps you to talk, go ahead.'

'It's thanks to you,' François said, 'that I am beginning to feel a lot better about myself, about not being really what you would call normal.'

'Thanks to me?'

'Yes. I used to feel ashamed about wanting to dress up like this. I felt like some kind of freak. But then you told me to do my own thing and not worry about conventions. And then I realised that it doesn't matter what you are, as long as you don't hurt anyone or…' He paused again, glancing at Jacques, who was swirling his brandy around in the glass, looking as if he wasn't even listening. 'I still don't know what I am, but I'm having a lot of fun finding out,' François ended, smiling shyly.

'But dressing up in women's clothes, is that a new thing?'

'No. It all started years ago when I was doing a *stage* at the *sureté*,' François said. 'That's the special branch of the police force. I worked with the guys on the drug squad and they often had to dress up as women, because they were going to drag clubs undercover, and then, well, I started to really enjoy it, the dressing up, I mean. And I got lots of praise for the way I looked and for my figure. But of course, I had access to the best wardrobe in Paris. And I was lucky enough to fit into my mother's clothes. Did you know,' François said, looking at Margo with great excitement in his eyes, 'that she has a huge wardrobe of the most beautiful vintage fashion?'

'Yes, I've seen it.'

'I've been borrowing from that for years. It's been such fun.'

'So there is no Paquita, then?' Margo said, feeling a little disappointed.

'No. I am Paquita. I work as a singer in this drag club at night. I have quite a good voice, you know.'

'He used to be a choirboy,' Jacques said. 'I think that's where it all started.'

Something suddenly occurred to Margo. 'That voice,' she exclaimed, 'that lovely singing the other night. It was you, wasn't it?'

'Yes,' François said modestly.

'Such a beautiful voice,' Margo said.

'Thank you.' François smiled happily. 'And you said you thought it was good enough to be a CD, remember?'

'Yes, it is, definitely.'

'You don't know how right you are,' François said. 'I have – I mean, Paquita – has been offered a record deal. Isn't that exciting?'

'But that's fabulous!' Margo exclaimed. 'I'm sure you – she'll – be very successful.'

'If it works, I can give up my boring old job at the ministry,' François said.

'That's fantastic,' Margo beamed.

'Mother will be ecstatic,' Jacques said dryly.

'But one more thing,' Margo said. 'Last summer, that dress – the Galliano.'

'I borrowed it, yes,' François nodded. 'There was a special jazz evening at the club, you see, and that little black number was perfect. I didn't think she would notice, I thought she was going to wear the navy Yves St Laurent that night, but she must have changed her mind.'

'She certainly did,' Jacques said. 'And it wasn't much fun to have to explain it to the police.'

'She called the police?' François asked, looking appalled. 'Oh, *mon Dieu*, I'm sorry.'

'More tea?' Margo asked, lifting the teapot.

'No thanks, dear Marguerite, I think I'll have a cognac instead.'

'All right.' Margo refilled her cup. 'It's kind of sad to find out that there's no Paquita,' she said. 'I thought you might be very happy together. She – I mean *you* – are very pretty when you're her.'

'Thank you,' François said, pouring brandy into his glass. 'But she's not as beautiful as you, my dear Marguerite.' He looked at her while he swirled the cognac around in his glass. 'You have the most beautiful body – slim, long limbed, like a dancer. Especially in the nude.'

'What?' Margo nearly dropped her cup.

'In the *nude*?' Jacques growled, shooting out of his chair and grabbing François by the lapel of his dressing gown. 'What do you mean?'

'Please.' François pulled out of his grip. 'Let me explain.'

'Explain what?' Jacques demanded, looking angrily from his brother to Margo. 'That you and she…?'

'Don't be silly,' François chided, sitting down again, smoothing his dressing gown. 'There's nothing between us. I happened to see Marguerite when she was swimming.'

'At the weir,' Margo said, staring at him, trying to take in his latest revelation. 'You mean,' she stammered, '*you're* the peeping Tom? Oh God! Gráinne and I were talking about that. We knew there was someone lurking in the bushes spying on us, but I thought it was Bernard. Thank God I didn't say anything.'

'*Merde*,' Jacques mumbled, sinking down on his chair again. 'Tell me I'm dreaming. Tell me this is not really happening.'

'Peeping Tom?' François said. 'Sounds worse than it is – *was*, I mean. It was not really like that. It was more like looking at something beautiful. Like a painting. It didn't turn me on. Or off,' he added with a laugh. 'It was just, well, curiosity, I suppose. It was interesting to look at two women that were so totally different.'

'*Two* women?' Jacques exclaimed.

'Gráinne,' Margo whispered. 'Oh bloody hell.'

'She is also quite attractive,' François said, taking a sip of cognac. 'But more full-bodied and heavier than you.'

'Can we stop this now?' Jacques pleaded. 'I'm beginning to feel quite ill.'

'What's going on?'

They all looked around at Milady standing in the doorway tying the belt of her white silk dressing gown. 'What are you all doing here in the middle of the night?' she demanded. 'And Jacques? When did you arrive? Why does nobody tell me anything?'

Jacques rose and kissed his mother on the cheek. '*Bonsoir, Maman*,' he said. 'I arrived very late and didn't want to disturb you. I had to talk to Marguerite. We have things to discuss.'

'Of course you do,' Milady said, sitting down on the sofa beside François. 'You have a lot of things to sort out. But François, what are you doing here? I thought you went to bed hours ago.'

'I went out later, after you had gone to bed,' François said.

'And then,' Margo started, 'later on, I heard something and I thought someone was breaking in.'

'And I went out to investigate,' Jacques filled in. 'And I discovered François, who was arriving home. So then when we had sorted all that out, we came in here for a drink.'

Milady looked at them, and one of her eyebrows shot up. 'Really?' she said.

'That's right,' Margo nodded. 'That's what happened.'

'I see.' Milady started to get up from the sofa. 'Well, it's a great relief there was no burglar. I can go back to bed then.'

'Good night, *Maman*,' François said.

'Good night,' Milady said as she walked to the door. She stopped for a moment, turned around and looked at François. 'I just wanted to say to you, darling…'

'Yes?' François said.

'If you wanted to borrow the Galliano,' Milady continued, 'why didn't you just ask?'

There was stunned silence, during which they all stared at Milady.

'What?' Jacques said. 'You knew?'

'Darling boy,' Milady sighed. 'So like his father.'

'My father?' François stammered. 'Did he…was he…?'

'Oh yes,' Milady nodded. 'Except *he* preferred Givenchy.'

*

'What are you doing?'

'Packing,' Margo said, folding her navy pullover.

'At this hour of the night? I mean, the morning,' Jacques said.

'I have to get out of here. I can't stay another minute. This family is beginning to get on my nerves. Talk about dysfunctional,' Margo muttered. 'I'm afraid that if I stay, it will rub off on me. I've already found myself oddly attracted to Justine lately.'

'Very funny.'

'I just have to go. Where is my passport? I thought I had it a minute ago.' Margo rummaged in her handbag. 'Here it is.'

'Where are you going?'

'To England,' Margo said, taking her passport out and putting it back in the bag. 'I'm taking the early morning Eurostar train to London. Didn't I tell you?'

'So you did.' Jacques put his hand on one of Margo's. 'But I thought that after last night, we…you and me…'

Margo looked up from her task. 'You and me what? I thought I made myself perfectly clear. I can't marry you, I will *never* marry you and that's final.'

'I know. So you said. But, well, then we…'

'We what?'

'We slept together.'

'So? We just slept. Nothing happened.'

'That's it,' Jacques said. 'Don't you see? I have never just slept with a woman before.'

'I don't know what you mean.'

'There was no sex,' Jacques murmured, stroking her cheek. 'Just you and me and the baby. Sleeping. I want to keep doing that. Sleep with you for the rest of my life. And I don't care if we're not married. I just want to be with you.'

Margo looked at him and wondered why he had to look the way he did. It would be easier to resist him if he was unattractive. And she had to resist him, resist the urge to fall into his arms and tell him how much she loved him and that he should stay. But it would lead to disaster and she would eventually find herself yet again in a relationship that didn't work, this time with a small child.

'No.' She shook her head. 'I don't believe you. Once we're together, you'll start demanding things. You'll tell me what to do, and before I know it, there I'll be again.'

'Where?'

'Stuck,' Margo said, putting her underwear on a pile on the bed. 'Pyjamas,' she muttered, 'and my dressing gown. I have a lot more clothes than when I arrived, that's for sure. Maybe I can put them in that carrier bag from the supermarket.'

'Stop it,' Jacques ordered, taking her hand again and holding it in a tight grip.

'Go away,' Margo snapped, pulling away. 'Just get out of here and leave me alone. I know what I'm doing and where I'm going, and I'll get there a lot quicker if you just leave me alone.'

'Oh, I see,' Jacques said. 'You want to be independent. You want to be this heroic single mother, don't you? You want the baby all to yourself, so that people can see how bloody marvellous you are. And you don't want to share him with anyone, not even me, his father.'

'You want to be a father?' Margo said. 'How do you know you'll be any good at it? Do you know anything at all about children?'

'Do you?' Jacques demanded. 'How do you know you'll be any good as a mother?'

'I'll be all right,' Margo said. 'Most mothers seem to cope very well, so don't you worry.'

'I'm not worried. I'm sure you'll be an excellent mother. Really dedicated and caring.'

'You bet I will,' Margo said. 'I know I will. This is the biggest challenge of my whole life.'

'Poor little baby.'

'Why?'

'How terrible to grow up as somebody's challenge.'

Margo stared at him. 'You don't know what you're talking about.'

'Marguerite,' Jacques said, 'listen to me for a moment.'

There was such sincerity and concern in his voice that Margo's determination crumbled. She didn't know what to do or say, and unable to fight him any more, she let him take her hand and lead her to the bed.

'Sit down,' he said, 'and listen.'

'All right,' she sighed and sat down. 'I'll listen.'

'I grew up without a father,' Jacques said, sitting down beside her. 'I know what that is like. This baby happened because we made love.'

'Well, yes, I realised that,' Margo said, trying not to sound ironic. 'Go on.'

'It's not his fault.'

'Who's fault?' she asked, confused.

'The baby,' Jacques said, pointing at Margo's stomach. 'It's not his fault we made him. It's not his fault you don't love me and don't want me to share your life. But I want to be there when he grows up, and he'll want to have a father. I know that's not what you want, but don't you think it's just a tiny bit selfish to want him all to yourself?'

'Selfish?' Margo said.

'Yes,' Jacques said, anger creeping into his voice. 'You said you always wanted a baby. Why? So you could play with it and dress it up and show it off to your friends like a doll? And the child would love you and only you for the rest of your life? And what are you going to say when he asks where his father is? Have you thought of that?'

'No, I...' Margo started.

'No, of course not.' Jacques shrugged, got off the bed and picked up his coat he had left on the floor earlier. 'You haven't really thought of anybody but yourself.'

'Where are you going?' Margo asked.

'I'm leaving,' Jacques said, putting on his coat. 'You don't want me, so what's the point of staying? I'm not going to beg you. You don't have the courage to leave everything and come with me, and maybe I didn't have the right to ask you in the first place. I can't promise you life with me would be easy. I can't offer you anything but my love. So, as that doesn't seem to be enough for you, maybe you should go and start a life on your own. At least that way you won't be disappointed.'

'I suppose,' Margo said, feeling suddenly bleak.

Jacques walked back to Margo and touched her cheek with his finger. 'Marguerite,' he whispered. '*Adieu, mon amour.*'

Unable to move or speak, Margo watched him walk away. But as he opened the door, she suddenly regained the power of speech.

'Wait,' she said, her voice hoarse with emotion.

He stopped. 'Yes?'

'Don't go.'

*

410

The room was in darkness. Margo tiptoed across the carpet to the big bed. 'Milady?' she murmured softly. 'Are you awake.'

The shape in the bed stirred. *'Comment? Qui est là?'*

'C'est moi, Milady,' Margo said. 'Marguerite.'

'Oh.' Milady coughed and sat up. 'Is it time for breakfast already? Did I oversleep?'

'No, it's early.'

'Pull back the curtain, I can't see you.'

Milady shaded her eyes as Margo pulled back the heavy curtains, flooding the room with bright sunshine.

'What time is it?' Milady squinted at the Cartier carriage clock on her bedside table. 'Seven-thirty,' she said in an aggrieved voice. 'Why are you waking me up at this hour? I never wake up at seven-thirty.'

'Milady,' Margo said, sitting down on the edge of the bed and taking Milady's hand. 'I came to say goodbye. I'm leaving.'

'Leaving?' Milady asked shrilly, sitting bolt upright and staring at her incomprehensively. 'What do you mean? Where are you going?'

'I'm going to England. To stay with my brother for a while. Then Jacques and I—'

'Oh.' Milady looked calmer as she sank back against the pillows. 'To visit your brother. For the weekend, yes? You'll be back on Monday?'

'No.'

'No? How do you mean? Oh, I see. Tuesday? You'll be back on Tuesday, then?'

'No, Milady, I'm not coming back,' Margo said very gently. 'I'm leaving for good. I'm going away with Jacques.'

Milady stared at her without a word for a long time while the Cartier clock ticked and the traffic noises from the street below increased in volume. 'I see,' she said very slowly, her eyes narrowing. 'It's Jacques, isn't it? It's all his fault, as usual. I thought something like this would happen if he came back. I knew he would stir up trouble.'

'There's no trouble,' Margo said. 'On the contrary, I think it's all rather wonderful.'

'Wonderful?' Milady demanded. 'What's wonderful about it?'

'Jacques and I…we…' Margo stopped.

'Jacques?' Milady said shrilly. 'Jacques? What does he have to do with all of this? You're going to marry François. I thought it was all settled. We'll have a small, discreet wedding in a few weeks and then you will live here, and then little Josephine will be born in the spring and we'll have the christening at the château.'

'No, Milady, we won't,' Margo said gently. 'There will be no wedding.'

'Just like when François was christened,' Milady murmured, looking dreamily into space. 'Charles de Gaulle came to that one, you know,' she continued proudly. 'Did he tell you?'

'Eh, no, he didn't,' Margo said, wondering if she should ask François to call a doctor.

'Well, he was invited in any case, but he had to cancel at the last minute because of some small problem in Algeria. Or was it Indochina? Can't remember. I only know that I thought it was very rude of him.' Milady's eyes focused on Margo, and she seemed to be back in the present again. 'What was it you said, my dear?'

'Milady,' Margo said very slowly, holding the older woman's hand in both of hers, 'please don't be upset. I am not going to marry François.'

'He forgot to ask you? But I *told* him, I know I did. Wasn't that what we were talking about earlier?'

Oh God, she's confused, Margo thought. 'Don't you remember, Milady? He did ask me, but I refused.'

'Yes, but you said you'd think about it. So I thought…'

'Please, Milady, listen to me,' Margo said in a near sob. 'I have to go. I want to live with Jacques and our baby. He is the father, after all. Didn't you tell me not to do what you did? Did you not say that what you did ruined a lot of lives? Yours and Jacques's father's and Jacques's? Lives, I mean,' she ended awkwardly.

'Lives,' Milady murmured, rolling her head sideways and closing her eyes. 'All those lives. Wasted.'

Margo leaned forward and stroked Milady's forehead. 'But now we have a chance to undo some of the pain,' she said softly. 'For Jacques, in any case. Don't you think he deserves that?'

Milady didn't reply, and Margo could see a tear roll from the corner of her eye. Milady turned her head and looked at Margo. 'What about Josephine?' she whispered. 'Will I never see her? Never hold her in my arms? Never hear her call me *Mamie?*'

'Of course you will. As soon as she – or he – is born, we will let you know. We will come and visit you often.'

'You're a fool, Marguerite,' Milady suddenly said so sharply Margo jumped. 'You should have married François. Jacques is no good, just like his father. But I can see that there's no stopping you. Go then,' she said, shaking off Margo's hand. 'Go and be damned. But don't blame me when it all ends in tears. And don't come crawling back looking for sympathy. Or money,' she added nastily.

'I wouldn't dream of it,' Margo said, getting up from the bed. 'I'm sorry you feel like this. I thought we might part as friends after all that has happened between us, all we've said to each other.' She paused, not knowing quite what else to say.

Milady looked at Margo with an inscrutable look in her hazel eyes.

'Well, goodbye then,' Margo said. 'Goodbye, my dear Milady. I hope that you won't think too unkindly of me.' She was about to open the door when she heard Milady mutter something from her bed. Margo turned around. 'Did you say something?'

'Yes,' Milady said. 'I wanted to tell you...I wish...oh, never mind.'

'What?'

'I wish I had your courage.'

*

'What did she say?' Jacques asked as they were leaving the apartment. 'Was she very upset?'

'Yes, she was,' Margo said. 'But then, so was I. Even though we've only known each other a few months, I think we have come to understand each other. I'll really miss her and I think she'll miss me too.'

'We'll keep in touch with her. And once we're settled, she can come and visit. What have you got there in that big pink bag?'

'Baby clothes,' Margo said, peering into it. 'Your mother has been buying out Baby Dior. There are these adorable little dresses. I just couldn't leave them behind.'

'You'll have to give them all away if it's a boy,' Jacques said as he pressed the button for the lift. 'Or he'll end up like his Uncle François.'

'Oh, François,' Margo exclaimed, turning back toward the apartment door. 'I have to say goodbye to him.'

'I already did for both of us,' Jacques said, pulling her back. 'He's gone to the office in any case. And he sent you his love, along with this.' Jacques showed Margo a flat parcel wrapped in brown paper and tied up with string.

'Oh yes, the gift. He said he was making me something and it would be ready soon.' Margo took the parcel and turned it around. 'I wonder what it is? Looks like some kind of picture. Maybe he painted something himself?'

'It had better not be a nude painting of you,' Jacques murmured. 'Or I'll have to go back and strangle him.'

'Maybe it's a print of the château? Wouldn't that be a nice memento?'

'Lovely.' Jacques peered up through the lift shaft. 'Where is that lift?'

'It's coming,' Margo announced. 'I can hear it creak. Yes, here it is now.'

The lift came slowly down and finally stopped at their floor. Jacques opened the wrought iron doors and loaded Margo's luggage inside. When the lift started again, Margo found that with all the luggage, she was squashed close to Jacques. They looked at each other for a moment and Margo found herself wondering how she could possibly have forgotten how luminous his eyes were. Jacques took her by the shoulders and kissed her softly on the lips. 'Why?' he murmured. 'Why did you change your mind?'

'Because of what you said.'

'That you were selfish?'

'No. It was that last word.'

Jacques frowned. 'Which one?'

'*Adieu*,' Margo whispered. 'I know that in France you only say *adieu* when you know you will never meet again. That's what your mother said to your father when he died. She whispered *adieu* in his ear and closed his eyelids.' Margo sighed, leaning her forehead against his chest, feeling tears prick her eyes. 'And when you said it to me, I knew I couldn't bear it if we never met again.'

'Neither could I,' Jacques said and held her close.

The lift stopped.

'Will we go back up again?' Jacques murmured into her ear. 'We could stay here and just go up and down, and up.'

'No, we have to get out.' Margo got out of the lift, walked through the lobby and opened the heavy entrance door. She turned around and looked at Jacques, who was slowly closing the doors to the lift. 'Come on,' she said, 'or I'll miss my train.'

When they were standing on the busy street, Margo looked around for his car. 'Where is it?' she said. 'Where's your car?'

'There,' he said, 'right in front of you.'

'What? Where? I can't see it, just that big horrible van.'

'That's it,' Jacques said. 'Don't you recognise it?'

Margo looked at it again. 'It's the van from the château. The one you use when you go to competitions.'

'That's right. And it's my home now.'

'What? You live in this...this...?'

'Yes. All my stuff is in the back and I sleep on one of the bunks. Quite comfortable, really. There's plenty of room for you. But don't just stand there. Get in.' He opened the door to the passenger seat.

Margo stared at him. 'Is this it?' she asked incredulously. 'This is what you meant when you said you had nothing to offer but your love? You expected me to live in a truck?'

'Why not?' Jacques said, lifting one eyebrow. 'What's wrong with it?'

'Everything,' Margo said, walking away.

'Where are you going?' Jacques asked.

'To get a taxi.'

'But I'll drive you. I said I would. Come on, Marguerite, I was only joking. Did you really think I was going to ask you to live with me in this? Don't you trust me?'

'No,' Margo said and came back to climb into the passenger seat. 'I said I love you, nothing about trusting you.'

'You're such a realist, my darling,' Jacques said, and after having put Margo's bags in the back, lowered himself into the driver's seat. He turned the key and drove the van expertly into the busy traffic.

'Where are you going after you've left me at the station?' Margo asked.

'To Normandy,' Jacques said, turning the van down a narrow lane. 'A shortcut,' he said, swerving to avoid a motorbike.

'What are you going to do there?'

Jacques shrugged. 'I was going to look at this property. But I'm not sure I can afford to buy it. I'm just having a look, really. Maybe in a few years I can buy something like it.'

'But I thought you sold the horses?'

'I did, and got a very good deal. Enough to buy a small place somewhere. So, my darling, once we have decided where we want to live, we can buy a small flat or maybe even a little cottage.'

'Good.' Margo sighed, feeling suddenly tired. She put her head on his shoulder and yawned. 'But let's not worry about that yet.'

'*Merde*, we're stuck,' Jacques muttered as the traffic came to a grinding halt.

'But we have plenty of time and we're quite near the station.' Margo said. 'So,' she continued, 'where is this house you're looking at? The one you can't afford?'

'At the coast. Near Deauville. Nice place. If I could raise the money to buy it, I would set up a yard for event horses there. But it's only a dream.'

'Let's dream for a while,' Margo said sleepily. 'Tell me more about this place.'

'It's very nice. An old Normandy farmhouse. Beautiful, with beams and the original fireplaces. It's recently been done up and it's very cosy inside with lovely views of the sea.'

'Sounds really wonderful.' Margo yawned again. She suddenly caught sight of the parcel on the floor and bent down and picked it up. 'I might as well open this,' she said, undoing the string.

'What?'

'The present François gave me.' Margo struggled with the wrapping. 'He wrapped it up so well, I can't...there, I've got it.' Margo took away the last of the brown paper. 'How nice,' she said. 'That's so sweet. A lovely memento.'

'What is it?' Jacques said, putting the van into gear and rolling slowly forward as the traffic started to move again.

'A painting.'

'One he painted himself?'

'No,' Margo murmured, looking at the picture. 'It's one of the paintings from the dining room in the château. A copy, of course, but lovely all the same.'

'Oh? Which one?' Jacques pressed his foot on the accelerator as the traffic started to flow faster.

'The Holbein,' Margo said. 'Portrait of Christina, duchess of Milan. Jacques!' she exclaimed as the van suddenly swerved. 'What are you doing?'

The van came to a screeching halt at the curb, accompanied by loud hooting from the cars behind them. 'Show me that,' Jacques breathed and snatched the painting from Margo. He peered at it, his face pale with emotion. 'Oh yes, he whispered, 'it is. It's the Holbein, all right.'

'I know.' Margo sighed. 'What a nice gesture. And that one was the best of the whole lot. You can hardly believe it's a copy.'

'That, *mon amour*,' Jacques said softly, 'is because it isn't.'

The battered camper van travelled along the motorway, the soft rumble of the engine barely audible over the sound of someone singing a popular French song on the radio. Margo looked idly at the countryside gliding past the windows, the music and the rough bouncing of the van preventing her from sleeping.

'*Ca va?*' Jacques asked, putting a hand on her knee.

She turned her head and looked at him as he drove through the heavy traffic. 'I'm fine,' she said. She was still holding the painting on her lap and she looked at it again, trying to take it all in.

*

'Are you sure?' she had asked incredulously as they sat in the van, staring at the painting.

'Of course I'm sure,' Jacques had said. 'That art dealer wouldn't take that one. He said it was too

421

difficult to copy and impossible to sell unless it was purchased legally. He wouldn't touch it.'

'Did François know that?'

Jacques shrugged. 'I have no idea. I'd say he thought it was a fake. Why else would he have given it to you?'

'I think it was very nice of him all the same,' Margo murmured as she looked at the painting again, lifting it up to see it properly. 'It was painted in 1538, you know,' she continued. 'In Milan. The Duchess Christina was one of Henry VIII's prospective brides and Holbein was sent to paint her.'

'How come you know so much about it?' Jacques asked.

'I read about it in an art book while I was at the château. I was so taken with this painting and I wanted to find out who this woman was.' Margo peered at her face. 'Have you noticed how she seems to move towards you as you look at her? Her face is so alive. I wonder if Holbein wasn't a little bit in love with her. It's a beautiful portrait,' Margo continued, 'really exquisite. But I suppose I'll have to give it back.' Something fluttered to the floor of the van as she turned the painting. 'Look,' she said, bending to pick it up. 'There's something here. An envelope.' Margo opened it and unfolded the stiff pages. 'Looks like some sort of document. The French is very difficult. I can't quite make it out.'

'A certificate of ownership,' Jacques said, peering over her shoulder. 'Signed by François and witnessed by a lawyer. My God, he knew it was the real thing.'

'And the owner is…' Margo looked at the letters, trying to understand the legal terms in French.

'Madame Margo Hunter,' Jacques read. 'Who's that?'

'Me, you dummy,' Margo said. 'He's given it to me.'

'Mon Dieu, c'est incroyable!'

'Yes. This is what he was talking about when he said he was preparing a gift.' Margo looked at the painting again, unable to understand the full impact of it.

'What's in the other envelope?'

'Which one?'

'That one on the floor.' Jacques picked it up. 'It was attached to the other one. Here, you read it.'

Margo opened the envelope. 'It's a card,' she said, opening it up. *'Dear Marguerite,'* she read out loud, *'Hope you like my little gift. I thought you both deserved a memento from the family. All my love and best wishes for the future.* It's signed Paquita,' Margo said, 'and dated two weeks ago. How sweet. He must have planned this a while ago. He must have guessed you would come back for me.' She looked down at the painting again. 'If I sell this, it will be a considerable nest egg. But I don't think I could bear to be parted from it now it's mine.'

'Even if you don't sell it, it could be an excellent collateral for a loan,' Jacques said casually.

'Really?' Margo said, lifting one of her eyebrows.

Jacques laughed. 'You looked just like my mother when you said that. But we'd better get going,' he said and started the engine again. 'You'll miss your train at this rate.'

'I think I've already missed it,' Margo said, looking at her watch.

'I'm sorry. What are you going to do now? Do you want me to take you to the station and try and get the next one?'

'No,' Margo said. 'I have a better idea. Take me to Le Havre. I can get on a ferry there. And it's near Deauville, so...'

'What?'

'Well, it wouldn't hurt just to look,' Margo laughed.

*

'We should be at the exit soon,' Jacques said.

'Yes, I think so,' Margo said dreamily.

'You sound sleepy.'

'Yes, I am.' Margo suppressed a yawn. 'It was a rough night.'

'There's a motorway station up ahead. Do you want to stop for coffee?'

'No. Please, no; I *really* don't,' Margo said, a hint of panic in her voice. 'I *hate* those motorway stations.'

'All right, we'll keep going then. But I'd like you to try and wake up and have a look at the map. I'm not sure which exit to take.'

'Just keep going for a while,' Margo said. 'There's quite a bit to go yet.'

'All right.' Jacques turned his attention to the road and Margo relaxed again, looking at the view and thinking about the past few months. 'You know,' she mumbled, 'I was thinking that if the baby is a girl I might call her Gráinne – as a middle name, of course,' she added hurriedly when she saw the look on Jacques's face.

'Hmm,' he muttered.

'She'd love it.' Margo suddenly smiled. 'And God, how she'd laugh if she had been there last night. I can't wait to tell her who was spying on us when…' Margo stopped. 'No, maybe not.'

'I should think not,' Jacques murmured. 'Look, it says Caen over there. That can't be right.'

Margo picked up the map. 'No,' she said, 'it isn't. We've gone wrong somewhere.'

'What?' Jacques demanded. 'We've gone wrong?'

'Yup, that's it.'

'*Merde.*'

'Couldn't agree with you more.'

'Shit,' Jacques snapped, 'don't you know how to read a map?' He glanced at her sideways, his mouth pinched into an angry line.

Margo looked thoughtfully at him, then down at the map. 'No,' she said, 'as a matter of fact, I don't.' On an impulse, she picked up the map and began to tear it deliberately into small pieces.

'What are you doing?' Jacques exclaimed.

'Getting rid of this,' Margo said as she wound down the window and scattered the pieces like so much confetti behind the van. 'Find your own way. I'm going to sleep.' She closed the window, leaned her head against the back of the seat and closed her eyes. 'Wake me up when we arrive,' she muttered sleepily.

There was no response from Jacques. Margo half-opened her eyes and met his glance. 'What?' she said.

Jacques's smile was tender. 'Nothing,' he said, 'just...*je t'aime, mon amour.*'